ALL
the
SHADOWS
of the
RAINBOW

Thanks to one of my biggest fans!

Imanna Arthur

The Vampires of New England Series

ALL
the
SHADOWS
of the
RAINBOW

Inanna Arthen

By Light Unseen Media
Pepperell, Massachusetts

All the Shadows of the Rainbow
The Vampires of New England Series
http://vampiresofnewengland.com

Cover and book interior designed by Vyrdolak, By Light Unseen Media.

This is a work of fiction. Names, characters, places and incidents are either the products of the author's imagination or are used fictitiously, and any resemblence to actual persons, living or dead, business establishments, events or locales is entirely coincidental.

Perfect Paperback Edition
ISBN-10: 1-935303-15-5
ISBN-13: 978-1-935303-15-2
LCCN: 2013913328

Published by
By Light Unseen Media
PO Box 1233
Pepperell, Massachusetts 01463-3233

Our Mission:
By Light Unseen Media presents the best of quality fiction and non-fiction on the theme of vampires and vampirism. We offer fictional works with original imagination and style, as well as non-fiction of academic calibre.

For additional information, visit:
http://bylightunseenmedia.com/

Printed in the United States of America

0 9 8 7 6 5 4 3 2 1

1955

1

Diana's return to the stone house off of School Street went as unnoticed as her absence had been.

She surveyed the area carefully from above to make sure there were no witnesses before ghosting to the ground and solidifying. The only live creatures whose body heat glowed dimly below her were small wildlife and a cat hunting them in the weeds overgrowing Thomas' stone circle. She nervously recalled what Thomas had told her about other vampires being undetectable to them. But the property *felt* empty—neglected, undisturbed, and half-wild, the new spring foliage expanding into formerly clear areas. She saw no sign that anyone had come closer to the house than the access road. Her old Chevrolet stood hubcap-deep in the smooth unmarked patch of snow that lingered under the north shadow of the house.

All her normal self-awareness and memories had returned, for the first time since she'd walked into the woods four months earlier. As she regarded the dark windows in the moss-stained granite walls, she recalled the last few grueling months of the athanor construction. She and Thomas had spent every waking moment working in the decrepit Schuller house until they collapsed in exhaustion to sleep on its bare floors, deserting this house to collect cobwebs and dust. Now Thomas and the Schuller place were both gone. The only evidence of their two and half year long magical working was a foundation hole full of rubble, Diana's vampiric state, and, she reflected somberly, a couple of new gravestones in cemeteries. For the first time, Diana began to truly appreciate Thomas' words about memory becoming a burden as the years accumulated but vampires remained unchanged. Standing there listening to the haunting echo of spring peepers in the distance, she made a decision.

I won't dwell on memories—ever. The past is past, and I have an unending future ahead of me. I'll always look forward. No sentiment, no nostalgia. It's the one luxury that I can't afford.

She reflected on her resolution for several minutes, allowing it to fully sink into her consciousness and Will. Then she squared her shoulders, dematerialized, and slipped through the crack of the bolted back door to solidify inside the kitchen. After taking a look around and some deep sniffs of the air, she lit a kerosene lantern and went to check the pipes. There had been water in the cistern when she left—given how cold it came from the tap, she guessed that much of it was still frozen. The interior of the house, with its thick stone walls, was at least twenty degrees colder than the mild air outside. As soon as she completed a cursory walk-through of the rooms, where she found nothing out of place, she started a vigorous fire going in the massive kitchen woodstove.

She occasionally paused to wince and rub her behind—both her buttocks and her ego still smarted from the recent encounter in the woods with Her Ladyship and the rest of...whoever they were. Thomas had called them the Tylwyth Teg, the Welsh name for the Fair Folk, or the Fae. Diana still wasn't sure she believed all the mythology about those beings, but she could no longer be skeptical about their existence, or their power over her. They had ruthlessly kicked her out of her self-pitying mope, laughing uproariously at her whining. The one whom Thomas had called Her Ladyship had ordered Diana to clean herself up and start acting like a responsible human being. As conflicted as her feelings toward the Teg were, Diana knew she was indebted to them for their intervention. She had no idea yet just exactly what she *was* going to do now, but rejecting civilization and rationality hadn't been a solution to anything.

She'd always been glad that the fictional cliché about vampires having no reflections was nonsense, but now she avoided the small bathroom mirror. She couldn't bear to confront the image that had spawned a local monster legend *(all covered with hair, one glaring eye?)*, even though her conscience nagged at her to do so. She found some turpentine with her alchemical supplies, and it dissolved, somewhat painfully, the blackened, peeling layer of pine pitch on her face and hands. But her dark hair was so hopelessly matted into sticky, hardened dreadlocks that she finally located a pair of scissors and cut most of it off. She ended up with the boyish gamine look that was rather in fashion for the art and theatre crowd. The turpentine got rid of the last bits of pitch, and by then the kettle of water she'd put on the stove for a bath was boiling.

She burned her filthy, pitch-stained clothes, what was left of them, and spent the rest of the night cleaning the house top to bottom—all except Thomas' study, which she left closed and untouched. She was a little surprised that she wasn't hungrier, but—she winced at the memory—she had drunk more from the boy in the barn than she should have, and that had been right before the February snow storm. Evidently freezing solid had put her into a sort of suspended animation. Before she went to bed at dawn in her own room upstairs, she made a list of things to do the following afternoon. She'd wasted far too much time.

"Next time, fill out a card so we know you're going away," grumbled the postmistress as she heaved a large cardboard tray of mail onto the counter.

Diana stuffed handfuls of mail into the shopping bag she'd brought without stopping to look at it closely. "Has anyone been in asking for me?" she asked, keeping her tone as idle as possible. The postmistress was not one of her greatest fans, disapproving of Diana's cohabiting with Thomas to begin with and scandalized when Diana moved in with Moira while Thomas so ostentatiously courted the dilettante artist, Catherine Jorgens.

"For *you?* Not that I know of," the postmistress sniffed.

Main Street looked the same as always, with one exception—Moira's beauty salon was still vacant, its windows covered with heavy brown paper taped to the inside. Diana could only bear to take a quick glance before she turned, blinking away tears, and walked rapidly north past the public boat ramps and ferry dock and on to Holliston House Inn. The Inn was half-hidden with painters' scaffolding as the Wilkinsons spiffed up the three-story façade for the coming season.

Mrs. Wilkinson was delighted to see Diana, and immediately asked where she'd been. As much as she hated fibbing, Diana had a plausible story ready, about needing to get away and visiting family. She managed to keep a straight face when Mrs. Wilkinson told her how lucky she'd been to miss the blizzard, historic even by Maine standards. "Why, the whole coast was shut down for three days! It was that bad!"

"Yes, I read about it in the papers."

Mrs. Wilkinson tsked sadly over Thomas' move to France. The Wilkinsons were among the few people in Pepperell who had sincerely liked him. "And I'm so sorry about Moira Waterford," she added. "I know what good, friends the two of you were." She managed to fit a universe of meaning into the tiny pause before "friends."

"Thank you. I'm surprised no one has adopted her thriving business, with the town growing and the economy improving."

"Oh, I'm sure it won't be empty for long."

"Is there any word about..." Diana hesitated.

"Her young assistant, the Beauvais girl?"

"Yes, Carole."

Mrs. Wilkinson shook her head sadly. "Still in the sanitarium, and even worse, from what I've heard."

"Worse?"

"Oh, completely deranged, raving about all kinds of wild things. Witchcraft, werewolves, I don't know what all. Her family actually tried to call in an exorcist."

Diana stared. "You're kidding."

"The diocese refused, apparently. But the family has moved down to Portland to be nearer to the sanitarium. Of course, she had such a horrible shock, losing her fiancé like that. That poor Crothers boy, only twenty-one, supporting his whole family, and still thinking about college and improving himself, and then to be blown up in that horrible fire—didn't he do some work up there for Mr. Morgan?"

"Uh…yes, he did, for a couple of weeks…" It took a moment for Diana to answer, she suddenly felt so chilled. Was Carole raving about vampires when her medications wore off? Maybe she wasn't as insane with grief as everyone thought. Brent's death had stunned all of them, Diana and Thomas not the least…*because it was all our fault. We fouled up and he paid for it. And we never found out how much he told her…*

"Are you all right, Miss Chilton?"

"Oh—I'm sorry. I was just thinking about poor Carole."

Mrs. Wilkinson shook her head, her expression momentarily tragic. Then she snapped back to a business-like mien. "Alma Patton in the Assessor's office says that you own all that property now, is that right?"

"That's correct. And there's an escrow account to pay the taxes, so she won't have to chase down any more pesky liens. I'm sure the town will be relieved, with that shiny new school going up."

"Will you be living back there all by yourself? Or are you making other plans?" She paused, fixing Diana with a piercing look.

"I have no plans to develop the property, or sell it, if that's what you're wondering. But live there year-round?" Diana was silent for a moment. "I haven't decided what I'm going to do, Mrs. Wilkinson. I just got back, and…well, life has been pretty crazy the last six months or so. I have a lot of thinking to do." *And even more thinking, after this conversation,* she added silently.

Dusk was falling by the time Diana finished her business in town, and she walked west on School Street toward the hilly region where she now owned some five hundred acres of land. She'd intended to walk only until she found someplace she could duck into the bushes and dematerialize without being seen, but she was so deep in thought, she kept on for nearly three miles. The information about Carole worried her. *Maybe I shouldn't stay here. Maybe I should go someplace else for five years, or ten years, until the details fade in people's memories…* But where would she go? Back to Boston? As far as she knew, she was still a member in unblemished good standing of the Order of the Silver Light, the three hundred year old magical group in which she had been born and raised. Would that still be true if they found out what had happened to her? But Thomas had been a member, as had her mentor, Levoissier, who was something quite extraordinary indeed.

I'm just a white-livered coward. I don't want to have to explain to everyone, and deal with all their reactions. Could I just not tell them? Or would they know, the minute they saw me? There was no way to answer that question except by testing it out in person.

9

A bat flitted by her ear and startled her out of her deep reverie, and she looked around in confusion for a moment, she'd been so oblivious to how far she was walking. She realized that she'd lived in Pepperell for three years, and she'd never seen this stretch of the road except from a car or from the air. Nothing waited for her at the end of it but a cold, empty house with no neighbor for two miles in any direction. *Thomas said I'd need a place to call home, but this isn't it. What am I going to do here? Plant a garden, spend my nights sneaking up on cows?*

She had a feeling that the Teg would intervene forcefully again if she attempted to isolate herself the way Thomas had done. But more importantly, she desperately wanted to find other vampires, those whom Thomas had mentioned or any others. She also intended to somehow track down her former covenmate and lover Gregory Fitzhughes, who she had last seen walking down this very road on his way to join their mentor Levoissier in Montréal the previous June. She couldn't do either of those things if she was too nervous to set foot outside of midcoast Maine.

When she got back to the house she dumped out and sorted through the bag of mail. Most of it went to feed the stove, but there was a small stack of envelopes left to open and read. She had letters from her parents in France and several friends in the Order. The Board of Bread and Roses, the charitable foundation she had launched with her trust fund money at the tender age of twenty-one, had sent its quarterly reports. There was nothing from Gregory. The last letter she opened was from Phoebe Hudson, a somewhat dilettantish member of the Order whom Diana had mentored as a Novice. Along with her usual chirpy gossip, Phoebe asked rather plaintively if Diana might consider attending the Order's Beltene festivities this year. Diana, to her own surprise, was sorely tempted, but uncertain it was the best choice for her first interaction with other magicians of Adeptus and Magus grade. The tone of the request piqued her curiosity, however. It almost sounded as though attendance for this year's Beltene was in danger of falling below quorum.

That would be a shame, she thought archly, and had to smile, remembering her attempt to explain this unashamedly licentious celebration to a wide-eyed Moira. ("Orgies and everything?" Moira had said. "I mean, in the Twentieth Century."). The date was only two weeks away. Boston offered all kinds of potential, provided she could handle the sensory overload of a major city. If other magical adepts would recognize her as something no longer human, she might as well find out and get it over with. Even more important, someone in the Order might be able to give her some leads as to the whereabouts of Gregory or Levoissier. She went to find some notepaper and a pen to send an RSVP.

As she'd expected, the car refused to start, and needed to be towed and serviced before she could drive to Boston. Diana wondered if she could travel that far semi-materialized, but the practical barriers seemed daunting. Getting the car repaired made her miss Brent as poignantly as she had since his death. Her memory too vividly evoked the image of his bright red crew cut and sweat-shiny, painfully young face, his cheery voice saying, "You have any trouble with the car, you bring it here, nothing I can't fix..." With effort, she forced both the image and the pain from her mind. The car's problems proved minor, and within ten days Diana was southward-bound, firmly pushing her apprehensions to the back of her mind.

She hadn't done much driving since she'd changed, and she had a number of close calls when she overcompensated or miscalculated. By the time she reached the Massachusetts border, however, she had adjusted to driving with her enhanced senses, reflexes and strength. In Boston, she took a room in the Hilton and spent a day walking around her usual haunts, accustoming herself to the sensory impressions that were so familiar and alien at once. Only after she had begun to feel somewhat less out of place did she call Phoebe, who was overjoyed to hear from her.

"Diana, you just can't *imagine* how much everyone has missed you!"

Diana had to smile—Phoebe lived life on a high vibrational level, to say the least. "Well, that's always nice to hear. I missed all of you, too."

"Are you coming back to live in Boston now, back for good? You gave up your apartment, where are you going to live? I can't *believe* you gave up your apartment, it's impossible to find a place in the city now."

"Well...it's a long story." Diana wasn't sure how much to reveal about Thomas giving her his property—how would she ever explain that? "Right now I'm staying at the Hilton, and I haven't really thought about what I'll do next. I haven't been back to the Motherhouse yet. Are they holding Beltene there this year?"

"I haven't heard anything different. Lot of stags this year, though. People just aren't excited about it the way they used to be. It doesn't feel right."

"I heard that a lot of members have left the city."

"Oh my god, the *country*. And they're not even coming back for the festivals. The House in France is bigger than here now. It's crazy."

Diana pondered this. If Phoebe had heard any rumors about the magical working and its blowback, she was certainly playing innocent. She was silent long enough that Phoebe cleared her throat delicately. "Sorry, I was just thinking."

"Oh, that's all right, I'm sure it must feel very strange to be back in the city after so long."

"It really does. This is my first trip…home in three years. I hardly ever even went to Bangor, while I was up in Maine." She could almost hear Phoebe, a confirmed urbanite, shaking her head incredulously over the phone.

"Well, listen. I'm having some people up for cocktails in a couple of hours, a sort of pre-Beltene loosening up kind of thing. Why don't you join us? It's mostly people you know. I think there will only be one or two you haven't met before."

Diana hesitated, feeling a qualm at the prospect of meeting a whole group of magical people at once. But Phoebe's invitation would be a good way of dabbling her toes in the water. How Phoebe's friends reacted in a casual social situation would give her some clues about what to expect at the Beltene ritual a few nights from now. "Sounds fun, I'll be there with bells on." Only after she hung up the phone did she think, *Oh, damn…what on earth* do *I have to wear?*

2

By 8:00 p.m., Diana was pressing the buzzer outside of Phoebe's apartment, so nervous that if she'd still had a pulse, it would have been racing. As it was, her imitation of life, as Thomas had called it, was authentic enough to supply shaky hands and a wildly fluttering stomach. It had been so long since she'd worn even modest high heels—especially brand new ones—she was wobbling on her feet like a debutante, and she prayed that she'd gotten all the store tags off the sapphire blue cocktail dress.

The door opened so abruptly, Diana started back and almost turned an ankle. Phoebe, frothing with pink satin ruffles, stared at her blankly with her mouth making a little O of surprise. Taken aback, Diana said, "I'm not too early, am I?" Phoebe's face suddenly went through a series of expressions like rapidly flipping pages of a book: recognition, embarrassment, slight confusion and exasperation.

"Oh! Diana! I didn't…I'm sorry…no, you're not early at all, we've been waiting for…I mean…oh, how stupid of me, come in!"

Diana stepped carefully into the apartment's tiny entryway, and almost unbalanced on her high heels again when Phoebe flung arms around her shoulders in an exuberant hug.

"Oh, it's *so* good to *see* you!" she shrilled into Diana's right ear, as Diana flinched with pain. It wasn't that, however, that made Phoebe stiffen slightly and pull back, her brow creasing. Diana watched her warily. "Are you okay? You feel…"

"What?"

Phoebe's eyes were searching Diana's face and arms in bewilderment, as if she wasn't sure what she was even looking for. "You feel very…*cold*. Did you walk?"

"Uh…yes," Diana improvised. "I've been away from Boston for so long, I've been walking everywhere, just getting back into the groove of it all, you know."

"Oh." Phoebe kept on staring for a moment, then she gave her head a little shake and smiled brightly. "But your *hair!* What have you *done* to yourself?"

"You don't like it?"

"It's just so *different*, that's why I didn't recognize you. But come in, here, let me take your wrap, and get you a drink. Art's mixing for us tonight, you can just *imagine* how hard I had to twist his arm..." Diana trailed Phoebe into the living room, where about half a dozen guests all turned expectantly toward them. She knew everyone present except one young man, and yet each smiling face echoed the confused reactions that had just flickered across Phoebe's. As each man or woman met Diana's gaze, she saw the smile falter, the brow crease, the eyes darken with momentary doubt. Then each guest blinked and smiled again, but the cheerful greeting seemed forced, and no one else proffered a handshake, far less a hug. Diana sternly repressed a powerful impulse to dematerialize on the spot.

"Diana, you'll have a Gibson Girl, right?" Phoebe was already waving to Art, who reached for a martini glass from the bar setup on the long sideboard against one wall.

"Actually, I'd like a Scotch and soda," Diana said, without thinking.

Art and Phoebe both stared at her, then Art grinned. *"Well,"* he said jovially as he swapped glasses with a flourish. "So that's what comes of living out in the back woods for three years. Would you like a cigar to go with that?" He snapped his fingers over the glass and a puff of gray smoke swirled out of it, reeking distinctly of Havana Gold.

"Phew, Art, stop that," Phoebe said, wrinkling her nose.

"That's what you get for dating an alchemist—and letting him tend bar at your parties. So where's my leather armchair and brace of hounds?" Diana bantered back, and several people laughed. *Good,* she thought, *maybe everyone will relax and stop trying to figure out what about me is bothering them.*

They did, or least they pretended to. "Wherever did you get that *chic* haircut?" teased Evelyn, whom Diana just barely remembered as one of the Novices admitted shortly before her departure in 1952.

"Oh...I just got sick of washing it in the rain barrel, so I found a rusty pair of scissors and chopped it all off." This largely truthful statement evoked another burst of laughter.

"For a minute we thought you'd turned into one of those Beats," Art said as he handed Diana her drink.

"Or run off to join the Actors Studio and go on the stage. Are you going to start reciting poetry for us?" asked Calvin, a slight blond man who was virtually glued to Evelyn's skirt; they had been admitted in the same group of Novices.

"Oh, please. I have been reciting things every day for the last three years, in multiple languages. I'm taking a break, thanks." She sniffed at her drink—Art wasn't as mischievous as Gregory by any means, but his party cocktails occasionally had surprising effects.

"Reciting things every day?" Fran, a contemporary of Evelyn and Calvin, set down the drink she was holding and took a half step toward Diana. "Could you…could you tell us a little bit about your working? I don't mean—" she added hastily as Phoebe made a reproving sound, "I don't mean anything confidential, of course. But it's just…we've heard all these hints and rumors…"

"Hints and rumors?" Diana's words came out more sharply than she intended, and Fran's cheeks grew pink.

Calvin cleared his throat, obviously coming to Fran's rescue, and Diana wondered when she'd gotten to be so intimidating to these younger members, who were far from Novices. "We've just heard that you were doing something very ambitious, something with a very long scope. Naturally, we've been curious to hear some of the technical details. My mentor said no one has done a working like this for a century."

"Where did he hear about it?" Diana was genuinely bemused. Calvin glanced around at the others and shrugged helplessly. Diana took a sip of her Scotch, relieved that it seemed to have no magical effects aside from a faint undertaste of cigar smoke. She thought she could make a fairly astute guess as to the source of any hints and rumors, and struggled not to fume. So was Phoebe, Diana saw from the corner of her eye; she was furious that her guests were prying. But Diana, seeing the intent expressions around her, wasn't surprised. *They're spooked. They can feel that something is off, and they want some explanation that makes sense to them. Maybe I can stop all those imaginations from running off over the horizon before someone hits on the truth.*

"Look, it's okay," she said finally, with a nod at Phoebe. "I don't mind talking about it—Phoebe's heard a little, and there are other people who were in on the whole plan. You all know what not to ask, and what not to repeat."

Several people nodded; Fran appeared to be holding her breath. Diana tried not to fidget under the weight of their undivided attention. "All right… we needed something that would collect power in small increments over a long period of time as we focused energy into it. So we built an athanor…"

"An athanor?" Calvin sounded as though he wasn't sure he'd heard her correctly. "You mean one of those ovens for processing alchemical compounds, like the one at the Motherhouse?"

"Art's got one of those," Evelyn said.

"This had a sealed core, though," Diana said. "It took six months to build, we barely made our deadline. We were working every day, setting in every brick ritually, one by one."

"Oh my *god*," Calvin said.

Diana went on for some time, explaining the elaborate magical construction of the athanor itself and the pattern of the daily workings, although she left out some fairly large details. Among those was the actual purpose of the working, any information about Thomas, whom she referred to only as "my partner," and the final outcome. She knew her listeners were biting their tongues to keep from asking questions about these glaring omissions, but they were all too experienced and too well trained to break taboo.

When she stopped talking, there was a thoughtful silence. Fran let out a long sigh. "It's hard to even imagine. Three years! I'm envious, on the one hand, but on the other…I don't think I could do that. I really don't."

"So, was it all worth it?" asked Evelyn, who was studying Diana's expression more intently than Diana was comfortable with; she perceived that Evelyn was the most psychically gifted person in the room. She glanced around at the curious faces, unable to snap off a glib reply, and took a hasty gulp of her second glass of Scotch.

"I guess not," Calvin said wisely.

"Oh, I wouldn't say *that*, exactly," Diana said. "But we didn't get the results we were hoping for."

"I'm sorry," Fran said. "After all that work, and all the time you spent on it…"

"It was a big gamble, and you know how those go," Diana said.

"Would you ever do anything like that again?" Evelyn asked.

It had never occurred to Diana to frame the issue quite that way, and she gave it a moment's serious thought. "I don't know. I wouldn't rule it out, but…I'd have to consider the Intention very carefully. I'm not sure I did that enough before we started this one. We sure raised power, though. And I learned a lot, I have to admit that."

"Who was it who said you learn more from your failures than your triumphs?" Art said.

Calvin chortled. "The New York Mets?"

"Besides them." Art rolled his eyes.

Diana braced herself. "I seem to recall hearing some such bromide from Levoissier, a few times." She saw no reason to repress the acid edge in her voice, but regretted it when the room abruptly fell quiet. Evelyn and Fran exchanged uneasy looks. "What? Did I say a dirty word? It's not carved into the lintel of the Motherhouse ritual room that no one dare speak the name of my former mentor, is it?"

"No, of course not," Phoebe said hastily. "It's just that…"

"He gives you the willies, I get it. And you all call yourselves magicians."

Fran waved a hand, looking flustered. "We've all been told that it's not respectful, that's all. I know you worked with him, Diana, but the rest of us… well, my mentor dressed me down eight ways from Sunday just for asking questions about L-Levoissier."

"Mine, too," Calvin said. "And that was after I was raised to Adeptus."

"Anyway, Levoissier isn't around Boston now," Evelyn said. "He left more than two years ago."

Diana took a smaller and slower sip of Scotch. "Seriously, though. Have any of you heard any…hints or rumors about where he might be? Is he with one of the Order's other Houses—San Francisco, or France, or Chicago?"

Phoebe looked at Art, who just shrugged. She turned back to Diana. "There's a new House, you know, it just opened up, in Providence. In fact, Roderick Vale has gone down there to serve as their P.M. They practically begged him."

"Roderick Vale left Boston? You left this bombshell out of your letters, Phoebe." Diana scowled at her friend, who flung up her hands.

"It just happened. The Providence House was only chartered at the Vernal Equinox."

"Well…" Diana suddenly laughed. "I've been monopolizing this conversation for the last hour, and I'm the stranger in town. Come on, fill me in on what else I've missed. Have any of you visited the House in France recently? What's their new Motherhouse in Paris like?"

That opening got her off the hook for quite a while, as the others filled her in on gossip about who had been initiated to the next level, who had left, who had moved to France or Providence or San Francisco, who had gotten married or divorced or had a baby. She fielded a number of curious questions about Pepperell and what it was like to live up there. After a little while, she sat down in a chair, noticing that the rest of the guests, even as they chatted happily, had shifted somewhat away from her. It wasn't an obtrusive movement, but as the group settled into seats or corners, Diana was like the thumb to their fingers.

As the lively conversation bubbled on, however, Diana was repeatedly distracted by the one person who had been silent since she arrived, except for an occasional nod or short comment. It was the young man she didn't know. While everyone was riveted to Diana's story about the working in Maine, and during the bustling chatter of gossip, the young man had remained in the background, and there was no opening for Diana to ask his name.

But as time passed, Diana's curiosity about him steadily increased. He was without doubt the most gifted and magically powerful individual present, after Diana herself. She could feel energy coming off his aura in pulses, like a slow heartbeat. If Phoebe had invited him to this gathering, he must be connected with the Order, but Diana was sure she had never seen him before. His eyes were so dark brown, they appeared black, and he was watching her with such intensity, she had glanced back at him half a dozen times before the rest of his face registered. All she could remember at first was eyes. He had thick curly dark hair that seemed to be trying to escape from his scalp, full lips and a rather large nose, but to balance those eyes, it needed to be.

Phoebe circled the room offering canapés. As she took one, Diana said casually, "I don't think I know the boy sitting by Calvin. Is he from the Boston Motherhouse?"

Phoebe looked over at the boy in question, gasped in horror and clapped a hand over her mouth—by this time she'd had three of Art's martinis. "Oh, I'm so *sorry!*" she said, in a tone of voice that would have served if she'd accidentally maimed someone's child. "Of *course,* I *completely* forgot, and he wanted to meet *you* just *desperately!* Here—" Putting the tray of canapés at great risk, she gestured with her free hand at the young man, who had deduced that he was being discussed and came to join them.

"Diana—this is David Hofstein. David, Diana Chilton. David came out here from the San Francisco House two years ago, that's why you haven't met. But now he's...um...I'll let him explain, actually." Flushed to the roots of her light brown hair, Phoebe corrected the tray's list to starboard in the nick of time and bolted for the kitchen.

Diana looked up at David inquisitively. Now that he was suddenly in touching distance, he seemed stricken by shyness and wouldn't meet her eyes. "Pleased to meet you," she said as brightly as she could. "Have a seat, why don't you. Tell me why you wanted to meet me so badly."

David flung himself into the chair next to her, making an impatient motion with his oddly large hands. "Oh, that's Phoebe, she always exaggerates everything. I'd just heard people talking about you—good things, I mean. About your foundation and all that."

"Bread and Roses. I haven't been active with them for a while, you know."

"Still. They're an example for the whole city. And then there was...well... you know. That trouble you were in."

"Oh, so people talk about that, do they?"

He turned towards her and that ferocious look was back in his eyes—at such close proximity, it almost seemed tactile. Diana thought that if she tried to stare him down, she'd end up with a migraine. "Only the ones who agreed with you, who thought you were right and the Council treated you like dirt."

"I see..."

"I'm quitting the Order, that's what Phoebe got so tongue-tied about. She didn't have to be embarrassed, I'm not making any bones about it. It's the right thing for me to do."

"Okay...then you won't be at Beltene, I take it?"

"Not sure I would have gone anyway. But no, I'm done, I'm out. Phoebe just asked me here tonight because we're good friends, and you would be here."

"How long had you been with the Order?"

"About six years. I went through all the training in San Francisco, then my mentor for Adeptus decided to come out here, and I just tagged along. I didn't have any ties in California."

"So you're Adeptus grade?"

"No, I—" he sighed heavily. "I was supposed to go through initiation two months ago. But I came off the retreat knowing it just wasn't the path I was meant to take. My mentor was pretty disappointed, but she said she understood."

Diana just nodded. It wasn't uncommon for members to hit a crisis point and leave just before reaching Adeptus. Something about that particular transition had a way of forcing issues. "So where do you think you might be going from here?"

"Hey, it's a big world. The Order isn't the only game around, you know. And plenty of people work solitary."

"None of which answers my question. You're lousy with talent, and don't try to deny it. If the Council wasn't all but drop-tackling you to keep you from leaving, there's got to be something you're not saying."

He grinned, a little sheepishly, which suddenly made him look rather appealing. He had very white teeth. "They weren't happy when I turned in my resignation. Of course, I don't have your *chutzpah*. I didn't tell them everything I was thinking."

"About what? You must have some serious beefs to get this far and then throw it all to the winds."

"Yeah, well…probably not their fault. The Order is what it is, I can't expect it to change. But I just realized…" he leveled an almost shifty look across the room toward the other guests as he trailed off, and leaned toward Diana, lowering his voice. "I just felt that I wanted something more practical, you know? I wanted some way of applying magic to the real world, use it to solve real problems. Something like your foundation does, except using magical techniques. I don't know, does that sound idiotic?"

For some reason, Diana's mouth had gone dry. *Déjà vu*…a mocking voice in her mind echoed. She licked her lips uneasily before she could answer. "I don't think so, not at all." She was afraid to say anything else. It was as though the floor had tilted, like a funhouse. David leaned even closer, and her fingers tightened on the chair arm involuntarily as she firmly resisted pulling back from him.

"That trouble you got into? Somebody told me that you were pushing the Council to—" he broke off as she shushed him, not even understanding why. She'd never been hesitant to talk about her censure and what led to it before now.

"I understand what you're saying, believe me. But this isn't the kind of conversation we should have at a cocktail party, David."

"I know, but—" this time another voice cut him off.

"Hey, what's going on over there? Are you two conniving some sort of subversive plot in the middle of Phoebe's living room?" Art's voice was louder than it needed to be, and there was a hard note underneath the humor. Suddenly affronted, Diana stiffened.

"Of course not, don't be silly."

David stood up and took a step toward Art, and Diana was alarmed to see that his lips had turned white, the sign of real anger.

"Are you calling Miss Chilton a subversive? Or me? It's none of your business what we're talking about. The jackboots don't go with that sports jacket, *Arthur.*" He somehow made the name a scathing insult. Art's face flushed deep red.

"Don't you pull that sh—that nonsense with me, David. Diana had enough trouble ten years ago, and she finally got her head on straight, she doesn't need you pulling her off into any more crackpot radical schemes."

"Excuse *me*, Art!" Diana would have been angrier if she hadn't been so astounded by this sudden eruption.

As though too furious to speak, the two men locked eyes in the kind of glare Diana imagined preceded a knife fight in Sicily, not that she'd ever seen one. She stood up herself, just as the electric lights flickered—probably in the whole building, given the combined abilities of the combatants. The floor shivered, and all the glasses on the sideboard rattled musically. Phoebe drew in a sharp breath.

"Boys, *stop it,*" their hostess said in a voice completely unlike her usual trilling deference. "Art—if you—if those bottles start—don't...you...*dare! Either* of you!"

After a few tense moments in which Diana was genuinely unsure what might happen, etiquette prevailed. Art stepped back, shrugged his shoulders as though his jacket was too tight and turned to walk into the kitchen, muttering something under his breath which Diana was very glad no one but she could hear. She'd never have thought Art was anti-Semitic. Maybe he and David had squared off before. Phoebe made an impatient sound, threw down the small towel she'd been holding and followed him, shutting the door behind her. Deflated, David looked back at Diana. "What the hell?" he whispered. "What made him think we were—" He broke off as she urgently shook her head, afraid that any more furtive exchanges might get someone else started. The room was very quiet, and Calvin had put his arm tightly around Evelyn's shoulders. To break the shocked stillness, Diana went over to the sideboard to put her empty glass on a tray.

"You know, it's getting pretty late," Evelyn said. "I need to be at work in the morning, and you're teaching a class, aren't you, Fran?"

"Well, not until...I mean, yes, I probably should be getting home."

"Oh, for gods' sake, don't everyone rush out while Phoebe is in the kitchen," Diana said. "She'll never forgive you."

"I'll go," David said. "I'm really a fifth wheel in this crowd now, anyway. I knew that when I made up my mind to resign." He stuck out his hand. "I'm glad I got to meet you, Diana."

The others murmured politely in response as David tersely said good-night, with a wave half over one shoulder at them. He walked rapidly down the short hall to the spare room to get his coat. Diana, mindless of what anyone thought, hurried after him.

"No, wait—" She caught his arm as he emerged with his coat and pulled him across the hall into Phoebe's bedroom where there was a phone with a pad of paper by the bed. "Give me your phone number, at least."

He stared down at the paper and pencil she pushed against his chest. "Why?"

"We need to talk. After Beltene would probably be best."

"Well..." he slowly took the pencil and scribbled briefly. "I'm looking for a job, so I'm not home very much."

"I'll keep trying."

His mouth crooked into a half-smile. "Pushy, aren't you? My Bubba warned me about girls like you."

Diana couldn't repress a short laugh. "I kind of doubt that."

𝕷ate the next afternoon, Diana was still brooding over the cocktail party an hour after she'd woken up. She couldn't shake the uncomfortable suspicion that the little tiff between Art and David had been her fault. Doubtless there was some history between them which had nothing to do with her, but she was sure that her presence had made everyone tense. She felt more apprehensive about attending a large ritual than ever.

She finally remembered that she had asked not to be disturbed, and checked with the front desk for phone messages. To her surprise, Phoebe had called several times.

"Oh, Diana, I just wondered if you'd like to meet for lunch, but I guess you were out."

"Yes, I'm sorry. I still don't know whether I'll be staying here after Beltene or not, but I thought I'd look at the apartment listings." This was technically true, she'd just happened to be reading them at 4:00 in the morning.

"It's pretty grim, isn't it? The only places worth considering have waiting lists a mile long."

"There are options, though."

"It would be wonderful if you stayed. Can I make an appointment now for lunch tomorrow? Fran would like to come along, too, if that's all right."

Diana was so astonished, it took her a moment to reply. "I'd love to, and Fran is welcome to come. I'd enjoy getting better acquainted, I barely know her."

"We can do some shopping, too. You mentioned that you hadn't brought much with you. We'll be in the hotel lobby at noon, okay?"

After she hung up, Diana sat looking at the phone for some minutes, wondering if she could trust her own assessment of any situation these days.

3

Over the next few days two lunches, a long shopping trip and an evening of cocktails in a small lounge all went congenially, although people still seemed a little uncertain around Diana. Those who got together with her repeatedly, like Phoebe and Fran, seemed to shrug off their feelings and relax into normality by the second or third meeting, at least as far as Diana could tell.

Nevertheless, the night of Beltene, Diana arrived at the Motherhouse with considerable trepidation. Very few people would be present whom she knew well—in fact, she thought she had seniority as an Adeptus over everyone except Daniel Cobert, who as the new Presiding Magus was officiating for the ceremonial portion of the night. Of the other Council members still in the Boston area, all were visiting the first Beltene celebration of the House in Providence. Diana sternly refused to speculate on how recently they'd decided to do so, *en masse,* and why—Providence was the first new House to be established in fifty years, after all.

When she cautiously greeted Daniel, his reaction was no more perspicacious than her friends'. His unctuous smile disappeared for a moment and he raised his eyebrows, then seemed to dismiss his perceptions and turned to greet the next attendee. Diana heaved a small sigh of relief, although Daniel had never been the brightest star in the Order's magical firmament.

She wondered if she would be left a wallflower for the first time ever. It happened—the rule about Beltene was that participants never questioned what took place after the lights were extinguished at midnight. You simply accepted whatever did or did not ensue—one partner, several consecutively, several at once, or none at all.

The ceremony itself was a bit dull. With everyone in the customary masks and toga-like drapery, Diana honestly wasn't sure who some of the participants were—a significant number had become Novices during the three years she'd been away. She saw immediately what Phoebe had meant about there being a lot of stags—the term the Order used for male participants who outnumbered the women present. With so much attrition and so many relative newcomers to the Order's traditions, Diana detected much less tense excitement than she was used to. *I really am a relic,* she thought wryly. *I'm actually thinking, "it's not like the old days."*

For her, the intensity of the smells and sounds were highly distracting and not always very arousing. She'd been careful to hunt earlier that evening, so she wasn't bothered by blood thirst despite the close quarters. But her apprehension was proving justified. Insofar as the ritual constraints allowed, the other people in the cavernous hall were drawing away from her. One man, whom she hadn't seen before everyone was garbed and didn't recognize from what parts of him were visible, seemed to be staring at her rather intently—at least, she caught him looking away when she glanced at him at least half a dozen times. Initially he was on the far side of the room from her, but as people moved in the steps of the ritual, he alone kept shifting closer.

Diana had completely forgotten that when the lights were extinguished, she would be able to see in the dark. She was a bit startled at how self-conscious she suddenly felt, not because anything was going on that she hadn't seen many times, but because she knew that no one else present realized they could be seen. Diana recalled what Thomas had said about darkness giving an illusion of privacy. The mild intoxicant in the chalice wine had no effect on her whatsoever, and she felt, not just awkwardly out of place, but rather like a voyeur. She sat down on the thick carpet and turned toward the wall behind her, frustrated and embarrassed at once, and regretting that she'd agreed to attend. There was a lot of movement around the room, as usually was the case at first, so she didn't realize she was being approached until someone knelt behind her and put his or her hands on Diana's shoulders.

She started, then relaxed as the hands slid down her arms. Whoever it was seemed to be utterly fascinated with the coolness of her skin. Diana sat still for several minutes as the hands roved over her body, less sensuous than curious. Finally she turned around to face her inquisitive partner, and as she'd guessed, it was the man who had been watching her all evening. He hadn't removed his mask, and that wasn't per custom. She could feel his fingers trembling, as though he was both afraid of her and irresistibly attracted despite himself. Now that he was closer, she thought he seemed familiar, but she couldn't quite connect the way he smelled to her now, and the way his warm skin glowed to her night vision, with what she remembered of people she'd known in her old life. He had learned all he could by caressing her skin, and he leaned in to kiss her, at first tentatively and then harder and more aggressively. Diana couldn't identify him by taste or feel, either, and decided to stop worrying about who he was and just enjoy this unexpected pairing for all it was worth.

Her unknown partner kept both of them occupied for several hours, and his lovemaking was similar to his initial approach—exploratory, as though he was collecting information about her, inside and out. Diana felt something of the same inquiring mood, however. Beltene etiquette denied participants the right to ask a partner's name. She got the feeling that this man knew how badly she wanted to know who he was and was amusing himself by refusing to tell. That may have been an illusion, but it was odd that the only scrap of clothing he never took off was his mask. She wanted to abandon herself to the intense pleasure he was giving her, and found this annoyingly difficult. The intoxicant would have helped, of course, but an even greater hindrance than sobriety was the fact that Diana kept thinking, almost obsessively, about Gregory. It was as though something was persistently reminding her of him, and she didn't know what that could be. Several times, Diana took the lead, pushing the man down and fucking him astraddle as hard as she dared without revealing her real strength, but no matter what she did, he wouldn't speak or even moan out loud.

No one else approached the two of them, and when dawn came, Diana was as exhausted and sleepy as the rest of the circle. Some people left the ritual chamber, either to retire to a private setting or to preserve their anonymity, but the masked man seemed in no hurry to leave. Eventually they fell asleep, curled up against each other on the deep, soft Oriental carpet, along with those others who were too satiated or blissful to move from the hall.

Diana wasn't sure what awoke her, and for a moment or two she blinked groggily at a blurred rectangular outline of light that seemed to be hanging in space. The apparition resolved itself into daylight shining around the edges of a window blind on the wall thirty feet away. She remembered then where she was, and sat up slowly, wondering what time it could be. She usually didn't awaken before mid-afternoon, but Beltene revelers seldom slept so late, even with chalice hangover. Those who'd stayed frequently went out for late breakfast or lunch together, taking a sly glee in picking some highly conservative venue and feigning nonchalant normality. She looked around and saw the masked man sprawled on his back next to her, snoring softly. His mask was askew, and as she pondered whether she could get away with tugging it off, he stirred, and suddenly sat up with a gasp, groping to his side with one hand. She remembered that for him, the room was still very dark, and she clasped his hand. He started but didn't pull away.

"It's all right, I haven't gone anywhere." She kept her voice low, because there were a dozen or so other sleepers in the room.

"What time is it?" His voice was gravelly and he was slurring his consonants—the intoxicant hadn't been inert for him.

"Gods, I don't know. I'm not sure why I woke up." It would have been nice to awaken to bird song and bubbling brooks on May Day, but what she dimly heard, through the thick exterior walls, was the traffic on Beacon Street. "Are you hungry? I thought maybe we could go somewhere and talk."

He glanced toward her. "I'm starving," he finally said. "And you're right, we do need to talk."

With those words, Diana recognized his voice, and a shock ran through her. She started to speak, but caught herself until they'd left the ritual chamber. She got to her feet, and he followed suit much more clumsily, groping for her hand. She led him cautiously around their sleeping peers to the changing room at the side of the hall. *He does know I can see in the dark,* she thought. When they were inside the changing room and had closed the door behind them, Diana turned on the light, both of them wincing despite the dim wattage intended to spare the eyes of those walking in from the darkened hall.

"All right, you can take that mask off, Jack."

He grinned then, and pulled off the mask, tossing it jauntily aside. "Ya got me."

"The minute you opened your mouth, finally. No *wonder* I couldn't stop thinking about Gregory all night. I was with his best friend! So what gives with the Lone Ranger gag, anyway, and why even bother? Do you think I have x-ray vision or something?" The light humor in her tone was entirely dishonest.

His grin disappeared, and he glanced at the door. "We don't really want to talk here. Let's get dressed and go someplace private."

4

They went back to Diana's room at the Hilton, because they couldn't talk in a public setting. Jack wanted a steak with all the trimmings, and Diana obligingly ordered him one from room service.

"I thought you were in Colorado," she said after the food had been delivered.

"I was."

"Obviously you didn't quit the Order, after all. Now I feel silly."

"Is that what you thought?"

"That's what I assumed—but so did nearly everyone else. You just disappeared. No one reported seeing you at one of the other Houses and nobody heard boo from you. What else would we think? So what happened?"

She had to wait for a reply because Jack was chewing steak with great élan, washing it down with gulps of Coca-Cola. "I took a leave of absence, that's all," he said finally. "It wasn't anyone else's business. I was mad as hell at the Council for what they did to Gregs and I just needed to cool off."

"Why didn't you speak to the Council on his behalf, then, if you were so mad?"

Jack gave her a quick mirthless grin. "You mean like you? I didn't have your connections, sugar. I tried and got told to shut my face or get the same boot Gregs did. I wasn't ready for that, I'd just made Adeptus. Besides, I was flat broke. My dad offered me a job with his firm out in Colorado, so I decided to go out there and work for a while, just to get flush. I've been back here a couple of times to see Gregs, I just didn't come into the city."

"Gregory didn't tell me you came back here to see him." Diana felt a little miffed, although she realized that she should have guessed Jack had been in touch. That explained why Gregory knew that Jack was out in Colorado back in 1952, and why his tone had held no rancor when he'd mentioned his old friend.

"That's Gregs. He never was a talker, that's why the Council was so fouled up, thinking for one second that he'd go blathering secrets around. Everyone who knew Gregs knew how screwy that was."

"There was something else behind all that, I know it."

"Yeah, well, you made enough noise about it then to make them damned uncomfortable. I'm surprised they let you off so easy."

"I was formally censured, Jack."

"I'll say it again—you got off easy, from what I was hearing. Roderick always had a soft spot for you. Take it from me, anyone else would have been banished along with Gregs. Of course, maybe they were too scared of you."

"Scared? Of *me?*" Her startled reaction wasn't exaggerated.

Jack just grinned at her and applied himself to his food. Diana was silent, letting him eat in peace. He looked like he needed it: he was considerably leaner and hard-muscled than she remembered, and his dusty brown hair was already thinning at the crown and receding from his temples. It was no wonder that she hadn't recognized him by feel, although she should have remembered his unusual hazel eyes, the colors of a muddy river. He hadn't commented on her failure to order any food for herself, and she was letting that topic hang between them.

When he'd all but licked his plate clean, Jack sprawled back in the armchair where he'd sat to eat, heaving a blissful sigh. "Well, thanks for buying me lunch," he said with a teasing half smile.

"Anything for old times sake. But you know what they say about a free lunch."

He grinned. "Yeah, I know, you're full of questions, aren't you?"

"And you're not?"

His grin faded. "Maybe just a few."

"You're not running off to any appointments or anything, are you?"

"Well, no, but...truth is, I don't really have anywhere to stay at the moment. I just blew into town a couple of days ago, and I've mostly been sleeping on sofas. The rest of the Order is as surprised to see me as you are, so I don't feel terribly welcome."

"Sorry to hear that. The Hilton would take a dim view of you sharing the room with me, I'm afraid. We'll be tossed out for indecent behavior."

"I know."

After they'd looked at each other for a moment, Jack wearing his most insufferably endearing puppy-dog face, Diana heaved a loud sigh. "I *suppose* I could hide you for a night or two—if you promise to be discreet."

"Swear on a thousand gods, they'll never know I'm here." He straightened up. "Okay, now that we've got that settled—who wants to start?"

"I'll start. Have you heard from Gregory since last June?"

Jack blinked. "Last June? No. No, honest, Diana. We didn't really keep in touch, y'know? I'd heard from him...let's see. It's been more than a year now. He told me that he'd seen you again, and he told me you'd gotten divorced, but you weren't free yet. That sounded cock-eyed, but I knew I'd be wasting my time asking him what he meant. I got the message, between the lines, y'know, that he was hoping he'd pick you up on the rebound somehow."

"He might've, too, if he hadn't fouled things up. So you didn't hear about him selling his house in Manchester and moving on?"

"What? No. Shit. I was going to go up there and see him."

"By now, there're probably three new houses on the lot, or at least the foundations."

"Jesus. What gives? Where'd he go?"

Diana hesitated automatically. There was no reason not to share information about Gregory with Jack—all three of them were Adeptus rank and practically siblings in the Order. But it wasn't Gregory's confidentiality that restrained her. Thomas' voice echoed in her memory: *One doesn't talk casually about Levoissier...* Then she stiffened. *He can kiss my ass,* she thought, recalling the way she'd seethed at Gregory's news in June.

"He's back with Levoissier," she almost snapped. Jack gaped at her, his expression a portrait of utter stupefaction. After a moment in which her friend seemed incapable of composing a spoken response, Diana said dryly, "You're wearing about the same look that I did. I can't verify this news independently, mind you. I'm only repeating what Gregory said."

Jack finally closed his mouth and swallowed so hard, even a mortal would have heard the gulp. "When did this happen?"

"When I saw him in June, he was on his way to some mysterious rendezvous up in Canada. He had to get up there without anyone's help—he was thumbing rides, he said—and meet Levoissier in Montréal. Of course, where they went from there is anyone's guess—the moon, for all I know. Except that the whole Order seems to be migrating to France these days—or at least Providence."

"Well, not exactly, they were just leaving Boston, because—" he broke off and looked at her sharply. "You *know* why because."

"You tell me."

Jack rolled his eyes. "Diana, let's not beat around the bushes, okay? I'm not trying to be cute, I just haven't had a chance to talk yet. Because of your working, of course, the one that turned on you."

"How do you know about that? Nobody else here seems to, and you've been out in silver lode country." Her eyes narrowed, and she saw him draw back a little. "Did you get one of those warnings?"

"Well, I—I got *a* warning."

"From *whom?* Levoissier?"

"Jesus, Diana, don't give me the third degree! It's not my *fault!*" As she glared at him, trying to control herself before he fled the room, he flung up his hands. "From Gregs, but it's not what you think. He didn't tell me any details. He just said he was helping you with something he was afraid might get out of control in a really big way, and I should be aware of it. He said he took down his athanor to break the connection, just in case."

"But why did he tell you, what did you have to do with it?"

"I helped him build his athanor."

Diana sagged. "Oh. But...why didn't he tell *me?* Why didn't anyone warn me and Thomas, if so many people knew—"

"Would you have listened? Would you have stopped it? *Could* you have stopped it?"

"I suppose not."

"Did it really turn, Diana? See, I really don't know. All I know is..."

"Is what?"

"All I know is what I see," he said softly. "And feel. And sense from you. I know what you are now."

She studied his solemn face for a moment. "If that was true, you wouldn't be alone with me."

"I'm not afraid of you. I don't get that kind of feeling from you, at all. And I ought to know, after last night, wouldn't I?"

"So what am I, Jack, since you're so smart?"

He shrugged. "Okay. Vampire?"

She looked away from him. "Am I the last person in the Order to find out about this? Is that why everyone's been shying away from me since I came back—everyone else has known all along that—"

"—that there are vampires running around and you're one of them?" Jack broke in. "Hell, no. I'll bet most people in the Order are more skeptical about the supernatural than your average church-going Christian. But you see...I've met one, a vampire, I mean. A couple of them, actually. They usually don't come out in the open and let anyone know, and you can see why. You practically get lynched for selling comic books these days. How long would a vampire last if he showed up on *The Tonight Show?*"

It was Diana's turn to stare open-mouthed, her voice choked off by conflicting emotions of stunned astonishment, betrayal and anger at the unfairness of it all. "But—where did *you* meet other vampires? How did you recognize them, and why did they let you know they were real? Thomas said he knew others, but he wouldn't tell me anything about them, no names or where they could be found or what they look like, nothing. He just said we'd probably cross paths sooner or later, and some kind of vampire etiquette prevented him from breaking their confidence."

"I can't tell you much more, Diana. Besides, I don't know very much, probably not even their real names, or at least the names they'd be using now, and...I don't remember everything I knew."

She blinked. "They blotted your memory?"

"Some of it. I asked them to."

"You *asked* them?"

He nodded, his eyes distant.

"Gods, Jack, there's a hell of a story here, I can see that."

"There is, but not a tenth of the story that you've got. Is *this*—" he reached out and touched her hand, and she knew that he meant her cold skin—"what you wanted, Diana, or was it just a side effect?"

"It wasn't what I thought I wanted, but…the Sidhe always know what you really want, that's what Gregory told me, before it all even started. I didn't know…vampires…had anything to do with it until I got to Maine. And even when I knew, I never thought I wanted to *be* one. Gods, I…I should have known better than to get involved."

"So, how *did* you get involved, then?" Jack was studying her intently, and his voice was quiet in the way he got when he was so focused that he begrudged the energy to speak more loudly. "Tell me, Diana. If you think your whole adventure is gossip fodder, you're wrong. Everyone knows that something's happened to you, because they can see it, and feel it magically. And they're spooked, I won't lie about it. But these are the same people who got the shivers around Levoissier, and no one knows *what* he is. They don't know what you are, exactly, they just know that you're something different now, something else. I only know because I've seen it before, and not one person in ten thousand can say that, at least not who remembers the encounter afterwards. *You* know what I mean. So tell me what happened, and how Gregs was part of it."

"If I tell you all that, will you tell me about these vampires you met?"

"As much as I can, I swear."

"Did you meet them in Colorado?"

"No, it was here."

Diana was silent for a while, thinking. She was remembering the stifling afternoon, not quite a year ago, when she'd sat at Moira's kitchen table spinning the whole fantastic tale out to her, while Moira let cigarette after cigarette burn out, forgotten, as she listened entranced. She didn't think the affair would strike Jack as quite so exotic. She drew in, from habit, a deep breath to compose herself. "All right. You're sure you don't want another Coca Cola or something? We're going to be here a while."

He shook his head, smiling a little. "If I get parched, I'll get a glass of water from the bathroom. Should I worry about how thirsty you are?"

She smiled grimly. "I'm good for another day or so. I might order something chocolate from room service later on, though." She considered for a few moments. "I better start back when Gregory was expelled from the Order, in forty-seven. I don't know if that's really when it all began, but that's when I started consciously taking the actions that put me on this path." She launched into the story of how Levoissier recruited her as an apprentice after Gregory and Jack had both left the Order.

5

It was late afternoon by the time she finished her story—Jack had a great many questions. What struck Diana about his reaction, though, was that he didn't seem as interested in vampires or the physical destruction of the spell's turning, or the apparent reality of the Tylwyth Teg, as she'd expected any magical person to be. He seemed wholly absorbed by another aspect of her tale entirely.

"So...tell me more about this idea of yours that started the whole thing—this crazy idea you had that there's some kind of secret cabal out there pulling strings? Did you really think that?"

"Come on, Jack, you know I thought the Order had some level that was working politically. I still think they were exerting some pretty suspicious influence during the war. How else did Stephen manage to spend three years on a tin can gunboat and never see action? And I think the Order must have helped Thomas fake his 4-F and get into the civil defense command up in Bangor."

"You said he was a lawyer, and loaded, he didn't need the Order for that."

"Maybe not, but it's still fishy, and he admitted they'd helped him in the past. Those are just examples, there's lots more—all little things, but they'd have to be, or they'd be noticed."

Jack shrugged. "So why didn't you keep on pushing it? I know, I know, you were censured—but then Levoissier took you under his wing, that made you gold. Wouldn't he have told you if you were on the ball?"

"You're kidding, right? Levoissier? Tell me anything I actually wanted to know?"

"My, aren't we bitter, though."

Diana snorted. "Jack...you have no idea."

"We're getting off the point."

"So what *is* your point?"

To her surprise, Jack got up and paced across the hotel room, then back, scowling. He stopped in front of her, hands behind his back. "You mentioned something about asking Thomas Morgan if he'd ever thought about starting an underground group himself. He said it was impossible for something like that to be completely secret and do any good. I think he was bulling you about that."

"What do you mean? You mean he really does know about groups and he was just lying to me? Oh, Jack, I really don't think so—"

"No, I'm not calling him a liar, not about that. But I don't agree that you have to be public to work real change. I think it is possible to exert influence and still be unknown and unseen. What it takes is..." he started pacing again, and Diana watched him, frowning. She wondered if the ritual intoxicant had quite worn off yet. "What it takes is power, and resources," he went on, his voice rising a little. "And you've got those now, Diana! I mean, you always had money, but you never used any of it. You gave it all to that white elephant of yours—"

"Ex*cuse* me?" She bristled at this characterization of Bread and Roses, even though she had stepped down from its Board three years ago.

"Oh, hell, I'm not saying it didn't turn out pretty well, but it just sucked you dry, you gave it everything you had. And for what? It didn't make you feel good about yourself. You said it, you just got more and more overwhelmed and frustrated, because no matter how big your charity grew, it could never do more than scrape the surface. You couldn't feed and house everyone on the planet, educate every child and bring about world peace. But nothing less than that would have satisfied you, in the end."

"Well..." Suddenly irritated, she fumbled for a reply. "So what? Would Bread and Roses have done any better if it had gone underground and operated like some kind of—"

"No, no, no, I'm not saying that. It's great, for what it is. But it wasn't really what *you* wanted. I always thought that, and now I can really see it. And now this working of yours, you know—Morgan was right, what he said to you, about it not being a failure at all. You did get what you wanted, what you've always wanted. You've got power and you've cut free from all your ties, including Bread and Roses. They're flying on their own, you're free, your conscience is clear. Now you can do what you really were meant to be doing, what you've wanted to do, right from the start."

"You mean—"

"I mean found another group, a totally different kind of operation, one that doesn't plod away at street level, that attacks everything that's wrong with society right at its roots."

Diana studied him silently for a moment. "Sounds like a tall order."

"What did you go to Maine for, then? What did you go through all *this* for?"

"I didn't choose it, Jack! Thomas told me that he didn't know of any groups and he didn't want to start one. That was the end of it. I got involved with the working because..." She hated to admit it out loud even now. "I was just drunk with the idea of that much power. I couldn't even think about what I'd use it *for*. I just *wanted* it. And the worst thing is, I was the last person to know that.

Thomas saw right through me before the end of our very first conversation. Levoissier knew it, that's why the bastard set me up to meet Thomas in the first place. Even the Teg knew, damn it. *Everyone* knew that I was nothing but a power hungry egomaniac wearing the sheep skin of a do-gooder."

"Oh, that's ridiculous. You're no egotist! Diana—" Jack came rapidly back to her chair and dropped down to one knee, taking hold of her hands as though he was going to propose to her. Diana drew back a little at the intensity in his eyes. "Don't you see, that's what's wrong with the world now, the wrong people have all the power, and the people who *should* have it, think they don't deserve it, or can't handle it, or that it's wrong to even want it. Women, y'know, *women* should have the power, then maybe we wouldn't live in a hell of faceless corporations and wars."

"You remember what Lord Acton said. Doesn't power change people?"

"Nuts to Lord Acton. I never believed that bullshit. Did someone die and make him God?"

"Of course not, but I think a lot of people have observed independently that power tends to corrupt people who get it."

"Because the people who go after it, and get it, want it for evil reasons to begin with. Who's ever proved that someone like Hitler or Stalin, or Ford for that matter, were one bit different before they got hold of a lot of power over people? All those slobs you see griping and complaining on their way to and from work, and stabbing their coworkers in the back to get ahead, and gypping the little old guy in the corner store out of ten cents every time they can get away with it—what do you think they'd be like if someone gave them a million bucks and put them in some big office?"

"I suppose so, but—"

"But then there are people like you. You have a trust fund, for god's sake, but you didn't grow up into some white-fingered society lady."

"Well, I didn't exactly have a normal upbringing, did I?"

"Neither did Stephen lah-di-dah Winthrop, your precious ex-, and look how he turned out. No, you're just naturally principled, Diana. You deserve what you've got, because you can handle it."

"That's a very flattering thought. Not everyone would agree with you there."

"Nuts to everyone agreeing."

"So who died and made *you* God?" He scowled at her and got up, pacing back and forth a few more times. Watching him, Diana felt uneasy. "Jack, I think you need to calm down a little. Maybe the day after Beltene isn't the most auspicious time to discuss something this...serious." When he threw his arms up in an exaggerated shrug, she went on, "Is there some kind of hurry? And where are we going with this, anyway? So, I've got power, or that's what you think. So what? What's it to you?"

He went back to the armchair and sat down again, finally—Diana thought he must have been getting tired by now. "It's obvious. I'm asking you if you want to start a group, a movement, whatever you'd call it. With me. And other people, we'll find more. With someone like you at the core of it, we won't be like all the associations and guilds and unions out there. We'll be something different. We'll be what you've been looking for. Remember what they say about searching the world over for what's in your own back yard? You've been looking in corners for your own tail. It's been a part of you all along."

"You want to co-found this thing with me?"

"Yes!"

"You mean you want to be a vampire, too."

He blinked. "What? No! I never said that."

"But, Jack—that was my whole idea when I went looking for Thomas Morgan, don't you remember? Anyone can found a group. I was looking for immortals, or at the least, people with an extended lifespan. I may have been disappointed, but my rationale for that hasn't changed. If the group's members can't survive more than a generation, the whole thing will fall apart. How can you and I change that, if you're mortal and only good for a few decades? What's going to make this group so different from all the others?"

He leaned toward her. "*You*. You will be the continuity at the core of this group. You're what will hold it together."

"While everyone else gets old and dies, and I keep having to train new people who do the same, over and over? Wow, what fun for me."

"Don't take such a selfish view, Diana, for god's sake. I might change my mind, I'd have to get used to the idea. I don't know very much about it, and I'm not ready to give up steak dinners for a liquid diet. Oh, yeah, I know you guys can eat food, but I saw the way you wrinkled your nose up when room service left the tray."

"So political idealism is trumped by fine dining?"

Jack shook his head, looking frustrated. "Why are you dodging this?"

"I'm not dodging it, Jack, it's just…this is all coming at me from out of the blue, and I guess I need some time to think about it. Before this morning, I never thought I'd see you again. I came down here for Beltene, and also to see if magical people would run screaming from the room when they saw me, which is almost the case. What are you doing here?"

Jack shrugged. "Same as you, I was asked—Daniel sent me a note. I think he was just trying to reel in as many absent members as he could so he'd have something to preside over. That self-important ego of his would never recover if his first major ritual got cancelled for lack of attendance—especially a Beltene."

"But all the way from Colorado, with no place to stay? Come on. What did you do, leave everything behind and hitchhike all the way out here?"

"I didn't have much to leave. I've been living in my parents' basement. And I took the train, for your information. Trouble is, the train ticket cost most of what I had."

Diana sat back in the chair, frowning as she pondered the possible significance of all this. *Seven years and seven years,* she recalled Gregory saying. It had been seven years since she'd last seen Jack, and now they'd simply run into each other—and he knew about vampires. Where the Teg were involved, was there ever any such thing as a coincidence?

"What?" she heard Jack say, and realized that her expression must be unsettling to say the least.

"I don't *know* what, just yet," she said, because "nothing" would be dishonest and evasive, and Jack deserved better. "Look, Jack, we can talk more about your idea, all right? You promised to tell me about these other vampires you met. I'm assuming none of them was Thomas, or you'd have said something—wouldn't you?"

"No, I never met him, but I have to confess: I'd heard of him. Not by that name, but when you described him, I realized who he was."

Once again, Diana could only stare at him, even as she chided herself for being surprised by anything at this point. Thomas could hardly know other vampires without their knowing him, but apparently, these other vampires didn't share his respect for discretion. "Go on."

Jack's bombastic attitude had deflated. "I think I'll get a glass of water," he mumbled, and Diana waited patiently while he went to the bathroom, unwrapped a glass, filled it at the sink and returned. The glass sloshed a little water on the carpet when he sat down, and Diana realized that his hands were shaking. She raised her eyebrows but didn't say anything to call attention to her observation. Jack cleared his throat and took a deep breath.

"You understand, I've never told anyone about this. Not Gregs, not my mentor, no one, not ever."

"It stays in this room, I swear."

"I know. I didn't mean that so much, just that—you keep jumping to the conclusion that people haven't been telling you things. It's not like everyone knew this but you, and I sure don't want you to think that Gregs was holding out on you. He really didn't know."

Diana nodded. "I appreciate you telling me that." She realized that he was stalling, and refused to feed into it.

"It was during the war. I had a leave, in October of forty-three, but it was only five days, so I didn't have time to go out and see my folks. We tied up in New York City, and I took the train up here to see Gregs, but that was about all I could do except goof off. I didn't have a girl waiting for me or anything like that, and most of my other friends were in the service or out of the country. You were totally taken up with Bread and Roses. I was at loose ends, so I just went to bars and got plastered with other servicemen. I didn't even pick up any of the good time girls, that's how pathetic I was.

"I was up until all hours, because I hated to be home and just sleep. The second night I was in some dive at about three in the morning, and I noticed this fella standing across the room. The way he was dressed, and the way he acted, he wouldn't have stood out in a crowd anywhere, but for me, he might as well have been tap dancing down the bar. I couldn't tell you anything specific, you know—there was just something different about him. I was pretty drunk, and that made me stupid, so I was staring at him a lot, trying to figure out what it was that bugged me about him. Finally I realized that he was looking back at me. Then he came over to where I was sitting. 'Got a problem, pal?' he said, but he didn't say it the way most guys would. It almost sounded like he was reciting a line. He had this cultured voice."

"What did he look like?"

"Well, that was another thing. He didn't look like he ate his Cheerios, that's for sure. Thin, not too tall, smooth skin, moved like a dancer—had that sort of…girlish feeling. Like Peter Lorre playing the fairy in *The Maltese Falcon*. But he was a lot better looking than Lorre."

"Okay, but, come on—blond, brunette, redhead? White, Negro, Oriental? Can you give me a *clue?*"

"Oh, well, white, dark hair, gray eyes—a lot like yours, actually—clean shaven, pale. Looked a little like a frog, if I had to guess his nationality."

"Did you find out his name?"

"He gave me *a* name. But you're getting ahead of me."

"Sorry. So, 'got a problem, pal'—then what?"

"I just mumbled something. He looked like I could have mopped up the floor with him, but I wasn't fooled. I could just feel the power coming off him, and he knew it, which was even creepier. I could see this curiosity in his eyes, he couldn't figure out why I picked him out when no one else in the room did. What was I going to say, 'hi, I'm Jack, I'm a magician?'"

"Nothing like cutting right to the chase."

"No, thanks! All I wanted to do was get out of there, but I didn't know what I'd do if he followed me. I was about ready to piss in my pants. But then something outside caught his attention. His head jerked around, and he looked at me and the door a couple of times, then he jumped like he'd gotten an electric shock, and he was just—gone."

"Gone? You mean he literally vanished?"

"I don't think so. I think he just moved that fast, plus took advantage of my being distracted, because I kept looking at the door, too, to see what he was looking at. Anyway, I'd had enough by then. I went up to the bar and paid my tab and asked the bartender if there was a back door. He'd seen me talking to that guy, and he just waved me out through the kitchen. 'Keep an eye out, sailor,' he said. He asked if I wanted him to call me a cab but I didn't want to spend the money, I had a room only a couple of blocks away.

"The back door opened out into an alley, and right away I was sorry, because it was darker than an old cellar out there. They turned all the lights off that late, like Boston was going to get air raids or something. I was standing there trying to get my bearings, and that's when something grabbed me from behind."

"Mr. Got a Problem Pal?"

"Turned out not, although that's what I thought in the first few seconds. It was so fast, and whatever grabbed me was so strong, I couldn't even take in a breath to yell. I was in a one-armed chokehold, and the guy's other hand was yanking my head sideways, and then I felt something clamp onto my neck, and there was this horrible *tearing* feeling…" Jack paused, swallowing hard. "But then he let go of me, and suddenly there were other people there and I was in the middle of a wild fight. I couldn't see anything, but I could hear grunts and curses and the sounds of fists hitting flesh, and a body slamming into the wall, hard—you'd have thought bones were breaking, from the sound of it. Then something hit me and I blacked out."

Jack took a long drink from his water glass, and Diana could tell he wished it contained something a lot stronger. "I woke up tied to a chair in a room someplace."

"Tied to a chair?"

"Not…it was just a loop around my arms and body, like they didn't want me to wake up and jump up without them knowing. Someone was standing right next to me, a little behind so I couldn't see him right away. I wasn't blindfolded or anything like that. Across the room there was a little group of people, and they were talking to some…character…who was tied up a lot more thoroughly than I was. It was a woman, doing the talking. She was taller than you, had one of those lean, hard bodies like female athletes have, not sexy at all but she looked like she could handle herself. Dark, kind of swarthy skin, the kind of woman who shaves more often than I do—you know the type?"

"I think so," Diana's tone was a bit wry.

"Hey, I'm not trying to be smart-alecky, just descriptive. You wanted to know what they looked like. I heard someone call her Janna or Janice…but not quite that. It was an unusual name, so I probably didn't hear it right. There were three guys standing with her, and then the one from the bar was standing next to me. He saw that I'd woken up and put his hand on my shoulder, that's how I saw who he was." Jack paused a moment. "That's all I actually remember."

"That's it? You mean they blanked your memory out?"

"Yeah."

Diana's brow creased. "But, Jack…how do you know that? You said you asked for your memory to be erased. If you don't remember asking—"

"I saw them again—well, the one from the bar, and one of the guys who'd been standing across the room. I think they were following up to see if their memory-blanking had taken, and whether I was going to blow their cover. Apparently, I'm very resistant to whatever it is that they do. It might be because of the magical training, I don't know. But when I told them what I still remembered, they admitted a few things to me. I swore up and down that I'd never breathe a word of it to a soul—but I have this feeling that you wouldn't be included in that promise."

"Why?"

"Because I'm sure they'd want to know about you, which means they probably would want you to know about them."

Thomas had said essentially the same thing, but Diana still pondered it dubiously. "So, they claimed that you asked for your memory to be erased?"

"I believed them. I had this very uncomfortable sense that I'd seen something…ugly. I know that sounds like a strange thing to say when I was in the Navy, and there was a war going on. But I was never in the thick of the action there—like your precious ex-, somehow I always seemed to be stationed someplace pretty safe. You won't hear me complaining about that! But I just had this feeling…" he shuddered, to Diana's amazement. She'd never thought of Jack as squeamish.

"Did you ask them what that might have been?"

"Yeah. Yeah, they told me. They said I'd walked right into an ambush, basically—oh, not of me, they were staking out that block tracking down some kind of rogue vampire. They said they had to destroy him, and I saw it. They didn't give me any details. I didn't want any. I did feel a little less—sticky—once I knew what was bugging me."

"Rogue vampire…Thomas never mentioned that."

"Sounds like there's a hell of a lot he didn't mention."

"He seemed rather confident that I'd run into some of these other vampires sooner or later and learn the answers from them. You said they gave you names?"

"The one who was in the bar said his name was Avery. The other one introduced himself as Ned. They didn't give any last names. Ned was the one who did most of the talking—I had the feeling that he was glad to have someone he could be honest with. Avery was quieter, and he kept giving Ned looks, like he was saying too much, although he didn't drop any bombshells as far as I could tell. He's the one who told me that there were only a small number of them, but they did a lot of different things in the normal world, and he even knew one who was an attorney, and did a lot of progressive political stuff. That Ned had quite a talent, though. He could open locks—not pick them, just open them, like magic." Diana looked up sharply. "Yeah, he'd just put his hand on the doorknob, and bingo. That's how they got into my room." Jack grinned weakly. "Have you got any special talents like that?"

"You want to see me dematerialize?" Diana hadn't mentioned that in her long story—like Thomas, she felt somewhat reticent about this particular gift.

"Ha. You're kidding, right—*Jesus.*" As Diana reappeared, slightly off kilter to the chair so that she dropped onto the seat and made the springs squeak, Jack's face turned almost gray. "Don't *do* that. I can't...I can't believe...is that for real, or did you just make me see that?"

"It's for real. I don't *need* to open locks. I just go through the cracks. Come on, you're an Adeptus, you've been around the magical block a few times. You knew Levoissier, for gods' sake."

"I know, but...don't tell me you didn't bat an eyelash the first time *you* saw that."

"It's amazing, isn't it?" She smiled wryly. "Well, I can see that I'm going to be sleeping alone from now on."

"Well, no—I mean, I didn't expect that—god, Diana, just give me a minute."

She smiled faintly, and glanced past him at the window. The sun had set while they talked, and she was feeling the change. "Are you hungry? We've been talking for hours. We could order something up for dinner. I wouldn't mind something sweet, myself. Or we could go out, there's no reason we have to hole up in this stuffy hotel room. Do you need to go pick up your things anywhere?" All Jack had brought with him was a small overnight bag that he'd had at the Motherhouse, and most members of the Order brought at least that much with them for big rituals.

"No, I've got everything with me. I traveled light, because I thought I might be going back home after a couple of days."

"Have you changed your mind about that?"

"Well...that's kind of up to you."

"Ah. Are we back to your idea of plotting world domination, then?"

He didn't smile. "Well, Diana...what *are* you going to do? You've given up Bread and Roses—"

"Not exactly, Jack. I did think I might get back onto the Board of Directors."

"Be serious, Diana. You've got way too much vision to be happy with that."

"And you're proposing, what, instead? Just the two of us, and you think we'll accomplish more than Bread and Roses does with a staff of fifty and a million-dollar budget?"

"And all the red tape and oversight that comes with it. We'll be operating under the radar—we won't have to follow anybody's rules. We'll be using influence, money—"

"My money."

"To start with. But more than that, we'll be using magic—and that, I can contribute to, as a full equal."

"And the, continuity, so to speak? My vision was a secret society of immortals, or at least, long-lived adepts who could continue their work for generations. Will you sign on for that? What if I say that I need you to step up to that level, at least eventually?"

He looked down uneasily. "Like I said…I need to think about it. Maybe you can understand why, after the story I told you. And your description of what it takes to change isn't exactly a sales pitch."

"I agree with that." She sighed. "The last time I made a magical commitment…"

"I'm not asking you for a formal vow. This isn't a working, not like that."

"I know." She was silent for a moment, thinking about the past four years and everything that had happened. *It's all brought me to this point,* she thought, *as anti-climactic as it seems after what I went through, and what I hoped for. The Lady kicked me out of the woods, literally, and as soon as I got home, I got invited to come down to Beltene, and there was Jack, and here we are. Thomas would say it's the hand of Providence again—or of the Lady. Either way…* "All right, Jack. Let's give it a try." She extended her hand toward him, and for a moment he just stared at it incredulously.

"You mean it?"

"Mind you, I'm not even sure where we'll start, let alone where we're going. I hope you have a lot of ideas, because I'm open to hearing any plans you suggest. And I should warn you: I have another agenda, which is going to take up some of my time and energy. I need to find other vampires. I have too many questions to ask and puzzles to unravel. If you can accept that, then let's shake hands and talk about what we'll do next."

Looking stunned, Jack reached out, grasped her hand and gave it a firm shake. "Then we're in business."

"For the greater good, I hope. Now, do you want to go out or order in? I need chocolate."

"**Are you sure** this is the address?"

"Positive." Jack frowned up at the modern steel-and-concrete eight-story edifice, most of which was occupied by an insurance company. Diana had wanted to see the bar where Jack had first encountered Avery, but that establishment had been on the first level of a three-floor nineteenth century brick building. Its twins still lined the opposite side of the street, and even the back alleyway remained intact. But of the original building and bar, not a trace was left.

Jack peered across the street and pointed at a small shoe repair shop in one of the storefronts. "That place has been there since the Depression. Let's see if they know anything."

The shoe repair shop smelled of old leather and fresh glue. Despite its tidy front counter, business did not appear to be booming. The wizened proprietor, gray tufts of hair framing each large ear, greeted them with the rigid smile of someone whose dental plates tend to slip. Diana looked around and selected a handful of assorted shoelaces and a couple of tins of polish. As the proprietor rang up the sale, she asked casually, "That big shiny skyscraper across the street sure seems out of place. How long has that been there?"

The proprietor rolled his eyes. "Not long. Wasn't happy to see that go up, no, nor anyone else around here. Blocks all the morning sun."

"Wasn't there a building there before, just like this one? With a bar on the ground floor?"

"Little joint called Sully's," Jack added. "Nice place."

"Oh, lord." The proprietor's face fell into tragic lines. "That whole building went up in flames, musta been, oh, forty-eight. Terrible thing. Killed eight people. Gutted the place, nothing left but the walls. They tore it down, and a couple of years later, up goes that thing. Lots of folks thought they should leave the site for a memorial, a park or something, but you know how it's been since the war. Build, build and build some more, anything for a dollar."

"It wasn't arson, was it?" Diana quailed at the thought that the building's destruction might have some connection to the vampire activities Jack had run into there. But the proprietor shook his head.

"No one ever thought so. Some drunken fool on the second floor fell asleep with a cigarette in his mouth, firemen said."

"What a tragedy," Diana said. "Well, thank you."

"I guess that's the end of that," Jack said as they crossed the street to where Diana's car was parked. "What are you going to do with that stuff, anyway?"

"Bread and Roses will hand it out to needy men."

"Oh, of course." Jack hopped into the passenger's seat, but Diana stood for a moment, looking helplessly up and down the street around the tall building. "There's not going to be anything here, Diana."

"It's just...do you think they took you far from here? You said you had a room within walking distance..."

"I have no idea. They could have had a car. You claim you can fly, not sure I believe it, but who knows how fast or how far they could have moved?"

"I know, but...gods. If only memory blanking worked both ways. If I could just undo what they did to you—"

"It doesn't and you can't." Jack shut his door with a solid thump.

Diana sighed heavily. Jack's story had sounded more like low-level gang activity than an organized group with either superpowers or a lot of money. Logic suggested that they couldn't have gone too far—they might have been upstairs in the same building. But that meant nothing, twelve years after the fact. The vampires Jack had met might not even be in the United States any longer, far less in Boston. *I'll just have to stay alert and pay attention. Thomas said, we tend to cross paths more often than chance would dictate—and chance doesn't seem too operative in my life now.*

Jack rolled down his window. "Come *on*. I promised April we'd be there by four. You really don't want to stand this girl up."

"April? You found us a magician named *April?*"

Jack didn't smile. "Wait 'til you meet her."

6

It was a tribute to American craftsmanship, Diana thought wryly, that the Formica tabletop wasn't buckling from the sheer psychic energy shooting across it from every direction.

It was June 12, 1955, and the first formal meeting of their clandestine coven which had, by Diana's conservative estimate, more raw power than the entire Council of the Order of the Silver Light. It had taken some weeks for them to reach this point due to Jack's concern for complete secrecy.

"We don't need to rush this and start off half-cocked. It's important that we don't leave any clumsy traces that will give us away."

"Give us away to whom, Jack? What are we going to be doing, that anyone would actually take seriously? The U.S. government doesn't believe in magic, and the police only harass people for telling fortunes."

He hadn't answered her right away. "Okay—then let's be sure we establish a solid foundation to go on with. Let's put it that way."

Their first solid foundation was a derelict house surrounded by warehouses and industrial buildings in the Boston suburb of Woburn. Using several layers of dummy trusts and corporations and two different proxies, Diana had transferred the title of the house to what appeared to be a lien-holder in New Jersey. To avoid any public utility records, they set up a camp stove in the kitchen, lugged in jugs of water and dug a deep hole for a privy in the dirt floor of the cellar. A fireplace would warm the main room enough for winter meetings. They surreptitiously reinforced the board fence that ran around three sides of the tiny lot, then added magical protection to both the house and the boundaries.

The four of them were sitting around the wobbly kitchen table Diana and Jack had rescued from a pile of trash on a curb, on mismatched chairs of similar origins. An assortment of candles and kerosene lanterns sat around the room.

They all knew why they were here. Jack and Diana had met several times with each of their recruits separately. It had taken Diana a couple of days to catch David at home, and his job search had borne fruit, although he wasn't very excited about keeping the books for a small warehouse in Somerville. His initial wariness at her invitation quickly blossomed into enthusiasm when they met and she could explain their plans in more detail. Their fourth member, April McFarland, had been as eager as a Thoroughbred at the starting gate from the moment Jack introduced her to Diana. Tall and statuesque, with irrepressible waves of the most vivid flaming red hair Diana had ever seen, April's riveting appearance still shone dim compared to her aura of magical energy that even surpassed David's.

Neither David nor April, as yet, knew more about Diana than her history with the Order and Levoissier. She'd decided to get to know both of them better before she sprung vampires and the Fair Folk on them. April herself was rather mysterious. She had never been associated with the Order, and yet she clearly had had years of training, and good training, too. Jack evaded questions as to how he had met April, and April responded to inquiries simply by smiling and saying she "pled the Fifth." As with many other things concerning Jack, Diana was letting it pass—for now.

"But you see the focus of what we're going to be doing." Jack was finally wrapping up a long review of Bread and Roses and Diana's search for a magical group that worked politically. "Grassroots and direct community efforts are fine, for limited results. Or for emergencies. But just like Diana said—" Diana had, indeed, gotten a few sentences in here and there "—that stuff is superficial, band-aids, and it never lasts. We're going to go far beyond that, or not beyond, but beneath it. We're going to work at influencing the roots of power, the actual decisions and actions. We're not going to challenge power directly, we're going to make it change itself. Power protects itself, confrontation makes it stronger. You have to bore into it, like a weevil, or infect it, like a virus. That's what sabotage really means, sawing through the floor underneath your enemy before he even knows what you're doing. We're invisible to these people—they'll never see it coming."

"So we're…magical saboteurs?" David said.

"Yes! But that's only for starters. We'll eventually get way above that level."

"What do you mean, above?" April said. "In what sense? Do you mean actually infiltrating governments and seats of power ourselves, or well, not us per se but people who join us later on?"

Jack shook his head. "No. We aren't going to go near that kind of thing. We're keeping our hands totally clean. Don't you see, that would just play into all the paranoia that people have about underground groups already, all the xenophobia and fear that make the masses such willing puppets for demagogues like Hitler or Stalin or Mussolini. Millions of people already believe governments and boards are infiltrated, they really believe stupid shit like the Jews running all the banks, or Communists are taking over school boards, or the silly comic book publishers have some grand plan to corrupt youth. Trying anything like that in reality would probably just backfire. We need to do things that no one would believe or imagine are being done. We need to make the most trusted agents of authority do exactly what we want them to, without their even realizing themselves that they're not following their own will."

David, April and Diana all exchanged looks. "What?" Jack said impatiently.

"It just feels a little...manipulative," Diana said, as the other two nodded.

"Of *course* it's manipulative! That's the whole *point!* What, you really think all those idiots should just be allowed to go on happily robbing the rest of us blind, starting wars and writing laws to suit themselves? If that's how you feel, then let's disband this group and go home now, and I won't bother any of you again."

"Damn it, Jack, keep your shirt on. We're never going to get anywhere if you're going to blow up every five minutes. Sit back down."

Jack thumped back down into his chair. "Look." He was obviously making a great effort to be reasonable. "We need to be *unashamedly* manipulative, yes. Our whole objective is to change the hearts and minds of men with the political and financial clout to make the right decisions, the decisions that benefit everyone, not just the generals and fat cats. We're going to be pushing people just enough so they go in a different direction—not even conscious of what they're doing until it's too late to reverse it. If we pick the right people, and hit just the right historical fulcrums, there's almost no limit to where we can take this. They'll be little changes that have a domino effect, but yes, it does mean manipulating people's heads."

"Be honest, Jack. You're flat out saying that the ends justify the means," Diana said.

He slammed a hand on the table, making them all jump. "I am *not!*"

Before Diana, who was suddenly angry enough to stand up herself, could react, April said, "You said we'll need to hit just the right people, just the right pivot points. How will we know what those are? That sounds like nine tenths of the problem in itself, identifying what to aim at."

"That's a very good question," Jack said, looking pleased, and Diana relaxed back in her chair, sighing. "We're going to be spending a lot of time on that, no doubt about it. We'll use divination, we'll use perception and meditative projection techniques, we'll do a lot of good old-fashioned research and investigation. We won't work magically until we know exactly what we're targeting. And we might, if everyone agrees..." he paused.

"You want the suspense to kill us?" David finally said.

Jack took a deep breath. "I have some...*enhancements* that I'd like to suggest we try. But I think I'll wait to discuss those. We haven't even done a basic ritual together yet. Let's do some very small projects and evaluate the results."

Once again, his three listeners exchanged glances, but this time their shared thought was, *sounds like a fair enough suggestion.*

"All that information-gathering sounds like a lot of work, though," David said. "I don't mind telling you that I didn't do well with that kind of thing in school. Math was more my line."

"Don't worry," Diana said. "Some of this is work we can hire out. In fact, I've already talked to a couple of research assistants who thrive on this sort of minutiae-mining, and one of them works for a couple of P.I.s, so he can access public records and all kinds of things."

"Can we trust them?" April looked dubious. "With all you've gone through to keep this house secret, and no phone, it just seems that hiring assistants—"

"They won't know why they're collecting clippings and news for us. And even if someone did get suspicious, what could he do? They don't even know this group exists, apart from me."

"How will they get in touch with us, then?" David asked.

"They won't. I pick up a portfolio from them once a week at their office. If I don't show up, they have an anonymous drop box to mail it all to."

David frowned. "What do they think the information is all for?"

"I said that we're setting up a specialized wire service for journalists. I'm paying them a lot, they're not going to risk a steady income stream by getting all curious. Confidentiality is part of their job description."

"Are you already doing this?" April looked startled.

Diana reached down to the floor by her chair and heaved a large leather portmanteau with straps onto the table. Jack said, "We've been collecting news for a month. It takes a while for patterns to start showing up."

April snorted a half-laugh. "We're going to need a file clerk. And don't look at me."

David also looked skeptical. "We can't trust all that stuff, you know that. The newspapers print nothing but disinformation, at least when it comes to anything that counts—labor, foreign policy, atomic bomb tests—you know what's happening on the fifteenth, right?"

"The big atomic attack safety drill, I know," Diana said. "Massachusetts isn't participating in that."

"It's all a plot, it's just to scare everyone," David went on. "What better way to make sure that no one is this country dares to question the government, or even wonder if communism might not be totally evil, or suggest that anything here needs changing, if the whole population can't think about anything but bombs wiping us out any minute? A terrified nation turns into sheep, they'll do anything the Army and the White House say. If we take all our information from the papers and official channels, we're just playing into the whole game."

"That's why we're not relying on that except as a starting point," Jack said. "We'll be using magical techniques for our fact-checking. We'll always be a step ahead of the status quo. We know better than to take anything at face value. But we do need the news to find out where things are starting to get troublesome, while they still don't appear serious enough for the authorities to lock down information."

"Are we always going to be working in this little...hovel?" April sounded only mildly curious, but she wrinkled her nose slightly. Jack gestured toward Diana.

"Oh, sure, someone brings up housekeeping and you give me the floor. No, April, at least I hope not. I'm going to be scouting around for some better locations—hopefully some that are a bit more secluded, so we don't have to be so careful coming and going. This is just the first one I could play all the financial games with. Eventually we may want electricity and a phone, too. We don't have to stay right in the Boston area. I can check out Worcester or Lowell, for example."

"Well, I've got to keep my job," David said uneasily. "My apartment is just a studio and the rent isn't too bad, but I don't want to be living on the streets, and I'm about one paycheck away from that. I don't have a car, and neither does Jack."

"I can cover your expenses, David, you know that," Diana said. She was covering Jack's, although neither of them ever mentioned it.

"No, no, that's okay. I appreciate it and everything, but I really don't need a...I mean..."

"A woman to support you?" Diana said dryly, and David flushed.

"Maybe we should all just live together," April said. "After all, it would make things a lot easier."

"And make us more conspicuous as a group," Jack said. "Believe me, we thought of it."

"Still," Diana said, "It's something we can keep in mind, down the road. Eventually we may be far less conspicuous staying together all the time than constantly coming and going to a meeting place—and our meeting place will be a lot safer and more secure with someone living there. But for now..." she sighed. "David, I respect your principles, but please let me know if you need anything, and don't just suffer in stoic silence. I inherited my money and my will names Bread and Roses as my chief beneficiary. You wouldn't have to feel badly about it."

David stared stiffly down at the table. "You know what people say about Jews," he said softly. "I'm perfectly capable of taking care of myself. I don't have to mooch off of anyone."

In the long awkward silence that followed the three non-Jews in the room struggled to think of something to say that didn't seem offensive, and failed miserably.

Finally Jack said, rather loudly, "Nobody here believes any of that crap about

Jews this and Jews that, so let's forget about it. Those Nazis and anti-Semites are the first ones in our cross-hairs, and we all know it. The same goes for the people who hate Negroes, or Catholics, or homosexuals, or any other scapegoat."

"It's not the same thing," David said.

"I didn't say it was. Look, we all need to agree on our priorities, David. We're not crusading against any one kind of injustice or bigotry. Those are just the poisonous fruit that you see. We're going to dig up the whole stinking, nasty weed by its strangling roots. All these individual causes are just distractions. That's exactly why people fight and fight against them and get nowhere."

The two men stared at each other unflinchingly, but the pure antagonism that Diana had seen between David and Art was missing. Nevertheless, both she and April were pressed up hard against the backs of their chairs, and a sudden cold draft made all the candles gutter. Something was passing between the men, but Diana couldn't interpret it. Jack's expression was earnest, almost pleading. Suddenly David's shoulders sagged and he sank back in his seat.

"Okay...okay. I see your point."

"Well, good. Don't think I'm minimizing. Anything but."

"I know. I guess you're right. I guess that's why I'm here."

Diana let out a long, noiseless sigh of relief, but a new doubt had kindled in the back of her mind. *I think I've severely underestimated Jack. Just because I don't feel obvious power around him doesn't mean he hasn't got something. It just means he's learned how to hide it—and that's much more impressive.* He obviously had some abilities to influence people directly that she hadn't seen since she'd broken ties with Levoissier. Abruptly, she recalled his story about the vampires he'd met in 1943, and his claim that he was resistant to their memory blanking. At the time, Diana hadn't attached much significance to that part of Jack's story, she'd been so emotionally involved with the fact that he'd met other vampires at all. Uneasily she wondered if any of her own recent decisions might not have been entirely voluntary on her part. She didn't think so, but...*oh, gods, I hate second-guessing myself!* She blinked as she heard Jack speak her name, and realized that it was the second time.

"Uh, Diana? Are you with us?"

"Oh—sorry. I just got lost in thought for a moment." She forced a weak smile around the table, but avoided meeting Jack's eyes for more than a second.

"I was saying, I think we should all try a short working, just to see how our energies mesh. Nothing ambitious, just an attunement, and maybe we can try that little trick with the candle that they teach in the Order—April, you haven't done that one, but it's pretty simple."

"I've done something like it. It's a basic technique."

"Okay, then." He looked around the table, meeting each of their eyes. "Are we ready?" They all nodded.

They got up and filed from the small dining room, where the table was set up, across the hall into the larger front parlor, which was entirely empty, cleaned and swept. Diana, last in line, closed both doors behind them. Jack carried a single candlestick, which he placed in the center of the floor. They all sat down cross-legged on the floor around it.

"No robes or anything?" David asked.

"We'll feel that out as we go," Diana said. "We may not need any accessories for the kind of work we'll be doing." She hoped so; the two years of ritual work in Maine had left her heartily sick of hand-sewing magical robes, and somehow she doubted that April did needlework. She and Jack had magically cleansed and consecrated the entire house, with special attention to this room, several times over the last two weeks, and Diana could sense that they'd done a good job. It felt very comfortable as a magical space—more than that, it felt *safe*. Just from the way the others were relaxing as they opened their psychic awareness, she knew they felt the same.

Jack reached forward and pinched out the candle flame, plunging the room into thick, palpable darkness. "Five minutes, tune in," he said quietly.

Diana closed her eyes, so she could no longer see the room and the warm bodies of the others glowing to her vampire vision. She shifted so that her limbs were symmetrical and her spine straight, hands cupped and just touching on her crossed legs, and she sensed the others around her doing exactly the same thing. But they were adjusting their breathing, deepening and slowing it until, by instinct, they were inhaling and exhaling in unison. Diana could imitate them, but it was distracting, and easier to cease bothering with breath at all.

She was already in a deep enough trance that Jack's voice sounded oddly hollow, and she knew he was going to speak before she heard him.

"Connect."

Tendrils of energy, like extensions of their hands and arms, expanded from each of them into a circle around their seated bodies, twining and thickening until they were knitted together in a web that connected and enclosed them. Diana had done this hundreds of times before, and yet somehow this felt different. The enveloping harness of etheric energy building around them was almost tangible, and it was growing much larger and denser than she'd felt before. She had the odd sense that it was taking on a physical presence, so supportive that if she'd lost her balance and fallen backwards, it would have held her up. It was instantly intoxicating. She wanted never to stop feeding this, wanted to keep on building it as far and as long as they could make it grow. She wondered if it was actually visible, not like energy or light but like the ectoplasm mediums used to produce in séances. But opening her eyes went against the flow, she didn't want to see. She was so deep in trance, and so intent on the moment, that she wasn't capable of asking herself what this could mean. Connected as closely as they were, she could feel the others' minds, at least superficially, and they also were completely and unquestioningly absorbed in what was happening, although they shared Diana's delighted astonishment.

It seemed like a very long time passed before Jack finally said, "Focus." Unthinkingly, they each shifted into the next step of the pattern. The result was instantaneous, totally unexpected and profoundly shocking. It was as though four sections forced apart from each other with great effort had suddenly snapped back together and completed a whole that had yearned for reunion for eons. Everyone gasped aloud, flinching as though there had been a deafening sound. They had become a single entity. Their bodies were paralyzed; they were locked into a flood of power pouring through them, as though they'd contacted a high-tension power line. They had achieved, although Diana only understood this consciously after it was over, perfect magical unity.

Diana smelled hot wax and felt heat on her face, and then Jack said, "Ground." With more effort than usual, all four of them cut the flow of energy and directed it down into the earth below them, slowly regaining feeling and movement in their muscles as their minds cleared. Her eyes still closed, Diana had a vague sense that something wasn't right. Just as she finally took in a breath, and choked on greasy smoke, David said, "Oh, *shit.*"

They all opened their eyes then, and reacted to the fact that the room was on fire—or on the verge of it. The magical exercise which Diana, Jack and David had performed dozens of times was intended simply to light the candle. Typically, a good percentage of tries resulted in nothing but an ember or a little smoke rising from the wick. Their candle, which had been almost new, had melted completely, leaving the empty candleholder standing in the middle of a large puddle of flaming liquid wax. Bright yellow light flickered on the walls of the room.

They hadn't even thought to bring in a container of water, far less a fire extinguisher. April ran to get a pan of water from the kitchen, but there was no time, and Jack pulled off his shirt, bunched it up and used it to vigorously beat out the flames before the scarred wooden floor caught. This risky maneuver worked, although he hissed as burning paraffin splattered on his bare skin. April returned with the water, into which Jack stuffed his wax-soaked shirt just to be on the safe side and then poured water onto the floor, which spat, bubbled and steamed like a hot skillet. It had been a close call.

It took some time for all of them to stop shaking and regain their equilibrium, even Diana, whose imitation nervous system, she discovered, did not like scary burning floors. But as they cleaned up the mess, drank some water and ate some cookies to help ground and center themselves back into ordinary reality, a deep sense of excitement began to bubble up among them. It was taking a while to sink in, but they were starting to understand that the four of them were such perfect complements to one another, their individual power was amplified a hundredfold. None of them had foreseen it.

It was getting late, and David needed to be at work in the morning. April didn't have a job as far as Diana knew, but she wasn't a night owl. They sat at the table, planning to leave separately at intervals after carefully checking outside to avoid being seen exiting the house. Diana, of course, would dematerialize and meet Jack at her car parked about a half mile away, so she had to stay until David and April were gone. April was giving David a ride, and Diana privately wondered how long it would be before she persuaded her new covenmate to move in with her—wherever she lived.

"Tomorrow, we'll try our first real project," Jack said. In the candlelight, his eyes almost seemed to glitter, like they had facets, and this was unnerving.

"What is it?" David asked, yawning.

"Something very small to start. I'll explain it all in detail. We're too tired to get into it now."

"With luck, we won't set whatever it is on fire," April said.

Jack laughed. "We'll see."

Diana sat alone in the dark house after Jack had gone, giving him time to walk ahead, since she was able to cover the distance much faster. As she thought over the evening's events in quiet solitude, she began to feel a little uneasy. A coven could experiment, adding and dropping members, for years and never even approach the kind of synergy that the four of them had stumbled into, apparently by pure chance. That was why it bothered her—it didn't seem as though it possibly *could* be chance. If their meeting had been arranged somehow by something beyond themselves, what was the purpose? Where might this end up taking them? *Where the Teg are concerned, is there ever such a thing as coincidence?*

7

They assembled at the house the following night, a bit later than the first meeting had commenced. As they settled around the table, Diana observed with wry amusement that the anticipation level was significantly higher than she'd detected before the Beltene ritual. She wasn't surprised. The feelings they'd shared last night were among the few things she'd ever experienced that she would sincerely describe as better than sex.

"All right, Jack, let's hear it," David said. "What is this 'project' that you've got for our first step at saving the world?" They were all smiling, but David's tone was only half humorous.

Jack had a sheaf of papers face down on the table in front of him, and now he turned over the top four and passed one to each of them. "This. This is the letter that was sent out to parents. It's an event being planned at a church in Malden. It's not being widely publicized, but there have been some flyers and so on posted in the neighborhood."

There was silence as they all read the papers, David and April tilting their pages to catch the dim candlelight and squinting.

"A book burning?" April suddenly blurted out, sounding aghast. "It says 'Book Swap,' but they're going to *burn* them?"

"You haven't heard about these?" David's voice had a note of world-weary cynicism. "They've been doing them all this year, all over the country. Mostly the American Legion organizes them—and you know what *they're* like."

April shook her head. "I'm not quite sure what you—"

"There are no Jews in the American Legion, put it that way," Diana said dryly. "Oh."

"'Crime and horror comics have been scientifically proven to cause juvenile delinquency, morbid thoughts, moral degradation and loss of intellectual rigor.'" Diana read from her paper. "'Sensitive children are deeply disturbed by the images they see although they may not display this disturbance to their parents. Many families have been shattered when a child was led to acts of cruelty or delinquent behavior after reading these comics...' Well. Jumping Jehosaphat. I'm running for a can of gasoline and a match right now."

52

"It's nothing to laugh about," David said. "Start by burning comic books and who knows where it will stop. Who knows *if* it will stop?"

"It says they're going to give the kids a wholesome book in exchange for their comics," April noted.

"Hence 'book swap.'" David made it sound like felony fraud.

"It's not happening for almost two weeks, though," Diana said. "So…what can we actually *do* about it? *Can* we do anything about it?"

"Wrong question." Jack was smirking.

"Well, sorry!"

"After last night? From now on, the one question we'll never ask ourselves is, 'can we do it?' There's just one relevant question: *'How* do we do it?'"

"I can think of another one," April said. *"Whether* we should. Let's not forget that."

"Agreed. But we'll figure all that out before we even start working magically. After all, it would be pointless at best, disastrous at worst, to start working if our Intentions aren't all in alignment." He didn't glance at Diana when he said this but she fidgeted uncomfortably as he spoke. He looked around the table at each of them. "Does any of you really believe that we should not attempt to prevent a book burning? Specifically, this one?"

They all glanced at each other and shrugged. "I don't know how concerned I really am about this thing, but who needs it?" Diana said.

"Good." Jack turned over the rest of the papers in front of him. "Now, here are more details about what's going on. It's really the brainchild of this minister, Reverend Porter. He gets on a roll constantly about 'protecting our children,' he's done a bunch of anti-communist rallies, he's spear-headed campaigns to get teachers fired from the schools—quite a fireball. He's got a little cluster of followers, mostly mothers in his church. They're taking care of all the logistics. Trouble is, it's all on church property, which gives them some exemptions from city regulations."

"They still have to have gotten a burn permit," Diana said.

"They already have one."

"Can we get the permit yanked?" David asked.

"Maybe. That's not the tack I would take, though."

"Why not?" April frowned. "That would stop it, wouldn't it? Isn't the simplest and most direct solution the easiest to pull off, and the most certain to succeed?"

"Don't you remember what I said last night, about getting to the roots? Sure, we could throw a few simple monkey wrenches and probably stop this event from happening on the twenty-fifth. But Reverend Porter and his cult would just reschedule, and probably find a location on private property where they wouldn't have to worry about permits. Not to mention the ammunition we'd give them to whip up a whole case for the fire department being infiltrated by godless communists. No...we need to aim directly at Reverend Porter."

"What—you mean break his leg or something, so he'd have to cancel?" Jack groaned, and April winced and then scowled at him.

"Were you not listening last night? Reverend Porter could light a bonfire from a wheelchair, that won't stop him or his supporters. No, what we need to do—and this is something *only* we can do—is change his *mind.*"

There was a long silence as they all, even Diana, struggled to grasp this notion. There was a big difference between Jack's sweeping generalities about influencing the minds of the powerful, and the prospect of influencing a very real and passionately committed person right now.

Finally Diana said, "How?"

"That's exactly what we need to figure out."

Jack had a lot more information about the Reverend, including his personal history, his previous campaigns and crusades, the texts of a few of his sermons, and several photographs. They spent an hour or more going over it all, and considering possible courses of action. Their subject was so fervent, emotional and fanatical, simply changing his attitudes by mind control didn't really seem feasible, at least not, as Diana said, without inflicting brain damage. "We don't actually want to *hurt* anyone, obviously."

Jack hesitated. "Well...not for something on this scale, anyway."

"Oh, come on, Jack!"

He waved a dismissive hand at her. "Think, people, think!"

"Do you think he'd be affected by nightmares?" April asked. "Something like..."

"Nuremburg." David said. "The Nazi rallies. Make him dream that he's Hitler, or something like that. Give him nightmares that he's presiding over something evil, shake his conviction that he's one of the good guys in all this."

"We'd have to do it every night for a week, or as long as it took," April said. "He could shake off one dream, but nightmares every night? It would have to wear him down."

"I don't know, though," Diana said uneasily. "I've known cases where nightmares every night...didn't make the dreamers change their course."

"Besides," Jack said, "he's already taking a lot of heat from opponents about book burnings and fascism and free speech and all that sort of thing. There was even an editorial in one of the local papers. His defenses are way up in that direction. Remember what I said about power feeding on confrontation? Anyway, if these sermons are any guide, he'd interpret nightmares like that as just being Satan's way of trying to weaken his resolve."

As they all considered this, David said "Satan..." softly, his brow furrowing.

After a moment, his lips started to curl into a very odd smile, half gleeful and half embarrassed. "I've got an idea. But I'd hate for anyone to be offended."

"Oh, gods, *now* you've got my attention," Diana said. "What? Come on, offend us."

"I don't *think* anyone here is a Christian, right?"

April just snorted. Jack said, "Sorry, David, but—confirmed atheist and proud of it."

"Not me. My parents raised me Pagan. I'm going straight to Hell."

David grinned. "Okay…then do you think that Reverend Porter truly believes? Or is he one of those hypocrites just using his religion as an excuse to throw his weight around and bully people he doesn't like?"

"What a loaded question." Jack chuckled, then sobered. "Much as I hate to give him the credit…yes, I do think he really, sincerely, believes."

"Which makes this little problem ten times harder, of course," April said.

"Or maybe not," David said. "If he really believes…do you think he'd listen to Jesus?"

For a moment they all stared at him open mouthed. Then Jack threw his head back in a roar of laughter, and one second later they all followed suit. When Jack managed to control himself, wiping tears from his eyes, he choked, "Mr. Hofstein—you are a genius. A fucking genius!" He got up, went around the table, pulled David to his feet and dramatically kissed each of his cheeks with loud smacks.

"Oh, cut that out." David shoved Jack away from him, but he was grinning. "It might not work. He might still think it's a trick by Satan."

"True, but we can give it a try. It's the best idea we've had. And for sure, it will shake him up." He went back to his chair and dropped down into it. "So—first things first. What does Christ the Lord look like?"

⊙hey agreed that Reverend Porter almost certainly visualized a brown-haired and blue-eyed Savior, and spent a long time discussing just exactly what their first attempt at an implanted dream would entail.

"We shouldn't go overboard," Jack said. "Too much, and he'll reject it as a fantasy or a ploy. It has to be just enough." They all agreed, but it was April who pointed out that the emotional content of dreams was often far more important than their imagery.

"I've had some of the most bizarre dreams you could think of, and I just woke up thinking, what the heck? But my worst dreams…I couldn't say what they were really about. I just woke up from them shaking all over, or cringing with shame, or crying, and I didn't even know why."

"I agree with that," David said.

Finally they were ready to move into the other room and make their very first attempt at remotely influencing a mind. They took one candle with them, but they'd learned their lesson from the night before. Even though they had no intention of trying to ignite anything consciously, the room now contained a large bucket of sand, a fire extinguisher, and a fire blanket in case anyone's clothes started to flame. They sat on the floor cross-legged, and went through the same preparation and attunement as the night before. When Jack spoke the word "focus," once again they felt themselves instantly bond together into a single magical unit. But this time the shock was less, because they were prepared for it.

It was partly like a two-legged race, negotiating in unison with three other Wills that tugged this way and that as their owners' thoughts faltered and focused. But it was also partly like riding some vast entity made of pure magical energy—as if, Diana felt incredulously, they had saddled and bridled the dragon, that immense core of power which she and Thomas had so foolishly tried to joust with in Maine. She didn't think there was any real association with that formidable adversary, but their union as magicians amplified their single strengths so much, it felt almost that overwhelming.

They sent their combined consciousness out toward their target, and in less than a moment had found him. Their perception of the Reverend and his bedroom had weird multiple levels, reminding Diana in part of how things looked to her when she was dematerialized, and yet partly as transient and malleable as a vivid daydream that she was inventing from her imagination. It took effort to maintain sensory awareness, and peripheral details faded in and out, as though only direct attention kept them in existence.

The Reverend was in bed asleep, his chubby body sweating under a light blanket although the early summer night was cool. His breath wheezed slightly. He stirred a bit, perhaps sensing their presence. Having planned in advance what they would do, they enfolded their minds around Reverend Porter's and fed the images and emotions they had carefully constructed into his sleeping brain. He moved restlessly, and almost awoke, and they pulled back, clumsily because they were still colliding with each other. Diana had a sudden mental impression of astral Keystone Kops and clamped it down immediately lest it be transferred to the Reverend, let alone her covenmates. Their synchronization would require some practice in the field before it was quite perfect. Reverend Porter muttered something, shuddered and turned over, the springs of his bed squeaking. He was dreaming, they realized—dreaming their dream.

When Jack said, "return," his physical voice sounded like a staticky radio heard from a distant room. But they were back before he got to the second syllable, a transition so fast they felt slammed into their bodies, as though they had dropped into them from ten feet above. After Jack said, "ground," it took considerably longer for them to return to normality than it had the night before. Of course, they didn't have an emergency and a shot of adrenaline to speed things along.

Although it was nearly midnight, and David had work in the morning, they all sat for a while around the table, slightly stunned by what they had done. They didn't talk much, for there was little to say. They didn't need to verbally compare notes. They would have to wait for the outcome of their efforts before they could evaluate their success, and this was only their first attempt. But there was one thing troubling Diana.

"Jack—are we quite certain that we've completely grounded this thing?"

His face took on an oddly guarded expression. "What do you mean?"

"I'm not sure, exactly. I just have this peculiar sense of…dragging, I guess. It feels like we haven't completely closed the working, like we've left something behind. April and David, do you feel—" she broke off because both of them were nodding.

"I thought maybe we were leaving some connection in place with Reverend Porter because we'll be repeating this, and building on it," April said. "When it's all done with, then we'll clear it."

"I know, but…this feels like something more than that."

April and David glanced at each other and shrugged. All three of them gave Jack inquiring looks.

"Something you're not telling us?" David asked.

"Come on, Jack. I did a cumulative working that ran for eighteen months. I'm having attacks of *déjà vu* here and I don't like it."

Jack appeared to be struggling for a reply, and finally he threw his hands up with an exasperated sigh. "All right! Yes, we are building something permanent—very slowly and incrementally. A sort of network, or web, that we can keep on using as we expand our influence outward. Think of it as a sort of magical telephone line system. We're going to need it. We can't start from the bare ground every time, that will seriously limit what we can do."

"Why didn't you say anything about this before?" David said. "It makes sense, but I don't mind telling you, it's a bit creepy to have you doing something with the magic that all of us are invoking, and not tell us what you're doing. What, did you think we wouldn't know? What are we, a bunch of Novices here?"

"Of course not! It's just…I mean…" he fell back in his chair and groaned. "I wasn't sure it would work at all. We'd have talked about it, I swear." He looked earnestly around the table, meeting each of their eyes. This time Diana *felt* it, a pressure in her forehead when he looked at her, and she glanced away. Neither April nor David did likewise. "Come on, people," Jack was saying, "don't say that you don't trust me. We're all here for the same reason, aren't we?"

"It just makes me a little uneasy, that's all," Diana said.

"I got the idea from you. You've done this before."

"Oh, right, and look how that turned out." David and April had both turned curious faces toward her, and she squirmed. She knew that they were picking up things about her when they connected magically, and she could perceive through that same connection that they weren't sure just exactly what they were feeling. She was going to have to explain sooner or later, but she'd have preferred it not to be because Jack spilled the beans in an argument.

"This isn't the same thing," Jack said. There was a tense silence as Diana studied the table, struggling to keep her anger in check. "Diana…look at me, all right?"

She gritted her teeth and deliberately raised her eyes to meet his. But her challenge went unmet. She felt no pressure or any other hint that he was trying to pull a fast one on her. She realized then that he simply didn't want the other two to start wondering why she was avoiding his eyes and get suspicious, and cursed herself for playing into his maneuver.

"Let's just keep everything above board, all right?" She kept her voice calm only with great effort. "We're handling too much power here to allow any room for error, and we're all peers. There aren't any Magi sitting at this table. I don't think basic honesty is too much to ask."

"Oh, I completely agree," Jack said fervently, and a little too quickly. He looked at April and David, who wore uncertain frowns. "I'm sorry," he said in a voice that throbbed with sincerity. "I was wrong not to tell all of you exactly what I was doing when I guided the working. I won't hold anything back in the future. I *promise*."

"Oh, just forget it," April said. "It's not *worth* all this fuss, really. I think past history may be clouding the issues here." She shot Diana an unfriendly look.

David yawned. "Am I the only one here who needs to sleep?"

"We're going," April said. "Come on." As they gathered their things in the kitchen, she added, "You know, David, I live closer to your job, if you want to stay over at my place, you won't have to get up so early…" If David replied, Diana didn't hear him.

She and Jack gathered up their papers and personal items, set things to rights around the house and extinguished all the lights except one lantern in the kitchen. As Jack was about to leave, Diana said, "Jack. A word." He stopped and looked back at her, hands in his windbreaker pockets and his body posture telegraphing resigned patience. This did not sweeten Diana's mood. She stepped up next to him, even if that meant she had to look up.

"You absolutely have *got* to stop using mind control tricks on members of the coven."

He affected a look of bewildered surprise. "What? Mind control? What are you—"

He got no further. Diana grabbed fistfulls of his windbreaker and shirt, picked him bodily off the floor and slammed him into the wall as he squealed. His dangling feet kicked, banging the wall hard enough to gouge the plaster.

"Don't. Even. *Try* that bullshit on me, Jack!"

"All right, okay! Lemme go!" His heart was racing and he'd broken out into a clammy sweat; he seemed more frightened than Diana would have considered justified. But she'd never shown him her full strength before. "Please...you're choking me..." He could have faked the strangled wheeze, but his eyes were bulging. She let him drop, and he fell to his knees, heaving gasps.

"Get up." She was already regretting her momentary loss of temper. He clambered back to his feet and raked a hand through his hair.

"I didn't mean anything by it, Diana. I was just trying to grease the wheels, keep things moving. I know David and April are solid, I know they're dedicated to what we're doing. I don't want stupid little misunderstandings to get in our way. Molehills into mountains, you know how it is, you say one little wrong word, it hits someone crosswise and everything goes off the rails. David and this anti-Semitism thing for instance, it's like waving a red cape for him, but we're no anti-Semites, we're on his side."

"No excuses, Jack."

"I'm not making excuses, I'm just saying—"

"*No excuses,* and it doesn't happen again. Or I'll tell them you're doing it."

He stared at her, frozen, and she saw anger sparking in his eyes. "You wouldn't."

"I would. I'm getting increasingly uncomfortable with what you're hiding from us. You want us to trust you? Why should we? One more foul-up like tonight and those two will walk out, no matter how hard you try to mesmerize them."

"I'm not the only one keeping secrets, sugar. When are you going to tell them they're in a coven with a vampire?"

"I will, when I'm good and ready. But that's not the same thing. That doesn't directly impact our magical work. You're using our work for your own ends, Jack, and that just can't go on." He scowled down at the floor. "You're right, we all have secrets. Maybe if this first project actually succeeds, we can have a celebration dinner and come clean about our pasts. I'll drop my bombshell, David can tell us just how they're trained out in the San Francisco House, we can play *What's My Line?* with April our Mystery Guest, and as for you..." She folded her arms, studying him thoughtfully.

"Me? Come on, Diana, you've known me since I was fourteen."

"I knew you when you were fourteen. You're not the person I remember. I'm pretty confident by now that you spent the last seven years in Colorado doing a lot more than work for your dad. I'm dying to hear more about it."

He hunched his shoulders and mumbled something.

"Didn't catch that," she lied.

"I said, maybe sometime."

She suddenly felt tired, and acutely aware that she was overdue to go hunting. "Well...I don't want to belabor this further. But I want your word, Jack. No more mind-control, or dissembling, or sneaking around behind the backs of the rest of us. It's not ethical, and it's not fair. We don't deserve it." After a long silence, she said, "Look at me."

He did. "Okay. My word. I promise." The heavy and very frustrated sigh which punctuated this made her believe him. She turned and dug into her handbag on the counter for her keys. "Here. Take the car back home. I'll be out for the rest of the night. Don't wait up."

8

heir meetings on the next two nights were shorter, since they didn't need to spend much time on discussion. They gathered at the house late enough that their target should be sleeping and started their working as soon as everyone had arrived. By Wednesday, the third night, they had to wait for some time, as it seemed that Reverend Porter was having some problems with insomnia.

"Do you think we could pull off a waking hallucination—make him think Jesus is actually appearing to him and lecturing him while he's fully awake?" April looked thrilled at the possibility. "I'll bet you dollars to doughnuts he's on his knees praying his heart out. The timing would be perfect." But Diana was dubious.

"I don't think we're quite up to that yet. We're still not staying together when we project over to his room. If we blow it, we lose him entirely. He'll just decide it's the devil doing it, or worse, some kind of communist brainwashing plot. He's about three sheets to the paranoid wind already."

"And it's much harder to create a believable hallucination than a convincing dream," David added. "People don't think critically during dreams, but they treat hallucinations like every other real world event. I agree with Diana, we're not ready."

April pouted but conceded their points.

David begged for a break on Thursday. "I'm sorry, I just can't do another late night. I can barely stay awake at work and I don't want to make dumb mistakes and get fired."

Jack considered the idea of skipping a night and just shook his head. "It may not matter. I'm not sure we needed to repeat this at all. We designed the dream suggestion as a sort of infinite loop, anyway, because the idea was that he'd dream it all night. For all we know, reinforcing it over and over is redundant. He may just go on dreaming it indefinitely."

"Oh *gods*." This possibility had never occurred to Diana. "That's like psychological torture! Shouldn't we stop it at some point?"

"Sure, when we get the results we want. Honestly? I don't have a lot of pity for the jerk, myself. Do you?"

"There are people I have lots worse grudges against, and I still wouldn't

curse them to have the same nightmare every night for the rest of their lives."
Hearing it phrased like that, David and April looked as aghast as she felt, and
even Jack appeared taken aback for a moment.

"Let's wait and see what happens. We're inventing this from thin air, Diana,
there are no rule books. We'll learn as we go. Okay, we'll skip a night and meet
again on Friday. Get some sleep, David."

When Diana awoke late Sunday afternoon, she was surprised to see
Jack sitting in the chair by her bed, his crossed feet propped on the edge of the
mattress and a smirk plastered to his face. A little groggy, Diana sat up, blinking.
"What are you grinning about? What's happened?"

Jack brandished a champagne bottle. "Suc-*cessssssss!*" He turned the word
into a jubilant crow.

"What? You mean Reverend Porter?"

"Get up and put on your party dress. I'm calling April and David now that
you're awake. David will be delighted not to have to meet late on a work night."

She climbed out of bed, excited and exasperated at once. "What's *happened?*
Is the comic book inferno called off? If you don't tell me, I'm going to break
that bottle over your head!"

Jack hugged the bottle to his chest. "No, no, no! You know how far I had to
drive to find this? Stupid Massachusetts doesn't allow alcohol sales on Sundays."

"Did you leave the car with a full tank? You have five seconds, lover. Five...
four..."

"The so-called Book Swap is cancelled. Not postponed, down for the count
and out. And the good Reverend, rumor has it, has gone on retreat."

Diana put a hand over her mouth. "Retreat?"

"He wasn't in the pulpit this morning, an assistant minister subbed, to
everyone's surprise. No one knows when Reverend Porter plans to be back."

Diana sank down on the edge of the bed. "Mother goddess," she whispered.
"It *worked!* We *did* it!"

"Yes, but...should we neutralize the dream now, just in case it's still
haunting him?"

Jack flipped a dismissive hand. "Let him stew in it, the son of a bitch. You
saw his record, you know how much trouble he's already caused for plenty of
honest, hardworking people—this comic book thing was just his current atrocity.
Believe me, there's a whole crowd of people we should invite to celebrate with
us, if we could, and they'd love to."

"I know, but..." She sighed. "I still think we should ground out the spell
and neutralize the connection. It only seems fair."

"And what if he just bounces right back to his old ways? Nah, keep him on
the run, I say. You know how these fanatics are: if he thinks he's survived an
attack, he'll be ten times as arrogant."

"Maybe that's not our business. It's not like we're the Greek Furies, Jack."

He smiled slyly. "No? Maybe we are."

Diana was a little disconcerted that neither David nor April seemed to share her concerns about their dream pursuing Reverend Porter indefinitely. They were ebullient at Jack's news.

"Serves him right, the misogynist s.o.b.," April chortled. "Jack, you skinflint, why did you only buy one bottle of bubbly?" She drained her glass.

"It was all I could afford, princess. That's the good stuff—at least as good as you can get in Portsmouth, New Hampshire."

"Then let's go out on the town, come on!"

"We better be careful what we talk about in public," Diana said.

David was watching her thoughtfully. "Do we have another project lined up?" April slapped his arm.

"Oh come *on*, David, take five minutes to savor this, for pete's sake."

"I am. But it's only the first one. Jack laid out some pretty ambitious plans."

"I've got some ideas," Jack said, shaking the inverted champagne bottle vigorously over his glass. "But we can talk about those on Wednesday. Diana gets the portfolio from our research department on Tuesdays. And by the way, don't wait for me to come up with every target. If any of you spots something you think would make a good project, speak up and we'll look at it."

On Tuesday afternoon, Jack accompanied Diana to the little building on Washington Street in Brighton where their researchers had office hours two days a week. She got the portfolio while Jack waited in the car, and they drove to a small shaded parking lot a few blocks away to look through some of the clippings and notes. An early heat wave made the bungalow they were renting in Cambridge, in the guise of a newlywed couple, stifling hot by this time of day. They'd stopped at a newsstand for a stack of regional and foreign newspapers.

Diana was studying a story taken from a wire service printout, still somewhat sleepy; she didn't fully wake up until after the sun set. Heat and humidity didn't affect her, but the potent sunlight, on the day of the Summer Solstice, was another matter. She felt as though she was walking around with weights on her head even wearing dark glasses and sitting in deep shade. It had also occurred to her only today that their victory over the book-burning minister had coincided with the first anniversary of the athanor blowing up and Brent's death the previous summer. It required a lot of mental energy not to think about that disaster, as well as avoid speculation about the possible significance of the date, and she was paying no attention to the pedestrians on the sidewalk a few feet away. Jack, whose seat was on the street side of the car, had his chin propped on one hand, and was gazing out his open window deep in thought.

Diana looked up in bewilderment at a sound so strange, at first she didn't realize it had come from Jack—it sounded like a cross between a gasp, a gulp, and a huff. She looked to her right, squinting because for her, the sunlight on the sidewalk was like looking straight into a spotlight. It took her a moment to register Jack's expression and posture. He was hunched down in the seat, as though trying to hide, and his face was so pale, his light brown eyebrows appeared to have been scrawled on his forehead by a cartoonist. His lips were trembling.

"Mother goddess, Jack, what's wrong?" Diana's first thought was that he was having some kind of seizure.

He sucked in a breath, rubbed his face with both hands, and then rolled up his window. "Let's get out of here."

"Why?" But she was reaching for the starter, since Jack's state left no room for doubt. She could smell his fear.

"Left, left!" he said as she pulled to the parking lot entrance, and she turned when she could and headed on down the street, bewildered but waiting for Jack to calm down before she asked any more questions. It was getting into rush hour and the traffic was heavy, but at this time of year, the sun wouldn't set for several more hours. After a few blocks she turned sharply off Washington onto one of the residential side streets and found a spot where she could pull over.

"All right, Jack, spill it. Do you need a doctor? A police officer? A drink? What *happened?*" She could hear that Jack's breathing and heartbeat were returning to normal or she'd have been more solicitous.

"No, no, *god* yes. But not around here." He sighed heavily, letting his head drop back on the top of the seat. "I'm sorry. I was just…that was the last thing I expected. You're going to kill me."

"I am?"

Jack swallowed hard. "I saw…I saw one of *them*. I'm dead sure of it. It's been twelve years, but…I know it was him."

"One of—*What?* You mean the other v–"

"Don't say it! Not out loud."

"Jack…are you sure?"

"Positive. I'll never forget them, never."

"But…" She struggled with frustration, even as she tried to understand how Jack must feel. "Jack, you *know* how much I want to find these people, and you never said you thought they threatened you–"

"I know, I know! I said I was sorry. I recognized him, and I just…I just flipped, that's all."

Diana twisted around to stare out the back window, as though the vampire Jack saw might have followed them. For a moment, she fought down an impulse to jump out of the car and run to the corner to look wildly up and down Washington Street. "It doesn't make *sense*. It's broad daylight, and it's the Summer Solstice! The number one day of the year when a—when one of us would avoid going outside if we possibly could, and you say he was just walking down the sidewalk, right in the sun?"

"He had dark glasses and a hat, like you."

"Then how could you possibly be so certain he's the same man?"

"They were wearing hats and dark glasses the last time I saw them. And besides..." he shuddered. "I've *dreamed* about them. For twelve years! I remember their profiles, their jawlines, it's not like they *change*, they don't age!" His voice dropped to a whisper. "He glanced at me, I think he saw me."

"Did he seem to recognize you?"

Jack shook his head. "He was wearing a coat. Not a suit jacket, a *coat*. It's ninety degrees! And he was walking like something was chasing him, almost a run."

"But still...why in the world would he have been out walking around at all?"

"Well, *you're* out."

"I have to go out during office hours, I don't have any choice—oh. Right." She turned to look behind the car again, then sagged against the back of the seat with a resigned sigh. "Damn...it's too late to go back and try to find him. He's long gone. Jack..."

"I don't want to do that, anyway. Sorry, but you're on your own with this one. I'm just a nice juicy *hors d'oeuvre* to you guys."

"I'm not even going to dignify that with a denial," Diana said sullenly as she started the engine. "I don't even know what they look like. Talk about a needle in a hay stack. How can I find them if you won't help?"

"Didn't you say you could spot them because of their not having any body heat? And you can tell they don't breathe or have a pulse, right?"

"I can't see body heat in blazing sunlight. And I can't pick out the one person with no pulse from a crowded sidewalk." She saw an opening and peeled onto Washington so fast, the tires squealed.

"I've tried to describe them to you. I can't take a photograph of my memory."

As she waited for the third traffic light to change, something clicked. "Wait a minute...maybe you *can* give me a picture. I can't believe I didn't think of this before! Jack—would you be willing to work with a police sketch artist? You know, the ones who work with eyewitnesses to create likenesses of suspects?"

"Well, sure...Jesus. I never even thought of that."

"I can ask our research team to recommend one. They work with police and the courts, they'll know who's really good. Then I'll have something solid to work with. I can even see if the police will let me look through their books of mug shots."

"Somehow I don't think they let themselves get arrested very often, but you could try."

"Which one of them was it, that you just saw?"

"It was...the one who called himself Ned. The friendly one."

"The one who did all the talking."

"Mostly, right." Jack shuddered again.

Diana glanced at him. "He's the one who blanked your memory, isn't he?"

"I'm not saying anything more about that."

They continued in silence for some time. Diana was pondering, once again, the story that Jack had told her on May Day, and something now struck her. "This is the real reason you left Boston seven years ago, isn't it? You didn't even get out of the service until forty-six. You came to rituals and meetings at the Motherhouse, but outside of those, I hardly ever saw you around. I just thought you were busy working or running with a different crowd than I did. But after Gregory left in forty-seven, you hung around for a year. So you didn't leave just because you were mad about his banishment, at all."

"I told you I was broke, remember?"

"So what were you living on from forty-six until forty-eight? No, you left because you saw something. You saw one of them." He didn't answer. "That's why you wouldn't work with Bread and Roses, no matter how desperate you were for a job. It would have meant spending too much time in the city. I never even suspected what kindred spirits we were, just because you were so scared."

Jack sighed heavily. "You'll have to change your name to Sherlock."

"And you'll have to change yours to Mr. Contrary."

"How so?"

She laughed. "Well, Jack—I can't figure for the life of me how you can be so bugged by vampires and still be sleeping with one."

He smiled weakly. "Me, neither. Are you complaining?"

"Not a bit. Just wondering."

"I didn't leave Boston just because of that. Heck, all my friends were here, Gregs, the Order. I didn't want to move all the way out to some hicksville in the Rocky Mountains. They hear the word magic and all they think of is card tricks or rabbits pulled out of top hats. But I wasn't fibbing about being flat broke. I'd lost three jobs in a row. I was going to have to do something, or I'd have been eating in your soup kitchens and sleeping on the Common. Seeing... one of them was just the last straw."

They'd gone a few more blocks before Diana said, "I'm finding it hard to believe that Colorado was such a magical wasteland as all that. You haven't been in retirement for seven years, Jack. I'm not that obtuse."

"That's another story. I don't want to get into it now. It wasn't in Colorado, anyway."

They were getting near Cambridge and their temporary home. "Do you still want that drink?"

"Oh, yeah."

9

heir euphoria over the averted "Book Swap" was short-lived. It turned out not to be as easy to identify targets and influence them as Jack had confidently believed.

Their clipping service included both left and right wing publications, as well as odd underground or radical periodicals. But the clipping service and local newspapers weren't giving them much grist to work with. It was two weeks before a leftist newsletter covered a local issue that seemed promising. The school board of a Boston suburb was planning to terminate the contract of a popular high school teacher, who had not been granted tenure, and rumor had it that she was suspected of communist affiliations. The school community—faculty, parents and some older students—were in conflict, with strong emotions on both sides.

Jack invested in some second-hand clothes that transformed him into a very convincing reporter and visited the town, asking questions and collecting gossip.

"She's a pinko, she's a wonderful teacher, she should get married, she's probably a lezzie, she's a lousy teacher and the commies are just exploiting this to recruit kids...but most of the people aren't too interested. 'We elected the school board and they know what they're doing,' is the general consensus."

"'She should get married?' What, she's supposed to just stand on a corner with a sign and take the first offer? She's single and supporting herself, and that makes her a Lesbian? What a bunch of jerks," April said.

"You make it sound like being a Lesbian is bad," Diana said. "That doesn't have anything to do with being a good teacher."

"Um...that's not what any school board would say, though," David said. "She'd be fired just for that. But nothing stops them from firing her for being a communist. That's happening all over the country, it's not even illegal." He looked at Jack. "So, is she? What evidence do they have? What are we stepping into here?"

"I don't know, but they aren't presenting anything as evidence, and you'd think they would if they could."

"How many members does the school board have?" Diana asked.

"Seven, and I'm gathering that five want to terminate, two are holding out."

"Any one ringleader really pushing for it?"

Jack could only shake his head and shrug. There was a long thoughtful silence.

"Why the dark frowns, people?" Jack sounded impatient as he looked around the table at them. Diana watched him closely, eyes narrowed, but detected no attempts at psychic coercion on his part.

April finally heaved a sigh. "I just don't know. There doesn't seem to be anything to...to get hold of. We don't know a lot about the board members—"

"I do have some information, names, photos, some short bios, from the school department."

April gave him a glare that would have blistered the wall behind him if he'd ducked. "Don't interrupt me. Men always think they can interrupt women." Jack scowled and waved at April to continue.

"It's not Reverend Porter, where the whole thing was his baby and if he abandoned the plan, it was all over. I'm sure every one of these seven men— they're all men, right?"

"Nooooooo, three women, so there, cupcake. Ow!" April had kicked him under the table.

"I'm sure all seven board members have completely different reasons for their opinion and different degrees of assurance in their decision. That's a lot to try and work on. They outnumber us, for god's sake."

"Get used to that," Jack said, rubbing his shin. "You're right, this isn't Reverend Porter. How many one-man shows do you think we'll get—and what's the point of bothering with that kind of small potatoes? The Book Swap was just for practice, and so is this, really. People, we're just warming up here. We're nowhere near out of the gate."

"I think April makes a good point, though," Diana said, and David agreed.

"Well, look. Let's give it a try and see what happens. It won't hurt to try."

"Won't it?" April muttered, but she shrugged.

"Can we see the rest of your information?" David said.

They went over the facts Jack had collected about each member of the school board, and everything else he could tell them. Finally they all agreed to make a first attempt, and moved into the next room to go through their usual procedures, aiming for this new target.

They had improved tremendously since that first night just two weeks earlier. Their synchronization was smoother, if still not flawless. They were refining their skill at communicating nonverbally, through their mental connection. Jack no longer spoke their cue words out loud. They had been practicing at every meeting. After each night's discussion, they went into the work room, tuned in and connected, and projected outward. They honed their perception, collected information, and sometimes nudged small animals or birds into activity and tried to control their movements.

All the Shadows of the Rainbow

They had a keener rationale for this consistent training than dedication and discipline. It *felt* good. Diana wasn't the only one of them who thought it was at least as good as sex. They were meeting three times a week without a specific project ongoing, and already wanted to meet more often. It hadn't occurred to any of them that their magical union was becoming addictive. Diana had spent two years on a project that required working every day, and the rest of them, especially David, had not yet started to neglect other priorities.

But tonight, for the first time, they found themselves at a loss. They located each board member easily enough. They'd learned that it was just as easy to manipulate a mind that was daydreaming, reading, listening to a radio or watching that new mass trance-inducer, the television set, as one that was sleeping. But April's doubts proved right on point. Each individual board member had a completely different level of emotions about the issue and a different way of interpreting it—and then there were the two who sympathized with the teacher, and needed to be encouraged, while the coven planted uncertainty and hesitation in the others' minds. When Jack finally called them back, after a much longer time than they'd ever spent on Reverend Porter, they felt exhausted, over-extended and a bit futile.

The school board met on Monday night, and some of the more fervent parents planned to attend the meeting and speak on the teacher's behalf. None of the faculty dared to take a stand. The coven met again on Friday, Saturday and Sunday nights, pushing themselves and their subjects as hard as they could. But not only were they getting some push back, they were dismayed to see unexpected effects. Some of the members reacted to the implanted doubts by stubbornly reinforcing their own positions, and several got on the phone with each other to talk worriedly about the upcoming vote, and bucked each other up in their resolve. Violent thunderstorms on Sunday night added more chaos to the coven's efforts, both energizing and distracting them.

The coven met during the actual school board meeting on Monday night. When they projected themselves to the grade school assembly hall, where the meeting had been moved due to the public clamor, they almost were forced outside by the tumultuous energy of the crowd. It wasn't a large number of people, but the protesting parents were strident, a few actually tearful, accusing the school board and arguing angrily with each other. The board members, faced with such emotional confrontation, reacted by digging in to their positions harder than ever, and the sympathetic two were tending toward termination just because the whole issue was causing them so much stress. Eventually, the board ordered the room cleared so they could go into executive session and vote. The coven pushed hard but only succeeded in raising the already high irritation level among the members—two of them broke out into recriminations and nearly came to blows. The final vote was six to one for termination.

Jack called the coven back, and once they'd grounded and opened their eyes, they sat in dazed silence. Finally David said, "Oy vey."

"Funny, I was just going to say that." Diana's voice was hollow. "That was like…"

"Like trying to herd a swarm of bees with our bare hands," April said. "That poor teacher. Can we do anything for her?"

"She'll get another job. There's a teacher shortage, they're building schools everywhere."

"Not if she's blacklisted as a commie, Jack."

"It's risky for us to get involved openly with a case we've tried to influence, April. You're smart enough to know that."

Diana said, "I'll see what we can do."

"Have we found our limits, maybe?" David said.

Jack blinked. "Not at all! Sure, we've learned something here, something very important. We need to start influencing much earlier in the process, before emotions get too engaged. Either that, or we need to work *with* the emotions, and not just come in from left field. I definitely picked up that we could have inflamed those feelings even higher, quite easily."

"And what good would that have done?" Diana said. "You're suggesting that we incite mayhem and riots?"

"There are circumstances where that might work. Not this one, but I can imagine possibilities, definitely. Sometimes people *need* to be stirred up."

"Property damage, people getting arrested, hurt, even killed…not my definition of success."

"Nor mine," David said. "Most of the time, it's the underclass, the ones we're trying to help, who get the worst of it. The wealthy and the ruling class have ways to profit from chaos."

"I can see Jack's point, though," April said. "He's right: complacency, fear, laziness, the ruling class and oppressors all profit from those, too. For god's sake, Diana, you didn't name your foundation after a peace movement, did you?"

"Okay, okay. But this isn't the nineteen-tens anymore."

"Thank god for that. There would have been no women on the school board, instead of three."

"All of whom," David said, "wanted to fire the teacher, if not tar and feather her. See, that's the problem, women are even worse than men when it comes to enforcing the status quo on other females. You think they'd have felt differently if the teacher was a young man?"

April's cheeks had flushed. "Well, that might be true for Jewish women, David, but in general, that's bullshit. Those women were probably just intimidated by their husbands. All those upstanding middle-class men are wife-beaters behind closed doors, everyone knows that."

David shoved himself back on the floor away from the rest of the circle. "I didn't get that sense from them, at all. They seemed to be very independent-minded, indeed. And suddenly you're the big expert on Jewish women, are you?"

"Of course not, but..." April abruptly turned to Diana. *"You're* divorced. How did your husband treat you?"

"Now wait just a goddamned minute! Leave my marriage out of this, it wasn't representative of a single thing."

"And why are you pretending to be married to Jack, right down to the cracker-jack-box wedding ring?"

Diana glanced in confusion at the 24-carat gold ring on her left hand. "You *know* why, April—no legitimate rental agent would rent a house to an unmarried couple, and I wouldn't trust the ones who would. It's just a lot easier for a married–" she broke off as April made an expansive *There, you see?* gesture to the whole group.

Jack straightened up, raising both hands imploringly. "People, people, people! For god's sake, let's not turn on each other! Think about what's going on here! We just fouled up, and now we're all snarling and spitting at each other like wet cats. Now, come on, cut it out. Do we need to ground some more? No? Okay, let's have our milk and cookies, go home and get some rest. We can debrief when we're calmer."

They acceded to Jack's wishes, rolling up the small rugs they each had to sit on now that their sessions were much longer, and putting things away. But instead of sitting down at the table with the rest of them, David stuffed a few cookies into his jacket pocket and left, mumbling that he still had time to catch the bus. April sat at the table with her forehead propped on both hands, looking either furious or on the verge of tears, possibly both. Abruptly, she too got up, took her things and departed.

Diana and Jack sat and looked at each other in silence for a few minutes. "Failure does not become us," Diana finally said.

Jack waved a casual hand at the back door. "They'll get over it."

"I hope so. You would have to recruit a redhead, wouldn't you?"

"Now don't *you* start with the offensive stereotypes." He rolled his eyes. "She's a fireball."

"But at least she's consistent with her themes."

"That's fine, as long as her themes don't pull all of us off-track. Hey, I'm not arguing that women's rights aren't important. But it's like a lot of things, it's a by-product of the whole system. The great failure of activist movements for centuries has been their focus on one subsidiary issue. They don't get to the core."

"But they have changed things, Jack."

"On the surface."

"Oh, come on! If nothing had ever changed on a deep level we'd all still be living in a feudal monarchy."

"There are plenty of monarchies in the world, and plenty of empires and dictatorships. What's changed? People say the Roman Empire fell? Nuts to that. It's still here. Only difference is that instead of Caesar it's run by the Vatican."

Diana started to reply, then decided she just wasn't up for a big emotional debate. The results of tonight's endeavors were too disheartening. "Jack, don't preach to the choir. I need to go out, and I need to think for a while. I'll see you later." Jack looked a bit miffed but just shrugged at her.

10

She left the car keys for Jack and traveled dematerialized low over the roofs of the city, still bustling and busy at this relatively early hour. She touched down in a narrow alley off Washington Street in Brighton, and made sure there were no witnesses before she materialized fully and strolled out to the street, joining the college students and other pedestrians walking in both directions. She looked much like a college student herself, and a police officer on the beat nodded politely to her as she passed him.

She had been coming here every night since the Solstice, looking for any sign of the vampire Jack had spotted—or thought he'd spotted. Their researchers hadn't yet found a sketch artist, but for now, Diana was just scanning for any figure that had no body heat. She had to keep moving, because standing in one place for more than a few minutes would look suspicious, especially if she was noticed repeatedly at 3:00 a.m. She could have scanned a larger area from the air, but streetlights and the ambient warmth of sun-baked pavements obscured the faint body heat sign from above, and trees and buildings blocked an overhead view of the sidewalks.

As a result, she covered a lot of miles on these outings, randomizing her routes, walking through various types of neighborhoods, and exploring areas that she would have picked herself as likely hiding places. She was propositioned more times than she could count, questioned a couple of times by a beat cop when she got careless, and followed on several occasions. The stalkers she led into deserted alleys and tapped for that night's dinner, and that was the sole material reward of her lengthy walks. Not once did she see a figure that was not surrounded by its warm aura of infrared light.

The failure of the coven's project tonight made her usual fruitless search even more discouraging. Logically, she knew there could be a dozen vampires walking the streets and the odds that she would happen across one in her aimless wanderings were small. She assumed that other vampires would recognize her via the same clues, but would they notice what they didn't expect to see? And if they did notice, would they approach her, or avoid her?

But it wasn't merely her dampened mood that made her cut tonight's quest short and head back to Cambridge. She had something else on her mind.

73

She was glad to see the car parked in the driveway of the little bungalow and lights in the windows—no black-out drapes like the Woburn house, they wanted to appear as normal as possible to the neighbors. Fortunately the neighbors never saw how Diana got in without a house key.

She materialized inside the kitchen and called quietly, as she always did, "Jack, I'm home." She knew he was working in the tiny bedroom that also served him as an office and study, because she could smell him, and hear his breathing and the muted scratch of his fountain pen. Despite her consideration he still gasped. "Sorry to startle you," she said as she walked out of the kitchen and down the short hall.

He turned in the straight-backed chair he pulled up to a small desk in the room. A goose-necked writing lamp brightly illuminated the desktop while the rest of the room faded into shadows. "You're back early. No luck, I take it?"

She couldn't decide if there was a baiting undertone in his voice or not, and chose to ignore it. "The evening seems to be a wash-out all around." She walked over to lean against the wall next to the desk facing him, and glanced down at the notebook he'd been writing in. "You've been refining that script a little."

He scowled and closed the notebook. "Don't snoop, it's not polite."

"What, we have secrets from each other?"

"I keep personal notes, nothing sinister about that, they're just personal. And look who's talking. Your journal is encrypted and coded."

"I write in Gregory's cipher, just like you do. After all, there are only three of us in the whole world who know it—well, by now, probably four." Her final words dripped acid.

"Well, I can't make heads or tails of it."

She smiled. "Learn Welsh."

"Oh, is *that* it? Jesus, that will fool the FBI surveillance guys."

"At least the non-Welsh ones."

He grunted, carefully screwing the cap back onto his fountain pen and replacing it in its slim flannel cover. "I suppose you want to hash over tonight's debacle."

"Not at all. We'll talk about that as a group. My thoughts can wait until then. I did have something I wanted to ask you, though."

He studied her warily. "Go ahead."

"I actually feel rather stupid for not noticing it before, but I guess I haven't been paying attention. This coordinated magic is a whole new game for me, I've never experienced anything like it. It takes a lot of concentration. But...that network sort of thing you talked about a couple of weeks ago. You've been... working on that, haven't you."

"What do you mean, working on it? I said right at the outset that we'd be developing and building that. It's fundamental to the goals we'll be aiming for."

"I wish 'we' had anything to do with it. This is something you are doing, Jack."

"Now wait a minute." He stood up, shoving his chair away roughly with his knees. "Are we back to this again? Why are you so suspicious of me, Diana? Why don't you trust me?"

"I'm just asking, Jack. We, as a group, aren't doing anything conscious with that network, or web, or whatever you want to call it. It's never even been mentioned again. But tonight...I don't know, maybe it was because we were struggling so hard, and getting so much resistance, I became a lot more aware of the energy surrounding the whole situation. That web has grown. It's grown way beyond anything we've purposely put into it. We haven't sent our deliberate Intention out beyond the boundaries of the greater Boston area, but I'm feeling tendrils of this thing stretching for hundreds of miles. And it's not like a web. It's not even like your telephone wire analogy. It feels more like...like the roots of a huge tree."

"And why is that bad? I don't get you. Yes, it's growing. Yes, I've been stretching it out—but I'm not doing anything that conflicts with all of our Intentions. I've just been guiding the pattern overall because the three of you are focusing so hard on the immediate goal. Diana—" His voice raised a little, and his eyes became intense. "Don't you realize how much power we're all generating here? We're barely tapping it yet. I'm not just going to let all that dissipate like water down a storm drain, I'm going to direct it. Except I'm not, not really. This...root system, as you say, is growing on its own."

"So every time we've met, all these practice sessions we've been doing, you've been taking all that power and—"

"No! I'm not *taking* anything! I'm just shaping our collective energy toward our future goals, the goals we've all agreed on." His shoulders slumped. "Why don't you believe me?"

"I don't know." She leaned her head back against the wall, suddenly exhausted, and wishing someone had followed her tonight. "Maybe I'm just shell-shocked by what's happened during the past three years. But here we are again, you're not being completely honest with the rest of us and then you insist that your intentions are honorable and we're being unfair not to trust you."

"I'm sorry. I'm just not used to explaining everything I'm doing every step of the way. For one thing, it makes me self-conscious, and then I hesitate and mess things up. This is all new to me too, you know. I barely know what I doing here, it's like...like steering an avalanche, or trying to surf on a tidal wave. Sometimes I feel like I'll be swallowed alive if I do the slightest thing wrong. I can't decide if it's terrifying or ecstasy. But I know one thing, I don't feel like we dare stop now."

Diana was silent, reluctantly recalling her thoughts the very first night: that it was as if they had harnessed the dragon, done the very thing which she and

Thomas had set out to do. Once you had grabbed hold of something like that, how could you ever let go? "I feel the same way. But I can't speak for David and April. What if they perceived the same thing I did tonight?"`

"I'm sure they'll ask about it, if they did."

"Jack, *we* should ask *them* what they felt and what they think about it. Don't just let it hang there. Let's tell them what's going on and ask them what their perceptions are, at our next meeting. We're all peers, Jack, but everyone is treating you like a leader."

"I haven't set myself up that way, I've never claimed to be superior to the rest of you."

"No, but you're adopting the role by default, and we're all—all right, I know that *I* am letting you do it mostly from sheer laziness. And you certainly have charisma, Jack."

"Oh, bullshit. Compared to April? Come on."

"Don't be disingenuous. Charisma has nothing to do with looks and you know it. April worships you."

"Oh, bull *shit!* She's sleeping with David, for god's sake."

"Well, not tonight." Diana couldn't help smiling. "That's why I wasn't sure I'd find you at home."

Jack just snorted. "Oh, man, you are miles off on that one. April is way out of my league—at least that way."

And I'm not? Diana thought, but she repressed the words. "Someday you're going to have to tell me how you met her."

"I will." He looked away and fidgeted for a moment as she crossed her arms and watched him steadily. Then he looked back at her. "Okay. You win, you're absolutely right. When we meet on Wednesday I'll bring up the whole network question first thing. It will probably evolve even better if we're all aware of it. I just didn't want people to be distracted."

Diana knew that was the best she was going to get from Jack at this moment, and restrained herself from any expression of skepticism. "That sounds like a good plan. Hopefully we'll *have* more meetings, after the way David and April slunk out tonight. You know, I still don't even know where April lives."

"She's got an apartment—part of a big old Victorian, actually. Over near the Harvard campus."

"My goodness. That's pricey real estate around there. Is she affiliated with the University?"

"No, but…" he sighed. "Look. I haven't said anything because April swore me to secrecy on pain of mutilation and death, almost. But I'm sure David knows some of this by now, and it's stupid to leave you out. All this secrecy about April—don't take it personally. She just doesn't want her parents to find out where she is."

"Her parents? She's well over twenty-one. Who are her parents?"

"You mean you've never heard of *the* McFarlands of Park Avenue?"

"No. Should I have done?"

"That will score you a few points with April, right there. She hated being rich and upper class, and she gave her parents a ton of grief as a kid. She'd sneak off to jazz bars, she smoked marijuana, she was picking up guys when she was thirteen. Mummy and daddy bailed her out a dozen times."

"I'm surprised she wasn't shipped off to some girls' boarding school in the Swiss Alps."

"I guess her parents would have been too embarrassed that they couldn't handle her. She was supposed to make her formal debut at seventeen and flat out refused to do it. She left home the day before and took a train to New Mexico to join an artists' colony. She always looked older than her age because she was so tall. That and her hair were what made her stand out, and she cut her hair off and bleached it or dyed it black. She wasn't too proud to stuff her clothes so she looked fifty pounds heavier, either. Her parents must have spent thousands of dollars on detectives trying to find her, but she managed to keep one step ahead of them until she was twenty-one and could tell them to kiss her ass. Of course, she had the magic to help with that."

"And that's not all the help she had."

Jack hesitated, but he didn't immediately attempt a glib denial. "She met people in New Mexico, right away. You're right."

"The dominos are tipping fast. You also met people in New Mexico, and that's where you met April. Right?"

He glanced over his shoulder quickly, as if he feared someone might be eavesdropping, and just nodded. "She came into a trust fund when she was twenty-five, but before that she was waiting on tables and reading palms. Yeah, you're right, we were working with...with the same group. I'm not at liberty to say more than that."

"If you mean a group like the Order, I completely understand. But it does give me pause, Jack. If you and April have obligations to another group, are you free agents? Is there a conflict of interest here? Is there a conflict of interest with you still being, technically, a member of the Order?"

"No, no, it's nothing like that. We're just not supposed to talk about the group with non-members. We're not even supposed to mention its name. But they're the right kind of people, don't worry about that. This is no dark cult or black magicians or anything."

"I can't imagine you having any patience with a cult. And if they trained April, they must be good."

Jack looked at her solemnly for a moment. "They are."

"Are you both still active members?"

"It's not like the Rotary, Diana. You're still a respected member of the Order and you didn't attend a ritual or a meeting for three years."

"That's true. Well…I understand some things a lot more clearly now—like why you couldn't save a dime living in your parents' basement. You were running off to New Mexico half the time." He grinned sheepishly. "But I won't pretend that I'm not seething with curiosity. I do appreciate why you can't say more, but…" she groaned in exaggerated frustration.

"I'll introduce you someday."

"Promises, promises."

He grinned. "Now you know why I'm not concerned about April quitting, and I don't think David is going anywhere, either. I've got something entirely new for us to try on Wednesday, anyway."

"New?"

"There's no point in our beating our heads against a wall. That just teaches us to expect failure. I think it's time to try that enhancement that I mentioned in our very first meeting."

"Oh, yes…I'd forgotten about that."

Jack sat back down in the desk chair and pulled open one of the drawers to remove a sheaf of papers. He handed it to Diana. "Here's some literature to read over. I'm going to get copies to David and April tomorrow, I hope, so we'll all be up to speed by Wednesday."

Diana read the first paragraph of the top page, which was an extract of an article from a scientific journal. "Lysergic acid diethylamide…LSD?"

11

hey met early on Wednesday, as soon as David could get there from work. He and April had cooled off and made up, both of them apologizing to Jack and Diana for their abrupt decamping on Monday. "I couldn't believe how badly that vote turned out, it just knocked me for a loop," April said. "Have you found out if we can help the teacher, Diana? She's not even going to have a reference from those creeps."

"I'm sorry, I'm drawing blanks so far. I can't think of any way to explain how I'd know about the situation. And another teaching job? They don't call it blacklisting for nothing."

They spent some time going over the entire project and comparing perceptions and opinions. Jack didn't have to introduce the topic of the magical network. Both David and April had perceived it and they'd been discussing it on their own. Diana was mildly surprised that neither of them seemed the least bit suspicious. They were both excited at the discovery that their regular practice was producing such unexpectedly far-reaching results.

Finally they had exhausted both topics. Jack went into the kitchen and returned with a wooden box that locked with a key, like a jewelry box, and set it on the table in front of him. They all stared at it riveted, as though they expected it to pop open and spray the room with some sort of toxin. Jack sat back down and chuckled. "It's not going to bite, honest. Did you all have a chance to read over the papers I gave you?"

They nodded. "Pretty heavy going, some of it," April said. "I can't honestly say I understood all of it."

"Well, you're not a biochemist. You got the gist of it, though."

"I'd heard of this stuff, LSD." David sounded curious. "I just thought it was some new psychiatrists' cocktail. I didn't realize it was a hallucinogen and all these other things."

"Now, we've all worked with mind-altering substances before. It's part of the training for Adeptus grade in the Order—at least, I assume they have the same training in San Francisco, don't they, David?"

"Well, we took some interesting concoctions, that's for sure. Something with mescaline, and also opium."

April said, "I've taken peyote, but oh my god, did it make me sick."

"This won't make you sick, I promise. It's very smooth."

"Have you tried it?"

"Of course." He grinned suddenly at Diana. "I don't have to ask about your experience level, after that *thing* that Gregs cooked up and talked us all into trying."

"Oh, yeah, the one that rendered us all unconscious for three days? I vividly remember walking barefoot on the surface of the sun. For hours."

"And the moon, and the planets—all eleven of them."

"Gregory never did tell us what was in that. I'd still love to know."

David looked amazed. "You mean you didn't get thrown out for that? Man, the San Francisco house would have had you keelhauled."

Jack laughed. "We were all teenagers, so I guess we got some slack for being young and stupid. Anyway, Gregs was Mr. Untouchable because of who his mentor was—"

"And said mentor was just bursting with pride, by the way, at this precocious achievement—"

"Diana's parents stood up for her, and I just said they made me do it."

"A defense you used quite a lot, as I recall."

When everyone but April, who only wore a sarcastic smile, stopped chuckling, Jack sobered. "Trust me, this isn't nearly so extreme as some of what you've already experienced. But it is…different."

"But, Jack…different or not, I'm not sure how you see this helping with the situation we just ran into with the school board. Based on my experiences with consciousness-altering drugs, this won't help our ability to focus—just the opposite, in fact."

"Yes, I was trained that these drugs are meant to help you push boundaries and let go of all control," David said. "We were barely holding it together on Monday as it was."

"Two answers to that. One is that I don't mean for us to use enhancements for influencing, although they may have their place even there. This will chiefly be for gathering information. Remember when I said that we'll need to start working on situations earlier? We can't do that if we're relying on conventional information sources, or even ordinary divination. This—" he tapped the top of the box. "This will help us see the patterns that lie underneath the patterns, layer after layer down. We can identify objectives before they're obvious even to the people involved with them."

"And possibly prevent the situation from even developing," Diana said. "It seems a bit risky."

"No more than what we're doing now."

"And your second answer?" April asked.

"Given the magical synergy that the four of us have, these drugs might have an effect on our focus and connection that none of us can predict." He fished a ring with several small keys out of his pocket, selected one and opened the box. It was an antique pharmacists' lockbox filled with tiny glass vials set into velvet-lined sockets, unlabelled and containing what looked like clear water. Four of the vials were amber in color.

Diana reached over and took one of the amber vials, holding it to the light. "Where did you get this—the drug, I mean."

"I have some connections from New Mexico. That's how I found out about it. Getting this drug isn't easy, but fortunately a modest amount goes a very long way. I thought we'd start small for the first time—"

"Oh-oh," David said. "Remember what happened the last time you said that?"

"Yes, but we all know what we're capable of now. And we have fire extinguishers. Are you ready? The colored vials are one hundred micrograms, that's less than half of a standard dose."

The other three looked at each other. "There's no point in talking it to death, not with this sort of thing," April said, shrugging. "The only way to know whether it's a helpful idea is to try it out."

"I'm game," David said.

"After touring the solar system with Gregory, anything else is a walk in the park." Diana tossed the vial and caught it with a wry smile, privately wondering if the drug would affect her, and how much. Some intoxicants, like alcohol, were effective, and some, like the herbal stimulant in the Beltene wine, weren't, and she never knew which it would be without testing it.

Jack laughed. "You may not be so sure about that later. But come on. It takes a couple of hours to peak." He handed David and April amber vials, closed and locked the box and led them into the work room.

They sat cross-legged on their rugs and uncapped the little vials. "Tune in first," Jack said. "We'll wait for the drug to kick in before we connect."

"How long does that take?" Diana asked.

"You'll start to feel it in about twenty minutes."

"What does it taste like?" April, remembering peyote, wrinkled her nose slightly.

"Nothing. Nothing at all. It's in distilled water."

No one else had a question and they went through their routine, the three mortals present slowing their breathing, all of them clearing their minds and centering their consciousness between earth and sky. On Jack's silent cue, they quaffed the contents of their vials in unison. The room temperature liquid was so tasteless, it was hard to be sure they'd actually swallowed something.

They meditated silently, waiting for Jack to cue them, and it wasn't long before Diana knew that she wasn't immune to LSD. The first odd effect it had was to make it feel like something was bubbling up from the base of her spine to the middle of her forehead, making her sinuses itch and teasing her to laugh. She was also becoming aware of visual phenomena, bright swirling colors that twisted and spiraled and moved continuously on the edges of her vision. But that was just the froth of a much greater sensation that everything around her was expanding outward, with a dizzying sense of release on all sides. She opened her eyes for a moment and the walls of the room were covered with tiny scarlet and flame colored moths running down the peeling plaster like a waterfall, and the candle flame was changing color in pulses. She heard April make a soft sound like a stifled laugh, and closed her eyes again, because she knew that Jack was about to give them their cue.

"Connect." It didn't sound like Jack's mental voice, and it didn't sound like just one voice. She had no time to wonder about this because when they united their magical energy, as they had done dozens of times now, everything changed.

It wasn't the totally synchronized unity of their connection, the sense of having become something much greater and more powerful than simply themselves times four. They were well used to that by now. But this time the sense of their connectedness extended far beyond that. Until now, they had been able to keep their inner selves—their minds, feelings and thoughts—more or less defended. Suddenly that was impossible. Diana had the odd sense that they had all joined hands, and then that they had somehow merged bodies into a sort of group hug, and then that their bodies were passing through each other's and blending, as though they all could dematerialize like she did. But at the same time, she knew this was an illusion because she could still feel her cupped hands in front of her. She was breathing, not because she needed to, but because she couldn't resist joining in with the matched intake and release of breath of her three covenmates.

Then she was thinking four sets of thoughts, rapid and simultaneous, and as impossible to understand as four radios blaring on top volume at the same time. She wasn't even sure which were her own thoughts—and these weren't merely words, but memories and images. If she considered one of the others, she saw him or her in fifty different forms, flicking past like book pages or the frames of a movie. She saw David as a baby, as a little boy, standing at a polished podium wearing a yarmulke and reading Hebrew characters from a scroll, carrying books in a shabby high school hallway...and then with a long gray beard and deep wrinkles, but she would always recognize those piercing black eyes. She saw April at fourteen dancing in a bar with black jazz musicians, at eighteen reading fortunes in a tawdry Southwestern tourist trap, standing blindfolded and wrapped in a shroud waiting for an initiation ceremony to begin, marching at the front of a crowd and shouting angrily, speaking on a lighted stage before a bank of microphones, white streaks now rippling through those flaming red waves of hair...

Jack sent them another mental cue, "Look outward." They all did, as one, and saw, glimmering around them, their network, their web, not as a static image, but alive, filled with power, and expanding. As they watched, it was growing before their eyes, thickening, sprouting more nodes and branches, stretching further and further from its beginning place.

They followed the network, feeding it energy and watching it in fascination, but over and over they ran to the end of a tendril and suddenly were engulfed in a scene that it touched. These scenes tended to have disturbing qualities: a man beating his wife for flirting with the landlord, the board of directors of a factory discussing how to get around their union contract and cut wages, a small mechanics shop furtively dumping waste oil into the river behind the building...there seemed to be an endless array of these. Like Diana's images of her covenmates, these situations fanned out on a whole timeline, and it wasn't obvious what was past, present and future. The three seemed, impossibly, to exist at the same instant. While all of this went on, colors and images flooded and swirled around their visual fields constantly, and it was very tempting to just forget about anything else except watching the light show unfold.

They had no sense whatever of time passing. Time simply *was,* in a way that Diana had rarely encountered. But eventually, the quality of their shared experience changed. As a brilliant starry sky fades before the onset of dawn's light in the east, they slowly returned to a more normal frame of reference. When Jack finally sent them the cue to ground, Diana felt completely disoriented. She opened her eyes and found that she, and all the rest of the group, were sprawled on the floor, in various positions but as limp as discarded socks. There was some residual visual effect, but mostly, she had a sense of disappointment, like a child awakening from a dream of Christmas morning to remember that it's still only December first.

It took quite a while for them to reach a point of getting up and returning to the dining room. Their usual cookies were wholly uninteresting, although David, Jack and April all got cups of water from the jugs in the kitchen. They sat in silence for some time, lost in their own thoughts, and Diana realized that April and David were directing a lot of long, considering looks her way. Not until this moment had it occurred to her that if she had been able to see her covenmates so clearly, it was very unlikely that they had not been able to see some things about her.

As if their minds were still linked, April yawned, looked at Diana, and said in a tone of casual curiosity, "So. What the hell are *you?*"

"Looks like the cat's out of the bag, lover," Jack said, but his tone was mild—he was still in a rather blissful state. David was looking at Diana expectantly.

"Can I explain it all on Friday? I don't think we're up to any serious discussion tonight."

Her three covenmates all nodded agreeably, which, Diana knew, was not the reaction she'd have gotten under any other circumstances. *Damn,* she thought, but it had been inevitable, and rather surprising that neither April nor David had twigged before now. She should have anticipated that enhancing everyone's magical perception wasn't going to leave any of them with many secrets.

Or almost any of them. Only later on, as she was processing the entire event and writing copious notes in her journal, did she realize that she had gotten few images and impressions from or about Jack.

𝔒hey met on 𝔉riday to talk over their first enhanced session.

"I had to call out yesterday," David said bleakly. Not only did LSD leave quite a hangover, they hadn't adjourned and gone home until 3:00 a.m. Their session had run for eight hours. "And the normal dose is two and half times that? I'm not going to be able to do this every night."

"David, at some point, you're going to have to choose your priorities. It may not be possible to do what we're doing and hold down a nine-to-five."

"I've got to eat. I don't have a trust fund."

Diana said, "If you know accounting, I bet I can find you something with flexible hours, or maybe you can just freelance. We hired in an accountant when Bread and Roses was first starting up. That's not charity, David, every smart person on earth uses contacts to get work."

"I know where there's a vacancy for a Social Studies teacher," April said bitterly.

"April, let's quit beating that into the ground, all right?" April glared at Jack and subsided. "Okay, people—comments, analysis, critiques?"

They spent a couple of hours comparing notes on their conclusions, but they didn't need to talk much about the session itself. They instinctively knew that they'd all perceived the same things, or very close to it. There was no mystery as to how LSD-enhanced workings would supply them with information. The big question was how to puzzle out just where the real-world timeline stood in relation to their perceptions, and whether, when and by what angles to step in and try to influence it.

"Again, it's going to take some experimentation," Jack said. "We'll pick the likeliest possibilities and see what happens."

"There's a theme to the situations this web is homing in on, isn't there, Jack?" Diana said. "It's not just neutral or random information. You've tuned it, like a receiver, and very carefully."

Jack rolled his eyes. "Well, of *course* I have. Or would you rather be trying to pick the trends and problems we're looking for out of all the information in the known universe back to the beginning of time?"

"So what are your frequencies? Be specific."

"Violence. Prejudice. Hatred. Oppression. Exploitation of the weak. Abuse of power, mostly—on any scale, from kicking puppies to mass murder."

David said, "You mean...evil."

"If you want to be incredibly banal about it, I guess so. But that's just how *we* think of it. No one sits around rubbing their hands together and chortling about how evil they are. They always think they're doing the right thing for someone, even if it's just for themselves."

David chuckled. "Maybe we *should* wear robes for our workings. How about tights and red capes?"

"Hey, anything that gives you a boost. I'll pass, thanks."

They were all smiling at this, but April turned to Diana and the table immediately fell silent. "Okay, enough business. You promised to explain what we saw in our session on Wednesday night. Come on, I know you saw a lot of stuff about me and David. And it's not as though we haven't both known right from the start that there's something pretty unusual about you. You aren't pale, cold and clammy because you have thyroid problems, and we'd noticed that you hardly seem to breathe at all, which is really unnerving. But *vampires?* Like Count Dracula? Tell me that was a hallucination, because it's damned hard to swallow."

Diana wasn't sure how to begin—Jack hadn't been so aggressively skeptical. To her surprise, he spoke up.

"It wasn't a hallucination, and she's not the only one. There are others, and I've met them. I think you're demonstrating exactly why Diana didn't just make an announcement, first thing. You'd never have believed it."

April looked flustered. "Well...it's not that I'm narrow-minded, for god's sake, but...damn it, Jack, it is pretty incredible."

"I know it is. Would you like her to show you some of the things she can do?"

"Wait a minute, Jack. Let's not start off with the parlor tricks." Diana turned back to David and April; he looked avidly curious, she still appeared guarded and doubtful. "Four years ago, I was just like you are now. I'd never have believed it, either. I'll tell you the whole story of what happened. Then, if you want some more evidence, I'll show you a couple of things." They both nodded agreement, and Diana launched into a somewhat condensed version of the account she'd spun for Jack on May Day.

Condensed or not, it took some time to finish, and David and April both had a lot of questions. When she finally concluded, David said, "Well, I don't need any more proof. I'm just glad to finally get the whole picture. I knew there was something different about you—I mean *really* different—the second you walked through the door at Phoebe's party."

"And so did everyone else," Diana said glumly. David nodded, his smile wry.

"Well, I'm not so sure," April said. "I'll grant, you're obviously strange. And at least you're not trying to sell us on coffins and bats. But this is quite a tale. Show me a parlor trick or two, go ahead."

"All right. Give me your hand." April pulled back from her, frowning. "Come on, don't chicken out now. You want something that couldn't be faked, right?"

Swallowing hard, April extended her hand. Briskly, Diana took a firm grip of April's wrist, turned it so her inner forearm was facing up, and touched two fingers of her free hand lightly on April's skin. It looked like she was taking a pulse, but she was being very careful to avoid any veins. Before April had time to react, she *opened* where her fingers were in contact. Blood welled up and splashed in drops on the Formica table top.

David gasped, and April let out a little shriek, partly from the unpleasant sensation of *opening* and partly from shock at the sight of her blood running freely down her arm. She tried to pull away but Diana tightened her grip.

"Let me close it, because it never stops on its own. You'll bleed out from this little wound." She concentrated and *closed,* then let April's wrist go. The smell of fresh blood was making her head reel, and she sucked the blood off her fingers and then dabbed up the drops from the table and licked that off, as well. She glanced to her right, saw that April had turned faintly green, and sat back, clearing her throat and wiping her hands on her skirt.

David handed April a handkerchief, craning his neck to peer at the puckered red bump as she wiped off the blood and clamped the handkerchief down on it as though it was still bleeding. "You don't bite?"

"No biting, no pointy teeth. It would be highly impractical, anyway. Convinced?" she asked April.

"I, um..."

"Show them that other thing you do," Jack said.

"You want April to throw up *and* faint?"

"I'm not about to do either, thank you very much—oh, *fuck.*"

Diana reappeared while David was still spluttering, "Oh my *god,*" in a half-laugh. "*That's* how you get around without a car! That's how you get in here when the door is bolted on the inside! I understand a *lot* of things now."

"I'm glad you're amused." Diana gave April's unsmiling face an uneasy look. "I guess the main question now is, can you two still work magically with me, now that you know? It's not like anything has changed, after all..."

"Sure," David said. But April was silent.

"Maybe you need time to think about it?" Jack said.

"I don't know, I...I don't want to be all prissy, but this is...a lot to take in."

"It is," Diana said.

After a silence, Jack said, "What I'd *like* us to do, if everyone agrees, is meet tomorrow and try a full dose of LSD, and see if we can use that to find our next project—something off the radar, completely outside the news media or general knowledge. It needs to be tomorrow so David can recuperate for his job."

"Thank you," David said.

"April, if you find that you can't make it tomorrow, for any reason, give me a call and we'll...well, we'll figure out what to do." April just nodded, avoiding Diana's eyes. She left without saying anything more. Jack gave David a ride back to his apartment.

12

April never told them what internal reconciliations or conversations with others she may have had, but she appeared at the house in Woburn on time the following afternoon. "I'm in," was all she said.

Jack had suggested they meet even earlier, since a full dose session could take around twelve hours. "It might not necessarily be longer, just more intense—but it's different for different people, and we may as well allow as much time as we can."

He turned out to be right. Their first full dose session was very similar to the test session on Wednesday night, just a little longer and much more intense. But this time, they attempted to focus on identifying possible goals, which required mental processes not harmonious with the drug-induced state of mind. Their synchronization wavered considerably, until Diana almost had the Keystone Kops feeling of their very first working. It didn't help that as soon as they followed a tendril to a situation and tried to read it, the tendril sprouted more divisions and grew off into new directions, apparently stimulated into growth by their mere attention to it. They did, however, glean several possible situations to look into. One in particular got their unanimous vote to try and influence, and they had their researchers do some sleuthing locally to pick up more fine details.

A textile factory owner in Lawrence, named Klinghoeffer, had stuffed his payroll with French Canadian and Puerto Rican immigrants. Most of them spoke little English and a number of them were not United States citizens. This left them fearful for their jobs and reluctant to say anything about their Dickensian working conditions and abysmally low pay. Some union organizers from Lowell had begun meeting with the employees and attempting to unionize the shop. Klinghoeffer, who seemed more like an organized crime boss than a CEO, had spies among the employees and a gang of thugs he was using to intimidate his workers from attending union meetings. He also had influence in the community, relatives on the local newspapers, friends on the police force, and to make matters as bad as possible, he owned much of the tenement housing in which his workers lived.

"You'd think it was the nineteenth century," David said as they collated all of this information over the following week. "Maybe we should just report this one. The jerk is flagrantly violating federal laws, we could report it to the state attorney general's office, if he's got the cops in his pocket."

"The union organizers tried that," Diana said. "The workers won't back up the allegations because they're too scared. They can meet and vote, the owner can't stop them from doing that, but chances are they'll be afraid to vote yes."

"Free elections, in this country, are a myth," April said. "All that nauseating bullshit about how 'free' Americans are, and it's crap. Sure, if you're white, male, Protestant and rich, you're free as a bird. Anyone else, forget about it."

"You're dead right on that," David said. "So, what can we do about this?"

"I see two alternatives," Jack said. "One, we can attempt to make the workers less fearful and more confident, or maybe just angrier."

"So they burn down the factory that employs them?" Diana said. "Not really a big step up for them."

"Or we could focus on this Klinghoeffer, try the same thing we did to Reverend Porter. After all, that one did work."

"No kidding. He still hasn't been heard from," David said.

"Or we can do both. This is a lot to try and push," April said.

Diana shook her head. "I have a feeling that was one reason we muffed the school board project. We were trying to do two totally contradictory things: change the minds of the members who wanted to terminate and encourage the two who supported the teacher. We ended up changing no one's mind and losing one of the supporters. What if we just make the workers more scared and Klinghoeffer confident and angry? I think we need to stick to one theme per project. The trick is figuring out which one."

"I guess you're right, I never looked at it that way," April said as David nodded in thoughtful agreement.

"I'd go after Klinghoeffer," Jack said. "Leave him and his goons alone and there will just be more trouble if the union vote does go through. Maybe we can get some of the pressure off the union organizers. They're seasoned veterans, they know what they're doing. A sneak attack on their opposition could be the best way we can help."

They all agreed on the logic of Jack's proposal, and designed an approach with the single goal of planting guilt, doubts, anxiety and hesitation into the minds of Mr. Klinghoeffer, his immediate executives and his gang of thugs.

They found that when they worked without LSD, they now were more focused and in command of more energy by several factors of ten, which was a heady feeling. That feeling was short lived, however. After four sessions of throwing everything they had at Klinghoeffer and cohorts, they had to admit that they'd run into a new dilemma. Mr. Klinghoeffer had a lack of empathy and conscience so absolute that he qualified as a sociopath. He was completely resistant to every influence they tried. His underlings were more receptive, but the thugs were thugs, motorcycle gang members and petty crooks who cared only for the money they were paid, and the junior executives in the firm were too afraid of their boss to disobey him. Nobody argued with Mr. Klinghoeffer. The factory was very profitable, so the one and only reason he would have questioned his decisions was not part of the equation.

Feeling as though they'd been flinging themselves at a brick wall, before the fifth session David suggested, "Maybe we need to keep him distracted somehow until after the union vote. You know those days when you feel that everything that could go wrong, does?"

For the next three days, Mr. Klinghoeffer's car broke down every morning, he hired cabs but was caught in traffic jams everywhere he went, he erupted into a nasty case of hives and the water main to his plush fifteen-room house in Andover burst and flooded the entire first floor. But all of this simply made him surlier, and more to the point, failed to slow him down. He didn't miss a single meeting with his executives or his thugs. With the union decision two days away, and the organizers doing well in persuading a quorum to vote in favor, one of the organizers' homes in Lowell was firebombed. By some miracle, no one was hurt, but the house was gutted.

The following night, the coven gathered in a somber mood.

"Things are getting serious," Diana said. "Should we try different tactics? Maybe try to find something we can use to get law enforcement involved, like some kind of evidence? Or should we just pull out? Maybe our interference is making the conflict worse."

"I seriously doubt that." Jack's expression was as grim as they'd ever seen him. "We tuned the web to home in to, as David put it, evil. Well, we sure found it. This Klinghoeffer is one hell of a piece of work. The question now is, how far are we prepared to go? Are we ready to do what's necessary?"

"Meaning what?" David asked. "How far do we have the *right* to go, after all? Just what are you implying, Jack?"

"We can't start and then stop with the job half done. What right do we have? I don't know if we can fairly claim a *right* to do anything that we're doing, even spying by magic, which, let's face it, is exactly what's going on. We *can* do it and we're the only ones who can, that gives us the right. Now people are in real danger of being seriously hurt, or even killed. If we're not willing to do whatever is necessary, we're handicapping ourselves."

Diana stared at him. "Are you suggesting that we actually murder people?"

"It's not considered murder during a war, Diana."

"That's the kind of thinking our enemies fall prey to. There are always alternatives to killing."

"Not always. And even when there are, you don't always have time. If you saw someone about to slit a child's throat, for example, would you hesitate one second?"

"Those old morals debates are straw men, Jack. Suppose it was another child holding the knife? Life is never that simple, and things are always connected in a thousand ways that we can't see."

"Wait a minute," David said. "When we met that first night, all you talked about was influencing the minds of people in power. I didn't sign up for this just to turn into some kind of magical assassin. That's nothing but pure black magic."

"We're not doing it for selfish reasons," Jack said. "Black magic is self-aggrandizing, it's done for greed or lust or power, to benefit just one person. We're not getting any personal profit out of this, it's all for the greater good."

Diana fidgeted uneasily, not certain that she held the ethical high ground in this debate. "Still, I think there's a line that we should only cross as an absolute last resort, and never happily."

"I wouldn't be happy about it, either. I agree with you. But in answer to your question, David, we have to be prepared to take extreme measures, if they're required. We can't set arbitrary limits on ourselves."

April said, "All these hypotheticals don't get us any closer to an objective for tonight's working. Is someone else's house going to be bombed? Is someone going to be shot next? Suppose we did want to remove Klinghoeffer—are we capable of that? Sure, we gave him a rash and whammied his car, but really putting him out of commission...what would we do?"

Jack's mouth was set in a tight line, and he didn't answer for a few moments. "Maybe that's one more thing that we'll just have to try out and see."

David sucked in a breath, and Diana stood up. "Mother of all the gods, Jack, we aren't going to try and kill someone as an *experiment!* Just to see if we can? Isn't that exactly what Leopold and Loeb said?"

Jack turned white. "We're not dealing with an innocent little kid, here, Diana, this man won't stop at maiming and murder himself. Besides, we wouldn't necessarily have to kill him. We could, I don't know, put him into a coma or something."

"How?"

"I don't *know,* I just..." he seemed to be weakening in the face of their resistance.

Diana slowly sank back into her chair. "I have a suggestion." When she had everyone's attention, she went on, "The big meeting is tomorrow night. If the workers vote to unionize, it will be on the public record, and however management reacts, the status quo will have changed. Klinghoeffer's only hope is to postpone the meeting somehow, and that's why he's attacking the organizers.

In fact, if you think about it, he's doing to them exactly what we've been trying to do to him." David and April glanced at each other uneasily; this obviously had not occurred to them. "So I suggest that we pull out all the stops and put shields and protection around the organizers and the main leaders among the factory employees. Let's keep them safe until tomorrow night."

After a long pause, Jack said "Agreed. That sounds like a good plan." April and David released audible sighs.

They pursued that plan, but their shielding wasn't put to a serious test. The next day, they learned that several of the thugs had been arrested by the Lowell police the previous afternoon before the coven's meeting had even started. They had left some very sloppy clues at the bombed house which the police easily traced, especially since one of the perpetrators had a long rap sheet for arson. The entire sordid story was front page news, and Mr. Klinghoeffer was confronted not only with the worst public relations crisis of his career, but some serious indictments. The workers voted to unionize, and it seemed certain that they would be doing so under new management.

The coven called a quick impromptu meeting at the bungalow in Cambridge to share the news, but this time they didn't feel as celebratory as after the cancellation of the Book Swap.

"Do you think we had anything to do with that at all?" David mused. "It almost seems like things would have turned out that way without our influence. I know we were sending Klinghoeffer bad luck, and we were trying to make his thugs foul up, but, still…how can we be sure?"

"We can't," Jack said. "We just have to have faith."

13

he factory project had taken considerably longer than Jack had expected, and he was eager for the coven to do another LSD session and look for new targets. "I think, however, that we may want to change our mode of attack." He refused to go into more details until their next session.

Their researchers finally put Diana in touch with a sketch artist who was both skilled enough to suit her and willing to work for a private civilian. Jack sat with him for two afternoons and ended up with finely detailed pencil drawings of the two vampires he knew only as Avery and Ned. He pronounced the likenesses as accurate as a photograph—so accurate, in fact, that after the drawings were finished, he refused to look at them again. On Diana's request, the artist did profile sketches, as well.

"That doesn't mean they'll look like this now," Jack said. "They could grow their hair long, shave their heads, even grow beards, at least according to you— who knows? If I were them I'd sure change my appearance a lot."

He couldn't recall the other vampires in the room clearly enough for a full sketch, but he did have the artist do a profile of the woman, Janice or Janna or whatever her name was. It was a striking face, with heavy, strong bones and a wide mouth, but Jack wasn't as sure of his memory in her case. The other two men he couldn't describe at all. He'd seen Avery and Ned again in his own lodgings and had gotten a much better and longer look at them.

But Diana was pleased to have the drawings, because at least now she had something concrete to go on. She was still making regular visits to the Brighton area and often to other parts of Boston as well. But she'd stopped searching every night and combined her quest for other vampires with her hunting forays, so she wouldn't feel that her time was completely wasted.

One day at just sunset she'd decided to walk around the Common, the theatre district and Tremont Street, which were close to the Beacon Street location of the Order's Motherhouse. A familiar figure emerged from a small restaurant just ahead of her, and Diana realized that it was Phoebe, dressed in the most up to the minute of evening chic. With a mixture of emotions, she slowed her steps, but Phoebe turned and saw Diana before she could step into a doorway or lose herself behind other pedestrians. Phoebe blinked in surprise and glanced furtively back at the restaurant entrance.

"Diana, what a…pleasant surprise." From her expression, she was lying her tongue black. Diana had expected Phoebe to be somewhat put out with her, but she was sensing something more serious.

"I'm sorry, Phoebe, I know I just abandoned you. I've been…well…I got involved in something I never anticipated, right after Beltene. I know have I should have called you, but it's been rather…" She hated making excuses. She'd met with Phoebe and some of the others a few evenings before the coven got organized, but since June 11th, she'd made no time for anything else.

"Oh, I understand, Diana." Phoebe broke in hastily, but she didn't sound as though she was rejecting Diana's apology. "We all know that you're doing something with David Hofstein and…" she dropped her voice almost to a whisper, "Jack Garrett. I've seen you a couple of times with him, Jack, I mean."

"You make it sound like he was on the ten most wanted list." Diana's tone was humorous but she was sincerely bewildered.

"It's not that, it's…well…it's Art."

"Art? You mean—oh, I get it. I could tell that there was no love lost between Art and David, at your party. But what does Art have against Jack? Jack was at Beltene."

"Art thought he shouldn't have been invited. Daniel asked Jack, and he apparently didn't check with the Council first."

"Since when does the ranking Magus at a big ritual have to?"

"Well…" Phoebe glanced behind her again. "I can't say anything more about it now. We have theatre tickets, and Art will be coming out any second, he was just visiting the washroom." She looked helplessly at Diana's expression and then tugged off her left glove and extended her hand. "We're engaged."

Diana blinked at the tastefully expensive diamond ring. "Congratulations. And that means you can't talk to me anymore?"

Phoebe looked on the verge of tears. "I'm sorry, I just—Art's being elevated to Magus next month."

"Really? They must be—very impressed by him." She'd barely stopped herself from sniping *they must be desperate.*

There was a long pause, because Phoebe was standing with her lips parted, as if she was about to say something difficult and was trying to find the right words. But all she could finally manage was, "Oh, Diana, I'm so sorry, but you've got to know…I mean, you must have known when you started…"

The restaurant door moaned open and Art stepped out and strode up next to Phoebe, reaching for her arm. "Sorry to take so long, honey, I—" He saw

Diana and stopped mid-step, his smile vanishing. Diana thought that he looked like a cheery housewife who had just opened a kitchen drawer and found a cockroach. "Diana," he said with a terse nod. Then he took Phoebe's arm so tightly, he must have hurt her, although she gave no sign of it. "We'd better go, we'll miss the curtain."

They turned and walked away toward Tremont without another word. Phoebe looked back over her shoulder once and Art tugged her forward, as though she was a balky dog on a leash.

Diana was so stunned, she stood on the sidewalk watching Art and Phoebe until they disappeared among the clusters of walkers. *I guess a few bridges have gone up in smoke, haven't they? And I never even realized it.* She wondered if all of Phoebe's crowd would act the same way, and for that matter, everyone in the Order. *Surely…surely…if I was banished, someone would have contacted me?* But she and Jack rented the Cambridge bungalow under an assumed name, and they'd been so secretive, no one in the Order had the phone number. Her parents and the Board of Bread and Roses only had a post box for her, and no one thought that was strange. She hadn't had a phone for three years in Maine.

She jumped when a voice next to her said, "Is everything all right, Miss?" She'd been standing still for so long, the doorman from the restaurant had come out to investigate.

"I'm fine, thank you." She hurried down the sidewalk and turned off on the first side street, wanting to get away from the bright lights and busy Common.

"**No.**" Jack stared at her blankly. "I haven't heard anything like that, official or otherwise. I'm…I'm completely thrown for a loop here."

"Have you talked to anyone in the Order since we four started meeting?"

"Well, no, I haven't. But doesn't the Order know your post office box? I mean, if they wanted to do anything formal…"

"You're the one who usually gets the mail from the post box. Are you absolutely certain that you haven't seen anything from the Council or the P.M.? Or even from one of my friends?"

"If I saw any mail addressed to you from *anybody*, Diana, I'd have given it to you instantly, my word of honor. I wouldn't hide your mail from you, no matter what I thought it was. Official mail from the Order isn't easy to miss—but I wouldn't throw away a circular from a used car salesman if it had your name on it."

Diana's shoulders slumped. "I'm sorry, I don't mean to imply that you would. I'm sure my parents would have gotten in touch, if only to demand to know what the hell I thought I was doing."

"Well, as family goes, they're not exactly on the clingy side."

Diana had to smile. "No kidding. 'Hi, darling, Provence is lovely, how have you been the past three years?'" Jack laughed. "But, still…"

"I wouldn't panic over it, Diana. Don't assume what you heard is the general opinion. I never really got along with Art."

"You didn't?"

"No, we, uh…we got into some pretty serious disagreements back before Gregs was banished. Political shit. He's about thirty degrees further to the right than William F. Buckley. He never approved of your foundation, you know."

"I didn't know."

"He thought you were just coddling wastrels and parasites who should go out and get jobs. But his was the minority view, so he kept it to himself. I'm kind of surprised Phoebe's latched on to him, but who can figure?" Diana just shook her head sadly, and Jack added with genuine sympathy, "Sorry about this splitting you two apart, though. I don't have any use for guys who make their girls choose between their husband and their friends, I think that's just plain slimy."

"He's being elevated to Magus." Diana's voice was just shy of catty.

Jack threw his head back in a long laugh. "Of course he is! He's perfect for that gang of stuffed shirts."

"Bread and Roses found jobs for all those so-called parasites, hundreds of them," Diana grumbled.

"Diana, just forget about it. We're playing for bigger stakes now than Art and his cronies will ever dream of."

Diana's mouth quirked into a half smile, as this sounded a little over the top even to her. "Depends on the dream. I suspect we're more along the lines of their worst nightmare."

Jack grinned. "Even better." He looked over his shoulder at the window, forgetting it was boarded over, and then at his watch. "Where are David and April, anyway?"

"What's your rush? We don't have a project."

"No, and we're not going to—not the way we've been doing. That's why this meeting is important."

Diana cocked her head and listened for a moment. "I don't know about April, but David just got off the bus."

"You heard the bus from two blocks away? Jesus, it gives me the creeps when you do that."

Diana laughed. "This is a very quiet street, Jack. Even you would hear those brakes if you were outside, and David's the only one who gets off at this time of day. You know, if you really wanted to—"

"Shut up," he said mildly. "I told you before, if and when I'm ready, you'll be the first to know."

"All right, I know I shouldn't pester you about it. But just bear in mind that only one of us has all the time in the world."

April arrived somewhat late, offering only a vague apology and no explanation. As they settled around the table, three of them were glancing at each other and at Jack uncertainly.

"I've been doing a lot of thinking about our work so far," Jack said. "A hell of a lot. And I'm sure all of you have been doing the same."

April shrugged almost imperceptibly as David nodded, his expression intent.

"I'd like to propose that we change our basic approach," Jack went on. "We've now taken on three very different projects, and we've gotten mixed results. We can't expect to have unbroken success, that would be unrealistic. But these projects are taking up far too much energy, work and time for the results we're getting. Extrapolate from all this, and we'll spend months working on one single issue at a time. That's just not effective. We'll never get anywhere at that rate."

"I don't think anyone ever suggested that magic was efficient," David said. "I mean, look at what Diana told us about that working in Maine she did. Two solid years, and all it did was rebound."

"Not only that, she's dead."

"Get lost, April," Diana said.

"So how do you think we could be doing anything differently?" David asked. "You said right from the start that we'd be influencing the minds of people in power. It's not like that's going to get any easier as we go up the chain of command, is it?"

"That's exactly it." Jack took in a deep breath. "I think I was off target with my initial ideas."

"You mean...you're admitting you were wrong?" April looked delighted. "Wait just a second, I'm going to go call the *Times*."

"Make that Ripley's Believe It or Not."

"All right, girls, go ahead and have your fun."

David said, "Can we hear your new plan?"

"Thank you, David."

"Yeah, you'd just know these men would all stick together, wouldn't you."

"Gods, April, just where were you before you got here tonight? Are you on something?" Diana leaned toward April and sniffed. "Oh good gods, you've been smoking marijuana, haven't you? You're higher than a kite."

"That's none of your business. We haven't got a project to work on."

"We've been doing practice workings every meeting! Is it too much to ask that you show up with your head on straight? I thought you were a better magician than that."

"Spare me the puritanical lectures, mom."

"She's got a point, April." Jack looked perturbed, while David actually appeared angry.

"Okay, okay. It's a long story. I won't do it again."

"Can we get back to the topic at hand?" David said, rather loudly, to Jack.

"Gladly. I've concluded that the big mistake we've made is to try and confront highly energized situations head on. It's like we wanted to divert a speeding freight train. Standing on the tracks and waving at it only gets us run over. But think far enough ahead, go down the tracks and find a switch and shift it, and the train will veer off onto another track all on its own momentum. Look, it's like that circus movie."

Diana shuddered.

"I didn't see that one," April said.

"It's got a train wreck. The bad guys stop a train with an emergency signal, and then a second train runs into it. One of the guys tries to stop the second train by driving straight down the track at it in his car, but it's too late, the train can't stop, he just gets demolished. Well, that's kind of what we've been doing. Reverend Porter stopped at our signal. The school board just wiped us off the tracks. And Klinghoeffer…we don't even know what happened there."

"That's a colorful analogy," Diana said. "But how does it apply to changing the course of history?"

"We're going to have to go back further in time and change things way before any crisis develops. Preventive action. By the time emotions have gotten engaged, the whole situation is too hard for us to steer. My thought is that we'll focus on elections, and on small decision points: hiring and firing by corporate boards, for example. And we're in a position to do that now, people. With the LSD and our network, we can see timelines and trends far in advance of their actual manifestation. We're the only people who can do this. No one will ever have the slightest suspicion that we even exist, let alone how we're pulling the strings." He smiled, and his eyes suddenly had that unsettling glitter again. "It's the ultimate conspiracy."

After a thoughtful silence, Diana said, "I wonder if we can be so sure that we're the only ones—and even if we're that invisible." She was thinking about her encounter with Phoebe, which had been bothering her ever since. She couldn't stop wondering whether Phoebe had been implying that people in the Order were somehow aware of more than the four of them assumed—or if there were some critical things that Diana didn't know about Jack's reputation. The latter suspicion was actually far less disquieting.

"I haven't detected a hint of that in our workings, and I've been looking for it. For god's sake, Diana, weren't both of us hunting for years for something like this? And we both gave up on it, didn't we?"

"Yes, you're right. Thomas told me the same thing and he'd been looking since the seventeen thirties. But there's a fine line between resisting paranoia and just being oblivious. Remember what I told you about Thomas and I being

98

completely blind to the effects of our working in the greater world? We were changing the plant life, we were affecting people, Gregory could feel what we were doing hundreds of miles away, and we couldn't detect it at all. Gregory said it was because we were in the eye of the storm we made, and he was dead right, as it turned out."

"But we're doing something completely different here. I can see why that happened to the two of you, but there are four of us, and we're spreading our consciousness out into the universe, not focusing it to a single point."

David said, "It just seems like it's going to be very tricky to keep track of our efforts. It's hard enough now to puzzle out those timelines, and what you're talking about, I can't see how we'll be able to use mundane methods to test our accuracy, or even know whether we succeeded. Suppose we are successful—how will we know for sure that we had anything to do with it at all?"

"It does seem very nebulous," Diana said.

"I know, you're right. All I can say is that I'm confident that we'll become more skilled and perceptive with time. People, we've only been doing this for a few weeks, and look at what we've already accomplished."

"Win, lose, tie? That's not even the trophy in a tic-tac-toe match," April said. "Reverend Porter might have been pure dumb luck for all we know."

Jack just shook his head, smiling. "Obviously we don't have a statistically significant sample. Let's keep working on it. I say we give it at least a year. Not only that, I think we should be meeting as often as we can. Maybe every night is too much to ask, but at least bump it to four nights a week."

"Uh, wait a minute…job? Paying the bills?"

Jack, who had been leaning forward towards them, looked down at his clasped hands on the table for a moment. "David, I think we may be at the fish or cut bait point here. If you really want to work with us…it's not a part-time proposition anymore." He looked up at David's troubled expression. "I respect your principles, I really do. But what's more important here? It's not like we can replace you, David. You know that. What the four of us have magically here, this is a one-in-a-million chance. If you leave, we're done. Every single one of us is as critical as one of these table legs is to the whole table. You're not expendable."

David's inner struggle was clearly visible on his face. "I don't want to be the quitter, but…"

"David, I'll help you find something more flexible," Diana said. "For pete's sake, let me do you the same courtesy I'd do for any magical peer who needed it. That's what Bread and Roses *does,* help men get jobs. You didn't have a job when I met you three months ago, it's not like you're giving up your pension."

David hunched his shoulders. "Well…it is a pretty crummy gig, anyway. Besides, they're not too happy that I've called out a couple of times already. They're probably going to fire me as it is."

"So who needs 'em?" Jack said. "It was just bad timing, if we'd gotten this group going sooner you wouldn't have committed to that sweatshop yet."

"Well..." David looked at Diana warily. "If you think you could help me find something..."

"I'm sure I can."

Jack beamed. "Great. But I'd like to suggest another big change, and this will make things even easier for you, too, David. April brought this up when we first started. I think we'd make a lot more progress if we found someplace where we could all be living under the same roof." As the rest of them exchanged looks, Jack said, "Come on. Diana and I are already sharing a house, and half the time you two are all but living together at April's. It's ridiculous for you to keep on paying for that apartment, David."

"You don't think we'll attract attention that way?" Diana said.

"Who cares? It's going to make it so much easier to really concentrate our energy. We can work every single night—no more worries about being seen coming and going, staggering our travel, catching the bus, driving home after an LSD session..."

"We could have running water and a toilet..." April said.

"I've got a lease, though."

"In this housing market? You won't have any trouble getting out of it."

Diana pondered, recalling how she'd argued Thomas out of his initial doubts about her living with him during their magical undertaking three years earlier. "I have to admit—it would make things a lot easier. The big challenge is finding a suitable place. We couldn't get away with a rental, four unrelated adults. We'll have to buy it."

"Is that a problem?" Jack asked.

"Not financially."

"I can go halfsies on it," April said. "I want to have some say in the decision, though."

"Of course, we all will. It's not going to happen overnight."

Jack looked delighted. "Then let's hold off on any more LSD sessions until after we get settled. There are too many big changes on the agenda, we need some stability for our next stage."

This made sense to all of them. They went into the next room and did a practice session, because none of them could bear to adjourn a meeting now without the sensuous and stimulating renewal of their magical union. But their coordination was shaky to say the least. They were distracted by the prospect of the transitions they planned, especially David, who had to relinquish the most, and Diana, whose mind couldn't stop churning over practical issues. The fact that April periodically lapsed into fits of giggles didn't help, either.

14

Most of those practical issues were strictly nuts and bolts matters of looking at realty listings, checking out zoning and local bylaws, and tapping one of the case managers at Bread and Roses to help David find more flexible employment. But Jack's new approach would utilize their research and clipping service far less than originally planned, and Diana decided to turn their skills toward some new ends.

In early August, she met with one of the researchers, a bespectacled young man named Brad Cooper, to go over that week's findings.

"Not too much this week," he said as she sat down in the chair opposite his desk. "Cops call this the silly season, but all the reports I'm seeing are pretty straight-forward. Stick-ups, car wrecks, bar brawls, drunks...you said you didn't care about flying saucers, right?"

"Probably not relevant. I may change my mind."

"You did say anything weird."

"Yes, but I want to keep that inside some kind of parameters. They need to be incidents that directly involve people or animals in some way." She hadn't wanted to be too specific with Brad about precisely what might signal, to her, that a vampire was active in the area, but she had mentioned victims with amnesia.

He rustled through his notes and then grinned for a second. "How about body-snatchers? Or a missing body, at least."

Diana sat up straighter on the hard wooden chair. "Tell me more."

"This came off a court docket. No other mention of it, so I'm sure it's being kept out of the news, probably with bribes. This rich old family in South Kingston, Rhode Island has filed some big lawsuit against the town. They claim the Department of Public Works has lost one of their ancestors."

"What was the DPW doing with one of their ancestors in the first place?"

"Moving a private cemetery. They're building a new school, and the town took the land by eminent domain but promised to handle transferring the remains. They dug up a sixty-year-old coffin, and lo and behold, it was empty."

Diana felt all her instincts go to high alert, but she tried to keep a reasonable grasp on her imagination. "A burial way back then, though? There may never have been anyone in the coffin."

"It wasn't *that* long ago. Looks like more than one elderly scion of the family remembers the funeral, including the dead guy's kid sister. They're on the warpath down there."

"Names?"

"Family name is Tillinger. They were pillars of Rhode Island before Roger Williams got there, to hear them tell it. Funny thing, though—that's not too far from that famous 'true vampire' case in Exeter, Rhode Island, the one where they dug up that girl to stop the whole family from dying of TB."

"Yes, I remember that." Her research had turned up that story, in numerous sources, very early on. "Tillinger…what was the name of the missing ancestor?"

Brad ran a finger down the page, squinting at the tiny print. "Edward Tillinger. Eighteen seventy-two to eighteen ninety-six, poor bastard. Probably died of TB, himself."

Diana ran her tongue along her suddenly dry lips. "Very possible…" *It can't be, can it? Twenty-four, just about how old Jack said his vampires looked…* "A nickname for Edward would be Ned, wouldn't it?"

"Yeah, I guess it would. Kind of old-fashioned now, though. Most guys these days just use Ed."

Diana nodded, trying to keep her expression impassive, although she knew she wasn't fooling Brad. "I'll take that one, thanks. I think I'll check this story out a bit more."

"Just watch your step. If the Tillingers think someone's snooping around, sounds like they're ready to shoot on sight."

"Don't worry about me. See you next week."

They were supposed to be looking at a house in Malden the following day, but Diana cancelled the appointment and drove down to South Kingston, arriving around 3:00. She knew it would probably be wiser to wait until the volatile situation calmed down—she doubted that the coffin had been vacated recently and she was sure the beleaguered DPW was entirely blameless. But she couldn't wait, even though she didn't dare risk asking anyone for help. She was going to find a picture of Edward Tillinger, if she had to materialize inside the family mansion and rifle their private records.

She didn't have to go that far, fortunately. She tried the public library first, but although several town histories discussed the Tillingers at length, none of them included a portrait or photograph of Edward, who wasn't even mentioned. He hadn't lived long enough to play an important role in town affairs. There was no historical society and she had no idea if the Tillingers had belonged to any fraternal organizations.

But the name of the defendants' attorney was on the report Brad had given her, and she discovered that it was the town counsel, who had an office in Town Hall. She inquired and found that the counselor was out of his office for the afternoon. He shared a secretary with several other departments, so Diana simply ducked into the ladies' room, dematerialized, ghosted inside the attorney's locked office and solidified. The desk was piled with case folders, and the folder labeled "Tillinger v S Kingston" was right on the top. Diana slipped the folder off the desk and paged through it. As she had barely dared to hope, it was full of minutiae related to the missing Edward Tillinger, possibly in an effort to raise reasonable doubt that he had actually been interred in that grave. As she turned over yellowed handwritten documents, a small, heavy photograph slipped from the folder and fell on the rug. Diana stooped down and for a moment felt faint. Looking up at her, somber-eyed, was the face so meticulously recreated by their sketch artist, the man Jack claimed had called himself Ned.

Footsteps clicked by and paused outside the door for a moment, reminding Diana that her position was perilous. She carefully replaced the folder exactly as she'd found it, pocketed the small photo, and dematerialized, not solidifying until she was outside and several blocks away from Town Hall. She was reeling from a mixture of giddy victory and guilt—she was stealing an irreplaceable family memento, after all, and town counsel would probably get into some hot water for losing it. But if Edward Tillinger was a vampire, the fewer records of his past that were left around, the better, she told herself several times. She wished she could have read more of the papers, to see if any biographical details about Edward offered clues that would help her trace him. But it would have taken hours to pore through the file and she couldn't have risked it.

She had learned two things: Edward Tillinger had died in Providence, not South Kingston, and he had been the victim of a murder which was gruesome even by the standards of the 1890s. Had he already been a vampire then, and attacked by a would-be vampire slayer, trying to cut pieces out of him as was done to Mercy Brown? He'd been found half-disemboweled in the middle of a slum street; a vampire might have recovered after a day or so and simply disappeared. Or did the grotesque nature of his death have something to do with his coming back as a vampire? She swore to herself that someday, somehow, she would find out.

1956

15

So, is the cake Kosher? And candles, no less. Someone's birthday?"

Diana shook out the match. "It's October third, nineteen fifty-six, David. Today is the first anniversary of our consecrating this house and moving in. I have no idea if the cake is Kosher, sorry."

"My god, already?" April dropped into the chair opposite David. "Hey, if we want to really celebrate, we should circle up, melt the candles and set fire to the frosting."

"The hell we will! I've been waiting all day for chocolate cake. Who wants to blow out the candles?"

"Well, Jack's got the most hot air. Trouble is, we'll still be waiting for him to finish blowing at midnight."

"Um, you'll pardon me?" But Jack was grinning at April. "Watch me make a liar out of you, babe." He took in a dramatically huge breath and then delicately puffed out the candles. "Control. It's all about control. Now Diana is the one you want handling the knife." He picked it up and passed it to her.

"I'm not sure I want to analyze that one too closely," Diana said wryly, as she sliced into the cake.

"He just means you cut right through the crap, Diana," David said.

"Oh, right. Sure he does." She sank into her chair, positioning a forkful of rich fudge ganache before her mouth. "Now shut up, I'm about to concentrate."

For the next several minutes she was focused so intently on the taste of chocolate that she blanked all other senses from her immediate attention. When she finally had exhausted the experience of that first bite, she picked up the chatter around the table slowly. None of it was about her; her facility for occasional sensory overload had long stopped evoking comment.

"Good cake," David said, indistinctly.

"Um. God, you remember that little dump we started out in? How did we ever get anything done there?"

Diana opened her eyes to frown at April. "I seem to recall that it worked very well, for what we needed. And I still own it."

"Good, we might want a really big bonfire some night."

"Not that this place is the Taj Mahal or anything," David said.

"We were lucky to find it. And Lexington is a good location—close to the city, but far enough out that we could get a nice big lot with no neighbors in earshot."

"You remember that farmhouse we looked at in Sudbury?" David said. "It's been torn down, there's a whole housing development going in there now."

"That's happening everywhere," Jack said. "The cities are emptying out, which says something about how toxic they are. All they do is concentrate the worst of humanity in the worst of conditions. It's no mystery why all these new families are abandoning them in droves."

"The ones who can afford it," Diana said.

April's fork clattered to her plate. "Jack, you're full of shit. Cities are the lifeblood of a civilized society. What kind of art and culture would we have if everyone still lived in little villages? Diana's right, it's not cities the white middle class is fleeing, it's the poor and minorities they don't want to live with."

"Don't put words into my mouth, April. I meant that *everyone* would be leaving the cities if they could. And I don't agree that art and culture require teeming hordes of people. Most writers, musicians and artists work in seclusion."

"Come on," David said. "Let's clean up and circle up, I don't want to argue tonight."

They picked up the dishes and plates and filed into the drafty old Victorian's large kitchen. Despite David's plea, Diana, April and Jack continued debating the worthiness of cities, eventually segueing into April's current obsession, desegregation and civil rights for Negroes in the South. During their magical workings, they were tuning into ugly incidents more often, possibly because their network now extended much further into the South and West. They had actually seen Emmett Till's murder before it happened, but had been unsure how much of what they saw was in the past until the crime itself was long over. It had been so horrifying, none of them wanted to believe it could be taking place in the Twentieth Century.

"April, I keep repeating this," Jack said. "The emotions are just too high for us to get directly involved. We tried, babe. Remember when we tried to nudge the university Board of Trustees to intervene more for Authorine Lucy? We nearly got blown out of the park, it was ten times worse than the school board fiasco. And that was just the fucking Board. We couldn't get anywhere near the mobs."

"I know, but—"

"You keep pushing this, April, but it's too volatile. We've got a good plan and we should stick to it."

"Besides," Diana said, "The violence really worries me. I don't want to risk making things any worse than they are. We found out how easily that could happen, too. Negroes are being brutalized and murdered often enough now."

"That's just *exactly* why we should be doing more. Goddamnit, Jack—"

David banged the dishpan into the sink. "There are a lot more atrocities out there than what's happening down South, April. The Negroes aren't the only ones needing help. We're not The Justice League of America. Now we're working on getting some of those congressmen who are opposing desegregation out of office, and we're seeing how hard just doing that is. You know what happens to people who keep making right angle turns—they never go anywhere except around the block."

As they talked, the four of them quickly and efficiently walked through the motions of cleaning up and putting away the dinner and cake things. They no longer were even conscious of the unthinking symmetry with which they worked, and they never stepped back to wonder at how unusual their coordination was for any group of people. It was yet another side effect of the magical work that now occupied a significant portion of every single day. Perhaps the endless verbal debates they engaged in, which included disagreements about the house itself and what chores had to be done when, fed their illusion that they were simply a house full of roommates. An objective observer would have gotten a very different impression, but there was no such observer. They never saw other magical people, and neither Diana nor Jack had made an effort to attend any gatherings at the Motherhouse.

When they had finished with the kitchen, without any spoken suggestion or agreement, they walked in tandem down a hallway and through a small parlor to reach the large room which they had adapted for their magical working space. A Twentieth Century addition to the main house, it seemed to have been intended as a small meeting hall or ballroom. It had a smooth wooden floor and a tiny platform or stage at one end. Now the windows were covered with three layers of heavy drapes, to prevent any chance of late night light attracting the attention of curious neighbors. The floor, scrubbed and waxed, had a painted circle with a six-pointed star inside it, and magical sigils painted around the outside. It had been David's inspiration to arrange standing iron candelabra around the room for light, which lent a somewhat church-like atmosphere, but the wrought iron had the advantage of being fireproof. Inside the painted circle they had placed four thin, narrow camp cot mattresses wrapped in plain cotton sheets. These had proven very practical given that not only their LSD sessions, but their ordinary workings often left them sprawled flat on the floor, and even sitting for so long could be uncomfortable.

The four of them walked into the room in single file, April in the lead simply by chance. She took a box of matches from a small shelf by the light switches and walked around lighting the candles, as the first person to enter always did. David was last tonight and had the tasks of turning off the light and closing the door. Each went to his or her designated mattress, and they sank down to sit cross-legged on them in a perfectly synchronized motion that a *corps de ballet* would have envied. None of this coordination was rehearsed. They seldom needed verbal planning by now, and they didn't need to discuss their sessions aloud, either. For the last six months, they had been meeting every single night, gradually increasing from four nights a week with occasional skips. None of them thought it ominous when skipping a night became unthinkable for all of them, no matter what happened. Only David had regular obligations outside the house; their nightly workings had become their reason for existing.

They did fewer LSD sessions now than when they'd started; they no longer needed the drug as much, and had progressed to taking double doses when they did use it. Tonight was a "straight" session, as Jack termed it. He still gave the signals for each step, but he didn't seem to do anything else to guide or influence what happened once they were in trance—at least as far as Diana could tell.

In unison, they relaxed, centered, focused, and dropped into the altered state where they could perceive the network they were building and follow its branches and tendrils to situations that called out to them. They had evolved a tri-part routine: first they checked on the progress of existing projects, and then they continued working on those which were still ongoing and unresolved. Finally, they focused on expanding and growing the tendrils further and looking for new potentials: changes or crises just starting to evolve or possibly not even germinated yet, which were still malleable and unformed enough for them to manipulate.

Had one of those nosy neighbors managed to peer inside a window, he would have seen nothing but four people sitting motionless in candlelight—for hours. But even though no one spoke aloud, communication flashed back and forth among them.

Bunderborg corporation board...Dyson elected...

Manchester school board...voted not to hire Jameson as principal...

Groenig's Steak House...let Negro staff who attended rally off with reprimand instead of firing them...

Winchester Board of Selectmen...fail on the by-law issue...try again?...major resistance from two Selectmen, maybe if one of them is voted off...don't see that in the possibilities, one's a lifer...count it as a loss for now...

Lyme school board...fail, fired teacher...election coming up, challenger for the red-baiter...push that?...let's wait...

They went on with this assessment for some time, shooting comments and arguments back and forth, until finally they took a short break, like pearl divers surfacing to hyperventilate again before diving even deeper. They stretched and yawned, repositioned themselves on their mattresses, and descended once more.

The longest and most uncomplicated portion involved the steady, concentrated "push" on each of their current targets, one by one. The last session involved communicating on a deeper level, as they attempted to evaluate what they were perceiving and place it in a timeline relative to their own. This was not easy, and the perceptions themselves could be stressful. Diana always hated it when they locked onto something truly ugly, like the murder of young Emmett Till or any other brutal crime. The visions then were searing, like a flashbulb going off in slow motion an inch from their noses. They blinded and burned at once, the compressed emotions screaming through the watchers' brains, and yet this fierce intensity never blunted the clarity of the perceptions. There was a unique horror in being forced to experience the unwatchable in detail far beyond what they'd have seen and heard in real time. Even worse, the more extreme the event, the less likely that they could influence or prevent it, unless it was still far in the future.

This repeated branding of their psyches, virtually every night, was one of the two things that had made their work so obsessive for all of them. The constant galvanizing reaction, *we've got to do something about this,* held them enthralled. What kept them from burning out and retreating was the phenomenon that had snared them all from the very beginning: the sheer pleasure that their magical unity gave them. If it wasn't a substitute for sex, it was certainly just as good.

They worked until they reached the limits of their ability to remain focused; fatigue and muscle cramps pulled their awareness back to their own bodies, and finally Jack called them to ground and center. They sat quietly thinking for a little while, talk unnecessary after hours of being connected mentally. They all rose as one, stretching, and Diana went around to extinguish the candles while Jack turned the electric light back on.

"Are you working at home tomorrow or on site, David?" Jack asked, yawning.

"On site. I've got another week on this job, they're on an October fiscal year, so I'm closing out the books."

"Lucky you," April said, wrinkling her nose.

"Hey, there are lots worse jobs. I kind of like this freelance thing."

"I knew you would," Diana said.

Back in the dining room, where it seemed like days since they'd had cake, they sat around the table for a few minutes to eat some crackers and drink some fruit juice—the first fresh apple cider of the year, from a local orchard.

"I've been thinking about something," Jack said.

"Yes, we know," April said. "You keep dragging us all back to it every time we circle up."

"It's not me dragging us back to it, babe. You really think that?"

Diana said, "No, I know it's not just you. It's pulling at us on its own, and hard. We can all feel it—come on, April. You know it's not Jack."

"But he's the one who's the most interested. The Presidential election, Jack? Be serious! It's going to be a landslide."

Jack folded his arms, frowning at the table. "Our network runs all the way to the West Coast, people—"

"Yeah, coast to coast, like NBC. But that doesn't mean we've got the whole country wrapped up like fish in a net. I think we've over-extended it a bit. We haven't really influenced anything farther away than the Midwest."

"Even if this election was closer, I don't think we're nearly ready to attempt anything on that scale." Diana felt a discomfort with the idea that puzzled her. "Maybe next time…let's keep on pushing smaller elections, work our way up to congressional campaigns and state governor races, see how much we can do with those. I think we'll need the network to be a lot older and heavier to really be effective. Eisenhower can't run for a third term, the slate will be wide open in nineteen sixty. Who knows what could happen by then?"

"It's way too late to even start with this one," David said. "People have already made their decisions, and there's a lot of energy there. Voters are quaking in their boots over communism and half the country is having fits about desegregation. They want Eisenhower to fix everything, and they're not going to be nudged in another direction."

Jack flung his hands up. "I know, I know. I just feel…but maybe I am tuning into something farther ahead. Trouble is…" he hesitated a moment. "I've tried looking at the nineteen sixty election, and I can't see anything there."

"That doesn't mean a thing, Jack. Our network has a mind of its own, and we see what it wants us to see." Even as she spoke, Diana knew she was rationalizing. Why wouldn't the network want them to see four years ahead? They'd perceived things that obviously would take much longer to fully develop. But they were all tired, and Jack yawned again.

"Well, forget it. So what is today, Wednesday?…April, it's me and you, and David and Diana, right?"

"If you say so, master. I hope you're in a necrophiliac mood tonight, because I'm dead beat."

"You're never *that* beat," Jack chuckled, putting his arm around her shoulders as they left the room. Diana watched David watching them leave.

When they were in one of the upstairs bedrooms they all shared randomly, with the door closed, Diana said, "Maybe you'd just rather skip it tonight, David?"

He had been sitting on the bed lost in thought, and it seemed to take a minute before he realized what she'd said, and why. Then his cheeks flushed a little. "No, no, it's not that…I guess I just have a lot on my mind. But not that much." He got under the covers, to Diana's regret since he looked so cute naked. But the upstairs rooms were cool for everyone but her on these chilly fall nights. She turned to face him, propping an elbow on the pillows.

"So tell me, what's on your mind?"

"Oh, I don't know…" he folded his hands behind his head, staring up at the ceiling. He was working his toes against the mattress nervously. "I just wonder sometimes…about what we're doing, that's all."

Diana's brow creased, but she wasn't entirely surprised. "How do you mean that?"

"Well, it's just that…sometimes I wonder if…if we're just kidding ourselves. About whether we actually have anything to do with what happens or doesn't happen."

Diana pondered this for a moment. "I suppose we can't really know that, can we? We can't know what would have happened if we hadn't tried to interfere with it, after all."

David relaxed a little, and she realized that he had been expecting ridicule or shocked denial. "I've been thinking this for a while now, but I hated to say anything."

"You must have been blocking it off, or someone would have picked up on it."

"I have been, and that's been slogging me down, too."

"I've been feeling that, a little. But I thought it might be because you're the only one of us with an outside job, and you were distracted by that." She turned onto her back, looking up at the ceiling. She tried to keep up with the cleaning, but cobwebs appeared so quickly in the early autumn. "Maybe we should be getting out into the world more. Gods know, you'd think I'd have learned that lesson. Getting so immersed in magical work that you lose all perspective can be a very dangerous thing."

"You stop thinking like other people, and you don't even know it. Pretty soon you stop seeing problems that would be obvious to any cowan, because you're just…not even on the same planet. And I don't think this is a problem only magicians have. There are lots of cases of little groups of people just walling themselves off and, well…"

"Going insane?"

"I don't want to say that, but there have been cults, and underground groups and things…you know."

After a thoughtful silence, Diana said, "You think that's happening to us?"

"I don't know. But I think we should talk about it."

"I agree. Tomorrow. You know, David, this is always an issue with magical work. We're taught that as Novices, first year. It's not like going out and confronting people or building a stone wall. You always have that doubt—that things would have turned out the same way no matter what you did, and at best, you psychically tuned in to what was going to happen, and decided to try and make it so because it was already a done deal. Automatic validation."

"Of course, and that's why we're also taught all kinds of ways to evaluate our work and eliminate wishful thinking and delusion. Trouble is, that applies to work on our own inner growth. I guess when I was so fired up about using magic to influence the real world, I never even thought about this being a pitfall. I wonder if Jack and April did."

"I wonder," Diana said, but she was thinking mostly about Jack. "We'll see what they say tomorrow. April seems to think that we should be doing something more concrete, at least about civil rights."

"I agree with Jack on that one. Besides, the Negroes aren't the only ones who get discriminated against. Sometimes I get a little sick of hearing about it."

Diana restricted her response to a sympathetic nod.

"But, hey," David said, half sitting up. "I feel a lot better getting that off my chest. I think I am in a necrophiliac mood."

"Gee, thanks. Just don't expect me to play dead, because there's not a chance."

"I sure hope not." He slapped the blanket lightly. "But you know, that's another thing. Doesn't it seem just plain nuts to be making out schedule cards for free love?" Diana laughed out loud, and he went on, "I'm serious! Wouldn't it make more sense for all of us to just kitten-pile or something all together, like Beltene? I mean, if the point is to prevent people from forming couples—"

"I don't think April would kitten-pile with me, sad to say. And anyway, would you really want to do that every night? It would stop being fun."

"It would not."

"I love chocolate cake, but I wouldn't want it three meals a day."

"I would."

"Oh, you're hopeless."

"I just can't help thinking that Jack cooked up this scheme so he could get into bed with April."

"You're not jealous, are you, Mr. Hofstein?"

"Jealous? I'm with you three nights a week, I should be jealous?"

"Aww, you're sweet."

"It's just not as equitable as it looks, that's all. The reaction of those two when you suggested we should do girl/girl and boy/boy as well...I mean, come on. It made perfect sense."

"I sure put my foot into that one...I mean, I wasn't surprised about April. She's never gotten quite comfortable with the whole vampire thing. But Jack? I always kind of thought..." She trailed off, realizing that her long-held suspicions about Jack and Gregory veered too far into gratuitous gossip.

"I try not to take it personally. Mostly. But I don't know how he got through all those Beltenes. Isn't it against the rules to be selective?"

Diana chuckled. "Those rules are something of an ideal to be aspired to, I guess. I don't know, you could be right. A year ago, Jack told me that April was out of his league, but the two of them do have a past. Besides, April doesn't exactly banish you to the armchair in the corner, now does she?"

David grinned. "Well, not all by myself." He ducked as Diana swung a pillow at him.

"Oh, enough of the heart-to-heart. You've got to go to work in the morning." She deftly moved under the blankets to straddle David, pushing his shoulders back down flat and bending down to wallow in a long, wet, probing kiss as he ran both his hands down her lower back and over her buttocks, tickling her labia from behind. She was caressing his chest and abdomen downwards, not too quickly because he was so deliciously furry and she liked the sensation. When she finally curled one hand around his erection, he broke off the kiss with a little hitch of breath. "You know, you get hard faster than any man I've ever known."

"Yeah, people keep telling me that."

Diana slowly pulled back under the sheet, running her tongue lazily along the curves of David's rib cage. She knew he had his head thrown back into the pillows, eyes closed, completely taken up with the sensation of her cool mouth. When she was just about at his pubic bone, she regarded his penis soberly for a moment and remarked, "You never seem to be nervous when you're with me. Why is that?"

"What?" He lifted the top of the blankets to peer down at her in bewilderment.

"Aren't you ever worried that I'll do something while I'm down here?"

"What, you mean, like suck my blood or something? Of course not. You'd never do that." He dropped the blanket and relaxed again, but Diana pushed up the covers with one hand.

"How do you know that?"

He just closed his eyes, letting his legs sprawl open a bit more. "I just know. I know you." He smiled drowsily. "Jack's scared of you, though."

"He is?"

"Um-hm." David sighed. "Idiot."

With that to ponder, Diana pulled most of David's erection into her mouth in one hard, tight move, sliding two fingers up his ass at the same time because she'd found that he liked that. This woke him up to groan appreciatively, and the conversation was abandoned. Unlike many men who were fast out of the gate, David could last quite a while when he wasn't tired. Tonight, however, it wasn't too long before he was sound asleep, curled on his left side as he always did. Diana didn't usually sleep before pre-dawn, and she lay awake, listening to David's soft breathing and the much softer rhythm of his heartbeat beneath that. She doubted she'd have been able to sleep if she were mortal. She was thinking too much about what David had said.

114

Ohe next afternoon, Diana and David asked Jack and April to sit down for a talk, which shifted the dynamics among them and got the immediate attention of their feistier half. To Diana's mild surprise and David's evident relief, their covenmates agreed with David's concerns.

"I've thought the same thing, sometimes," April said without hesitation. "I just wasn't sure how much I...I mean, how much it mattered." Diana wondered if she'd cut off "I cared" or something else. "It seems to be working, and remember, David, last summer when Jack proposed changing our whole approach, you pointed out that it was going to be hard to verify our results."

"You said that even before then," Jack said. "After Klinghoeffer."

"And you said we just had to have faith," David said.

"And you do, I mean, we all do. Think about it, people: isn't that how everything in life works? How many of our biggest decisions are based entirely on faith, in a sense—assumptions, wishful thinking, hopes, denying that we could be wrong? And even if it turned out that we weren't having an effect, we're trying, aren't we? What would you rather be doing?" April shifted uneasily in her chair, and Jack immediately pinned her with a hard stare. "Boycotting buses in Alabama? Come on, April. We're all here because we were so frustrated with the limitations of direct action. Isn't that so? Didn't every single one of us use almost the same words to describe our frustrations with monolithic institutions like the Order, and how much we believed that magic should be used for good? Isn't that why all of us are here? And how bizarre would it be, how totally beyond coincidence, that the four of us would have been drawn together, with almost identical feelings, *and* the one-in-a-million chance magical symmetry that we have, if something hadn't been pushing us together somehow? And if that could happen, why is it so implausible that we, in turn, are having a real effect?"

Diana looked down, feeling a sudden chill at Jack's suggestion that "something was pushing them together." *Where the Teg are concerned...*but she forced the thought from her mind. Why would they be concerned with this? They'd gotten their pound of flesh when Thomas unleashed the dragon into her. *No, they got Thomas' pound of flesh, your account is still open* something seemed to whisper at the back of her brain, and she caught a breath.

"Diana, are you with us?" Jack sounded impatient, and she realized she'd completely missed his last few sentences.

"I'm sorry."

David said, "Maybe if we could do some small test cases, things that we could independently verify..."

Jack shook his head. "David, you know that magic doesn't work like that. It would be a waste of time, and weaken our Intention toward our real goals. And besides, I don't even think it's possible. We'd have to know without the tiniest shred of doubt what was going to happen, before we could be certain that our influence was responsible for a different outcome. And we can't know that. But all those little exercises we've done on animals, and making people take wrong turns on sidewalks and that sort of thing: they couldn't all have been coincidences, or us seeing a few seconds ahead to what the animal or person was about to do anyway, could they?"

"I…I suppose not…but still, those are suggestive, not proof."

"Outside of mathematics, there's no such thing as absolute proof. You need to think more like a magician than an accountant."

David sagged back in his chair with a heavy sigh.

They talked for some time longer, and all of them agreed that they would take a couple of breaks from their work each week. They would see people outside their group occasionally and maybe even try something as drastic as go to a movie sometimes.

"It's not healthy for us to be so reclusive," Diana said. "When Thomas and I finished the athanor, and we could actually go into town, or see people socially, it was like being let out of jail. And that was after only six months. And it would sure make it easier for me to go on forays. I'm tired of sneaking out at 3:00 a.m., I feel like a kid running away from home—not to mention that the pickings are pretty slim in the wee hours."

David gave April a sly smile. "Some of us might even go march in a rally or a picket line, who knows?"

April bristled. "And why not? I might learn something we could use here, too."

For a moment, Diana thought that Jack was going to burst out shouting; his face tensed and his cheeks got a bit red. But as she watched him, he carefully smoothed his expression and relaxed the muscles around his mouth. "No reason why not. We certainly don't want to lose perspective. One thing I did want to mention, though: let's put even more effort into strengthening and expanding the network. I think you nailed it, April, when you said we were over-extending. If we want to try influencing things on a national level, we need a much stronger foundation for that. A year isn't nearly long enough."

David left the table and returned with a legal pad and some pencils. "Let's figure out a schedule so we know exactly when we'll have nights off and there won't be any confusion. You know—" he grinned impishly at Jack. "Like scheduling sex."

1960

16

So...are we all ready? Really ready?" Jack said.

"Four years,"

"And nineteen fifty-eight,"

"I think we're as ready as we'll ever be."

David, April and Diana had spoken with such perfectly matched inflection and timing that their words were as smooth as a single sentence uttered by one person. They did this so often now, none of them even noticed it, far less was surprised by it.

"We were ready in nineteen fifty-nine," April added. "After the fifty-eight elections? We were hotter then, than we are now."

Diana smiled. "We were pretty full of ourselves, at least. But we're a lot more focused now."

David looked thoughtful. "You know, the pundits all say that nineteen fifty-eight would have happened anyway. It's not uncommon for the opposing party to sweep the Senate or the House in a President's second term, especially if the public is unhappy."

"That's exactly what the pundits *would* say." Jack wore a self-satisfied smirk so much of time, he looked strange without it. "Nobody would ever in their wildest dreams guess what's really going on—and that's exactly how we planned it. You've brought this up before, David, and maybe it's true. The Democrats might have taken control of the Senate, sure—but made history doing it? *That* took a push."

"Maybe."

"Our resident agnostic," Diana said fondly.

"I just feel like 'faith' should apply to a higher authority. That doesn't mean I'm not giving our work my all."

"We know that, David. We all trust you completely."

Diana gritted her teeth; the avuncular attitude Jack had evolved since the 1958 elections was a bit too condescending for her tastes. It continued to surprise her that the other two weren't bothered by it at all; they seemed to enjoy the warm approval.

"I just kind of wish it was anyone but Kennedy," April said. "He's way too focused on communism, and besides, a Roman Catholic?"

"Hey," David said. "Don't knock the guy for his religion. That's what all the Republicans are doing."

"David, stop looking at everything from your own personal sore spots. A Roman Catholic will blast women back into the Dark Ages. Look at Kennedy, he's got a trophy wife, for god's sake."

"So you'd like him better if he married someone ugly?" Diana gave April a skeptical look. "Poor, poor Jackie. April, let's judge the man by his record, okay? Besides, we're going to push on all the Roman Catholics who will be voting *for* Kennedy because of his religion, so we better not be hypocritical about it."

"Look, he's not perfect," Jack said. "But no one would be. We worked hard enough to make sure it wasn't Lyndon Johnson, Christ, what a disaster *that* would have been. Veep is bad enough. But you think Kennedy is obsessed with communism? Nixon is a fucking Republican! He gets in, it'll be another war—and that means nuclear Armageddon now. We all know that."

"Nixon is campaigning on a 'peace and prosperity' platform," Diana said.

"Right. And every time some politician says that, you know they're just itching for another war. It's wars that build up the economy. And the economy is in the toilet now, so the citizenry will go along with anything that puts money in their pockets."

"Kennedy is pretty popular with the Negroes, April." Diana detected a hint of teasing in David's tone, but she doubted April picked up on it. "After he bailed out Martin Luther King Jr. in Georgia, he's gold with the Negro vote. You don't think he's going to keep building on that?"

"I'd love to think so. But who knows? These politicians are all alike—once he's elected, why should he give a damn?"

"Because he wants to get elected again," Jack said. "People, for god's sake, are we really arguing about whether we support Kennedy?"

"I'm not. He's our Senator, I voted for him," Diana said.

"I did, too, trophy wife or not."

"I'm not arguing," April said sullenly. "He's what we've got, and I don't want Nixon elected. God, that would be awful."

"Maybe we can influence Kennedy himself, once he's in office," David said. "Or members of his cabinet, his brothers..."

"His wife," Diana chuckled. "Behind every great man, after all...oh, for pete's sake, April, lighten up."

"We could try all of those things," Jack said. "But first, let's get Kennedy into the White House. That's the hard part. And it will be hard, people, I'm not trying to kid you. This whole election is balanced on the edge of a razor, and we're not the only ones who know that. That's why our Intention must be as pure as it ever has been." He slowly looked around the table at them, meeting each of their eyes for a long moment, his own expression not challenging but searching. "Is it? Count to ten before you answer."

Ten seconds later, four voices said "Yes," in unison.

Jack took some papers covered with scribbled notes out of a folder in front of him on the table and spread them out. "All right, here's what we're looking at. Michigan, Illinois, Missouri, California, New Jersey and Texas. We'll be working on every district we can, except maybe Massachusetts because that's a certainty, but these six are especially critical. From now until the polls close on Election Day: we're going to push and push and push."

They all nodded, studying the notes and sketched maps somberly.

April sighed. "I just hate the idea of pulling back on all the other things we're working on just to focus on this. Remember five years ago when you said that was one of the mistakes we were making, and how it was slowing us down?"

"I didn't say that was a mistake by itself. I said that was an undesirable result of the way we tried to work when we first started. When we aim at a goal this big, we have to cut back on the extraneous issues. They'll only distract us. We can get back to them in November."

"You know, Kennedy might win without our help," David said. "Between the Catholics, the Negroes, and they say Johnson is helping him with the South…there are a lot of Negroes voting this year who have never voted in a Presidential election before."

"Do we want to take that chance?" Jack shook his head. "People, this is what we've been working up to for the last four years. It's the elephant in the room: we can't dodge this, we *have* to work on it, and as long as we do, we may as well be serious about it and give it everything we've got."

"Are we going back to working every night? I'm closing out the books for three firms this month."

"I think it would be a good idea," Jack said. "Only for this month, David, until November eighth. And all straight workings, you won't be dealing with hangover. But you might have to stay celibate, if you want your beauty sleep—"

"Not a chance."

"We'll keep it quick for you."

"Speak for yourself, Diana."

Their laughter diffused the tension that had been building, and without further discussion they all rose from the table to head for the magical room. Diana, however, still felt an odd lump of anxiety in the pit of her stomach. They had been focusing on elements of this election for a year, but they'd had other projects as well. Now that they were turning into the home stretch, she suddenly

120

felt a qualm of fear, and she didn't understand why. *Because a failure might have a devastating effect on us as a group? Because there might be a backlash?* But their failure rate ran around twenty-five percent and it didn't seem to impact their mood. A Presidential election wasn't something that could blow up in their faces like the athanor—so Nixon won the election, so what? They'd just aim to influence him and his cabinet and go right on with their goals, wouldn't they?

She blinked as she realized that she was in the magical room and holding the box of matches. Her autopilot was so perfect by now, she had followed all the steps of walking to the room, entering first and starting to light the candles with no more awareness of her actions than a sleepwalker. *Which is not a good thing,* she chided herself as she struck the wooden match.

David switched off the electric lights and they sank cross-legged onto their cot mattresses, and immediately into their trance, heads falling back with the sensuous rush that accompanied their joining. But tonight, they all had to stay conscious of what they did, and follow Jack's guidance more than they had for several years, because they were altering their usual pattern. The projects they had been working on were pushed gently aside, and only the upcoming election was brought to the fore. For the next several hours, they teased that apart, following strands that applied only to this single objective, expanding and growing those as much as they could.

It wasn't easy, because the vast magical structure which they had built, in whatever reality it existed—Diana had never been able to determine that exactly—bore little resemblance to the "network" or "web" they'd begun in 1955. She wasn't sure what sort of analogy applied to it now, although tree roots came to mind—massive, unimaginably huge, almost infinite roots of something that made the World Tree of myth seem like a seedling. It was solid and yet dynamic, touching everything at once and yet shifting, releasing and taking hold in new places, changing from one night to the next. It responded to their attention but they didn't control it, and what they were able to perceive when they looked for information was entirely up to the root system itself. Diana knew that David and April also wondered whether they'd truly created this thing, as Jack believed, or simply opened their ability to perceive more and more of it over time. It didn't matter to April, but David shared Diana's skepticism that they had, or could, make something like this out of nothing but magical Intention. If they had made it, wouldn't they be able to control it?

These thoughts, however, remained firmly repressed for the hours that they worked, sending "pushes" down the complex twisting tendrils to multiply and feather into countless branches until each "push" ran up against a human will, a consciousness to tweak in the direction they wanted. There was nothing so crude as a single suggestion, since the "push" reacted to whatever it found in the target's mind. In many cases there was a push back, sometimes as resounding as a slammed door, and when that happened, they left that tendril alone. It was the receptive minds they looked for, and found—by the hundred. Eventually it would be millions.

Diana had thought it might be a little easier to work on just one goal, and a relatively neutral one compared to some of the passionate hatreds and violent impulses they encountered when they "pushed" racists, criminals and bigots. But when Jack called them all back, she felt more exhausted than usual. When she opened her eyes, she saw David rubbing his forehead wearily, while April blinked at the floor like a groggy cat. Even Jack's eyes had a slightly shell-shocked look.

They grounded and opened the circle, extinguished the candles and returned to the dining room table. "Okay, people, great start," Jack said as Diana returned from the kitchen with apple cider and a plate of muffins. Even she wanted something ordinary to eat, just for the comfort of it.

"Illinois is going to be a tough one," April said. "I think we're going to have to get creative there."

"We're not going to get California," David said.

"Ah-ah. No nay-saying allowed on the first try. No predictions at all, we just do it. April, we do need to be careful about tactics that can end up being thrown out in court."

"Yes, I saw what you mean," Diana said. "I don't think I like it."

"Hey, if it gets the job done."

David drained his glass of cider. "I'm hitting the sack, everyone. Good night."

𝕺he night of the election, they sat and watched the returns in an atmosphere of incredulity. Diana still found the immediacy of television somewhat unreal in and of itself. She was so used to waiting for the news coverage in the papers, even though television had been common for more than ten years now and had figured heavily in both the last two Presidential races. The coven had gotten a television shortly after they moved into the Lexington house and had even watched some of the televised debates between the candidates. Although the election was too close to call that night, the following morning newspapers announced the verdict: John Fitzgerald Kennedy, at the age of forty-three, was the thirty-fifth President of the United States, in the closest election for more than fifty years. The coven in Lexington shared their stunned reaction with a large percentage of the country, although for quite different reasons. Nixon himself didn't formally concede until that afternoon.

"Look at that." Jack appeared so awed, as he regarded the newspapers spread out on the table, that he struck Diana as humbled for the first time that she could ever recall. "An Irish Roman Catholic. You know—I bet we live to see a Negro elected President."

"I don't *think* so—not in this century, anyway," Diana said in a tone of mingled skepticism and regret. "Besides, I think a Jew will be next."

"There is absolutely no way that this country will ever elect a Jew for President," David said bitterly.

"Right now, I wouldn't say 'never' about anything," Diana said. "But I agree, I don't think that's going to happen in nineteen sixty-four."

"No, because in nineteen sixty-four, Kennedy will be re-elected." Jack's voice rang with certainty. He sounded delighted, but Diana felt a sudden chill clutch at the pit of her stomach, and she had no idea why.

"Don't jump so fast, Jack," April said. "Let's wait and see if we still want him to be re-elected in nineteen sixty-four. It's the morning after, we haven't even left for the honeymoon. As far as I'm concerned, Kennedy has a few things to prove."

"Besides, the honeymoon, as it were, is going to be delayed anyway. We saw that the last few nights—the shoes haven't all dropped yet. The Republicans aren't going down without a fight."

"We expected that, Diana. April's idea for Chicago was dicey and we knew it."

"It worked."

"Let's hope it worked," David said. "We're going to feel pretty stupid if that gets into court and fouls up the whole thing."

"We know some of it's going to come out," Diana said. "We saw it. I'd hate to be starting an administration with accusations of voter fraud shadowing my record."

"Oh, there's *always* accusations of fraud," April snorted. "Can you think of any election when the losers haven't tried to complain the other guys cheated? That's politics, for god's sake, not to mention that most of the time, it's true. All recounts do is lower the unemployment rate for a few months."

Jack laughed. "I wonder if they'll find out about the dead people who somehow managed to cast a ballot in Chicago."

"They will," David said. "We saw it."

"And why they'd complain, I can't imagine. We had a dead person voting here."

"Oh, shut up, April."

"And I was right, we're going to lose California. Nixon's getting it back on the absentee count. That whole huge state."

Jack shrugged. "Well, it was close, and it won't tip the final result. I have to admit, sending Nixon to campaign in Alaska last week was brilliant. Who did he think was going to vote for him up there, the Eskimos?"

"It was his idea," David said. "We just kept nudging him to think it was a good one."

"Too bad we couldn't send him someplace really far, like China," April said.

"Communist China?" Diana laughed. "No American Presidential candidate would even think about it. It would be political suicide."

"That's exactly my point. So, Jack, what do we do now?"

"I don't think we should keep on poking at this situation. The emotions have gotten pretty volatile and that usually means we'll just be banging our astral noses into the walls. Let's wait for all the dust to settle and see what happens. We can take a couple of nights off, we've earned it."

"Great," Diana said, "because I've got some things to do that I've been putting off for a month."

"Come on, Diana," Brad said. "I hate it when a client sits in my office looking like I just told them their dog got run over. It's depressing, and besides, half my clients are packing heat. Snap out of it."

"I'm sorry. It's not your fault, and I'm not armed, don't worry." Diana pulled herself upright; the curve-backed oak chair, a reject from some police department remodeling, was too uncomfortable for frustrated slumping. "It's just that…five years. Five years and zip, nothing, not a flicker of a rumor of a hint."

"Aside from the maybe, maybe not glimpse your friend had in fifty-five, the last verified sighting was during the war. The trail was pretty damn cold when we started."

She gave him a narrow look. "Too cold for you? Then you should have said so before you agreed to take my money."

He opened his mouth and closed it again. "No, I didn't mean that. I've cracked older cases. But there's just not much to go on, even with those drawings. And the name? Could be anything in the world. Where do we even start?"

"We can keep on checking the police mug shots…"

"Diana, in the last four years one or the other of us has looked through seven hundred and eighty-three books of them, in three states and New York City. The only solid close match we found was in Brooklyn in nineteen twenty-four, and your guy was probably still in diapers."

"Could have been his father."

"Sure, but we didn't find a trace of him anywhere. He was arrested, he made bail, he jumped bail and vanished. The name hasn't come up anywhere, they didn't have Social Security then, and talk about a long shot. For all we know he left the country. It's a sure bet that he changed his name. If that guy had a son, I'll bet the kid never saw his dad's face." Brad ran both hands wearily through his hair. "I hate to say it, but I don't think there's any point in going on. Unless you want to pay for teams in every state combing through newspaper files looking for that face, I think we just have to wait for something new to come up." He gathered up the drawings, copies of her own set, and replaced them in the file folder that lay open in front of him. "I'm sorry, but I'm too honest not to tell you when I'm licked."

"Okay," Diana said. "But you'll keep collecting the weird stuff, right?"

"I will. Speaking of which, and I'm not just being smart here, maybe you should try a fortune-teller."

"I have, actually," Diana said shortly, and Brad blinked. It was partly true; she'd been doing divinations herself, regularly, but it amounted to the same thing. She rose from her chair. "Thanks for your honesty. I'll see you next week for the usual report."

She was meeting David later at a coffeehouse called The Golden Vanity, which was near Boston University, and Diana didn't feel like going all the way back to Lexington in commuter traffic. She was in the neighborhood so often, she had obtained a forged student ID—not to get into bars, but to get into the university libraries, where she could spend a peaceful few hours. Occasionally she used her special skill set to ghost into the restricted sections looking for genealogy or history records, but usually she just found an interesting book and stayed out of sight. This afternoon, she felt too dejected to read, but once she had located an unused carrel, she took out her own set of drawings and spread them out on the desk. She could probably have reproduced each one to the last line by now, she'd studied them so long and often. But after four years, they were still the only clues she had. She'd hired a different sketch artist, to avoid arousing curiosity, to make several copies each of the original drawings of Ned and Avery and then alter them for various styles of head and facial hair, eyeglasses and sunglasses. She now felt that she might recognize either of them just by their noses and eyes, in the right conditions, and she'd had numerous false alarms when a close similarity held her riveted until she determined that the man had body heat and a pulse.

She didn't stay long in the library, since David liked to get to the Golden Vanity as soon as it opened. The venue tended to be standing room only when they featured popular musicians, and tonight one of their biggest new stars was performing, a young folk singer named Joan Baez. David was nursing a serious crush on her.

She was a little surprised to arrive at the Vanity and find April there as well, sitting with David in the back at one of the cramped tables shaped out of large wooden barrels. The Vanity had a seafaring ambience, with fishnets draped from the ceiling and a large ship's wheel hanging on the back of the small stage. The running gag among some regulars was that the decor served as a warning about the quality of the drinks, but Diana had tasted far worse in some of the dives she'd cased on her forays. In any event, the beverages weren't the attraction. Neither was the music, for April. After a couple of hours, the smoke in the room was thick enough to disguise the fact that not everyone was smoking tobacco.

"Where've you been?" David asked as Diana squeezed into the tight space between the chair and table—the barrels didn't leave a lot of room for customers' legs.

"Talking to the PI. I usually see him every week, but I skipped all last month."

"Say, what are you still meeting with them for?" April looked around furtively and slipped a pack of filtered Marlboros from her purse. Each paper cylinder had been emptied and stuffed with marijuana leaves, but the smell was a dead giveaway until the air got denser. She wasn't the only one who lit up reefer in the Golden Vanity, but this place didn't have the problems with the cops that Club 47 in Harvard Square did.

"You should wait on those, April."

"I know, Diana, don't hassle it."

"To answer your question, I'm on a private quest. It's no big secret, Jack's known about it since the start. It's just that no one else is very interested."

David had been alertly watching the first musicians come on stage; seeing that none of them was his idol, he turned back to his tablemates with a sigh. "Looking for other—you-know-whats?"

"Aren't you the coy one, though. Yes, other you-know-whats."

"Are there any?" April asked.

Diana leaned back against the wall. "The evidence is suggestive but there's no proof so far." David snorted. She had already scanned the dim room, as she did everywhere she went that wasn't brightly lighted, but every face and figure present had an faint aura of body heat.

The coffeehouse had filled very fast, and the atmosphere was already hazy. Despite the closeness of the tables, the ambient noise level made it unlikely they'd be overheard. They huddled over the table, surreptitiously passing April's illicit cigarette back and forth. The only customers likely to notice were those who were also looking around furtively as they shared something. They all had drinks for camouflage, beer and rather murky screwdrivers.

"We've been gossiping about our fearless leader," April said as she finally exhaled after holding a long toke.

"Really? Am I detecting subversion in our very ranks?"

"Well, I don't know. Does it seem to you"

"that things have changed since November eighth?" David finished as April took a sip of her drink. It was like a ventriloquist's trick of talking while drinking a glass of water, and Diana, already buzzed from vodka and marijuana, had to stifle a giggle. It took a moment for her to actually consider the question.

"I hadn't really thought about it, but you're right, it does. But wouldn't you expect things to feel different? In a lot of ways, we'd been working up to November eighth for the last four years. Jack was hot to try it in fifty-six and it just wasn't the time. We knew this year was it, and for the last month we've been doing nothing else. Now it's done. Accomplishing a big goal always changes everything, doesn't it?" She watched the other two frown over this in silence. "Well, what do you think has changed?"

"I don't know," David said. "But the last few sessions…we've been pushing on this, pushing on that, starting to get back to our routine before last month… and it's not the same."

"You mean you think we can't go back to what we were doing?"

April looked frustrated. "The whole thing doesn't feel the same. It's not"

"stretched into the future now the way it was." April nodded as David finished her thought. "It's like we can only see so far ahead, and then it just stops. The tendrils aren't growing right out like they used to."

April started; she'd forgotten to keep passing the cigarette, and it had burned down to her fingers. She shifted her grip and took a hasty drag, then passed the cigarette to Diana, who took a drag so deep, it burned the last of the leaves to the filter. She could hold the toke for a long, long time, and finally April asked impatiently, "Are you picking up on that at all?"

Diana exhaled, feeling a bit dizzy. "Yes. It is a little strange. I haven't had a chance to really look at it. But I planned to bring it up when we were all together. We should be talking about this with Jack, too." April and David glanced at each other, and Diana's brows raised. "You don't think we should talk about this with Jack?"

"I've just been wondering about a lot of things this past year," April said. "You know how long it's been since we did an enhanced session?"

"He keeps saying we don't need one," David said.

"I think his supply of the enhancement is getting low. But he's right, we've been doing fine without it."

"Maybe we need it now," April said. "I'm just wondering if there's something Jack doesn't want us to see."

Diana stared at them. "Such as what? April, you know Jack better than any of us. Are you saying you don't trust him? After five years?"

"It's not that," David said. "I mean, it's not, not trusting him, like we think he's lying or double-crossing us. We're just wondering if"

"something's going to happen. If Kennedy is going to do something, something really bad. And Jack is trying to protect us."

"That doesn't work," David said. "We're all peers, we need to be informed."

The room suddenly erupted into applause so enthusiastic that it hurt Diana's ears acutely. "Here she is, here she is!" David said, as a young woman with long black hair and a faintly Middle Eastern flavor of beauty walked onto the stage with her guitar.

"She's still got her shoes on," April said.

"Third number. You watch. She'll just kick them off, like she couldn't bear to sing with them on."

"I can't wait."

The room settled into dead silence as Joan Baez began playing the opening chords of her first ballad, which made two reasons the three of them had to postpone further conversation. David's eyes followed every motion of Joan's hands and mouth like a cat watching a bird through glass. Diana settled back to listen to the flute-sweet soprano, feeling both privileged to hear such a gifted performer and at the same time, slightly envious. *I wish I could do something like this. I'm so damned...ordinary.* Glancing sidelong at David's face, she wondered if she should let her hair grow. She'd kept it cut short, which was easy to manage and went along with the simple college co-ed style she affected for street clothes. April tended to a Katherine Hepburn look with slacks and blazers, which she was tall enough to pull off, and David had a closet full of suits and ties, although tonight he wore dungarees and an Argyle vest. But like dancers or actors, they spent so much time sitting on floors or meditating, they usually dressed to accommodate it. Diana had heard that some of their suburban neighbors referred to them as "those beatnik weirdoes."

After Joan had finished her set and departed amidst long and lusty applause, the chatter in the club rose again, and a trio of musicians playing vigorous sea chanties with a guitar and a ukulele took the stage. David heaved an exaggerated heartbroken sigh and sat back to chug his now flat beer.

"But we were saying?" April said.

Diana had to think for a moment. "I've caught Jack being less than totally forthcoming more than once. But I'm sure he means well, or I wouldn't have stayed with this for so long. I think he's been burned a few times, or had close calls, and that's made him overly cautious."

"I'd agree with that," David said. "But why don't we see more about him in the enhanced sessions? Is he hiding from us, or is he really that much of a non-entity?"

Diana only shook her head. "He does guide the sessions, and we all try not to focus on each other. What we do see is involuntary and unavoidable, and you notice, it's Jack who tries to call us away from that as soon as possible. We don't want to invade each other's privacy and get all distracted, and someone has to do it. Maybe he does that before we get around to him. I just don't *know,* David."

"Why do you say I know Jack better than the rest of us, Diana? You've known him since he was a kid. The two of you set this whole thing up. Don't you talk with him when you're alone?"

"I hadn't seen Jack for years before nineteen fifty-five. You're the one who worked with him out West. And the truth is, Jack and I don't talk privately very much. He keeps things pretty close. I talk to David more than anyone else in our group."

David raised his eyebrows in surprise. "But...what about sex, the nights when you're on the schedule? Don't you talk then?"

"Not like we do, David. Wham, bam, snore, that's Jack—at least with me."

April frowned so hard, her nose wrinkled. "That's...weird."

"You mean he's different with you? Well, that's your business. But as far as what we're seeing or not in our sessions, I don't think Jack *can* control this... structure, or whatever, that we've built. I don't think anyone could."

"I don't see how anyone could, either," April said. "But does that mean it's just stopping now on its own? The implications are scaring the shit out of me. If we can't see the future past a given point..." she suddenly picked up her glass and gulped down several swallows.

"We've never understood how that works," Diana said finally. "You know how hard it's been to look at those situations and figure out what was actually past, present or future. Maybe we can't recognize the future anymore. Maybe the world is going to change that much."

"And maybe it's what everyone is petrified will happen. Maybe Kennedy is going to push the button," David said softly.

"I don't believe that. I *can't* believe that. No one would do that."

"Jack thought Nixon would do that," David said. "And we didn't exactly scoff at the idea."

This plunged them into a sober silence, and they listened to the end of the folk singers' set in a dark mood that the energetic tunes did little to lighten. They left the coffeehouse earlier than most of the customers, since neither David nor April kept late hours.

"Can we give you a ride home?"

"Thanks, David, I'm going to be roaming for the rest of the night." The drinks and April's potent marijuana wouldn't facilitate hunting, but she hoped she could find something, because she was rather hungry. She kept on walking with her covenmates toward April's car, several blocks away, and David slowed a bit, touching her arm.

"Listen, I thought of something. This 'private quest' you're on...why can't you try using our network to tune in and find information? If these other ones are so elusive...I mean, you've been looking for five years now."

"Longer than that." Diana frowned. "Use our network?"

"It seems obvious, doesn't it? We see just about everything else on it, and what could it hurt?"

"I don't know, David...use our group work for my personal goals? That doesn't seem very ethical." As she spoke the words, she vividly remembered arguing with Jack long ago, accusing him of doing that very thing.

"I don't see why not. April sure homes in on anything related to desegregation that she sees. Sometimes I feel like I'm walking a dog that keeps running off after rabbits every five minutes."

"Hey, are you talking about me?"

"Of course."

"Always."

April snorted and strode on ahead, jingling her keys. They were nearly at the car.

"Well..."

"Unless you're worried about the rest of us seeing these other—others, too, and you don't want us to."

"There is that. Jack already knows, and he wishes he didn't. It's not that I mind, David, but I know that I'm not *supposed* to let anyone else know. I just don't want anyone to get hurt...or something."

"Even if I did pick up some information, I sure wouldn't be spreading it around. Nor would April, even if she believed what she saw."

"Maybe an enhanced session, if we ever do one again...I don't know. But it might be something to think about. I'm certainly not making any progress with the methods I'm using now. Even the P.I. has called it quits." She smiled sheepishly. "Thanks, David. I'll consider it."

"Come *on*, David, if you're coming."

"Better go, or you'll be calling a cab. See you tomorrow."

17

I t was a couple of days before all three of them worked up the courage to ask Jack for a meeting about the truncated timelines in their network. Diana wasn't sure why they expected a difficult reaction from Jack, but their apprehensions did not seem to be justified. He listened solemnly to what David and April said, and then looked at Diana, who simply nodded. Then he heaved a sigh.

"I was hoping it was just me. You're right, and I have noticed the difference. I just haven't wanted to think about what it could mean."

"Maybe we should adjust our approach a bit," Diana said, groping for something positive. "The network has always responded to what we were paying attention to, and for a month we paid attention to nothing except the election. We deliberately cut off everything else. Maybe the network is just cooperating with our Will. Maybe we need to drop that whole topic and look for projects with a longer scope."

"You mean, test it? See if it will show us *anything* that extends very far ahead?" David swallowed hard.

"Well, yes."

"I wonder, though, if there's another explanation." April sounded uncharacteristically thoughtful. She looked at Jack. "You know how you're always saying that we can't work with situations that are too emotionally volatile? Maybe that's the problem. The whole country is tipping that way. Maybe that's blocking us."

"It could be," Jack said, "but in that case, what's the solution?"

April floundered for a moment and finally raised her hands helplessly. "I don't know."

A memory came back to Diana as she, also, struggled to think of options: Gregory saying, *you're in the eye of the storm you've made...* In a clear voice that made the other three stare at her in surprise, she said, "We need to forget about Kennedy." Her three covenmates replied simultaneously.

"I'm sorry?"

"What do you mean?"

"Forget about Kennedy?"

She nodded. "I know we talked about pushing him, or his administration…I think we'll have to completely abandon those Intentions. We can push members of Congress, we can work on local issues, we can work on civil rights, but Kennedy, we leave alone. For some reason, that path of history has been closed to us."

"But why would that happen?" David appeared completely bewildered, while April nodded in agreement. Diana knew that April was just as happy not to focus on elections and governments. But she glanced at Jack and thought that for a moment, his expression was both guarded and furtive. It smoothed into a look of mild concern so fast that she couldn't be certain she'd read him correctly.

"I don't know why, David, but if we've learned one thing in the last five years, it's that we can't always pick our battles. We don't control the network, we just use it. We can't fight it and force it to show us things and do things that it doesn't want to."

Jack straightened up. "Diana, I think you've nailed it exactly. I don't understand it, either, but you're right. We've never controlled that network, and only sheer arrogance would imagine otherwise."

David caught Diana's eye and then looked at Jack. "Maybe we should try another enhanced session. Focusing on information is probably a lot more important than trying to push things without preparation. Maybe do several of them, re-orient ourselves to some new directions, in a way."

Jack hesitated. "I only have four doses of LSD left. My supplier had to leave the country last year, and I've lost touch with him. That's why we haven't done one for a while, I've been saving it for a crisis."

"This isn't a crisis—I hope," Diana said, "but no drug improves with age. Maybe we can find another supplier. There's a professor at Harvard that David and I have heard some talk about in the coffeehouses, someone named Leary. Apparently he's doing research with LSD, and some similar drugs—they're calling them psychedelics now."

"All right, let's look into that. Shall we plan an enhanced session next Friday, when David doesn't have to work the next day?" They all agreed.

Jack was yawning when he came into Diana's room around 3:00 a.m. that night, a little later than his usual time when they were paired up on the schedule. Diana had finished with the latest reports from Brad and resumed a book she was reading by then. "Well, it's about time. I was thinking I may as well have gone on a foray."

"Hey, babe, we're both night owls. I just had some notes to finish up." He pulled his shirt off over his head and stretched.

"Umm." She studied him skeptically. "I'm starting to feel like an old married lady, reading alone until hubby comes to bed."

"Oh, *God*. Don't even say things like that."

You never make April wait, Diana thought, but if she'd finally learned anything from thirteen years of fighting with Stephen, it was to keep that sort of observation to herself. Besides, she wouldn't want Jack to think she was jealous. *Of April? That would be ridiculous. And April crashes early and gets up at dawn.* Jack was pulling his pants off and almost lost his balance, as he did at least fifty percent of the time.

"What is this allergy you have to actually sitting down to take your pants off?"

"Oh, I don't know. Makes me feel old." He tossed his clothes onto the chair in the corner, and bare-beamed, pulled back the blankets and climbed onto the bed. On hands and knees, he straddled her and bent his head down to nuzzle at her cheek. Diana put the book aside and reached up to fondle his hair as he kissed her. He looked confused when she caught his shoulders and pushed him gently back.

"We never talk anymore," she said, keeping her tone light.

"What do you mean? Of course we talk."

"I mean about anything serious. We really are like an old married couple—one that's too used to each other, and bored to death."

He sat up. "That's crazy. Is something bugging you?"

She sat up, too, and watched him draw back a little. "Well, I don't know. Should something be? You know—we never sleep in your room. Not even April. Always someplace else. I'm really getting curious about what you're keeping in there."

"I don't have any secret stashes of anything. I don't even have much furniture in there, for god's sake. I just like to have a private space, is that a crime?"

"It doesn't make you a very good communard, that's all. None of the rest of us have a totally sacrosanct room of our own."

"You could have. What's stopping you?" His look was one degree short of a glare, but she saw him catch himself and shroud his emotions with an expression of wounded innocence. "You're wrecking the mood, doll. What's going on?"

"This is the first I've heard there *was* a mood. I'm just a little tired of the monotony, that's all. You come in yawning, you bang me, you pass out. Don't you ever want to have a little fun?"

"Fun like what?"

"Oh, I don't know...maybe I could tie you to the bed and tickle you—"

"What?" His voice went up an octave and a half and Diana winced. But she caught a sudden whiff of fear from him that intrigued her, as though she were a predator and had sighted an injured animal that couldn't escape. Her common sense lectured her to let things be, but something more perverse, with roots in a myriad doubts and questions and reservations, had taken over.

133

"All right, let's not go that far. But wouldn't you ever like to just lie back and relax and let me do all the work? Some men love that. You never have harem fantasies?"

"No, not especially." He'd sunk back on his heels, and she got on all fours, leaning towards him.

"Why not try it? Come on," she grabbed his shoulders and pushed him down flat.

"Hey, cut it out, that hurts!"

"Well, get your legs out from under you, then." She slid her arm under the crook of his knees and easily pulled his legs up and straightened his calves as he clutched at the blankets with both hands. His heart was pounding. "What's the matter, Jack? We've known each other since we were teenagers. You've been fucking me three times a week, at least, for the last five years. What are you so scared of?"

"Who says I'm scared?"

"I do. You're gasping like a beached fish." She straddled him, and he put his hands against her shoulders, trying to hold her back. She impatiently gripped his wrists and pulled his arms out to the sides—against her strength, he might as well have been an infant. His face paled, and she let go of him. "Maybe you just need to face your fears. It's me you're hiding from, isn't it?"

"Diana, don't—just—stop it."

"Stop what? What am I doing?"

"Let me get up, this isn't funny."

"I'm not laughing. I think you need to push yourself a little, that's all. Isn't that the first thing we learned as Novices—push past our fears, embrace the thing that scares us the most? You never used to have a problem doing that. In fact, sometimes I'm amazed you made it to your twenty-first birthday."

"I don't know what the fuck you're talking about. Let me up."

"Yes, you do. You've been terrified of this since nineteen forty-three. And there's nothing to it, honestly."

"Diana...don't even..."

She bent down toward his chest, deliberately avoiding his face or neck, which almost anyone would be protective about. "A little sip, that's all...just to prove that you don't have to be—"

Suddenly she was several feet away, up at the head of the bed with her back slammed against the wall, and she had no idea exactly what had happened. Her eyes were dazzled so badly she was blinded. She didn't know if she had recoiled voluntarily or been flung backwards by some kind of force. She opened her mouth to ask Jack what the hell was going on, but she couldn't draw in air to speak—her diaphragm was paralyzed. Why she didn't dematerialize

134

automatically, she wasn't sure, but she couldn't focus her mind enough to do so consciously. After a second or two, the muscles in her torso unlocked, and her field of vision started to clear, shrinking blobs of sparkling light bobbing around like balls floating on the surface of moving water. She blinked hard and slid down the wall, flexing her hands. Whatever had happened, it didn't seem to have damaged her, but it would have given Jack ample time to flee. He was still in the room, standing a few feet from the bed, watching her with a look that mingled fear, horror and chagrin. When he realized she was focusing her eyes on him, he began to stammer.

"I'm sorry, I...I'm sorry, I didn't think..."

"What...Mother of all the gods, Jack...what was that?"

"I just...don't even tease me about that, all right? I don't care whether I should work through my fears, this one is off limits. I mean it."

Diana squeezed her eyes shut and gave her head a hard shake. She was returning to normality with reassuring speed—at least, it was reassuring to her. "You've certainly been keeping *that* one under wraps, Mr. I Don't Have Any Secrets. That's a nifty little trick. Learn that one out in New Mexico?"

"Yes." He sat down in the chair, on top of his clothes.

"They train you in magical combat techniques, or is this just some kind of defense against vampires and other bogeymen?"

"I..." he looked away. "I didn't even know if it would work. They didn't know. They thought I was nuts for asking."

"Didn't you *swear* to me, that day in the hotel after Beltene, that you'd never told anyone what happened to you in nineteen forty-three? Was that a lie? You obviously told the New Mexico group something."

"I didn't! I didn't tell them I'd actually met...vampires. I just asked—hypothetically."

"Hypothetically. And they blithely said, sure, we'll teach you how to do this—what the hell *was* that?"

"It doesn't have a name. They just said that if I ever encountered something, supernatural, and, well...evil...I mean, something that wanted to harm me, this might give me time to get away."

"Or make whatever it was mad as hell. You couldn't run fast enough."

"I wasn't sure what it would do...I mean..."

"You mean you blasted me with that not even knowing whether it would hurt me or not?"

"I panicked, all right?"

"Don't yell, you'll wake up David and April."

"I didn't really think it would hurt you. I didn't think it would do *anything*. I just..." his face had reddened now and he couldn't meet her eyes.

In the heavy silence that followed, Diana studied every line of Jack's face and body. She'd once heard there were psychics who could read people by touching them, and she would have traded every dime in her bank accounts for that gift now. *Is he as vulnerable and off-balance as he looks and feels, or is this just another act?* In support of the former, his heart rate, breathing and ashen skin tone would have been hard to fake, even magically.

"All right, fine," she finally said with a resigned sigh. "I suppose I owe you an apology. I knew that was a huge sore spot for you and I was provoking you on purpose. No, don't ask why, I don't know."

"I have a right to ask why."

"I think the score is pretty even. My ears are still ringing."

"This comes back to the same old crap, doesn't it? You still don't trust me."

Diana got up and pulled on some slacks and a sweater, not bothering with underwear.

"What are you doing?"

"I'm going out. I still have a couple of hours before dawn."

"Wait a minute, Diana—"

She cut him off. "You know—I am done with this schedule thing. You don't have to come in here and think of England just to keep everything fair. What does it *matter* if we form couples or not? At least I know David enjoys his rotation nights. You just stick with someone you actually talk to when you're alone."

"What makes you think—damn it, Diana, this is totally unfair."

She dematerialized. Before she ghosted through the crack of the window frame, she heard Jack say despairingly, *"Shit."*

If David or April detected Jack's magical jolt, neither of them mentioned it. But even the most oblivious cowan couldn't have missed the stiff awkwardness between the two senior members whenever they couldn't simply avoid each other for the next few days. David was too tactful to ask Diana about it when they shared a room, but she did notice a few searching looks from him, as though he was hoping she might volunteer an explanation. Neither coven member expressed the slightest surprise when Jack uncomfortably suggested at dinner one night that perhaps the schedule was unnecessary and should be abandoned in favor of "more spontaneous choices."

"Well, good," April said. "I've gotten tired of that routine, myself. It was like filling out a chores grid in a dorm suite."

"And we don't bother with that for the chores," David said. "Talk about ironic."

With that settled, the tension between Diana and Jack eased until they were almost back on their old terms—at least superficially.

In the meantime, April had contacted one of her former neighbors near the Harvard campus, who talked to someone else, who knew another person, and returned to the Lexington house triumphantly with a fair quantity of pure LSD and something new, a drug called psilocybin. "This is supposed to be a lot more sacred, whatever that means. But I'd test some before we try working with it."

The enhanced session that Friday went far in calming Diana's nervousness. They let their altered consciousness and the network take them wherever it willed, without trying to push or influence anything, and that seemed to loosen the temporal blocks. They followed tendrils for seemingly irrelevant patterns and watched them unfold years ahead, not sure what any of it meant. Men walking on the moon? Outdoor concerts attended by hundreds of thousands of people, in the rain? There would be a war, obviously, but not, it seemed, a nuclear one. The new LSD was better quality than the drug Jack had been getting from his supplier and after a while it was nearly impossible to concentrate on what they were seeing with any kind of rational approach. They were simply along for the ride.

As they were starting the descent from the session's peak, Diana remembered David's suggestion. But their minds were still so closely merged, she felt too self-conscious to try probing a personal interest. Maybe she would try out the new drug in private and see what happened.

1963

18

The fifth and last night that Diana spent surveilling Boston Common and the surrounding streets was typical late November weather: chilly and raining. That made it easier to see body heat, but cut down on the foot traffic, and after almost a week, she suspected that she was wasting her time. She'd persisted because she couldn't bear to admit that she'd come so close only to fail again.

The previous weekend, she had been roaming the Common and theatre district, which she often did, although she wasn't sure what attracted her there. She rarely hunted in those neighborhoods herself, and the high level of tourism along with the proximity of the State House meant the whole area was well monitored by law enforcement. She had no reason to believe that vampires loved the theatre; Thomas had found crowded auditoriums unbearable. But she kept coming back.

It was already dark at 5:30 p.m., and she was crossing the Common on a walkway that ran parallel to Tremont Street. As she neared the northeast corner of the Common, she looked up at the pedestrians on the sidewalks of Park Street, beyond the Common's iron rail fence, and stopped so abruptly that a man walking behind her almost ran into her. She barely even noticed him as he shoved by her and hurried on, muttering. Her attention was locked onto the figure striding down Park Street—a figure that had no hazy aura of dim reddish light in her vampire vision. She squeezed her eyes shut for a second, scanned the surrounding people, and looked again, but there was no mistaking it. No matter how heavily clad, booted and gloved the walker, the bare face of every normal person in sight glowed, and she could often see a cloud of warm breath, especially from those who were laboring up the steep incline of Park. After all these years of searching, she was looking at a man who was as cold as she was.

If this was another vampire, he would be able to perceive her own lack of heat, but he didn't appear to have noticed her. He was walking rapidly, looking straight ahead, as though he not only had somewhere definite to go but was overdue getting there. He was about average height, swathed in a long dark raincoat and wearing a dark hat pulled low on his forehead. Diana couldn't tell if he resembled the drawings at this distance; all she could make out of his face was fair skin and a clean-shaven jaw.

She was so thunderstruck, for a few moments she had no idea what to do. She wasn't sure what would happen if she confronted another vampire without warning. How did she know he would be friendly? *He can't hurt me,* she told herself—nothing could, as far as she knew. But she had her covenmates to consider, and she still had connections and an investment in the ordinary world—an aggressive enemy could cause her a lot of grief.

As these thoughts went through her mind, the dark figure was approaching the corner of Tremont Street. Realizing that she might not be able to spot him again if he turned the corner, she began hurrying along the path. With so many people around, and the Common well-lighted, she didn't dare dematerialize or even move as fast as she was capable of, and she had to head for the exit gate by Tremont and Park. When she was on Tremont Street, she peered down the sidewalk. After an agonizing few moments, a little knot of walkers split up and she saw her quarry, heading away from the Common in the direction of Government Center. She trotted after him, dodging around other pedestrians awkwardly—it was the end of the workday and the sidewalks swarmed with people. She got caught in a little cluster of shoppers just before she was sure she saw the man turn right onto School Street, and silently cursed her short stature, holiday shopping and mystery men who walked like the devil was on their heels. A sudden memory of Jack saying that the vampire he'd seen in 1955 was walking fast only made her more desperate.

When she reached the corner and turned, she almost despaired at the number of people walking in both directions. She could estimate how far the dark figure might have traveled in that length of time, if he'd maintained the same pace. But she couldn't pick him out. Diana walked on, her eyes searching so intently that she got some odd looks from passers-by. But finally, she had to concede defeat. The man could have turned down a side street, entered any of the buildings, gotten into a car—there was absolutely no way to tell. Had he seen her, and been consciously hurrying to avoid her? Or had he been completely oblivious to her presence?

If he had gone into one of the buildings, he might eventually emerge. Diana meandered up and down the sidewalk for about a quarter of a mile in either direction, until it was nearly midnight. By then the pedestrians were gone, and no one had approached her. She spent the rest of the night circling the Common, Public Garden, and adjacent streets, but she didn't see the dark figure or anyone like him, and there was no indication that she had been noticed by anything that was more than human. At around 5:00 a.m., she was noticed by someone all too human, and she led him into an alley behind the Church of St. Paul and made him that night's dinner, leaving him in worse condition than her usual habit.

She met with the coven for a session the following night, but she was so distracted and impatient, she disrupted the entire night's work. When they returned to the dining room table afterwards, Jack dropped heavily into his chair and spoke for all three of her covenmates. "Diana—what the fuck?"

She told them. "I need to go back, people. I'm sorry, but I just…I just *need* to do this. Just a few more nights, if I don't see him again, or don't find out something, I'll give it up. He may have just been passing through."

"And what if you do meet them?" David looked alarmed. "What if you just go off with them, where does that leave us?"

Diana shook her head. "It won't be like that, David. I'll be lucky if they talk to me at all. They're not going to instantly embrace me into some kind of secret society and take me away, like the fairies stealing a baby. Besides, I'm committed to all of you, I won't just abandon you. At the very least, I won't do that without coming back here and talking to you all about it. If they won't wait for me to do that, the hell with them. But I know Thomas would have understood completely."

April shrugged. "I don't mind taking a couple of nights off. I'm kind of curious about this. I hope you find the guy."

"I'm sorry I interfered with the session. I should have told you I'd be so distracted before we started."

"You're excused this time," Jack said, "but don't do it again." She looked at him narrowly, and he smiled.

So, excused from her ritual obligations, she returned to the Common every night, sometimes scanning from the air, sometimes watching from roofs or ledges of buildings, but mostly pacing the sidewalks, in the hope that if other vampires were staying out of sight, they might see her. But not once did she detect any trace of a vampire, or sense any hint that she herself had been seen. She stayed out until nearly dawn, when the growing daylight made it too bright to detect body heat. The long, deadly slow hours fighting boredom and sleepiness did give her a lot of time to reflect.

She could no longer deny that their little cabal of would-be world-changers had been coasting for a long time—ever since the 1960 election. It was as though the core of their Intention had been lost, and they had spent the last three years pursuing inconsequential minor issues. They remained completely blocked from any magical insight or precognition into the thoughts or plans of their government. The coven had shared the numb fear of the much of the country when President Kennedy publically advised the population to build bomb shelters, when he approved military action against alleged communists in Vietnam, when he dedicated billions of dollars to building and testing nuclear weapons, and most of all, during the stand-off with the U.S.S.R. over supposed missiles in Cuba in 1962. It didn't matter if the missiles were really there (as Jack thought) or not (as David insisted). What mattered was that the United States had missiles and Kennedy could fire them. They had sat in silence for an entire day, afraid to turn on the television for hours, not sure what they should do, unwilling to try a session for fear of what they would see.

After the Cuban crisis had passed, Diana felt a hollow undertone to their sessions, and none of them seemed willing to talk about it. But in the year since then, all of them had begun to put more energy into non-magical interests, and their sessions had fallen to three nights a week because one or more of them was so often at a meeting, rally, or other event. It hadn't surprised Diana that her plea for a few nights off to search downtown Boston was accepted so readily by the coven. In February of 1962, David had been away for several days, going to Washington D.C. to join a protest against nuclear proliferation. He'd met some of the members of Boston SANE, one of the organizing groups, in the coffeehouses where he continued to attend the performances of Joan Baez and other folk singers. April had gone to Washington for a week only a few months ago, for the Civil Rights March for Jobs and Freedom in August. Jack's absences were briefer and more mysterious, but he spoke of meetings on college campuses with a nascent group called Students for a Democratic Society, and had showed the coven a long description of the group's aims and mission, *The Port Huron Statement*. Diana sensed that David and April were beginning to view her as a dilettante who didn't want to get her hands dirty with real political work, and this irked her considerably. But since nothing was ever said openly, there was no way to confront their attitudes.

It was light by 6:30 a.m., the streets and sidewalks already filled with early risers, and she headed back to Lexington, foggy-brained and weighed down with the suspicion that she had completely wasted five days and everyone else's time. She also had to be especially careful not to be seen in the air, and the more dematerialized she was, the slower she had to travel. When she finally got to the house, she slipped in through one of the upstairs windows, planning to go right to bed. But to her mild embarrassment, David was in the bed. He was awake, and when he saw her materialize, he sat up with a gasp.

"Oh, gods, I'm sorry, David—I didn't realize you were using this room."

He flopped back down with a sigh. "I shouldn't be so shocked to see you do that, after all this time. No, you didn't, sorry, I moved down here because Jack and April were going at it and I wasn't in the mood to listen." He patted the blanket. "Hey, come on over here. I've missed you."

She smiled, kicked off her shoes and got on the bed to snuggle up next to him as he put his arm around her. "Shouldn't you be getting up for work?" She touched the stubble on his chin, remembering the vision she'd had of him with a long beard. The hair was receding from his temples, and while she didn't see any gray yet, his dark curls were muted in bright light, like a forest seen through mist.

"I'm going in an hour later today. I was up late talking to April. I'm a contractor, they can't complain." His expression was sympathetic. "So, no luck?"

"No luck."

"And you're sure you saw him."

"Positive." Diana had expected David to initiate sex and wouldn't have minded, but he seemed very preoccupied.

"You never did try using the network to search, did you?"

"No, it just didn't seem right. Not only that, it didn't seem possible. To see things on the network, you have to *start* someplace. Jack's the one with the actual contact points to these vampires, and he'd run screaming in the other direction first. He knows how hard I'm looking, so he obviously isn't about to help." Her tone was bitter; Jack's long-ago words about just being an *hors d'oeuvre* to vampires still stung.

"What happened when you tried the psilocybin on your own? I know we decided it wasn't going to work for our sessions, but it seemed to me that it might help with what you're looking for. You put it really well, when you said that LSD was like a roller coaster but psilocybin was like being in the Hall of Mirrors."

"All prismatic, yes. I used all the rest of the supply April brought us, but I couldn't *get* anywhere with it. It's the reverse of the same problem: you don't need a starting point but without one you have no way to control where you go or what you see." She stretched, feeling very sleepy. "It is interesting stuff, though. I heard that a lot of people just eat the mushrooms and don't bother with the chemical form. Maybe that has a different effect."

"Could you tune into the network on it?"

"No. I've never tuned into the network outside of our sessions."

"Never?"

Something about his tone of voice made Diana push up on her elbow to look at him curiously. "Never. I can only contact the network when all four of us work together."

"Have you tried?"

She frowned at him. "A few times, but only tentatively. No, on my own, I can't feel it at all. It belongs to the group, David, it's not something any one of us can work with alone." His face was very thoughtful. "Why? Can you feel it?"

He shook his head. "But I've never really tried. I don't do personal work outside of our sessions, our group work takes everything I've got. I know April doesn't, either. I can't speak for Jack. He sure seems to spend a lot of time alone. But I can usually pick up when someone is doing magical work—I know when you are, for instance, I can feel the little ripples coming off of you. I've never felt that from Jack."

"Unless he's doing something while you're at work. Of course, he sleeps half the day, he's almost as bad as I am."

"He's in his room half the day, at least." David looked back at her quizzical frown and sighed. "Never mind. It just seems weird when something that feels so powerful and so extensive when we work as a group isn't even perceptible to us individually. We all helped to shape it, you would think we could at least *feel* it."

"Sounds like Mr. Agnostic is wondering whether any of this is real again."

"Again? When did I stop?" He chuckled and then his face grew serious. "Ah, I'm just thinking too much. I'm starting to wonder whether...whether there's any point in going on with this. It's been a year since we even could pretend we were doing anything significant—I've felt like we were treading water while a tidal wave was about to hit." Diana shivered. "We all seem to be going off in other directions. This was the center of our lives and now it's a hobby."

"Seven years and seven years..."

"What?"

"I'm just thinking of something Gregory said, that's all."

"I really wish I could have met this guy."

"You'd like him. I wish I could introduce you."

"It has been more than seven years since we moved into this house, hasn't it? Maybe we need a sabbatical."

Diana just shook her head. *The trouble is,* she thought, *this isn't the group that I envisioned. I'm the only immortal, and no one else wants to sign on. I knew this would happen...and Jack just brushed it off when I said so.*

As if he'd read her thoughts, David said, "You know, I feel like I'm getting old. I'm thirty-six. I've never married. I can just hear my mother: '*Nu,* David, when are you going to find a nice girl and grow up, be a *mensch?* When will I dance at your wedding? When am I going to hold a grandson?'"

"I've never heard you mention your parents. I thought they must have passed away."

"They may as well have—I'm dead to them, anyway. My mother sat *shiva* and everything."

"You're kidding! Why?"

"I quit university to join the Order, and I threw it in their faces. I was being a rebellious dumbass, and they couldn't handle it. Hey, I've got three older brothers and two of them are doctors, how's that for a stereotype? I'm sure my mother has all the grandchildren she could want."

Diana sighed. "Well that's too bad. Not that your brothers are doctors, I mean."

David smiled. "It's not like I feel that I need to prove anything because of that, but I have been thinking about it. What have I really done with my life?

I quit the university and I quit the Order. I even quit my first job here—okay, no great loss. Still."

"I guess magic isn't a much of a career path. It's something of a curse when that's your most outstanding talent. I can relate to that completely—I've had the same dilemma. I couldn't have children, I failed as a wife and I left the foundation I started. Now..." There was a long gloomy silence. "Well, this is a depressing start to the day. Top of the mornin' to ye."

David laughed. "I better get up."

"I'm staying right here. Thanks for keeping the bed warm for me."

"You're welcome." He yawned hugely. "Man, I'm glad it's Friday."

Diana was asleep before he'd left the room. But despite her weariness, both physical and emotional, her eyes popped open unusually early. She thought someone had called her name, and half sat up, listening. But no call was repeated and the only sound from downstairs was the tapping of April's typewriter. Diana looked at the clock, which read 1:30 p.m., and lay back down, but she couldn't even close her eyes again. Uneasy, she got up, pulled on a sweater and slacks and went to see if everything was all right in the house. David's room was astringently tidy, April's, as usual, looked as though it had just been ransacked by a burglar on Dexedrine, and Jack's door was closed. She listened for a moment and heard the unmistakable slow breathing of deep sleep.

She padded downstairs in bare feet and checked all the rooms before looking in on April, who had claimed a tiny sunroom on the front of the house as an office. April seemed to spend most of her time at home typing, writing letters to the editors of newspapers all over the country in support of various civil rights actions, and lambasting the segregationists. Since she'd inhaled Betty Friedan's *The Feminine Mystique* in March, she'd been writing about women's rights just as ferociously. She kept up a constant stream of letters to legislators on every level of government from town boards to the Oval Office, and contributed columns to numerous newsletters and weekly papers. She had adopted a pseudonym more to avoid her parents than to hide her identity, and wrote under the name of Alice P. Merrill. For a finishing school dropout, she wrote extremely well. She barely glanced up when Diana paused in the doorway, squinting at the bright light.

"Afternoon. You're up early."

"I thought I heard someone call me."

"Wasn't me." April hadn't stopped typing during this exchange, and she only did so now to pick up the large mug of coffee on the desk and take a long drink. She'd cut back on her marijuana habit in favor of enormous quantities of very strong coffee, and Diana suspected that she chased the coffee occasionally with amphetamines. "Could you hand me that *Washington Post?* No, today's, there, November twenty-second."

Diana tugged the newspaper out from under several others and passed it to April, wondering if she was going to be handed a folder of things to file in a moment.

"You know, I've been thinking," April said, still typing. "Whether we should move our whole operation down to New York."

"New York City? Whatever for?"

"Well, it's where everything *is*, you know." April paused, pulled the page out of the typewriter and studied it before setting it on a stack of typed paper to her left. "If we really want to be doing anything important, we can't keep on hiding out in little backwaters like this."

"Cities that size aren't conducive to magical work, April. The energy is much too chaotic."

"Long Island, then. Or maybe DC, outside the Beltway. I just think we need to get closer in to the real scene."

"It makes no difference at all where we work. Geography doesn't matter like that."

April shrugged impatiently. "We need to do *something*. We're sure as hell going nowhere fast, sitting here." She took another swig of coffee and looked up at Diana, who was surprised to see a sympathetic look in April's eyes. "No luck finding your guy, huh?"

Diana shook her head. April hesitated, as if she was about to say more, and then shrugged. "We all need to have a serious sit-down, soon, and do some brainstorming about where we're going from here." She rolled a new sheet of paper into the typewriter.

"Yes, I think you're right." It occurred to Diana for the first time that April's face was moving from beautiful to handsome, lines deepening on either side of her mouth and her jawline softening. There was no gray in those brilliant copper waves yet, but April had to be at least as old as David. Had she ever wanted children? Had she thought, like so many driven, talented women, that she had plenty of time for a family later? Or was she simply feeling the years and her life going to waste, just like David was?

The phone in the hallway rang; April had planned to install an extension in the sunroom but hadn't gotten around to it yet. "Could you get that?" she asked Diana, typing furiously. Diana went out and picked up the phone.

"Diana?"

Just from the sound of David's voice, Diana was on instant alert. "David, what is it?

"Where are Jack and April? Do you all know what's just happened?"

"April's right here working, and Jack's still asleep. What—"

"Turn on the TV, right now. I'm on my way home."

19

On the evening of Sunday the 24th, they all met around the dining room table to consider their position. Like the rest of the stunned nation, they had spent the last forty-eight hours either glued to the television or reading newspaper accounts. David and April had been watching the local NBC affiliate that morning when Oswald's murder by Jack Ruby was unexpectedly broadcast live coast to coast. Like any President, Kennedy had his detractors, and reaction to the assassination in Dallas was varied. That was no less true for the coven as among their neighbors in affluent Lexington. After they had assembled around the table, the television reluctantly turned off to eliminate distractions, they sat in glum silence for some time, no one prepared to open the discussion.

"This is what the network wouldn't let us see," Diana said. "All this time..."

"But we don't know why," April said.

David was staring down at his hands, pressed so hard on the table top that his fingernails were white. "Yes, we do." He looked up at all of them. "We couldn't see it because we didn't want to. We're the ones who blocked it off. Because this is all our fault."

"Oh, bullshit, David. How do you figure that?"

"Jack, there are two possibilities, and only two. Either we influenced the election in nineteen-sixty, or we didn't. If we influenced the election, then we changed the course of history, and that includes Kennedy's personal history. We're responsible for his being dead. If we hadn't pushed the election, he'd still be a Senator from Massachusetts, and he'd be alive."

"I'm sorry, David, but you're taking a idiotically simplistic point of view. Besides, I thought you were the one who didn't believe we were having a real effect."

"If we did not influence the election," David went on as though Jack hadn't spoken, "and then we failed to foresee something of this magnitude, even five or six years ago when we could still see far into the future, then obviously... we're full of shit. We've been kidding ourselves all along, and none of this is worth going on with."

"Well, you've been saying that for years."

"I agree with David," Diana said, and April looked up, her jaw set.

"So do I. Look, I wasn't that nuts about Kennedy. He was making some progress with civil rights, but mostly to cover his own ass. He was scared of the Southern Democrats and he wanted to keep everyone happy. He started this fucking space program, for god's sake—just to distract people from the fact that he was building thousands of nuclear missiles."

"The economy has gotten better," Diana said.

"Of course it has, Kennedy started a war. Remember," David looked at Jack, *"you* were the one who pointed out that wars are what raise the economy. That's what you thought Nixon would do."

Jack appeared unable to speak for a moment. "We are not to blame for Kennedy's death," he finally said. "That's just nonsense."

"Why didn't we see it coming? Why didn't we see it back in nineteen sixty?"

"Diana, that's just—"

"So if we're not to blame, you're saying that we didn't really have anything to do with altering the election results?"

"I'm *not* saying that, David, but…" he looked around the table. "Has it even occurred to any of you that we might have averted an even bigger catastrophe? That this might be a small disaster compared to what could have happened? Do you think that Nixon wouldn't have started World War III last year? Maybe we'd all be dead. Look, I'm sorry this happened. It's a horrendous thing, I feel for Kennedy's family, his little kids, but, people—when did we stop looking at the big picture? Isn't that our whole Intention?"

"Three years ago," Diana said. "That's when we stopped looking at the big picture—because we couldn't see it anymore. Damn it, Jack, are you the only one of us who doesn't realize that ever since nineteen sixty, we've done nothing but fritter away on meaningless issues? We've been spinning our wheels while Kennedy and Khrushchev took the whole world to the brink. That's not why we gave up everything and dedicated our lives to this project. At some point, you have to face reality. For us, that point was a while ago."

Jack hesitated, then threw his hands up. "Okay, say you're right, just for purposes of argument. We fucked up, we got Kennedy elected when we shouldn't have, and now he's dead. What are we supposed to *do* about it? Apologize?"

"We stop," David said, as April nodded emphatically.

"Exactly," said Diana. "Things have been slowing down for a year now. We've cut back on our sessions, people have been directing their energy and interests to other priorities…be realistic, Jack. It's not as though we've been blasting ahead full speed and this is some little set-back. Would you rather just grind to a slow halt by attrition? I'd rather close this thing with dignity."

Jack stared at all of them, his face working as though he was fighting not to break into hysterical sobs—although Diana didn't think for a moment that he was on the verge of tears. Just what sort of outburst he was trying to suppress, she wasn't sure—it could have been laughter or rage for all she could tell. "I think you're all reacting too fast. We haven't even tried a session since Friday—don't any of you even want to see whether the blocks are gone now, whether we can go back to really attacking the core issues? Look, I won't play stupid here. I've been frustrated, too, but I was willing to ride out the dry spell. Now Lyndon Johnson is President, everything is going to be different. Let's do at least one session and see what happens."

"No," David said.

"Things are too volatile," April said. "If the emotions were high after the election, what do you think we'll run into now? I don't need brain damage, thanks."

"Diana—"

"Don't look at me. I think trying a session right now would be insane."

"Well, then…in a week?" David, Diana and April exchanged glances, looked at Jack and shook their heads. Jack pulled himself straighter in his chair. "Just what are you all saying, then? Are you saying that you quit?" His voice was very quiet, in a tone more ominous than shouting.

There was a long silence. Finally David said, "All right, I'll be the bad guy. Yes. I quit."

"So do I," said April, in a huff as though she'd been holding her breath.

"We can't replace you," Jack said. "If you quit…you're killing the group. You're destroying everything we've done for the last eight years. Don't you want to think this over before you take a step that impacts all of us?"

"I have thought it over."

"I was ready to quit back in August," April said. "I was only staying here because I didn't want to let everyone down. I know none of us will ever have a magical connection like ours again. I know this was a once in a lifetime thing. But it's over now. There are more important things to work on, and we're just being self-indulgent if we avoid them because we're addicted to, to magical masturbation."

"Oh, I think *that's* a little harsh," David said.

"Well, sorry, but that's all it is now. We circle up for the rush, not because we're accomplishing anything. If it wasn't for that, we'd have broken up long ago."

Diana said, "I hate to admit it, but I think you're right."

Jack had folded his arms tightly. "So you all quit," he said without meeting anyone's eyes.

Their answering "Yes," was spoken in unison. Jack took a deep breath.

"Well, then." He stood up. "There's no reason for me to hang around here any longer. You've made your decision. I'm on my own."

As he walked out of the room, Diana said, "But...you don't have to *leave*, Jack. Where are you going?" He continued up the stairs without answering.

They sat at the table in shocked silence, not truly surprised, but sick at heart that Jack was reacting this way. They could hear him moving around in his room, and Diana could hear drawers and the closet door opening and closing. He didn't own much; Jack had never been acquisitive. Everything from the books to the kitchenwares belonged to the household. After about half an hour, he came down the stairs with his Navy duffle, fairly full, over his shoulder. He walked directly to the front door, opened it, and walked out without another word to any of them. He left the door standing open. After a moment, Diana got up to close it, as she knew he'd intended someone to do, and watched him walking down the road, heading toward the main part of town.

She closed the door gently and went back to the dining room, looked at David and April, and shrugged. David sagged in his chair, his head falling back.

"Oh, fuck."

"Where do you think he'll go?"

"I have no idea. I don't know what he has for money, I've been supporting him. If he had any other source of income than my...allowance, he kept it to himself."

"He can take the commuter train to Boston," David sounded as though he was trying to convince all of them that Jack would manage.

"Yes, or just hitchhike. And from Boston, he can go anywhere. He might have friends he can crash with, from these meetings he's been attending. Look, Jack can take care of himself."

David frowned thoughtfully. "I wonder what he meant when he said, 'I'm on my own.' We just want to stop the sessions, no one has to leave the house."

"Do they?" April said.

"Of course not," Diana said. "We paid cash for it, and the taxes are automatically deducted from an escrow account. You can all stay here as long as you want." She smiled awkwardly at them. "I have a feeling that won't be very long."

"Don't take it personally," April said.

"Well, I have no immediate plans," David said. "I've got to go to work in the morning just like always, and I still need somewhere to sleep."

"Do you think Jack might cool off and come back?" April asked.

"It's always possible, but I'm inclined to doubt it." Diana sat back down in the chair Jack had vacated. "I think...Jack has known this was over for a long time, just like the rest of us. This isn't as sudden as it looks. We just finally forced him to face it. Picking up his toys and walking away without any notice isn't exactly a new thing for him." April nodded, no trace of sarcasm in her expression. Diana looked up at the ceiling, struggling with a hollow sadness that reminded her of the end of their LSD sessions. "It's going to feel strange, not doing this anymore."

"Kind of a relief, though," April said.

"Well, you two are certainly busy. Maybe I'll help you with all your letter-writing and agitating, April."

"I'd love it."

20

ack never returned, and if he communicated with April or the mysterious magical group in New Mexico he had said they both belonged to, April did not mention it. Diana was somewhat mystified to receive a letter from the Order in mid-December, not so much inviting her to the Motherhouse's Solstice event as informing her that it was taking place. Presumably that meant she could attend, but she wondered why, after eight years of silence on both sides, the Order would initiate contact. Did they know that the coven had disbanded, and that Jack had disappeared? If so, how did they know? Her curiosity almost prompted her to go to the Solstice festivities, but one thing stopped her. The letterhead gave the name of the Motherhouse's current Presiding Magus as Arthur M. Brewster. The last time Diana had seen Art, she'd concluded that he preferred not to share the same planet with her. Had his feelings changed? Had his antipathy been entirely because she was working with Jack? Although she knew she was being a coward, she couldn't bring herself to attend just to find out. The memories of Phoebe's party and the way almost everyone had shifted away from her at Beltene in 1955 were still raw.

The three of them celebrated Solstice quietly in the Lexington house. They never tried a session on their own, knowing instinctively that without all four members, the perfect union of power and Intention they'd had was lost forever. Without their regular workings, Diana found herself at a loss. She considered getting in touch with the Board of Bread and Roses, but it had been so long, she scarcely felt she had any claims on them. She worked with April on writing letters and making phone calls, but without her covenmate's unflagging passion, she felt like she was turning into April's secretary. When she wasn't doing that, she was keeping house for them all—cleaning obsessively, cooking large dinners and even baking pies. She felt that she was simply jogging in place like a runner keeping limber before the starting gun, but she had no idea when the race would begin.

One evening in mid-January, while they were having dinner, David cleared his throat uncomfortably and said, "I have some news. I'm going to be moving to New York City in two weeks."

Both women stared at him, April with some envy, Diana blankly stunned.

"What's in New York City?" Diana finally said.

"I've been offered a new job, a very demanding one, and I've accepted." He took in a deep breath, and Diana wondered how long he'd put off telling them. "It's an organization called United Jewish Communities, a sort of federation of groups that raise funds to support Israel, and Jews here and abroad. The caseworker at Bread and Roses saw the opening and called me, she thought it was a perfect match. Evidently they think so, too."

"And so do you?"

He nodded. "It's a fantastic opportunity, and it…I think it's what I really have been looking for, for a long time. I've wanted to get more involved in supporting Israel since nineteen forty-eight, but being so estranged from my family, I thought pro-Israel groups might not…well. But they don't care about that."

April said, "Well, I think that's incredible, David. What is it they say, *mazel tov?*"

He grinned. "Spoken like a true *goy,* but close enough. Thanks."

Diana swallowed hard. "It does sound like the chance of lifetime. Congratulations. I didn't know you were looking for another job."

"I wasn't. This dropped into my lap, it's been very sudden. I only went down to interview with them last week. I have you to thank for it. You're the one who set me up with the caseworkers at Bread and Roses. They're very good, you know. You should be proud of them."

Diana looked down at the table, still absorbing the shock. "I am proud of them, and I'm certainly glad they've been so much help for you."

"Look, I'm sorry to be leaving. I'll miss both of you, a lot. I hope we can stay in touch."

She looked up, struggling with the lump in her throat. "Do you need any help with a deposit for an apartment or anything? New York City is an expensive place to live."

He smiled. "That's very generous, but moving money, I don't need. I've been living here rent-free for eight years, you think I haven't got anything put by? I could buy a house in the suburbs if I wanted to. But I won't even need a car."

Diana nodded. "Who wants dessert?" As she got up and headed for the kitchen, she heard April scooch her chair closer to David's.

"David, we should talk about this. I know some people in New York that I can put you in touch with…"

𝔒hey both saw 𝔇avid off at the train in Boston two weeks later. He already had a furnished apartment on the Upper East Side waiting for him. As she waved good-bye, Diana had to fight off swells of lugubrious self-pity.

Stephen…Gregory…Thomas…Jack…David…I couldn't hold on to a man if I tied him to my ankle with barbed wire. She hated herself for even thinking it, but behind that trivial whine was a deeper qualm. *When I complained to Jack that I'd hate to be the only immortal and lose everyone else over and over…I had no idea.*

She was just waiting for the April-shaped shoe to drop, and it didn't take long. April had been corresponding for several years with leaders of numerous civil rights activist groups, including the Student Non-Violent Coordinating Committee, The Council for Racial Equality and the Southern Christian Leadership Conference. She'd once spoken on the phone with Reverend Martin Luther King, Jr. She donated a lot of money to these groups and their projects, and Diana tactfully forbore to suggest that this might be the chief reason that white, upper class and wealthy April got so much of their attention. It seemed like a cynical observation even to her, but cynicism was getting hard to beat off these days.

Diana knew, because she was helping with the mail and filing, that these groups were all collaborating on something major in Mississippi that summer. In early March several Negro activists came to New England to speak on college campuses and recruit volunteers. April blithely offered them accommodations in the house, which sent Diana into a flurry of making up rooms and cooking meals. She sat in on the discussions around the dining room table, feeling not only like a fifth wheel, but a fifth wheel with a flat tire, and the guests largely ignored her. But she couldn't feel resentful. She clearly saw where this was going.

Not long after that, she got up in the afternoon to find April packing the files in the sun room into cartons.

"Moving to Mississippi?" She didn't mean to sound sardonic. She knew April's fervor was utterly genuine. April looked up, a little uncomfortable.

"You knew this was coming."

"Yes, I did. Are you leaving tomorrow?"

"Monday, and not Mississippi just yet. I'll be down there later, in the summer."

"The Mississippi Summer Project, registering Negro voters in a state where the whites don't admit they're even human. Sounds dangerous."

April stuffed file folders fiercely into an already over-packed box. "It is. That's why we're going." She looked up. "I'll probably be moving around a lot. I may not have a real address."

"What about this house?" Diana glanced around the spotlessly clean hallway. "You paid for half of it."

April shrugged. "The title is just in your name. Do anything you want with it, I don't care. I won't be coming back here." Diana noticed that April didn't seem to assume that Diana would be staying in the house.

"Can I help you pack?"

"Sure. Some of this is going to be shipped, so it needs to be sealed and labeled. The tape is there on the desk."

Her car's trunk jammed full and the back seat piled high with cartons and bags, April left so early Monday morning, Diana hadn't yet gone to bed. "If something comes up, and you really need to reach me, you can try the contact numbers for SNCC or CORE. I'll be at the orientation sessions in Oxford, Ohio in June, but after that, I have no idea."

"Thanks. I doubt I'll need to bother you. You've put your affairs in order very well. You look like you're heading back to college."

April laughed. "I don't need to. This is *real* education, the only kind that counts."

"Before you go, could I ask one question? And would you swear that you'll answer it honestly, or not answer at all?"

April's brow creased. "That's a little offensive. I'd never do anything else." Diana just looked at her silently. "What is the question?"

"Do you have any idea—any idea at all—where Jack is?"

April blinked in what appeared to be genuine surprise. It struck Diana that April hadn't given Jack a sustained thought since he left. "No, I don't, Diana. I swear on my very soul. I haven't heard a single word."

"Thanks. Just thought I'd check." As April started the engine, she added, "Good luck."

"Thanks. Good luck with your quest, too."

"My quest?"

"I mean finding those others, wherever they are. I'm sure you will." She pulled out of the driveway, leaving Diana staring after her open-mouthed.

The Lexington house was now so empty and quiet, Diana could hardly bear to sleep there. The little house in Woburn had been condemned and torn down by the city two years ago. She wondered if she should go back to Pepperell, Maine. She'd visited the property at least once per year, and she had hired a couple from Waldo, who weren't so familiar with Thomas and the town gossip, to clean the stone house and maintain the grounds twice a month and keep a general eye on things. They appreciated the income and did a good job, but she knew they wondered why she didn't even spend summers there. The two other houses left on the property were gradually going to ruin.

But Pepperell would have been even lonelier than Lexington, and Diana suspected that if she went back there, she'd end up getting kicked off the premises as solidly and painfully as the Teg had kicked her out of the woods in 1955. *All right,* she thought impudently, *give me a sign, then. Preferably one where I can still sit down afterwards.*

On Tuesday afternoon she got up determined to start packing some of the kitchenware and furniture to offer to Bread and Roses, which had a store house of goods to distribute to homeless and needy families. But before she could get started, the phone rang, and she answered it expecting a call for David or April. When she heard a voice say her name, she had to sit down suddenly in the chair by the telephone stand.

"Phoebe...it's, it's wonderful to hear from you. How are you?"

"Diana, I'm so glad you're home. I called twice earlier today but there was no answer."

"I'm sorry I missed you. But how did you get this number? It's not listed."

"Your parents gave it to me, when I explained why I wanted it."

"So you're allowed to talk to me now? You're sure your husband won't mind? Or are you calling from a phone booth?"

"Oh, Diana, I am so, so sorry about what happened that night. I've wanted to talk to you for so long, but...Art and I have been living out in San Francisco since nineteen fifty-five, we got married out there. We just moved back here in December."

"I had no idea. I think running into you was the last time I saw anyone in the Boston chapter."

"Do you think we could get together? I have some things I need to talk to you about, and I really can't leave the kids."

Kids? "Any time, Phoebe—tonight?"

"If you're free—Art has a Council meeting tonight, but we're living in his parents' house in West Roxbury until we find a place. You remember where that is, right?"

"Vaguely. Give me the address and name a time and I'll be there."

At 7:00 p.m. Phoebe ushered her into the toy-littered basement rec room of the modest Brewster homestead. Apparently the children were sleeping down here, Phoebe and Art had the one guest bedroom and things were rather cramped. Six year old Travis and four year old Elaine were in their grandparents' custody in the living room for a couple of hours, and were so intent on the television, they hardly looked up when Diana said hello to them. Phoebe had gained about twenty pounds, and in her somewhat tired housedress, looked like every other settled matron on the block.

"So what was happening when I last saw you? What on earth was all that about?" Diana asked when Phoebe had finally stopped fussing with coffee and cookies and sat down on the worn sofa.

"Well. It was because of Jack Garrett coming back here. The Council had heard some rumors that he was working with another group out West, and that group had banned him for unethical behavior."

"What?" Diana stared.

"It was all very hush-hush, because that information shouldn't have gotten back to us at all. I never did hear how the Council heard about it. This group is very secretive, they make the Order look like an open book. Then, after Beltene, some of the younger members went to Daniel Cobert and said they thought there was something very peculiar about you and they thought you might have turned onto a left-hand path or something. Well, all of us, your friends, we went straight to the Council and told them what nonsense that was, but while the Council was considering it, they issued a minute saying that no one should have any contact with you, or Jack Garrett, or David Hofstein, until all these questions could be cleared up."

"But why didn't the Council ever call me in for an examination, if they thought I'd turned left-hand path?"

"Because they dropped the whole idea before it got that far. For one thing, your parents called from France and read Daniel Cobert the riot act, and your dad is a Magus and on the European Council, so Daniel just about had his tail between his legs. But I heard they got some other information in support of you, too."

"I can't believe my erstwhile mentor would have spoken up for me."

"I don't know. This was someone else in France, I think. Art's keeping mum, but whoever it was obviously has some clout."

Diana started to say something and abruptly closed her mouth as a thought struck her. Like Art, she decided to say nothing more. She stirred her coffee, frowning darkly as she digested Phoebe's news. *Funny that I didn't hear from my parents about all that...* "But this thing about Jack..."

"Well, that's just it. There you were working with him, with David and this other woman, and you seemed so concentrated on what you were doing. The Council couldn't sort out the rumors from this other group, but they tried to get Jack to come in for an examination, and he refused. So the Council put him on Interdict, until he agreed to appear before them and answer some questions. That meant none of us were supposed to talk to him or be in circle with him, which made it very difficult to stay in touch with you or David."

"When did this all happen?"

"We were right in the middle of the whole mess when I ran into you that night. That's why Art was so rude. He was preparing for his elevation to Magus, he didn't want to cross any lines with the Council, and more than that, he was petrified that I would get into trouble for talking to you." Phoebe smiled fondly. "He's a little too protective, I'm afraid."

"So that's why I didn't hear a word from the Boston area Order all these years," Diana said slowly. "I was working magically with someone who was under Interdict."

"It was awful. I mean, we could have talked to you casually, if you were by yourself, but you practically never were, and then Art and I moved before everything was settled. I couldn't write, because…"

"Because we all lived together, and you didn't know where your letter might end up."

Phoebe sighed. "I felt just terrible. I missed you dreadfully. But Art wouldn't let me write, or even call."

"He's very protective, all right."

"And even more, now that we have little Travis and Elaine. He wants them raised in the Order, he doesn't want anything to cloud their chances." She smiled proudly. "They're both very gifted. It's already showing."

"I hope their grandparents have fire extinguishers."

"Oh, now, stop it. Most of the problems have been with breakables, and we've put those away."

"A wise move even with cowan kids." Diana's wry smile faded. "Did Jack know that he was on Interdict?"

"As far as I know. The Council sent him letters with return receipt requested, to your post box, because they knew he was working with you. He signed for them." Phoebe peered at Diana's expression. "You mean *you* didn't know?"

"He didn't mention it. Not that, nor any problems with the other group. He never said a word." *He lied to me,* she thought, feeling a cold lump sinking into her stomach. *That night I met Phoebe, and told him, he said he hadn't heard a thing about any issues with the Order…he bare-faced lied to me. And when I asked if he was still active with that other group…he didn't really answer, did he?* But this was beginning to clarify the mystery of why—if not how—Jack had blocked himself off during their enhanced sessions. Diana wondered just what "unethical behavior" he had been accused of. That could simply mean violating internal rules, but it could also mean a raft of far more serious infractions. She also wondered if April had known more than she ever let on.

"Well, I would never have believed for one moment that you would work with someone unethical, so I was sure you must have the real story. I didn't even think that you might not know." Phoebe shook her head in disbelief.

"I'm humbled by your faith in me. Protective Art, on the other hand…"

"Don't blame him, Diana. He was just sick about it. Before you left for Maine, he thought you were one of the most talented and principled members of the Order. He used to say you were the one woman who made him question the rule about only men qualifying for Magus. It was never you."

"It was the company I kept." Diana sighed. She was a little doubtful, recalling what Jack had told her about Art's opinion of Bread and Roses. But maybe she shouldn't put too much credence in that bit of gossip, after all.

Phoebe lowered her voice. "But that's why...*this*..." she rolled her eyes to indicate the ceiling, "is just killing him."

"Living with your in-laws?"

Phoebe almost whispered, "Art got involved in some...investments out in San Francisco. They turned out very badly, and, well...we lost our house and we're almost ten thousand dollars in debt. There we were with the children, and Art was pounding the pavement, like a laborer, and finding nothing, just nothing. Then the Boston Council nominated him for Presiding Magus, if he wanted to move back East, and we decided to move because his family is here. He's just gotten a good position with a firm, but we can't even afford to rent an apartment for a while yet. I hate to enroll Travis in the public schools. I never thought I'd come down to this, Diana, it's been so hard." She looked away, blinking rapidly.

Diana hesitated, then put her arms around Phoebe and hugged her. "I'm sorry, Phoebe. That's really a raw deal. Especially now that you have a family to worry about."

Phoebe sniffed and forced a smile. "I'm sorry that your group broke up, Diana, but honestly, it was such a relief when we heard that Jack had left, and we could talk to you again—"

"Wait a minute, though. This has been bugging me since December. How did the Order know about that?"

Phoebe looked puzzled. "Why, from Jack."

"The Order has heard from Jack?"

"He sent the Council a note when he left—actually, it was pretty rude, from what I heard. I understand the phrase 'fuck you' was involved. But the gist of it was that he knew that his presence meant we couldn't contact you or David, and he wanted the Council to know that you three had all quit and kicked him out—I'm sorry, but that's what he said—and he wasn't going to bother any of us ever again."

"Gentlemen, you're not going to have Jack Garrett to kick around anymore," Diana paraphrased Nixon wryly.

"That's pretty much what he said. The Council was a little nervous about just how final he meant it, but he didn't sound desperate, just mad. So Art sent you a letter about Solstice, to try and feel things out. He wants to smoke a peace pipe, Diana, honest. But I wasn't surprised that you wouldn't attend. Finally I decided it was my obligation to make the first move, and I got in touch with your parents to see if I could get your phone number."

"I'm glad you did, Phoebe. Thank you." Diana picked up one of Phoebe's cookies and held it under her nose, inhaling deeply. "Did Jack say where he was? Or where he was going?"

"Not that I heard. I don't think the Novice who opened the mail thought to keep the envelope or look for a postmark."

Diana took a bite of the cookie and closed her eyes, relishing the flavors of butter, brown sugar, chopped dates and pecans. The Lexington house floated before her mind's eye, and she saw, as if for the first time, the spacious upstairs rooms, the large back yard with its sturdy fence, the quiet country road. Lexington had very good schools. When she finally opened her eyes, Phoebe was watching her with amusement.

"You obviously love my cookies. I'll have to pack up some for you to take home."

"They're delicious."

"Your figure can certainly stand it. You haven't aged a day. I wish I knew your beauty secrets."

"Not having children to worry about."

Phoebe laughed. "Isn't that the truth! I swear, Travis gives me a new gray hair every day."

"They're beautiful kids, though. When is Art getting home from his meeting?"

"He's usually back by nine."

"Would you mind if I stayed until he gets home?"

"No, of course not. Why?"

"I have something to talk to you both about. I'm going to ask you to do me a really huge favor."

1965

21

The little town of Sheridan, Massachusetts reminded Diana a great deal of Maine. The sprawling mill complex that employed a large percentage of the population belched stinking smoke from its tall stacks, although not as malodorous as Maine's paper mills, and frequently flushed waste and dyes into the river, staining it pink or green. For several years now there had been grassroots agitating to curb industries like the paper mills or Sheridan's fiber and textile complex from polluting the air and water so freely, but Diana wasn't optimistic that these efforts would see any success. The escalating conflict in Vietnam had boosted the American economy into the stratosphere, and there were many other domestic issues to distract the public's attention. She knew that the Standish Mills were making fabric for the military, but even before they landed that contract they'd run twenty-four hours a day. Young Jerry Standish, who had only taken over the firm from his father the year before, was well on his way to millionaire row.

The comfortable familiarity of the town did nothing to ease Diana's knee-shaking fear about being there. Sheridan could be the end of a year-long journey that had begun when she'd signed the Lexington house over to Art and Phoebe, visited the Pepperell property once to check in with the caretakers and drop off her belongings, and hit the road.

She had moved in a slowly widening spiral outward from Boston, the location of the last known sighting, until she had eventually gone as far as Philadelphia, Syracuse and Burlington, Vermont. She'd given her car to Art and Phoebe as well, preferring to be as unburdened as possible. She hitchhiked, walked, or took to the air, dematerialized, never going far at a time, simply down the road to the next stop. She spent some time in New York City and tried to look up David while she was there, but he was out of town; apparently his job entailed a lot of traveling.

She spent hundreds of hours in coffeehouses, small stores, theatres that were little more than holes in the wall, student hangouts, anyplace where she could melt into a youthful crowd of beats, transients, musicians and people of similar bent who she could probe for information. She smoked a lot of grass, as marijuana was now called, but more worthwhile for her was saving the grass to share around. She learned very quickly that the worst way to seek information was to ask a direct question, since the subculture that was rapidly evolving among the alienated and disenchanted had a strong keynote of paranoia. Unknown people who asked bold questions usually marked themselves as possible law enforcement. Pulling out a pipe or papers and a baggie instantly erased that suspicion, but indirect queries still got better results.

Hunting had never been easier. In fact, hunting had never been less necessary, because sex was so casual, at least in those cities where many people allowed strangers to crash in their apartments, hotel rooms or storefronts. Anyone who seemed to be "one of the tribe" could stay for a night or a week or a month as long as they didn't hurt anyone and didn't rip people off. What somewhat annoyed Diana was the way that sex was not only casual, but more or less expected. Men in the crash pads seemed to assume that any unaccompanied woman staying there would sleep with them, and acted offended if they were turned down. This may have been why almost all the women of any age attached themselves to boyfriends, without appearing very choosy. "Whatsa matter, baby, you uptight?" was a question Diana got very tired of hearing. Imagining April's likely response helped her keep a sense of humor. But she seldom turned anyone down, because she could usually get dinner out of it, even if she had to be quick and not take much. Marijuana was a decent anesthetic, especially in the throes of passion, and blow jobs made great cover for a short drink as long as she was very careful about what she did. But drug use was becoming so ubiquitous, Diana often thought that she could have dematerialized in full view and no one would have given it a thought—at least not for several minutes.

She let her hair grow, and picked up and abandoned clothing as she traveled, adopting more and more colorful costumes. The coven's pioneering adventures with psychedelic drugs made it obvious to her whence came the inspiration for the brilliant paisleys, tie-dyed fabric and vivid geometric designs that were bursting into fashion as British Mod styles followed the Beatles to America.

It was a little disconcerting to see people dropping acid, as they called taking LSD, in such a random and recreational way. Of course, it was rare for street acid to be as strong as the LSD the coven had used, and frequently it was cut or outright phony. But Diana kept any sign of disapproval to herself. She had brought along what remained of Jack's supply, a little surprised that he had left it behind.

The LSD was the one thing she didn't share. She took doses only when she was outside of dense city neighborhoods and alone. Since Jack's departure, Diana had never stopped wondering if the network might still be in existence, and if so, whether it could be accessed or seen by any one of the coven, without the amplified power of their magical union. She hadn't attempted using the LSD on her own, after the psilocybin proved so unhelpful, and she'd never suggested it to David or April. But her efforts now simply gave her a fascinating light show without any hint of the magical reality in which the coven had worked. She was torn between conserving her supply and taking higher doses in hope of being able to perceive more deeply. But even a double dose didn't feel as though it was getting her anywhere near what they had contacted in their sessions.

By early April of 1965, Diana thought that she had probably personally verified the body heat status of a quarter of the population of the United States, and the complete lack of clues was wearing her down. Then, in the back room of a thrift store in Hartford, Connecticut, she finally heard what she had been hoping and praying and dreaming for since she'd left Maine a decade earlier.

She was sitting with half a dozen other people on sagging armchairs and several mattresses all covered in layers of variously colored blankets and sheets, below an incongruous assortment of posters that included Che Guevara, Lenin, and a battered print of Monet's *Waterlilies*. The man next to her, who gave his name as Diesel, had slept with her the past two nights and was completely oblivious to the fact that he was, by now, running about a pint low. His arm draped around her shoulders in a happy grip that occasionally fingered its way to her left breast as a joint went around the room. The conversation had been rambling from the Vietnam war and the protest march down in Washington in two weeks, to local gossip, to music, to the scene out in the Haight-Ashbury in San Francisco, which two people present, Miriya and Johnny, had recently visited.

"We're going back, maybe next month. It's where everything's happening. All the real people are going there. Love is building a new world, no one will need money, we'll all take care of each other. Johnny and I are going to get a place there." Miriya could have been all of seventeen.

"That's cool." Diesel sounded like he was talking in his sleep. He squeezed Diana's shoulder harder and said, *"You're* cool. You're *cold*. What's with that, baby? I never felt anyone as cold as you. Even your pussy is cold."

"Does that bother you? I can go away."

"Oh no, baby, doesn't bother me that much. It's just freaky."

Ryan, who ran the thrift store, laughed. "Sounds like this guy who was here a couple of weeks ago. He totally freaked this little chick out. She wouldn't ball him, went running out of here like a scared mouse. She'd been crawling all over him, too."

As stoned as they were, everyone's interest was intently piqued, but no one was as alert as Diana, who forgot to pretend to breathe.

"Why? What did he do?" Miriya's eyes were wide.

"Don't know. I wasn't paying attention. They were starting to ball, and then she jumped up and ran like hell, barely remembered to grab her clothes. Saw her the next day and she said he was ice cold and had all these scars. She said he had to be a zombie." Ryan shrugged. "I think she was wasted on something. He seemed pretty straight to me. Quiet, really polite. Wouldn't talk about what happened, so I forgot about it. Not my business."

With the approximate caution that she would use in defusing a bomb, Diana said, "That sounds like it could be my brother. He's been missing for months. We were both born this way, we just have a low thermostat. Doctors don't know why."

"Well, doctors don't know anything," Johnny said.

"He did look a little like you," Ryan said. "What's your brother's name?"

Fortunately, the pause while Diana scrambled mentally went unnoticed. "His name is Ned, but he's probably calling himself something else. He had a big fight with our dad, and we haven't heard from him since." The plaintive note in her next words was unfeigned. "I really miss him."

"Huh," Ryan said. "Well, this guy said his name was Troy something. Stevens?"

"Stevenson." Ryan's partner, Brenda, exhaled the name with a long cloud of smoke and passed the joint on to Johnny.

Diana rolled her eyes. "Our uncle's name was Troy."

"He was with a bunch of people heading up to Massachusetts somewhere," Ryan said. "Nature freaks, talking all about how they're going to start a farm or something."

"Organic gardens," Brenda said. "They're all vegetarians. They really sounded like they had their shit together, too."

"Do you know where in Massachusetts?"

Brenda frowned. "I remember they said it was close to Providence, on the state line there."

Diana heaved a sigh. "He's probably shaved his head or something, and I wouldn't even recognize him."

"Plenty of hair, but he has a beard now. You might not." Ryan laughed.

"No, he had a beard before. Look, I've got this drawing that his girlfriend did of him..." she pulled away from Diesel, who looked wounded, and fumbled for the bag she carried with her. Careful not to reveal that she had an assortment of drawings, she pulled out the sketch of Ned with a beard and showed it to Ryan and Brenda.

"Yup," Brenda said, nodding. "That's him."

It took a minute for Diana to get the drawing back, since everyone crowded around to goggle at the man who had sent a girl fleeing in terror from this very room. From their expressions, they weren't too impressed.

"You know who was talking to them for a long time?" Ryan said. "Cindy, you know, the chick who's living with Joey now?"

"Oh, yeah," Brenda said. "Yeah, she's really into herbs and things like that."

"Maybe she knows where they were headed to."

"Does she come in often?" Diana asked.

"Not really, but she waits tables at this little place over on Franklin Ave. She's probably there now."

"I know where it is, I'll show you," Miriya said.

"Wow, thanks."

Diesel stared blankly as the two women headed for the front door, Johnny trotting closely on Miriya's heels. "Hey, baby, are you coming back?" Diana just gave him a wave and a smile over her shoulder. "I mean, it's only her fucking *brother,*" she heard as the heavy glass door closed behind her.

Cindy remembered the group very well, and without hesitation rattled off the names of all five people, described the decrepit car they had been driving, and repeated every detail she'd been told about the town they hoped to get to without yet another breakdown on the road: Sheridan, Massachusetts. "They said it's out on River Road, north of town, this farm called the old Maugham place. I might come up and see it later this summer. Tell them I said hello, okay?"

It would have been a long way to travel dematerialized. The next morning, Diana hitched a ride with a trucker as far as Worcester, another ride from Worcester to Providence, and a third ride to Fall River. From there, she was close enough to Sheridan to make it by air, but she waited until darkness had fallen to avoid being seen. That wasn't her only reason for stalling the last leg of her trip.

She had to ask directions to River Road. The narrow, winding way alternated long straight stretches with sudden sharp bends which Diana guessed were deathtraps in waiting. There was nothing on the road but a state forest, marshlands, and farmland, with the road itself dead-ending at a large dairy farm after several miles. That reduced the traffic and the potential body count considerably. About a mile east of the dairy farm, she alighted and solidified before a sprawling old farmhouse with a barn next to it, built almost abutting the road. Open fields, which appeared to have been untilled for around five years, sloped upward behind and on both sides of the house. Diana was sharply reminded of her first view of Thomas's property and its vast overgrown stone circle up in Maine. She caught a whiff of distant wood smoke, and felt a pang of nostalgia.

A power line ran to a meter on the side of the house, but the light in the windows looked like candle and lantern light. A badly rust-eaten Ford sedan sat in the half-circle driveway. Diana took in a deep breath, walked up to the front door and knocked.

168

The door was opened by a tall woman with broad shoulders and a sturdy build, light brown hair rippling down her back to her hips. She held a kerosene lantern, but the entryway behind her and the front stoop of the house were both unlighted, and she squinted down at Diana's face.

"Yes?"

"Hello, uh, my name is Diana Chilton, and some people in Hartford told me where to find you…" she saw the woman's eyebrows rise. "Cindy? Cindy from the coffee shop on Franklin Ave? She says to say hello." The woman's face relaxed, but she seemed uncertain. "I'm looking for someone who was traveling with you. Troy? Troy Stevenson?"

The woman caught her breath, and then she raised the lantern and extended it almost over Diana's head, peering intently at her hair, her clothes and her face, eyes narrowed as though she was examining Diana for evidence of a crime. Sensing that she was undergoing some kind of assessment, Diana held still and tried to look earnest and unthreatening. The woman withdrew the lantern and stepped back.

"Come in."

Diana entered the house, looking around warily. Ahead of her to the right, a staircase rose into shadows, and opposite it, the hall opened into a wide archway.

"Are you, uh, Theresa Maugham?" Diana guessed from Cindy's description.

"Yes, but I'm called Avani here. That name belongs to a different life."

Diana followed Avani through the archway into an airy room that seemed bigger than the barn. A table made of planks laid across sawhorses stood at the far end of the room, where a massive woodstove was cold and dark despite the chilly night. Two bearded young men sat at the table on a bench that apeared newly hand-made.

"This is Diana Chilton," Avani said as the two looked up curiously. "This is Denny, my partner…" the larger of the two, built like a football linebacker with a shiny, prematurely bald pate, nodded. "And this is Ellie. Brigid's upstairs?"

"Doing something with the windows," Ellie said with a faint note of resigned patience. He reminded Diana a great deal of David, but his eyes were light brown and his hair a little redder.

"Is Troy upstairs, too?"

"No, he was out in the barn," Denny said. "Haven't seen him for a while."

"I think he said he was going to take a walk around the fields," Ellie said. Diana repressed a despairing sigh. She wasn't sure she could bear the suspense much longer before she was reduced to gibbering hysteria.

Avani put the lantern down on the table, flexing her back. All three gave off vibes of having done a lot of hard physical work recently. After a moment of silence, Diana realized that Avani and both men were giving her long appraising looks, just as Avani had done a few moments ago at the door. Then Ellie and Denny glanced at each other, smiling oddly, and Ellie gave his head a slight shake, his expression conveying something like, *well I'll be damned,* if Diana was interpreting it correctly.

"What was your name again?" Ellie asked.

"Diana Chilton. Did someone tell you that I was looking for you? You seem…it almost seems like you know me."

"Oh, no, no…not exactly." Denny said. He was starting to grin, and turned to Avani. "That's not quite it, is it?"

"No, definitely not."

"What isn't it?" Diana was completely confused.

"'Diana' isn't quite right. We'll have to ask Brigid. She'll know."

"You'll have to ask Brigid my name?"

"Maybe I should call her," Denny said, but Ellie shook his head.

"You know how she is when she's working."

"Would you like some chamomile tea?" Avani said. "Or would you like to try and find Troy, since that is what you came for? He may not come back to the house, he sleeps out in the barn."

"I would like to see Troy, if you wouldn't mind. I've come all the way from…" suddenly she was at a loss how to put it. *From 1955…*

"Go right ahead. Here, take a lantern."

Diana started to say she wouldn't need one, but paused. It was the waxing crescent moon, dark and chilly out, and the fields still had long patches of snow on top of what was undoubtedly mud. A normal person would want a light. "Thanks."

Avani showed Diana to the back door, which was at the other end of the front hallway. When the door was closed, Diana turned out the lantern and set it carefully next to the stoop.

She scanned the yard and the slopes all around, her eyes searching for a human shape. She could see the landscape perfectly well, glowing with the odd internal luminosity that things had to her night vision, but at first she saw no movement and nothing that seemed to be a walking or standing person. There was marshy ground to the west and the air was filled with the trilling of spring peepers. She took some deep sniffs of the air, but Thomas had told her that other vampires had no smell.

She started across the back yard, which was covered with long matted dead grass that squished under her shoes. Her attention was drawn to a light-colored mass a hundred yards ahead, and she realized it was a solitary boulder the size of a small house, one of thousands dropped all over New England by receding glaciers. A dark shape on top of the boulder moved, and she stopped. Someone was lying on the boulder, looking up at the night sky.

She swallowed hard and started toward the huge weathered rock, so riveted on the dark shape, she stumbled several times. She realized she should make noise deliberately and began scuffing her feet hard on the ground with each step. When she was about twenty feet away, the figure sat up, although she was sure he'd heard her long before. His back was toward her.

"Brigid? What is it?" She stopped again, and the man pivoted smoothly around to look at her. He froze for a moment, and she saw him glance quickly back at the house. She faintly heard a woman's voice calling something about a bed, and a reply, so the man on the boulder knew his housemates were safe. But she was suddenly humbled that his first thought upon seeing her was to check on his friends. *I might be another rogue vampire, after all...I didn't even think...* Embarrassed, she waited for him to say something, but all he did was stare down at her, as motionless as though he was part of the boulder.

They stayed like that for a long time. Diana wished she could see his face more clearly, but without the glow of body heat, all she could discern above his dark beard was his eyes, locked onto hers. She started to shake; was this a staredown? Was he challenging her? Was he waiting for her to do something? *I feel so fucking stupid...Damn you, Thomas, why couldn't you at least tell me some protocols?* But at least he hadn't jumped off the boulder and attacked her, or fled in the opposite direction.

At last she could bear no more and flung her hands up helplessly. "I'm sorry to bother you." She turned and started back toward the house.

"Wait! Just...wait, don't go." She turned back to see him step off the boulder into mid-air, drop ten feet and land as lightly as though he'd stepped off a curb. "Forgive me. I was...so shocked to see you, and then I was waiting for you to say something..."

His flustered tone reduced her terror by at least three quarters. "You're Troy Stevenson?"

"Yes." He didn't sound quite sure.

"Formerly Ned? Formerly...Edward Tillinger?"

He was silent again, but at least she knew why he was shocked this time. "Who are you?" he whispered.

"My name is Diana Chilton. I'm another..."

"I can see that. How did you find me?"

She opened her mouth, stopped, and suddenly laughed. "For that answer, you'll need a comfortable chair. And a drink. And a three-day blizzard raging outside." He smiled, and she said, "I've been searching for you for nearly ten years."

He stared at her for another long pause. Abruptly, he smacked himself in the side of the head. "This is ridiculous. A blizzard is beyond my control, but I can offer you a chair. Come on." He strode past her, but slowed his steps so that she was walking next to him, not trailing behind. "May I call you Diana?"

"Of course, don't be silly." *Well, he was born in 1872, after all,* she thought.

When they got to the back yard she trotted ahead to retrieve the lantern, and followed him to the barn's side door.

Just from Troy's body language, Diana intuited that the barn was his domain. A sizeable workbench along one wall and pegboards full of tools had obviously been cleaned and organized in the last two weeks, and the rest of the space was in similar transition. The steps to the loft above were uncluttered and recently repaired.

"Looks like the farm used this for equipment, not animals."

"And all of it long gone, unfortunately." Troy finished lighting the kerosene lanterns on the workbench and shook out the match, dropping it into a small can of water. "Avani says her great-uncle sold all the equipment off when he left the farm, and most of the furniture, too—just about everything moveable. The place was quite a mess when we got here."

"The old Maugham place...she grew up here?"

"No, but she spent summers here. Now she has a lease in her name, from her father. He inherited it."

"And you're all really going to start farming here again? Or, what did Cindy say, intensive organic gardening?"

"That's the plan."

There were several badly weathered Adirondack chairs in one corner, and Troy pulled two of them to face each other. "These were just sitting out in the back yard. I'm going to refinish them, eventually." They sat down in the chairs and there was another awkward pause. Now that she could see him in natural light, Diana couldn't stop staring at his face, almost in awe that after so many years of searching, she finally was seeing the person from her photo and drawings in the flesh. He actually existed. Of course, she had felt exactly this way when she met Thomas, but somehow, Troy had seemed far more ephemeral. She'd had a lot more concrete evidence for Thomas. A few times she'd even wondered if Jack had invented his whole story and made "Ned" up, sketches included. Troy seemed just as fascinated by her, but he had to be less amazed to be meeting another vampire, per se. His curiosity about her was more personal, and in that area, she had the advantage over him. She finally cleared her throat.

"Well, since I investigated you, hunted you down, sneaked up on you, gave you the shock of your life, and I'm much the younger of us two...it seems only fair that I start."

"You have the floor and my undivided attention. I have no obligations for the rest of the night, barring an emergency."

She talked for a long time, telling him about being raised in the Order of the Silver Light, her quest for immortals and the reason for it, how she had tracked down Thomas, the magical working and its outcome. He clearly reserved judgment as to the reality of magic, and seemed uncertain what to think about the possibility of the Fair Folk, the Tylwyth Teg. He appeared amazed by her description of her search for him and all that had gone into it, as well as the way she had tracked down Thomas. However, Diana didn't go into much detail about her work with the Lexington coven, feeling that she wasn't justified in breaking the confidentiality of Jack, April and David. Her work with them had no relevance whatsoever to vampires, and besides that, she could tell that Troy would be highly skeptical and didn't want to be diverted into any arguments. There would be time enough later on to show him some things that might challenge his assumptions. For now, she simply said that she had been working with a small group and they had broken up and gone their separate ways, freeing her to focus her energies toward locating other vampires.

She did, however, tell him Jack's story about his encounter in 1943, and the apparent sightings in 1955 and 1963. After what Phoebe had told her, Diana had started to wonder if Jack's story was entirely credible.

"Yes, I remember him," Troy said. "A painful example of pinpoint bad timing. He walked out into that alley at precisely the wrong instant."

"It's all true? Rogue vampire and all?"

"The only one I've ever met, although I'm told there have been others."

"What is a rogue vampire? Thomas said that we're very rare and scattered, and there are no rules or hierarchies. How can a vampire be a rogue if there aren't any rules to violate?"

"There are certainly implicit rules. Don't do unnecessary harm, don't behave so egregiously that you expose yourself and other vampires to the world, don't endanger or threaten other vampires. But if you wonder what gives vampires the authority to enforce standards of behavior on each other, that's something of a gray area. The majority of us have a certain code of ethics and we enforce it because we have the power to do so, and it's a matter of self-preservation."

"So…what did you do to him? Jack said it was so horrible, he asked you to erase his memory."

"It's not something you'd ever want to see. The only two ways of destroying us are burning and dismemberment, and since we'll always awaken and fight to survive, to our last trace of strength, this means being burned or ripped to pieces alive. We don't go into shock and we don't lose consciousness. It is dreadful, no question about it. On the other hand, this was a vampire who would have killed Jack and left his bloodless body in that alley within a few minutes had we not happened to have been there."

"Did he really ask for his memory to be erased?"

"Not exactly. We told him we would do it, and he said, for god's sake, yes, do it. When he realized how it was done, he changed his mind. But we didn't give him a choice."

"He claimed he was resistant to the memory blanking. Is that possible?"

"He seemed to have more memory than he should have had, but you know how hard it is to gauge that. Knowing in advance that one's memory is going to be tampered with probably mutes the results. I can't think of a single other instance in my experience when a victim knew what was going to happen. Jack wasn't completely resistant, but I did have some serious doubts about how effective I'd been. That's why I wanted to see him again."

"You really took a big risk."

He grinned, but his smile was humorless. "So Johanna told me. Emphatically. But I've learned that sometimes it's better to enlist allies rather than just manipulate people. Memory blanking can unravel."

"Was that really you Jack saw in nineteen fifty-five?"

Troy frowned. "What was the date, June twenty-first? Yes, I was in Boston then. It might have been—but I never noticed him, regardless of what he thought."

"And in nineteen sixty-three—"

"That was not me. I have no idea who you saw."

"Could it have been Avery, or one of those others?"

He shrugged. "It may have been. I haven't been in contact with them for a while."

"And how did you know Thomas? That one really makes me crazy. Thomas wouldn't give me the tiniest details about any other vampire. He just said that you existed, and that was all. Oh, wait—he did say one thing. He said one vampire he'd met, and I assume he meant you, could open locks by thinking about it. He said you were the most accomplished thief he ever met, and he thought there was nothing on earth you couldn't steal, if you wanted to."

Troy burst out in a real laugh at this. "No wonder my reputation is so tarnished! I'm an honest citizen now, I promise—well, mostly. I never steal merely for profit, at least. But as for Thomas, or David M. Brown, Esquire, as I knew him—he was my attorney, back in nineteen twenty-four."

"How did you find each other?"

"Oh, he found me. He was in the court when I was arrested and spotted me, and he knew I was going to need help. I was very grateful, believe me. That was the closest I ever came to exposing my nature to the whole world. I'm permanently in his debt."

"And you don't think that was an amazing coincidence? That the only other vampire in New York, most likely, one of the few others in the world, and an attorney, shows up at exactly the right moment to keep you from turning into a circus attraction?"

He shrugged, smiling. "What would you call it, magic? Life is full of coincidences, many of them far weirder than this. Reading supernatural meaning into them is the path to madness, or fanaticism—if there's even a difference."

"This is a vampire talking, remember."

"That doesn't mean I can't be rational." He leaned back in his chair, looking thoughtful. "I'm finding it hard to believe what you told me about Brown—Thomas, I mean. He became human? I've never heard of such a thing. You're absolutely certain?"

"I met him in person. There was no mistaking it."

"But you don't really know *how* it happened. You only know what he said."

"I wasn't there and he didn't go into details, so no, I don't know the exact mechanism. But..." she hesitated, frustrated. "Let's not get bogged down in pointless arguments. Obviously we'll have to agree to disagree on a few matters, at least until I can show you more evidence."

"You're right. I'm being more hard-nosed than I deserve to be."

"Anyway, it's your turn now."

"My story is much shorter than yours—especially since you've already ferreted out so much of it yourself." He told her about the odd experience he'd had with something visiting him at night, waking up next to his open grave, and leaving Rhode Island never to return.

"And you had no idea what had happened to you? You had to figure it out alone?"

"No, I didn't and yes, I did, and it wasn't easy. I had some very close calls."

"And you were...murdered, according to these court documents I read?"

"Not something I like to think about."

And you must have a very ugly scar, she thought, unconsciously touching her own lethal scar, left by the Teg's dagger. She decided not to ask about the incident in Hartford. It must have been humiliating for him, and he probably guessed that she knew, since she'd told him how she'd learned about the farm and her improvised fable about her missing brother.

"And you never saw anyone in your family again?"

"How could I? I was dead—and I perished in a way that left it impossible to claim that someone had made a mistake and pronounced my death prematurely. I missed them, but..." He shook his head. "It defies belief that my sister sued the town of South Kingston. I'd been gone for sixty years!" He sobered. "And now she's gone, too. She was the last of us."

"You have a slew of nieces and nephews, some of them sharing a nice fat settlement thanks to you."

He smiled sadly. "I know. That's why I can't go back to Rhode Island. I'm dangerously close, living here. But maybe that's why I decided to come here with Avani and her friends. It's almost home. Besides, they're going to need a lot more help than they know."

"How did you meet them?"

"Their car had broken down in New Jersey, and I stopped to give them a hand. I fixed the car, they told me where they were headed and why, and they invited me to join them. I had nothing better to do."

Diana nodded toward the tidy tool bench. "I gather that you're mechanically inclined."

"I hoped to become an electrical engineer before fate intervened. I thought I would be building power plants and inventing amazing devices for the good of humanity. I even applied for a job with Thomas Edison's firm." He smiled wryly. "I was turned down."

"Couldn't you still do that? If that's what you love—after all, Thomas practiced law for about two centuries."

"I've thought about it, but I completely change identities every ten to fifteen years. It hardly makes sense to spend four years getting a degree only to have to do it all over again a decade later. I've just adopted the guise of Troy Stevenson and re-engaged with the world, in fact. I've been lying low for a couple of years. I keep up with developments, as much as I can through studying and tinkering. I've even written some articles." He stretched, as the chair creaked in complaint. "So now that your ten-year-long quest is over, what are you going to do?"

Diana gazed around the shadowy barn. "I don't have the slightest idea. I was completely focused on finding you, or some other vampire, and for all I knew it would take decades. I never even thought about what I would do next."

"Would you like to stay here?"

"Can I? Are you sure you can extend that invitation?"

"Of course, we'll all have to agree on the final decision. But let me ask you something. When you arrived, how did people seem to react to you?"

Diana regarded his small knowing smile for a moment. "It was like they'd been expecting me—or someone like me. They said my name was all wrong."

"Did you meet Brigid?"

"No, just Avani, Denny and Ellie."

"No wonder you were confused. I don't want to explain too much second hand. But all of them have been saying that the Universe will send them the right people. They know they're taking on too big a job for the four of them. When they picked me off the side of the road in New Jersey, Brigid said, 'there's another one coming.' A complement or second half for me, she implied. Small, she said, but really strong, with dark hair. And the rest of them just nodded."

Diana sat in silent amazement for a few moments. "I...that's just...wow."

"I suspected that with your background, you wouldn't reject the idea out of hand."

"Well, no, of course not, but…they don't know a thing about me."

"They will, though. And when they hear about your work with your foundation, Bread and Roses—you needn't mention that you actually started it, of course—and that you lived in a communal household for eight years, they won't have many questions. You clearly are a hard worker. Destined or not, I think you're just what we need."

Diana mulled this over, uneasy with the idea that she had been "sent by the Universe." *Where the Teg are concerned…* but maybe their intentions were benign for a change. "You make a strong case for it, and I'm tempted. But it depends on the rest of the group. I haven't even met them all yet."

"We all talk over dinner every night. Eat with us tomorrow night and we'll discuss it together." His smile was teasing. "At length. For hours, probably. Be prepared."

The household had apparently retired by this time; Diana could see the back of the rambling house through a window by the workbench and no lights were visible. This sparked a minor qualm about Troy's suggestion. "Don't farmers pretty much get up and go to bed with the sun? It's not going to be easy for us to handle that schedule."

"Don't worry about that. I've already worked that out with the group, and I'll tell them that you have the same medical condition that I do."

"Which is?"

"Medical." He grinned. "Diana, you're not going to have to explain yourself here. As long as you contribute your share, you can do anything you want. You'll see. In my case, we've all agreed that I'll be doing a lot of work at night."

"Work at night? You mean, in the gardens and everything?"

"Why not? We won't be making a lot of noise. Power tools aren't on the priority list. And if there's one thing that we can do well, it's hand-dig gardens. What?" Diana had swallowed hard, suddenly remembering Thomas saying, *you're going to be amazed at how fast you can dig a grave now…*

"Nothing. No, you're right. Besides, I'm up a good part of the day, we don't need eight hours of sleep."

"Exactly. And we can eat just enough food at dinner to look ascetic but normal. They're vegetarians so we don't have to make excuses for avoiding meat."

Diana shook her head. "You're making it sound almost too perfect. I know there must be some catches somewhere."

"There may be some catches but I don't think there will be any fatal ultimatums. We'll smooth out any rough spots. And if it doesn't work out, well…on to something else."

As dawn approached, Troy offered her a safe sleeping spot in the barn loft. The accommodations were spartan—he had a naked mattress on the floor, ancient burlap sacks doubled over and tacked across the small front and back windows, and very little else. The loft would be stifling hot in the summer and freezing cold in the winter but that wouldn't bother either of them. After sleeping in scores of similar crash pads and back rooms over the past year, Diana felt almost at home. But Troy's loft differed from most of those spaces in two respects. For one thing, it was almost astringently clean, reminding her sharply of Thomas' meticulous habits and her own almost compulsive cleaning wherever she was living. April used to tease her about what a terrific housewife she'd be, and sometimes Diana couldn't repress a furious and sarcastic comeback, which April had found very funny. *Are all vampires compulsive cleaners?* she wondered now—Troy was only the third one she'd met, including herself.

But the second difference was more unsettling. In sharp contrast to the males in the crash pads, Troy displayed no interest in having sex with her at all. It wasn't merely his politeness—it was his entire attitude and body language. Diana felt that mentioning the topic would be an unforgiveable *faux pas*—and she couldn't understand why. She'd always assumed that the violence of her turning had destroyed her intimacy with Thomas, but now she wondered, *do vampires not have sex with each other? Or is it just me?* The story she'd heard in Hartford didn't sound as though Troy was simply homosexual, which she could have understood.

It wasn't that Troy didn't trust her, either—he fell into the coma-like state that served them as sleep before she did. But she lay awake later than usual, still trying to absorb everything that had happened that day. Her long quest was finally over, and she could hardly believe it. *Troy must have an encyclopedia's worth of things to teach me, just about being a vampire,* she thought. *I'll have plenty of time to sort all these mysteries out.* Maybe vampires just didn't have sex on the first date. After all, Troy had asked permission to call her by her first name.

22

When she awoke in the late afternoon, Troy had already left. Diana washed up as best she could at the tiny chipped sink's single cold water tap. She combed her hair and dressed carefully, wishing that she'd had a bath and washed out her clothes more recently. *Should I just walk into the house?* After debating for a few minutes, she hesitantly walked through the back yard and entered the house through the unlocked rear door, bringing along the lantern she'd borrowed last night.

As she came into the hall, a slender woman with a riot of carrot-colored ringlets and graceful long-fingered hands was coming down the stairs. She saw Diana and beamed. "You must be Troy's friend! Welcome!" Before Diana knew what was happening, she was enfolded in a hug, and almost forgot to hug back.

"You must be Brigid."

"That I am. Umm." She pulled back and looked at Diana, nodding. "Troy was right. You do feel just like him. So you'll be helping him work at night?"

"Uh…"

"I think that's such a wonderful idea, it's like having twice as many hours in the day. There's so little time, you know. The last frost day here is May fifteenth."

The hall was quite dark, and Diana could see a faint cloud of body heat around Brigid; but more interesting was the brighter glow around her belly, as though she was hiding a little sun behind her navel. "When is the baby due?"

"October, and I'm so hoping it's a Libra. Scorpio children are so intense! Of course, we'll be blessed whatever we have, but come on, I'm helping Avani make dinner. We call this the great room, isn't it amazing? Look at the space!"

"I know, it's the biggest room I've ever seen in an ordinary house," Diana said as she followed Brigid through the wide arch from the hall.

Ellie had disassembled the trestle table and was cutting 2x8s on the sawhorses with a hand saw. He had already stacked an impressive number of carefully trimmed boards against the wall, highest at the back to reduce any chance of the stack falling over. The aromatic scent of freshly sawn pine filled the room. No shades covered the newly washed windows; sunlight reflected off the white walls and worn floorboards. Diana tried not to squint.

"This is Ellie, my partner—it's really Elliott, but that just sounds like *The Untouchables.*"

"Ellie and I met last night, briefly," Diana said. "You're a carpenter?"

"Yep. Carpentry, cabinet-making, framing—for this I went to college."

"Useful skills. What are these for?"

"We're building raised garden beds, and we've got to get them done fast." With a nod, he bent back to his sawing.

"So, what do you do?" Diana asked Brigid. "Last night, I heard you didn't like to be interrupted when you're working."

Brigid rolled her eyes. "Oh, you should have called me!" she said to Ellie, who cheerfully snorted. "I'm a sculptor, and I do fiber art, but mostly I work with pottery and ceramics. I've got a kiln sitting down in my parents' basement that we're going to bring up here in a couple of weeks."

"Do you make things to sell?"

"Let's hope so," Ellie said as he set the board onto the stack by the wall.

"Is your kiln in New Jersey? I think Troy said he met you there."

Ellie laughed. "We were broken down by the side of the road in New Jersey. No, we're all from Delaware."

Avani called from the kitchen, "Brigid? Are you coming?"

"Oop, let's not keep Mama Bear waiting," Brigid said, grabbing Diana's arm and hurrying toward the kitchen, as Diana trotted to keep up with her long legs.

In the kitchen, Avani was cutting vegetables on a scarred wooden table, a heavy five gallon soup pot waiting on the gas range. It was immediately obvious why she didn't use the broad linoleum-topped counters: the kitchen had a plague of ants, not unusual for country houses at this time of year.

"Hello, Diana. I'm so glad that you're staying."

Brigid, who had noticed Diana's glance at the counters, brushed several ants onto the floor impatiently. "We don't want to use any poisons or chemicals. But that doesn't mean we want ant soup."

"They go away when it warms up, usually. The range uses propane?" She'd seen the tanks on the back on the house.

"And the hot water heater," Avani said. "But we're going to use sunshowers outside as much as we can. We need the electricity for the refrigerator, but we're trying not to use it anywhere else, unless we have to."

"What are sunshowers?"

"Oh, don't you know?" Brigid said. "You take these heavy black plastic bags and fill them with water and hang them up. The sun heats the water naturally."

"That's...rather ingenious."

"We're going to build a permanent one later with forty gallon drums. But we have to find some that we know never had toxic waste or oil in them."

"Makes sense." Diana pulled drawers open and shut until she found another vegetable knife. "Too bad you can't cook on the wood stove and spare the propane gas," she said as she started peeling an onion.

Avani stopped chopping. "You know how to do that?"

"I cooked on a wood stove for three years up in Maine. We didn't have electricity or running water."

"Far *out*," Brigid said.

"I never got the hang of baking in the thing, though. But you should taste my charcoal cookies. With delicious gooey centers."

Brigid laughed, but Avani looked quite serious. "I'm sure we could figure it out."

"Pies do better in a wood stove, anyway."

"Can you light it?" Brigid's eyes were shining. "There's some wood behind the house, it's pretty old, but it should still be good."

"Well, uh…sure, I guess. It'll be kind of hot for Ellie—"

"Come *on!*" Brigid dropped the knife and pulled Diana out of the kitchen by her elbow. "Ellie, you're going to need to move."

"What? The hell I am…"

The vegetable soup ended up simmering on the wood stove, while a large pot of brown rice and red lentils cooked on a burner of the gas range, where they'd be less likely to scorch. Ellie's muttered grumbles subsided as the house filled with the aromas of cumin and herbs.

A vehicle pulled into the curving driveway. From the noise, Diana thought it was a school bus at the least, but a minute later Denny and, to her relief, Troy walked in the front door. "We got the truck," Denny announced as though he was proclaiming that they'd won the Super Bowl.

"Did they take the car?" Avani called through a cloud of vegetable soup steam.

"Yes, but they didn't give us shit for it."

"No wonder, it wasn't worth shit," Ellie said, studiously marking a board.

"Mr. Maddox says he'll give us that old trailer, and all the composted manure we can use."

"Who's Mr. Maddox?" Diana asked.

"The dairy farmer, up the road," Brigid said. "He's really nice."

"We saved his ass, is why he's nice," Denny chuckled.

"You're not worried that he won't like a bunch of beatnik vegetarian organic farmers for neighbors?" Diana spoke humorously, but she was thinking of the abutters in Lexington, who never did thaw very much. In her experience, farmers tended to be conservative. But Denny guffawed.

"Hell, no. He remembers Avani from when she was here as kid, for one thing. But there's been developers sniffing around with the idea of turning River Road into the next Levittown, and Avani's dad lives in Florida and hates the place. Mr. Maddox is orgasmic that someone is going to farm here. He hopes we stay forever."

"He's going to sell us raw milk," Brigid said. "We're going to make our own yogurt, the way they do in Tibet."

"We're going to go get the trailer, and the first load of manure," Denny said. "No reason to bring the trailer back empty." He and Troy had left before Diana could catch Troy, to her exasperation.

The truck's engine hadn't started before Ellie said, "Diana, do you think you could help me with these long pieces? I need someone to brace the ends while I saw—"

Brigid drowned out the end of his sentence as she came down the stairs two at a time. "Diana, could you help me upstairs? I've got four more rooms to clean and I need another person on the curtain rods."

Diana stood agape for a moment, then said, "Can I hold boards for Ellie and *then* come upstairs and help you with the curtain rods?"

"Okay, that works."

Denny and Troy came in from unloading the manure just as dinner was ready, kicking off their work boots by the door. "Man, it's hot in here," Denny said. "Are you *cooking* on that thing?"

"The marvels of modern living," Ellie said as he lowered the table top, which Diana had the other end of, onto the sawhorses.

"We'll save on the propane," Avani said as she brought in a stack of handmade ceramic bowls. "Did you take all this time making just one run up the road?"

"No, we made three," Troy said.

"Just for starters," Denny added. "I'm tellin' ya, that is one big pile of shit up there."

"Well, good," Ellie said. "We'll put it to better use than polluting the aquifer."

"You two wash up." Avani lined up bowls on either side of the table and beckoned to Diana to follow her back to the kitchen for more, as Diana cast a despairing look over her shoulder at Troy heading for the first floor bathroom with Denny.

All six of them were soon sitting on the long benches at the table, now further from the stove than it had been the night before. Diana sat across from Troy at one end, casting him a quick nervous smile. The mischievous grin and almost imperceptible wink he gave in return did not reassure her. She quickly turned her attention as Denny, sitting beside her, took her hand and she realized they were all joining hands.

"Creator of the Universe, we thank you for your blessings," Brigid said. In unison, the other five joined voices in a chant: *"Om...namah...shivaya."* Each word had several notes and took up a full line of the chant. Diana could only listen, as she had never heard this form of the chant before, although she recognized the Hindu words. Troy joined in as fervently as any believer, eyes closed, his light baritone forming a perfect balance with Denny's bass and Ellie's tenor. *No wonder they decided he fit right in,* Diana thought, then quailed as she suppressed her smile.

No one noticed, as they released hands and Avani ladled up soup and handed bowls down the table, while the dish of rice and lentils was passed around. The four humans were ravenously hungry and there was no conversation until the second helping of soup was almost gone. Diana and Troy ate their small amounts in tiny sips and bites with many pauses, although Diana had to admit it was delicious. Eating food was easier with no nauseating cooked meat smell in the air. She only regretted that the household's healthy lifestyle banned sugar and chocolate. She probably would wind up smuggling candy bars into the barn and hiding them with her stash of Jack's acid.

"Now then," Brigid said, setting down her spoon. "We need to talk to Diana about what we're all about, and hear your story."

"Are you really certain that you want to stay?" Avani's face was so solemn, Diana felt a sudden pang.

Am I? The day had been so busy, she hadn't had time to think. Had Troy told them she was staying? But what else did she have to do? *What else do I want to do?* She had said it to Troy last night—she hadn't given a thought to what she would do after she found him, or any other vampire. That single goal had seemed so unattainable, it had filled her whole future. "Yes, I think I am. This isn't what I expected when I came here looking for Troy, but…I like it. It's just all…kind of new to me, that's all."

"Not really," Troy said, and Diana caught herself.

"Not living communally like this, but the whole, organic gardening thing. I'm going to have a lot to learn."

"Not to worry," Ellie said. "We've got books and things, and we'll teach you. Mostly it's plain hard work."

"And you've been working your ass off since you walked through the door this afternoon," Avani said.

"Have I? I feel like I've just been running from one thing to the next."

"That's about right," Denny said.

"You all seem to do it so well, though. How long have you been together as a group? Were you farming in Delaware?"

"Oh, no," Avani said. "We were sharing a place in Newark. We've known each other since college. But we've been working toward this for the past four years."

"We're the last hold-outs," Ellie said. "We had a group at the university, and after we graduated, about a dozen of us kept up meetings. But the rest of them gave up and drifted away, mostly to join the rat race and get married."

"They didn't share the vision," Brigid said. "They only thought they did. Finally it was just the four of us holding the circle."

"Then Avani's dad said he was going to sell this place for a housing development, and Avani told him she wanted to live here, and she'd cover the taxes and maintenance."

"It was a sign from the Universe," Brigid said. "Finally we could get out of the city, and live in true harmony with the earth."

"So, you just decided to become farmers? What did you major in at college?"

"Agriculture," Denny said. "I grew up on a farm in western Pennsylvania. But I didn't finish my degree. Farming is getting completely industrialized now, all drugs and chemicals. I figured there had to be another way. The problem is making it pay."

"Or at least live off the land ourselves, which isn't necessarily the same thing," Avani said.

"We're homesteading, like the pioneers," Ellie said. "But we aren't all aggie majors. I have a degree in history. Thought I was going to teach, for a while."

"Pre-nursing, but I just couldn't see myself in a hospital," Avani said. "Or toeing the AMA party line. I just wanted to help people, not become part of the system. I didn't realize that until I started doing some internships."

"What, like Candy Stripers?" Diana asked, and Avani nodded wryly.

"I grew up reading all those girls' romances about young nurses. But when I really got into it…I don't know. I just didn't have the stomach for it. But after I met Denny—" she laughed. "I thought about switching to veterinary science, for a semester. But that wasn't it, either."

"I majored in Fine Arts," Brigid said. "I just wanted to be an artist."

"But how did you get from all those different interests to running an organic farm?"

"Lots of talking, lots of reading," Denny said.

"Not just about this," Ellie said. "We hated what was going on in our country. The industry, the pollution, the way big soul-killing corporations are just taking over everything."

"The war," Denny said. "We didn't learn a thing from Korea, now we're right back in southeast Asia, destroying a culture that's thousands of years old, and for what? They want to be communist? Who gives a fuck, they're in Asia."

"Big business, that's who gives a fuck," Ellie said. "But I can't see what the big deal is with Cuba. Since when do we get to tell other countries what kind of governments they can have?"

Brigid waved her hands impatiently. "Lots of talking, that's for sure! But this is taking the next step. It's all about creating a different model for the world, becoming living examples. We're putting ourselves right on the lines to show that it can really be done, that there are other ways to live than commuting to some faceless office every day and coming home to two cars in the garage and a giant TV in the living room. We'll have a complete relationship with Mother Earth and Mother Goddess, every moment. We'll grow our own food and make what we need, the way the Shakers did, and the American Indians. What we're doing, it's sort of like magic, I mean *real* magic. I know you'll think that sounds silly…"

"No, no, not exactly. But what do you mean by that?"

"Breaking a new trail," Denny said.

"Or rediscovering old ones," Ellie added.

"Giving people a model to follow, something they might not even have thought of before." Avani had just returned to the table with a stack of books and small magazines she'd retrieved from a bookcase near the archway. "Or they have, but couldn't see how to change their lives to try it out. We'll show them. Like this—" and she reached over to hand Diana one of the books.

"Living the Good Life, by Helen and Scott Nearing," Diana read the book's cover.

"Have you read it?"

"No, but I've heard of it. Aren't these the people who built a stone house by hand up in Vermont?"

"You should read it, and these, too." Avani pushed the rest of the stack to Diana.

"Just for starters," Ellie said.

Diana looked through the stack thoughtfully. The eclectic and well-thumbed collection included Thoreau's *Walden, Let's Eat Right to Keep Fit* by Adele Davis, a thick tome about herbal and natural medicine called *Back to Eden,* J.I. Rodale's *How to Grow Fruits and Vegetables by the Organic Method, Stranger in a Strange Land* by Robert Heinlein and an assortment of *Prevention* and *Organic Gardening* magazines. "I read this one, at least." She held up *Silent Spring* by Rachel Carson. "Pretty scary."

"No shit," Denny said.

"Well…I'll read them, definitely, and anything else you've got. Thanks."

Brigid beamed at her. "So, tell us where you're coming from. Troy didn't say much, but I feel that you're following a path a lot like ours, aren't you?"

Diana was silent for moment. *More than either of us imagined,* she thought. "It does seem like it." As the others listened in rapt attention, she described her experiences with Bread and Roses, living in Maine and the communal household in Lexington. She said nothing about magic, vampires or the Order of the Silver Light for the time being, but dropped enough carefully chosen keywords into her narrative to make it obvious she was in sympathy with the group's spiritual views. She risked adding another statement. "I should confess that I'm a bit older than I look. It's part of the medical condition Troy and I have." Everyone nodded solemnly at this and no one asked how old she was or what medical condition conferred eternal youth. But perhaps, she thought, they'd noticed that everything about Troy except his appearance suggested someone much older.

185

When she finished her account, there was a minute or two of reflective silence. Brigid's eyes were closed and Avani, Denny and Ellie were watching her expectantly. Brigid opened her eyes and looked at Diana. "You are staying."

Diana looked back at Brigid's face, which was somehow serene and intense at once, and felt as though she was standing tip-toe on a threshold, about to step into another world with no turning back. But she felt no apprehension, just a deep excitement. "Yes. If you'll have me." She looked around the table, and a chorus of murmured assent replied.

"Then you'll need a new name," Brigid said.

"Okay…but why?"

"You just do. We all knew it the minute we met you. Now, I've been meditating on it—" *When?* Diana wanted to ask, but did not interrupt "—and it's come to me. Your name here is Raksha."

"Raksha?"

"Yes. It's Hindu. I thought Gaelic, but no. This is your name."

"It is," Avani said. "It fits you. That's definitely it."

"I, uh…what does it mean?"

Brigid smiled. "It means 'protector.'"

It took a moment for Diana to respond to this. "Raksha…all right." *Protector. How very strange…who will I be protecting?* She glanced at Troy furtively and he raised his eyebrows as if to say, *you've passed.*

"Why don't the men get new names? Hardly seems fair."

Brigid waved a hand. "They don't need them. It's we women who are taking on a whole new role. We're all equals here. We can't be equals in the outside world. We have to leave our old names behind. They're slave names. Don't laugh, it's true."

"I'm not laughing at that," Diana said, trying to suppress her grin. "I was just thinking of one of my old friends. She'd agree with you."

"Put your hand on the table—no, palm up," Brigid said. She laid her open hand on Diana's. Ellie, Denny and Avani placed their hands on top of hers, one after the other, and when Avani gestured to him, Troy did the same. "Welcome, Raksha," Brigid said, and the other four repeated in unison, "Welcome, Raksha."

They all resumed their seats. Diana looked down at her open hand, not sure what to say. But Denny said, "Okay, let's talk about where we are with the garden plans so far. Ellie, how are you doing with the beds?"

This launched the longest part of the conversation, on the work that needed to be done immediately, and there was a staggering amount of that. A long, long discussion, with diagrams, involved the positioning, sizes and composition of the raised garden beds. Denny thought they should have the equivalent of two acres of single beds built and ready to plant by May 15th. Before the beds could be started, that much land had to be cleared—without machinery.

"That's a lot to do in six weeks," Diana said.

"That's squat, if we want food for the winter and produce to sell," Denny said. "It's just a good start."

Troy caught Diana's eye. "We'll begin tonight. We can clear, at least, and pace out the beds as we go."

"This seems like so much to take on for six people," Diana said. "And you left Delaware thinking it would just be the four of you?"

"Oh, no. There are supposed to be eight of us," Brigid said firmly. "I knew from the beginning that there would be eight—like the four quarters and four cross-quarters. And here you and Troy are, already."

"And the other two?"

"They'll be here. The Universe will send them when it's the right time."

By the time dinner was cleaned up, the four mortal householders were sagging. They'd all been up since dawn. Troy and Diana, on the other hand, were just starting their work day. As they walked out into the back yard, Diana hissed at Troy, "What did you tell them about me?"

He was standing with his hands on his hips, surveying the land just past the half-collapsed picket fence that denoted the edge of the small back yard; they would start building the beds as close to the house as possible and push them out and up in concentric rows. "Nothing."

Diana crossed her arms. "Expand on 'nothing.'"

"I just said that we were old friends who hadn't seen each other in a long time, and we had the same medical condition that makes us light sensitive but able to see in the dark, and you didn't have anywhere else to go at the moment and you very much liked it here and you wanted to stay for a while."

"That is not nothing! Why didn't you tell me? I'd like to have gotten our stories straight."

He chuckled. "You shouldn't sleep so late." Before she could splutter a retort, he said, "Come on. Mattocks, spades, saws, and that big two-wheeled cart in the barn. Let's get started."

The work was tedious and strenuous, but it wasn't back-breaking or exhausting for Diana and Troy in the way it would be for their mortal friends. Diana had never felt as though her enhanced vampiric abilities were so profoundly *useful*. "It's almost as though, it finally seems to make some kind of sense," she said to Troy on one of their occasional breaks. They dug out the long grass, dug and pulled out saplings and brush, and trundled endless cartloads to the spot where a massive compost pile would be. When the trees to the east were starting to show as silhouettes against light the color of pearls, Troy stopped, stretched, and looked back at what they'd done so far.

"I'd guess that's about…a quarter acre."

"You're kidding! In one night?"

"We've been going steadily, and fast. Do you want to pace it out?"

Diana studied the broad expanse. The coven had looked at houses with quarter-acre lots, and they hadn't seemed very large. "I think you're right. Gods, we'll have two acres done in eight days!"

"And then the beds have to be built, and the soil prepared, and put in the beds, and then we have to plant...and we'd better not do too much at once. It will look very strange if we consistently achieve what's not humanly possible."

They left the cart and tools next to the barn. "Denny will be up soon, and he'll be picking up right where we left off. The others will all come out and help him off and on. When I get up this afternoon, we'll get more manure."

Diana looked down woefully at her stained jeans and mud-caked sneakers. "I need work boots. And work clothes. I didn't come prepared for any of this."

"We can get you those tomorrow, too."

Up in the barn loft, Diana sank down on the mattress, paging through *Living the Good Life*. Troy stretched out next to her and yawned. "Well, you've been accepted—Raksha."

"You don't have to call me that, you know."

"Oh, I think I better use it consistently. I wouldn't want to slip up. Is this the first time you've changed your name?"

"I am not changing my name permanently to Raksha, thank you very much. I've had initiation names, and I've used pseudonyms, but..."

"You'll get used to it."

"I suppose. I just can't shake this suspicion that I've been accepted because everyone believes the Universe sent me. I feel like I've been mistaken for a celebrity and don't dare disillusion everyone."

Troy chuckled. "They think the same thing about me. God sent me to fix their car. What does it matter? It's not like the Universe is going to show up, point at you and say, 'that's an impostor, get her.'"

"I guess not." She yawned herself and put the book aside. Birds were starting to chirp and sing outside and that always made her sleepy. Troy had rolled over to face the wall and already seemed asleep. She looked at his turned back glumly. *We might as well run a bundling board down the middle of the mattress.* Resignedly, she lay down and snuggled her back up against Troy's, too tired to feel rejected. "Troy, if you think I'm sleeping too late, get me up."

23

The days passed with breathless speed, because they were so busy and full. Denny, Ellie, Troy and Diana cleared the two acres, and a bit more, in six days of round the clock labor. They all worked together building the raised beds because the long boards demanded several pairs of hands to hold them in place while Ellie nailed them to their supporting stakes. They measured the beds out to thirty feet square because that was exactly one fiftieth of an acre, making it easy to calculate seeds and additives from a per-acre formula. The soil inside the beds was mixed with manure, leaf mold from the woods, lime, and various other components Denny scrounged and brought back in the trailer. He had worked out the ingredients of his growing medium as carefully as a chef planning the recipe for a new soufflé, and meticulously tested the soil using kits he'd brought from the University of Delaware Agricultural school. The saplings and small trees they cut down were sawn into stove lengths and went into a growing wood pile. The house was cleaned and slowly accumulated furniture, some of it made by Ellie and Troy, some of it found or bought at flea markets or thrift shops. Brigid's kiln and potter's wheel arrived and the kiln was set up in the cellar.

Diana and Troy never missed a household dinner and meeting, but their real nutritional needs presented a much bigger dilemma. Diana had drunk from animals at times, but she had never relied on that source as much as Thomas, and Troy showed her quite a few techniques and tricks for hunting, locating and drinking from animals, wild or domestic, which Thomas hadn't covered.

"I honestly don't understand how you could stay in the same area, and completely rely on human blood, for so long and not raise suspicions. Have you found a way to drink without leaving a mark?"

"No, I haven't. The trick is where you leave it." He gave her a puzzled look. "First of all, I pick the right targets. I usually would cruise around until some shady character tried to pull something on me. Some guy with rape or robbery on his mind isn't going to go to the police, no matter what happens to him."

"That's a good point..."

"The second thing is that I don't leave a mark in easily visible places, if I can help it. I usually incapacitate the target first, and then drink from some part of his body he can't see—middle of the back is good. All I have to do is pull his shirt up."

Troy raised his eyebrows. "That's…very ingenious. But I still think animals are a lot safer."

"I agree, but in the city, large animals aren't very accessible. I'm not heartless enough to eat people's pets. Besides, I love animals."

They'd moved into the farm too late to start seeds indoors properly, and constructing cold frames and a small greenhouse for next year were high on the list of projects. They planted the beds with corn, winter and summer squash, carrots, onions, potatoes, and lettuces, with tomato, cabbage, pepper and broccoli plants they purchased late, after the plants had been discounted at the nurseries. They tried planting one bed permanently with asparagus and another with strawberry plants.

The results were variable, as Denny had predicted would be the case the first couple of years. Not surprisingly, they saw most of the pests endemic to the area, and spent the summer testing all the organic solutions in their books. Diana surreptitiously tried a few magical attacks on particularly brutal infestations of potato bugs and squash beetles, and found that this was a trickier application of spellwork than she'd thought. She tried to refine her methods so as to whammy the bugs without killing the plants, but Nature supplied a relentless tide of voracious insects.

In mid-August Avani started canning, and they built shelving in the cellar for the squash and root vegetables. They ended up with not quite enough food put by to sustain six people for six months, but certainly a large amount. Denny wanted to prepare another five acres that fall to be ready for spring, and they'd already cleared the land, at a more measured pace than the first two acres.

Both Troy and Diana contributed financially to the household, mostly by paying the electric and propane bills or buying necessities, without ever mentioning where their money came from. The only one to comment was Avani, who told them she just didn't want anyone in the house dealing dope, because of the trouble that could cause. Troy and Diana assured her that no dope was being dealt by them, although all of them smoked grass and Diana still had the last of Jack's LSD, carefully hidden up in the barn loft. Brigid made beautiful pottery and by August, even as she burgeoned enough to make sitting at her wheel a challenge, she began marketing her wares in local stores and flea markets. Ellie occasionally found a carpentry job. But the gardens and house took up nearly all the time and energy they had. The four humans dropped into bed at the end of each day like stones plunking into a pond, while their vampire housemates slept only slightly less.

"Does it ever freak you guys out, that we do so much work at night?" Diana once asked Brigid and Ellie. They both shook their heads, and Ellie laughed.

"Are you kidding? It's fucking great. I don't know what we'd do without you."

"I feel like I'm in a fairy tale sometimes, like 'The Shoemaker and the Elves,'" Brigid said. "We get up in the morning and all this work is done. It's like magic."

After the gardens had been planted, Brigid began one project that was not strictly practical. Along with her more artistic work, she started to shape and fire heavy slabs of clay, making tiles about a foot square and an inch thick. She lined those up, unglazed, against the wall of the great room. Her housemates glanced curiously at the growing rows of slabs as they passed through doing their own work, but they knew Brigid would explain when the Universe prompted her to do so.

The explanation came after a carton arrived from a crafts supply store out West. That night at dinner, Brigid brought one of the slabs to the table along with several bottles of what turned out to be glaze in unusually vivid colors.

"This is my idea. Each of us will glaze some of these in whatever colors we choose, and I'll fire them, and then we'll make paths of them. We'll have rainbow paths, all around the house and leading out to the gardens and places in the woods. They'll make a sort of sacred trail that we'll walk on every time we go out to do our work. Of course, it will take a while to make all we need, but we'll just keep adding on to the path as I make more stones."

"A Rainbow Path?" Ellie said. "That's far out, Brigid."

"Very cool," Denny said.

"I like that idea." Diana touched the rough surface of the tile. "When can we start glazing them?"

"Tonight? I thought we could do them after dinner."

Denny and Troy meticulously set the tiles into place, starting with a path to the front door. They dug a shallow trench lined with fine gravel and spaced the tiles with sand between them, allowing them to flex with temperature and footsteps. "These could last for decades," Denny said. By the time of the first hard frost, there were over three hundred tiles in place, gleaming in the sunlight, surrounding the entire house. It was, Diana thought, like a magic circle, like Thomas's circles of crushed stone, binding and shielding what they all were building together.

"You're doing great, Brigid. You're almost there." The nurse-midwife had arrived half an hour ago, and Brigid was already dilated to ten centimeters. Diana had worried that the slender, fine-boned woman might have some problems with her first delivery, but Brigid's Irish genes and the months of hard work were easing her way. Diana felt strange to be in the birthing room with Avani and Ellie, but Brigid had wanted her there, and she was now positioned directly behind the mother-to-be, supporting her back. That took some doing. Brigid's feet were braced on the bed and she frequently strained back against Diana so hard that her hips completely cleared the mattress. Ellie and Avani each held one of her hands and they both had deep crescent marks from Brigid's fingernails, but neither of them flinched no matter how hard she squeezed.

"Okay, take a deep breath and push." Brigid's entire face coiled into a single grimace, her teeth in a gaping snarl. When she couldn't hold for another moment, she released her breath in a sound that was half groan and half howl.

"Again, Brigid. Just twice more, take a breath…"

The baby seemed to spill out onto the bed all at once, tiny face as contorted as her mother's. All her limbs waved in the air as though she was trying to swim to the ceiling. "It's a beautiful little girl, you have a daughter," the midwife said. She deftly scooped up the wet slippery baby and laid her face down on Brigid's stomach. Brigid let out several long cries, tears running down her face, and Ellie grabbed her, Diana and Avani in a spontaneous hug, crying, too. They all pulled themselves together as the midwife briskly worked over the baby, cleaning her with quick practiced strokes and tucking a little cap onto her head. The baby didn't cry until the cord was snipped, and then only for a few seconds. Her eyes were open, and her flat little tummy moved up and down as she breathed in the air of this world for the first time. The midwife wrapped the baby in a receiving blanket and handed her to Brigid, who gazed down at the tiny bundle as if she thought she was dreaming.

"A daughter…"

"And a Libra," Diana said. "The sun enters Scorpio tomorrow. Good thing you pushed so hard." Brigid started to laugh and then winced.

"It's going to be a couple of days before I can get back to work, I think."

"A couple of days? You deserve a good long rest, Brigid," Diana said.

"Raksha's right. You're a mother now. You need to take care of yourself," Avani said sternly.

"But the garden clean-up…in Africa, women give birth and go right back to the fields."

"And die at thirty-five. We're not in Africa. We'll manage just fine, Brigid, the canning is almost finished."

"Have you and Ellie picked a name?" Diana asked. She hadn't been able to take her eyes off the tiny face since the midwife had handed the baby to her mother. The sight of Brigid cradling the bundle of blanket made her arms ache with longing.

"Oh. Yes, we have." Brigid smiled fondly at Ellie. "Morningstar."

"Morningstar. That's lovely."

"We'll do a naming ceremony when Brigid is completely recovered," Ellie said.

The midwife said, "Let's clear out the room a bit and give mom some space. I need to check the afterbirth, and I've got a few more things to do. We're not quite finished yet." Avani tugged Diana out of the room.

Several nights later, Diana was sitting downstairs by the woodstove with Morningstar in her arms. As newborns went, their newest housemate was on the fussy side, and Diana had offered to take her and let Brigid and Ellie sleep between feedings. Troy came in, looking for her, and stopped, an odd expression on his face.

"You have the baby."

She raised an eyebrow at him. "Yes, I have the baby, and she's perfectly safe."

He came over and sat down. "I know, I'm sorry. Children make me a little nervous."

"Why? Surely you'd never harm one."

He looked away. "I'll tell you sometime."

"Everyone always says that to me. Tease." Morningstar stirred, and Diana bounced her gently until she settled. "I've been brooding too much, stupid me. Wondering what my life might be like if I'd had my babies, instead of losing them."

"I didn't know. I'm very sorry."

Diana sighed. "You know…I really feel like I'm home for the first time since nineteen forty-five."

"What happened in nineteen forty-five?"

"That's when I was initiated to Adeptus and realized that was as far as I was going to go." She glanced at his quizzical expression. "That's the highest grade women are eligible for. That's when it all started to sour. I got into trouble with the Order, I broke up my marriage, then I gave up my apartment and friends in Boston and ran off to Maine…it feels like I've just been bumming around ever since, with no idea where I was going or where I even wanted to go. Becoming… what we are, that was almost irrelevant. I'd have been just as lost without it. But now…I'm tired of magic, Troy. I'm tired of fighting all the time, crusading, always trying to *fix* things. All this digging and grubbing in the earth…there's healing in it. I never would have believed that if I hadn't come here." She looked thoughtfully up at the stained ceiling and unconsciously hugged Morningstar closer. "I feel like I'm home. I want to stay here forever."

Troy was silent for a minute. "If only we could. We can't stay anywhere forever, Raksha. We don't age. We can only stay for a while. Even if we extend the charade by simulating aging, eventually we have to say goodbye."

Diana looked down at the sleeping baby's face. "I guess that's true for all of us, isn't it? We only stay a while." She looked up at Troy, who was smiling faintly. "We're supposed to be out doing fall soil preparation, aren't we? The ground is going to freeze soon."

"I suppose it can wait."

"No, it can't. She's going to wake up soon and need to be fed, and I'll have to give her back to Brigid. I'll come out then."

𝕷ife in the house grew quieter in the winter months. Ellie had time to work on elaborate bas-relief panels he was making to put around the front door. Brigid kept busy, because her pottery sales picked up at the Christmas season, and she was beginning to sell hand-made clothing, as well. They didn't do anything as materialistic as exchange gifts, and unanimously agreed that cutting down a tree for decoration was unethical. But Diana and Avani brought in armfuls of evergreen trimmings and festooned the walls of the great room and the banisters of the stairs. They planned a "winter feast" on December 22.

Diana missed the Order's festivals more poignantly this year than she had for some time. She hadn't been in touch with any of the Boston House since she'd said good-bye to Phoebe and Art, and she couldn't imagine what they'd think of her current appearance, let alone her lifestyle.

The vegetarian winter feast had five courses and was two days in the making, and everyone's spirits were high afterwards. Diana and Troy, in a somewhat puckish mood, celebrated their own feast after everyone had gone to bed by visiting the dairy farm for a more luxuriously long drink than they usually allowed themselves. It would have been risky had Mr. Maddox and his wife not been spending Christmas with a married daughter. Their house was empty, with the hired hands only coming in for milking and chores twice a day.

The barn now had a small wood stove downstairs, mostly to alleviate Avani's concerns about their well-being during bitter weather, but not entirely. Even vampires preferred temperatures above the freezing mark, and Troy had been somewhat awe-struck by Diana's story about the winter she'd frozen herself solid in Maine. The heat rose and collected in the loft, making it almost cozy up there. They'd acquired, as free castoffs, two twin beds on actual frames to replace the lumpy mattress on the floor.

Everyone was taking a break from work tonight, so Troy and Diana had some unaccustomed hours of leisure after they returned from the dairy farm, blissed out and buzzed on cow's blood. They sat facing each other on the beds, comparing the vastly dissimilar manners in which each of them had become vampires, and how both related to the still different transformation which Troy had heard other vampires describe.

"I don't think there necessarily is a contradiction, Raksha. I think it may be a matter of degree. There's definitely evidence that something is somehow passed between us to initiate the change. Whether that's energy, or some kind of contamination, or an entity, I don't know."

"But you never heard of anyone else whose change involved so much pain. I don't want to sound melodramatic, but the agony is simply beyond description."

"I also never heard of a vampire who remained conscious during the process. We don't feel pain, and we don't perceive whatever the medium is, because we've died, or at least, we're in that twilight state between bodily death and the point beyond which a clinically dead person could not be resuscitated. You said you didn't continue to feel pain after you were unconscious."

"None, it cuts right off. But Thomas thought that the change wouldn't happen unless you were conscious for at least some of it."

"I know that the change isn't always reliable. But there are other factors to consider. You're indestructible, or so you say. We aren't. And we can't dematerialize. Perhaps we're only partly changed. Maybe you and Thomas represented the purest possible form of our condition."

"That makes sense, but it still doesn't explain why there should be any difference at all."

"No, it doesn't." He frowned, thinking. "I don't think that this entity you say you saw, that you call the dragon, can be objectively real."

"Well, you would say that."

"I mean, real as some kind of living thing. I think that was your mind's way of interpreting the power that was changing you."

"And the Teg?"

Troy smiled. "I'm going to have to reserve judgment until I meet them, I'm afraid."

"Ohhhhh, man. Be careful what you wish for."

"I'm keeping an open mind, believe it or not. I just can't give credence to this kind of thing without hard evidence. But evidence is the whole problem. We need to find other vampires to unravel these dilemmas. We just have too few examples to work with."

"Suppose there aren't any others?"

"Well, I've only been a vampire for seventy years, which isn't very long, and I've roamed most of North America. I've met seven others so far, and some of them say they know of more. I've wondered if we might be more numerous in other parts of the world, such as Europe."

"You never went looking?"

"I never had a clue to even start with. Look at what you went through to find me. Imagine that, with multiple countries and languages you don't know."

"Thanks, I'd prefer not to."

"Perhaps..." Troy's tone was cautious, "...when the time comes that we have to move on, we could go looking for them together." He watched Diana's expression change. "I know you don't want to leave here. But that day is inevitable. It's better to plan for it and meet it bravely than deny it."

"I know, I know you're right. You've been doing this a lot longer, I'm still getting used to it. I can't even imagine changing my name over and over, like you and Thomas. Jack and I rented a house under an assumed name and I nearly blew it a dozen times. I'd go to write a check and couldn't remember what to sign."

"You'll get the hang of it with practice. It's like being a good actor."

Diana shook her head, smiling. "You really want to travel the world with me? You wouldn't get tired of my company?"

"Lord, no. Why would you think that?"

Diana girded herself for a move that she had been considering for some months now. "Well, Troy...I've never felt the slightest twitch of interest or attraction from you, aside from general friendliness. I've been sleeping in the same room with you, even on the same mattress, every day for more than eight months and it's like you weren't even there. I must have jinxed myself, you might as well really *be* my brother. Are you interested in females? No shame, if you're not, but I've really been wondering."

He looked genuinely surprised. "I'm very interested in females. But I've thought...I never detected any interest from you."

"Then I've been hiding it pretty well. I think you're *very* interesting. You have the body of a gymnast and you move like a dancer, who wouldn't be interested? Of course, people do wonder why all you ever take off is your shirt when the rest of us all shower together and toss our clothes off whenever we feel like it. You've seen me naked, and maybe that's the problem. I know I'm no prize."

"Oh, I wouldn't say *that*."

Diana cupped a hand behind one ear. "What? What's that? Did I hear an expression of...of...what?"

Troy was smiling now. "More often than not, women who have been interested in me changed their minds when things came right to the point. It's not just the rejection, I'm not really that pathetic. But it's put me in danger of exposure more than once, so I've learned to be cautious. There are safer options available if I really need an outlet."

"That's true, but those options get pretty lonely. I've been celibate since I came here, Troy, and it's gotten very tedious. I haven't even gotten a quick bang while I'm hunting, because you convinced me that animals were safer. Now maybe you can shuck the sheep on a slow night, but me? The logistics are a little more challenging." Troy burst out laughing.

"I'll have to remember that if I'm ever desperate."

"I'm desperate now. I won't even try to be dignified about it. Are you waiting for me to be forward and jump your bones, is that it? Not a problem." Diana got up, crossed to Troy and deftly sat on his lap, wrapping her legs around his waist. He started to say something and she kissed him, long and hard with her tongue dancing into his mouth, her hands sliding around his shoulders and coiling up through his long hair. He returned the kiss with equal fervor almost immediately.

When they finally broke off, Diana said, "Oh, so *there* you are. There's somebody in there. Hello, sailor."

He smiled, looking a little dazed, pulled her closer and went on kissing her. She was pulling his shirt up and running her hands under it, following the lines of muscle and bone beneath his smooth skin. But when her fingers dropped to his fly, he broke off the kiss and caught her hands with his own.

"Let's not go too fast…it's not like we're in some alley somewhere."

Diana pulled loose from his grip and let her hand slide up the inside of his thigh. She could feel his erection and it seemed carved in stone though the soft denim.

"You don't want me to see your scar." He swallowed. "Come on…I read the police reports. I know what happened to you. I have an imagination, and I'll bet I've exaggerated. I'll show you mine." She pulled off her peasant shirt, which was all she wore above the waist, and Troy's eyes automatically shifted to her breasts. Diana drew her hair back from the right side of her neck. "You see? Thomas cut my throat in one swipe."

His eyes raised to the knotted white scar and he blinked.

"And Thomas' scar was even uglier. He cut his *own* throat."

"Oh, my god…"

"So you can understand why I'm hard to impress."

Troy tentatively leaned forward and touched his mouth to the white scar, then slowly ran his tongue along its length. Diana shivered. He went on to trail his lips and tongue along her collarbones and then down to her nipples, teasing and playing with each one, and she arched her back, bracing her hands on his knees behind her. His beard added a lot of intriguing collateral sensation.

He slowly sat back up, to her disappointment. She opened her eyes and straightened up herself. "Now what are you thinking about?

"You know…I've never had sex with another vampire before. There's simply never been an opportunity. The only other female vampire I've met is Johanna, and she…well. Let's just say that if she initiated it, refusal wouldn't be an option. But it would be all one's life is worth to make a pass at her."

"She sounds scary. I've never had sex with another vampire, either, if that makes you feel better."

"But I thought you and Thomas…"

"Not after I changed. We never even touched each other again." At his bewildered expression, she said, "There are reasons, but I can explain some other time. I've been very curious as to what it would be like, though. We can't hurt each other."

"Well, at least not up to a point."

"We can't hurt each other *accidentally*. We don't have to hold back…I wonder what else will be different?"

"Let's find out."

"Yes, let's." Without unwrapping her legs from his waist, she reached behind his back and pulled off her soft knee-high suede boots one by one, then undid the ties of her embroidered batik skirt and pulled it off over her head. She'd long since abandoned wearing anything underneath. "Do those jeans even *come* off? I won't believe it until I see hard evidence."

This time he didn't grab her wrists, but accommodated her as she unlaced and pulled off his boots, unzipped his fly and skinned his pants off, tossing them inside-out on the floor.

"So this is the scar you've been hiding so carefully all this time." She ran her hand lightly over the thick raised line of hard twisting flesh. "Yep, you can tell that was lethal. But I've seen worse." The erection that had quailed at the topic of scars was already back to half-staff. "Here, let me work on this for you…" Diana couldn't resist. She sucked his penis into her mouth, tongue spiraling around the top of it. It snapped to full attention so fast, she almost bit him by mistake. Troy was laughing—she'd moved so quickly, he was only half on the bed, and was grabbing the edge of the mattress to keep from slipping off.

"Such *enthusiasm!* Oh…oh, god…"

She slowed down a bit to allow him to savor it more, but he came within a few minutes anyway. "You were pulling my hair," she said, licking her lips.

"I'm sorry. You caught me by surprise. I don't usually finish that fast, but… god almighty."

"I hope you don't, and thank you. Now we have to start all over."

They eventually pulled both mattresses onto the floor because they kept almost rolling off the narrow beds. They tried out virtually every form of teasing and penetration they could think of with fingers and tongues; Troy came once more and he brought Diana to climax twice. But somehow, whenever they got close to actually fucking, they mutually veered aside to something else.

Finally, Diana pushed herself up and said, "Come on. We've been dancing on third base for an hour. Let's go for a home run." She used the silly metaphor for a reason: she herself felt a chill of nervousness at the prospect. It worked; Troy chuckled.

"Be my guest."

He shifted to lie flat, and Diana straddled him and guided him inside her too fast for either of them to think about it.

She had no idea what she'd really expected, but what happened amazed her. Something seemed to click into place, a little like the click she had felt that first time with Thomas. But it also felt like the bond she'd had with the coven during their sessions, that sense of being joined not only physically but on levels that transcended the physical. The rush of euphoria was dizzying, and she gasped. Troy obviously felt it, too, so it had nothing to do with being a magician.

"Oh...what...that's..."

"Don't talk."

She'd almost forgotten to move, and the smallest movement created such intense sensations, it was almost overwhelming. She could feel energy passing back and forth between them, almost tactile itself. As they went on, she felt compelled to shove against him harder and harder, and finally he sat up, pushed her onto her back, and rammed into her with a ferocity that he could never have considered inflicting on a human woman. She had to clench her teeth at the near-pain of it, and her fingernails were leaving scores in his shoulders, but it was wonderful. No human man had ever been able to approach this. She climaxed again, in shuddering waves that made her toes clench so hard, it hurt. He needed another minute or so, then they collapsed into a pile of tangled limbs on the mattresses, as limp as their discarded clothes.

Even as they lay quiet and motionless for some time after, they remained somehow interconnected, sharing energy and even emotions. It took some time for them to finally move apart, and then they did so only because they were so over-satiated, they were getting disoriented, and needed to find their own boundaries and ground themselves.

After a long blissful time, Diana said, "Well. Now we know."

It took a moment for Troy to respond. "There are no words to do it justice."

"I know." Diana heaved a deep sigh and turned on her side to face him, head propped on one hand. Her smile was impish. "Let's do it again."

𝕿he following day, it was back to chores, projects and tasks as usual. Until dinner, Troy was working with Ellie setting glass into frames for their hand built greenhouse, while Diana walked a colicky Morningstar so Brigid could work at her wheel. Recalling nostalgically how members of the Order played innocent in public after Beltene, Diana thought she was behaving with perfect decorum. As they were cleaning up after dinner, Brigid passed them and said with a sly smile, "It's about time, you two. I was starting to wonder." She headed for the basement stairs with a heavy load of freshly turned bowls to be fired before Troy and Diana could respond.

"Now that's creepy," Diana said. "How did she *know?* Are we acting different somehow?"

"Oh, probably," Troy said, putting an arm around her shoulders and nuzzling her hair.

"Be careful, I'm holding a baby."

"Yes, and it's very becoming on you."

Diana was amazed to realize that she was blushing.

On Candlemas in February, 1966, all six of them walked out into the back yard through crunching snow, Brigid carrying Morningstar swaddled in masses of blankets. They formed a circle, shivering, and Avani uncapped a small bottle filled with white wine infused with herbs they had grown that summer. None of them drank alcohol; this wine had a more elevated purpose.

"On this sacred day, one year after we dedicated ourselves to this path," Avani said, "we offer thanks for a prosperous season, for this beautiful place, for our lives and for the love we share. We've become a true family." She tipped the bottle and poured the wine into the snow. "Today we christen this homestead Rainbow Stone Junction."

1967

24

little store, named Heart of Light, had opened up on Swansea Road in May of 1967, selling posters, records, incense, Indian muslin dresses and second-hand oddities, and they did very well with Brigid's pottery and handmade clothing. In early November, Troy and Diana took the truck over to the store with a new load of wares, hoping they could extract payment for the last batch without exerting extra influence on the proprietor. The woman who had opened the place styled herself Tinuviel, a name from the fabulously popular fantasy books of J.R.R. Tolkien, and was so stoned most of the time, Diana doubted that vampiric influence could take hold.

They found that Tinuviel apparently had a new boyfriend named Stew, a biker with a hard head for business—which meant, Diana cynically realized, that he was probably a fairly heavy dope dealer. But if Heart of Light was his cover, he had an investment in keeping it out of trouble, and he paid them their commission to date while Tinuviel fussed over the cartons of new items. As Troy and Diana were leaving, several teenage boys entered the shop, one wearing an elaborately tie-dyed peasant shirt of Brigid's design, all of them with hair flowing at least to their collars. They nodded at Troy and Diana. Without comment, Stew led them to a little office at the back of the shop and closed the door.

Out in the parking lot, Diana let out a resigned sigh. "Why do I feel like this place doesn't have much of a future?"

"Hey, it's cool. They're just doing their thing."

A battered convertible was coming up Swansea Road from the center of town at much too high a speed; as it reached the store's parking lot, the driver slammed on the brakes, making the convertible fishtail with a squeal of tires. A young man in the back seat yelled "Fucking hippie faggot!" at Troy and hurled a half-full beer can that sprayed an arc of amber liquid over the road. It bounced off Troy's arm. "Join the Army, you cocksucking druggie freak." The convertible's engine gunned and the car took off in a spray of loose gravel.

"Yeah, I don't see you in uniform," Diana yelled after them, although she knew the car was out of earshot.

"Don't even hassle it, Raksha," Troy said, appearing completely unconcerned.

"We knew things would get worse after the mills were picketed last month, on the same day as the big anti-war march in Washington."

"I know. A lot of mill families have sons in Vietnam. It's divided the town into two factions that hate each other. People who babysat each other's kids aren't even speaking." Cars occasionally screamed by Rainbow Stone Junction hurling trash and epithets, too; she was sure that Heart of Light got a lot of harassment. No wonder Tinuviel had found a biker boyfriend. On the other hand, the Junction definitely had its supporters in town. Mr. Maddox remained a staunch ally, even if it was mostly from self-interest. Diana and Troy made no effort to fence-sit; when not dressed for the garden, they both were walking advertisements for Brigid's handiwork. Troy hadn't trimmed his hair or beard since he arrived, while Diana's hair had narrow braids with bright colored ribbons worked into them and hung to the middle of her back.

"It's the kids that I worry about," Diana said as they turned onto River Road, "little Morningstar and Sirena and Michael. All these straights are so shocked that commune kids see sex and drugs and naked people. I mean, horrors, naked people! But we kids growing up in the Order saw those things all the time, and we turned out just fine. It's the violence and hatred, like those assholes, that's what really hurts kids. I don't want our kids seeing that."

"You can't protect children from life, Raksha. They have to learn how to cope with it. Didn't you tell me that you thought you were a little too sheltered from that side of things?"

"There's a difference between understanding that life is hard for most people, and dodging beer cans and threats." She peered ahead as they approached the house. "Oh, look, what's this—more refugees from the Summer of Love?" A multi-colored VW bug with California plates sat in the driveway, listing slightly to one side although all its balding tires appeared fully inflated.

"At least we're getting a lot fewer of those than we used to."

"Thank the gods. You fascist, you."

The year before, in a spirit of generosity, the Junction had decided to open its doors to strangers who needed a place to stay and a meal. They'd set up some rooms and a bathroom on the east side ground floor as a crash pad, with mattresses and a rack full of clothes people could take or trade. Large pots of lentil or bean soup and loaves of homemade bread were always ready to feed hungry visitors. As word spread among the hippie subculture, more and more people descended on the house. It quickly became obvious that the Junction was attracting two kinds of people: those who wanted to help out and feel like a part of the dream, and the majority, who believed everything in the world was free for the taking and the Junction was just another playground to get stoned, high, and laid.

Young people from town came up to the house constantly to hang out, since rumors that you could get grass, acid, and sex there went around the high school with blinding speed. The Sheridan police made a number of visits, and the Junction members took to keeping their own stash of grass hidden inside a hollowed beam up in the barn loft, with Diana's growing hoard of Owsley acid. Seeing Rainbow Stone Junction written up in the papers for another police raid and more drug busts of visitors infuriated Avani, but none of them wanted to close their doors entirely. Too many of their visitors desperately needed and truly appreciated a safe place to crash.

The labor of tending the expanding gardens remained as grinding and continuous as ever. The Junction's family increased by immigration as well as birth. In early 1966 Cindy and Joey from Hartford drove up for their long-promised visit and stayed to help with the spring planting. They moved in permanently two weeks later, Brigid's prophesied seventh and eighth members. Cindy was promptly rechristened Sorcha, and two extra pairs of hands created an instant and significant easing in everyone's work load. But the visitors sometimes partied late into the night, which was hard on the early-rising gardeners and mothers. Some of the visitors pitched in to help, but most tended to get bored quickly and wander off into the woods to get stoned or drop acid. But it was the strawberry incident that made up the Junction members' minds.

In July of 1967, the Junction's third summer, two wildly painted VW buses full of people roared up to the house. Their dozen occupants, including several dirty and half-dressed children, tumbled inside, running though the building like so many puppies let out of a crowded kennel. Good natured and noisy, on the third day there, they dropped acid in the back yard, stripped off all their clothes and wandered nude through the garden beds. One of the men slipped and fell in the strawberry bed, the one that the Junction members had so carefully planted their first spring. Now in its third year, it was producing a bumper yield, one of their most successful crops that summer. He staggered to his feet dripping with crushed berries and red juice.

"Far out," he said as he tried to rub the berries off his very hairy chest. Two of the women jumped up into the bed and rolled around like horses in wet grass, kicking their legs in the air and coming up smeared with juice, their long hair full of smashed berries. The rest of the group joined them, rolling among the soft sun-warmed leaves, rubbing handfuls of berries onto each other, pulling up whole plants and smearing themselves with dirt and sticky juice. They began sucking strawberry juice off each other, and eventually the strawberry bed was a full-fledged orgy as the whole group fucked and wallowed in the carefully composted soil. By the end of an hour, they all had vicious sunburns, and the thirty-foot-square strawberry bed was a total loss. Not one single plant survived.

No Junction member, hard at work in the farther garden plots or in the house, realized what was happening until it was too late.

The two busloads of people were sent on their way that night, with many hard words on both sides. It was fortunate that Joey was nearly as large as Denny, and that the VW tribe, unlike some groups of roaming hippies, didn't have weapons. Avani stood between the two men and if anything was more daunting than both, making Diana think of a Valkyrie. The Junction members unanimously agreed to implement strict guidelines for guests: no one was allowed to stay more than one night without working in the garden or house for at least four hours per day, visitors had to keep their crash space picked up and sanitary, and no one was allowed inside until they'd given a name and some accounting of themselves. After a difficult transitional period spent turning people away and once, calling the police, the number of visitors reduced sharply and the crazy, anarchic or burned-out types mostly stopped appearing. Word got back to the Junction members that they now had a reputation for being "fascist" and "authoritarian." They all decided they could live with that.

Along with the eight Junction members and two-year-old Morningstar, who had inherited her mother's carrot-curl mop, some six to ten visitors usually sat down for dinner at the long tables and benches Ellie had built. Some of them were teenagers from town, and some were teens from much farther away, footloose wanderers who arrived by thumb. The Junction members asked no questions as long they behaved themselves, knowing that even the local kids often were fleeing homes that were nothing like *The Donna Reed Show*. Tonight fifteen people were eating vegetable stew, bean soup and dense bricks of bread and drinking herb tea with fruit juice. The couple who had arrived in the VW an hour or so earlier had the glassy-eyed look that Diana associated with some combat veterans. They had been on the road for ten days, driving from California.

"The Haight's dead, man," said the young man, who'd been introduced as Scat. "They did a whole fucking funeral, you know, motherfucking big coffin and everything. The death of the hippie. And it's no shit."

"It's really that bad?" Diana said.

"It's awful. It's all gone so bad," Scat's partner Misha said. "The Mafia has taken it all over, everyone's on speed now. We went up to this house we heard of in the mountains, it was all Hell's Angels and dealers. Everyone had guns and they'd get high and go out and shoot up the woods, blow up little squirrels and things. And they just thought it was funny. We left when they shot up a cat."

"Are you fucking with us?" one of the other visitors said, agape.

Misha shook her head emphatically. "There are some good places, but a lot of houses are like that. My best friend got gang raped, and no one cared. She went to the Free Clinic and they told her, don't go to the pigs because these freaks will come after you. So she split, I don't even know where she went."

"You can't go in the cities because the blacks are burning everything down. I had this friend, had a little place in Detroit, he got burned out, and the blacks beat him up so bad he was in the hospital for a week," someone else said.

"You know, it's fucking scary," Scat said. "Everything is going so crazy. It's like something was stirring people up on purpose. They say it's the commies doing it, but I think it's the CIA. It's like some kind of conspiracy is pushing people to get all worked up, and then they just blow. You can't understand what the fuck is going on."

"I know what you mean," Brigid said. "It doesn't make any sense. When did anger and destruction ever solve anything? People need to learn to love each other, and help each other, not fight. There's a war in Vietnam, how does starting wars in the streets help stop that?"

"I don't know, though," Joey said through a mouthful of bread. "You have to fight back, sometimes."

"This is more than fighting back, though," Scat said. "This is like, I don't know, like mind control."

"Aw, man, that's just plain crazy," a visitor said. "It's no mystery why the blacks are rioting, and why people are so fired up. Johnson and the pigs are fucking us over, it's come time for the Establishment to pay its dues. These big corporate fucks, they're going to find out what comes of killing babies and poisoning everyone's food and water. It's all coming down."

Troy leaned closer to Diana. "Are you all right?"

She realized she had been staring blankly down at her bowl of soup without moving ever since Scat had said *pushing people to get all worked up.* "Yes, I'm fine," she said, smiling at Troy. He frowned, obviously unconvinced. They were distracted when Brigid jumped up from the end of the bench to grab hold of Morningstar's head.

"Misha, no, she can't have that…"

"Why not?"

"She can't chew that…" Morningstar finally lost the ferocious battle to keep whatever it was in her mouth, took in a huge breath and let out a full-diaphragmed, outraged howl. "Please don't feed the children if you don't know what's not good for them," Brigid said over the din.

"Hey, don't talk to her like that," Scat said, as five other people jumped into the argument with opinions of Brigid's attitude, Misha's action and what was good for babies. The political debate was over for now.

The Junction now had a flock of chickens—for eggs, not meat—and herding the hens had proven excellent practice for what was involved in getting the visitors through clean-up and bunking down every night. When things were more or less quiet, Diana slipped out the back door. She needed someplace to be by herself and think.

On top of the big boulder, which was now surrounded by garden plots, she lay flat and stared up into the starless gray sky. This was not the first time a visitor had talked like Scat. She wasn't sure how much significance to place on it, because conspiracy theories and paranoia were rampant in America now. She had read and heard plenty of remarks from ordinary, middle-class people opining that outside agitators were driving the war protests, that communists were behind everything from drugs to rock music, that liberals were inflaming blacks to riot in order to push their "agenda." In chaotic times, it made people feel less helpless to imagine that someone, somewhere was controlling what's going on, even if their intentions were evil. This was basic human psychology, so why did she feel an icy stab in the pit of her stomach when she heard visitors in the house talk about it? *Jack, where are you?*

In the past two years she had tried several more times to use large doses of LSD to break through to the network. She'd used up all of Jack's supply, and when Owsley's acid hit the streets and she started hearing about it, she had begun collecting as many doses as she could whenever she had an opportunity to obtain it, several times taking rather large risks. It was indeed high quality LSD, but even a quadruple dose of it did no more for her than Jack's pharmaceutical-grade drug. Another person—a reasonable person, Troy would say—would have concluded long ago that the network simply was gone. But Diana couldn't escape the conviction that it was still there, just out of reach.

She'd worried about April when city after city erupted into violent race riots, wondering how much in the middle of things her former covenmate might be. This summer—ironically, the "Summer of Love" in San Francisco—had been especially brutal. Diana kept remembering April's ongoing obsession with Negro civil rights, and how she'd kept pulling all of them off on tangents in nearly every session. She remembered David saying, after that night at the Golden Vanity, *April sure homes in on anything related to desegregation that she sees. Sometimes I feel like I'm walking a dog that keeps running off after rabbits...* Their network had had a countless number of tendrils touching racial events and incidents. If anyone wanted to be tweaking those, and had access to the network...

"Oh, this is fucking *crazy!*" She spoke aloud as she sat up. Jack had left *because* he'd lost access to the network when they all mutinied, that's what he was so mad at them about, that's what he could never forgive them for. And the blacks had plenty of legitimate complaints and valid reasons for outrage. There was no reason to fantasize some kind of puppeteer influencing them to riot.

She dropped off the boulder. She had work to do. Even with the garden tasks almost finished for the season, the "night shift" had plenty to keep them occupied. Diana was helping Brigid with her clothing and pottery. Her alchemical studies finally had a practical use, as she concocted vivid and unique dyes and pottery glazes, and those took time to process; she monitored the kiln, stitched embroidery and decorations and mixed clay. Close to dawn, she prepared food for breakfast: baking bread or cooking a thick filling oatmeal porridge, chunky with dried fruit, nuts and seeds. When the babies were teething or colicky, Diana walked the floor with them so their exhausted parents could sleep. She had a thousand things to do. This was her family. This was real life.

A few days later, in the late afternoon, Avani came out to the greenhouse where Diana was putting together trays of garlic sprouts to plant in the beds before the ground froze. "Someone is here asking for you." When Diana followed her back to the house, she was amazed to see April standing by the potter's wheel, talking to Brigid. She hadn't changed much in three years; she dressed the same, was a little leaner and looked just a bit older. The only major difference was her hair, now cut to about shoulder-length, and framing her face in flattering curves.

"Gods, April, what are you doing here?"

"I was passing through and I thought I'd stop by and check in with you. I got your address from David." She glanced around. "Is there somewhere we could talk?"

Diana hesitated; at this time of year, privacy indoors was at a premium at Rainbow Stone Junction. But the greenhouse was fairly warm on sunny days. "Come with me. It's good to see you, by the way." Brigid watched them leave with open curiosity.

In the greenhouse, April perched fastidiously on the edge of a large crate. "Seems to be a thriving little concern."

"We're getting there."

April eyed Diana's long hair and flowing skirt with her mouth in a wry twist. "Raksha, huh?"

"You're standing in a glass house, Alice P. Merrill."

"Yeah, yeah. You just look so different, that's all."

"Life is change. But how have things been going with all your civil rights work, April? What have you been doing since Freedom Summer?"

April's lips thinned. "How is it going? They threw me out, that's how it's going."

Diana stared. "They...what? Who did?"

"SNCC. They threw out all the white volunteers and workers. It's all about 'black power' now, they don't want us lowly white folks condescending to them, or some fucked up thing like that." She got up and paced up and down the narrow aisle of the greenhouse, so that Diana had to squeeze into the space between two shelves to avoid being bumped into. "It's that fucking Carmichael, he's nothing but a misogynist, sexist, *racist* prick. Four years, and all the work I did, I got arrested in Mississippi, I got threatened with a beating in Alabama, all the coffee I made and the shit I mimeographed for them, fuck, all the *money* I gave them! I might as well have pissed it all down a sewer. None of it means shit, just because I'm a white girl from Manhattan." She stopped dead and nailed Diana with a glare. "You wouldn't understand. You'd be on their side."

"Oh, fuck you, April. You're just pissed off, don't take it out on me. It sounds like a bum deal, but I don't know the whole story."

"You're fucking right I'm pissed off. Who wouldn't be?"

"Aren't there other groups besides SNCC?"

"Ah, they're all going the same way. Carmichael says white people should be working to change other white people's attitudes and let the blacks take care of themselves. What good will that do? Isn't that what whites have done for the last century, write their plays and books for each other and have their little meetings in drawing rooms, and get all self-righteous, and then if they met a *real* black person they'd run screaming. How can we ever achieve racial equality if the races sit in their own corners and never work together?"

Diana shrugged. "I think you both have a point."

"They talk out of both sides of their mouths, one minute blacks can't do anything to help themselves because The Man keeps them down so hard and the system is rigged. The next minute, they're all, we don't need white people's help because we're strong and powerful and we just need to be left alone. So which is it?"

Diana wasn't sure what to say, and April went back to the crate and sat down with far less caution than the first time. "Well. I guess I just needed to get that out. There aren't too many people I can really talk to these days."

"Not like that, at least. That's okay, I'll wash down the walls after you leave." April gave a little snort. "I'm still not sure why you're here, though." Watching April's face, Diana wondered how many bridges she'd burned behind her over the years. Her family, the New Mexico group, their coven…what did April have left?

Finally, April said, "Well, I'm moving down to D.C., and I just thought, since I was coming back East, I'd look you up. David's in Israel, you know."

"Yes, I know. He's applying for citizenship. I guess he's not coming back. What's in D.C.?"

"The National Organization for Women wants me to work with them. They liked all the articles I was writing back in sixty-three and sixty-four."

"That sounds perfect for you, April. Now there's a group that won't ever throw you out."

"They better not." She hesitated. "I also wondered…if you ever heard from Jack."

"Not one single word. I've been dying to ask *you* that."

April shook her head. "He may as well have dropped off the face of the earth. I haven't heard, David hasn't, I've asked a few of our mutual friends…"

"How about that group in New Mexico?" As April paused uneasily, Diana said, "Did they really banish him, April?" She looked at Diana sharply.

"You're not supposed to know that."

"I realize that, but I do know. Is it true? And what happened?" After a short silence, Diana said quietly, "April. It could be very important."

April looked at her, her brow drawing into a thoughtful frown. "Actually, it was something like what you said happened to you in the Order of the Silver Light. He disagreed with some…protocols, and then he tried to magically violate the group's parameters. This group doesn't give second chances. They booted him out."

"You knew this and you never said anything?"

"It wasn't my business to say anything. Besides, I thought he got a raw deal."

"What was this protocol?"

There was a longer silence. "Oh, fuck it, I suppose it doesn't matter now. Jack may be dead, for all I know. That network thing he had us all building? That was a technique he learned in New Mexico. It's one of that group's signature pieces of magic. But the way it's designed, it can only be performed by a group of people. No one can make a network individually, and no one member of the group can use the network alone. Well, Jack thought that was stupid. He was trying to convince the Elders to develop ways for the network to be divisible, so different people could use it for different reasons."

For a moment, Diana couldn't speak. "You knew this, and you didn't say anything? You knew he was using us to build a network he was going to access alone, and you didn't say anything?"

"Diana, it's impossible! It can't be done! The very idea is a total perversion of the whole concept. The network belongs to a bonded group. It can't be used by one person."

"How can you be sure, April? It seemed to have a life of its own right from the start, remember? How can you be absolutely sure?"

April rolled her eyes. "They're always like that. It's an illusion, like a Ouija Board. Look. Imagine six people, say, each hold one end of a web with six spokes. If even one person lets go and walks away, the whole web is compromised. It just collapses, goes limp. And how could a single person possibly hold it up, all six ends stretched out and tight, all alone? And don't come up with any clever engineering answers because it doesn't work that way. It would be like levitating by pulling on your own shoelaces."

"Okay, I see what you mean. That's a pretty clear visualization."

"If you understand it, you're doing better than Jack. He simply refused to accept how the network functioned, and that's why he was banished. The Elders said he was displaying such a complete lack of true magical understanding, he basically wasn't fit to work with us."

Diana slowly walked to the end of the aisle. "What happens to the network if the group that formed it disbands?"

"It disintegrates, instantly, poof of smoke. It can't exist without the union that formed it."

She turned around to meet April's eyes. "So...you don't think it's possible for our network to still be...floating around out there somewhere—limp or otherwise?"

"No, I don't. When Jack walked out that door, that was the end of it. Anyway, it had been deteriorating for a long time, Diana, you know that. Those networks do that, they don't last forever."

"Did you ever try to access the network alone, or outside of one of our sessions?"

April shrugged. "No, but it wouldn't have occurred to me. I knew it wasn't possible."

Diana considered this. "Well...thank you. This is very enlightening."

"Look—"

"I know. I'll never say a word."

They both started as the greenhouse door opened and Troy looked in. "Oh. Excuse me. Avani said you were out here, Raksha, she didn't say anyone was here with you."

"April, this is Troy Stevenson, my other half here. Troy, April McFarland."

"It's a pleasure," Troy said, extending a hand. When April grasped it, her eyes widened, then narrowed, and then a look of comprehension crossed her face. "Um-hmm...I mean, pleased to meet you, too." She pulled her hand away rather suddenly. "Well. I probably should get going. I'm catching a flight out of Logan Airport and I have some things to do first."

"I'll walk you out," Diana said.

April paused by her rental car to look at the façade of the farmhouse. Her eyes slowly traced the brilliant swirls of color forming endless overlapping scenes, part *Fantasia* and part leftist political art, and more than a little inspired by psychedelic drugs.

"You like our murals? People just grab some paint and come out here when they have some spare time. We've been adding to it for a year now. We've had some very talented visitors, too. See that—" she pointed at the far eastern corner. "He's designing record album covers now."

April just shook her head with a wry smile. "This certainly isn't what I expected, Diana. You're the last person in the world I thought would just drop out like this."

"Drop out?"

"Well, look at you. You've gone native, you're living in a commune, political activism is the farthest thing from your mind. What would you call it? But don't feel bad. You have a lot of company." She got into the car, and then looked back at Diana, who was still speechless. "Oh, by the way. Congratulations on accomplishing your quest." Her mouth quirked into a crooked smile. "You and David. Must be nice to find what you've always wanted."

Diana went back to the greenhouse to finish loading the trays of garlic sprouts on the garden cart. When she got out to the bed where the sprouts were to be planted, Troy was waiting for her.

"She knows."

"It's all right, Troy. April was one of my covenmates. They all knew about me, and they knew I was looking for you. They won't tell anyone."

He relaxed. Sorcha came out to join them, and they set to work putting in the garlic. Diana was silent as she set in sprouts, thinking about what April had said. *What if Jack figured out how to access the network alone…what if that was his plan right from the start…and this thing with SNCC? If Jack wanted April out of that, if he wanted her to be safe, because…* "Oh, stop it. Just *stop* it!" She hadn't intended to speak out loud.

"Stop what?" Sorcha said in confusion, and Diana flinched. She'd been so absorbed, she hadn't realized anyone else was close. She had to apologize and flounder for some excuse.

"Um, okay." Sorcha bent back down to her work, and lowered her voice. "I think you do too much acid, Raksha. You want to think about the kids and everything, right? We need this to be a safe space."

Chastened, Diana didn't reply. She was conscious of Troy, at the far end of the row, listening intently to the women's exchange.

Troy had projects in the barn at night and Diana's were in the house, so they didn't get a chance to talk more until they retired to the barn loft as dawn approached. That area was now a little more comfortable, with posters, a rug, a couple of chairs and a small table, where Diana sat to write a journal entry most nights. They had pushed the two narrow beds together to make a single larger one.

"You've seemed rather preoccupied tonight," Troy said. "Did your friend say something that upset you?"

Diana put down her pen with a short humorless laugh. "You can always tell. She told me that I've dropped out."

"Ouch. She obviously isn't very perceptive."

"I guess from her perspective, I have."

"Because you're not marching in protests and organizing rallies?"

"Not just that. I guess I haven't told you much about what that coven was doing. It was all political, Troy. We were trying to use magic to influence reality. It was our whole lives, almost the only thing we did for eight years."

"And after all that, what do you have to show for it?"

Diana shrugged. "Nothing." He raised a hand as if to say *you see?* and she stiffened. "I know what you're thinking, that it demonstrates that magic is all a delusion. But I've shown you some things, I've proven that there's something to it."

"You shown me some clever tricks."

"They're not tricks, damn it—"

He made a placating gesture. "I only meant, handy little shortcuts, like the way you can break firewood, or make a candle light itself. Certainly, it's impressive on the face of it, but the practical applications seem rather limited. Besides, I'm sure there's a scientific explanation. It's just an area of science that hasn't been fully explored so far."

Diana flung up her hands. "That could be true. But science has certainly led to some terrible abuses. Just go down to the mills and look at the river, if you want evidence for that."

"That's industry, not science. Raksha, all these problems you're so concerned with come from a rejection of science, a rejection of rationality. Society allows scientific knowledge to be exploited by the wrong people. I still think that technology is the key to peace and prosperity on a mass scale. The world isn't big enough for everyone to live in homesteads and survive by subsistence farming. Rainbow Stone Junction is an idyll. There are more than a million people living in the metropolitan Boston area alone. Suppose every one of them wanted to live like we do? Could they?"

She looked down. "Of course not."

"I appreciate what we're doing here, but I think that ultimately, there has to be a happy medium, some meeting point between sane technology and a healthy way of living. Of course—" He laughed. "I don't have any idea what that is."

"When you find out, I'd love to hear more about it." She closed her journal and sat pondering.

"You know, I remember you saying that you were tired of doing magic, that working with the earth was healing. Are you really so unsatisfied with your life here, that your friend's words sting that much?

She turned in the chair to face him. "No. But I don't think that I *have* stopped doing magic, Troy. The night I first met Thomas, he reminded me that the deepest kind of magic, the very heart of it, is to change reality by changing yourself. That's what all the real magical systems teach. I didn't want to believe it. I fought and fought to use magic to change everything besides myself. But now…I think we are doing magic here, all of us. Rainbow Stone Junction is an oasis of sanity in a world that's going mad, and we're setting an example. We're holding things together, we and the places like us—and there will be more, a lot more. I can feel it, we're just the outliers, the pioneers. It's just like Brigid and Avani said on my very first night here. This *is* magic, and I didn't even see it."

He was quiet for a moment, looking back at her soberly. "I could agree with that—as a metaphor, at the very least. Certainly exemplars can be powerful tools to create change. But if you truly feel this way, why aren't you happy? Because you're not, Raksha. I can see it."

"Oh, Troy…I just don't know. Maybe I'll never be happy, maybe it's just impossible for me. But specifically…I've got this feeling that I have unfinished business. Something is just looming out there, and I'm going to have to deal with it somehow. But I can't get a bead on it. I just know that with every passing month, it seems to get stronger, and scarier."

He looked perplexed. "Can you tell me more about what this is?" She shook her head. "Something to do with this group, the one your friend April was in?"

"I can't talk about it, Troy, it would be violating confidence. At least, I can't talk about it yet, without knowing for sure that the group is the problem."

She was starting to feel very sleepy, and even as that thought became conscious, Troy yawned. "Let's get some rest. We can talk about this more."

1970

25

ay 16, 1970 was the day that Diana was finally sure. That was the day that she added the shootings of two students at Jackson State University to the diagram that now covered an entire wall of the barn loft. She had scrounged an end roll of newsprint from the local newspaper and tacked it to the wall in two long strips, six feet high and twenty feet long, then began entering circles with dates. The pattern had been obvious long before, but she could still question her conclusions. Only in the last six months had she tried predicting where new events might happen and making faint penciled circles on the diagram's future side. May 14 was the end of the wall; to go further she would have to turn the corner. But that was the last date she'd projected, and now every one of the circles had been filled with red, blue or black marker. She couldn't argue with a one hundred percent accurate outcome.

She sank down on the edge of the bed, staring numbly at the complex pattern of intersecting and branching lines with its hundreds of circles. She knew what was happening. She could guess, with a bone-chilling horror, what might be going to happen. But she still didn't know how it was happening, and more than anything else, what to do about it.

Oh, gods, Jack…where are you?

She'd started making the diagram after the Democratic National Convention in Chicago in August of 1968. The seemingly endless violence and conflicts of that year, punctuated by the assassinations of Martin Luther King Jr. and Robert Kennedy, kept her in more or less constant stress. But she could still rationalize that the events of 1968 were naturally unfolding from changes that had started years earlier. The civil rights movement was gaining power and momentum, leading to strikes and riots on college campuses in a battle for educational opportunities for young blacks. The race riots that continued to devastate poor urban neighborhoods were a response to the visible and flaunted prosperity enjoyed by the white middle class as the war-driven economy boomed. The anti-war movement was, obviously, a response to the war: never formally declared, disproportionately fought by blue collar and black young men. It was little wonder that hundreds of thousands of citizens, mainstream citizens, were marching and rallying in protest, when anyone with two eyes and a working brain could see that the government was blatantly lying while young American men and Vietnamese civilians were dying.

Things are changing, and that always creates chaos, Diana told herself. *There's nothing unnatural about any of this. The government is creating a lot of the outrage, even the civil rights battles would be more constructive if young black men weren't going to Vietnam and there wasn't such an atmosphere of mendacity and aggression coming from Washington itself. There's no reason to imagine conspiracies, there's no reason to strain for some kind of universal field theory to explain social upheaval. That's just paranoid.* She repeated these things to herself over and over and over.

The assassinations of King and Kennedy both gave her days of nightmares about President Kennedy's death and the sickening guilt she and David, at least, had felt at the suspicion that they were somehow personally responsible. But even then, she forced herself to think: *a war abroad no one wants, arrogant, patronizing leaders who hold their citizens in contempt, an oppressed underclass being told America is a land of opportunity while the white man's boot is on their necks—that's a recipe for revolution. There's nothing unnatural about it. The only surprise is that it's taken so long.*

But then the Democratic National Convention took place, with an army of 11,000 police, 6,000 National Guard and 7,500 United States military troops positioned in the streets of Chicago to face down 10,000 unarmed demonstrators. As American citizens were beaten, tear-gassed and shot at by armed forces, Diana staggered under a sense of *déjà vu*. At last the other side of the pattern had emerged.

Right from the beginning, the coven had noticed it: the push back. The first few times were unexpected and shocking, but they quickly found that it was a common result. Their influence would rebound and create an opposing effect—like the law in physics that for every action there must be an equal and opposite reaction. Sometimes the reaction went in the direction they wanted, but sometimes it was a ricochet, a blow back. This was so common that they were accustomed to seeing a quarter to a third of their attempts create random effects, often intensifying the existing situation rather than changing it. They'd learned to pull away immediately when they saw this happening and leave that tendril alone. But what if they hadn't done that? What if exacerbating a situation had served their purposes as much as altering it?

The school board that wanted to fire the suspected communist teacher. Push...push back. Mr. Klinghoeffer the union buster. Push...push back. Until they'd learned to immediately retreat, the outcomes had been disastrous.

She began mapping all the events that might be pushes, even if they would have happened anyway. *Wasn't that what Jack said about the Presidential Election?*

JFK might be elected anyway, but let's not take the chance? She marked the events that seemed to indicate a push back. Through 1969 and into 1970, more and more of those appeared, until it was roughly twenty-five percent, just about what they'd seen in their sessions. Police charged picket lines at the University of California Berkeley campus: push back. Police forcibly broke up a student occupation of buildings at Harvard: push back. Police and the National Guard fired on the unarmed hippies who created People's Park in Berkeley: push back. California Governor Reagan announced that he would stop campus demonstrations and disruption "if it takes a bloodbath." Push back. Students were shot by the National Guard at Kent State and Jackson State: push back.

Meanwhile, the possibly-pushed events themselves were growing ever more extreme. The demonstrations grew larger and the actions more drastic and out of control. In early 1970 the bombings began. A group called the Weathermen was supposed to be responsible for some of them, and this struck Diana because the Weathermen had splintered off from SDS, the leftist group that had interested Jack. But she didn't believe that Jack had joined SDS, and if he had any connection with the Weathermen and their bombs, she doubted that it was a straightforward one.

She realized she had been sitting on the bed staring bleakly at the diagram for some time, so lost in thought that a troupe of dancers could have tangoed across the room and she wouldn't have blinked. She sighed heavily; there was work to be done. There was always work to be done.

Brigid was at her wheel in the great room. Morningstar was sitting on the floor nearby, playing with some pieces of clay, her hands, face and clothes covered with ochre smears. Brigid and Ellie's new baby, Northwind, was sleeping close by in one of the large wicker baskets that Sorcha made. Brigid was deeply absorbed in turning something tall that wasn't cooperating, and she just nodded absently at Diana's greeting.

Avani was in the kitchen, shaping bread into loaves to rise. Lentil soup steamed on the stove. "It's about time," she said when Diana walked in. Her hair was bound into a single thick braid down her back and she wore a kerchief when she was cooking, which was a great deal of the time. "Those people from Philly split this morning, and they left a mess."

"Doesn't surprise me. They complained a lot about the rules. I'll take care of it. Are all the guys out in the gardens?"

"Yes, they started before sunrise. Lot to get planted." She set the last tray of loaves on the low shelf over the range to rise. "Hey, there's a new shop opening up in that little building where Heart of Light used to be."

"Really? That place has been empty for a year."

"Might have been legal issues."

"Poor Tinuviel. I knew when Stew got busted, she wouldn't be able to keep the place going."

Avani shook her head. "The cops did her a favor. He beat her, all the time. Sweet girl like that...I'll never understand why she would shack up with that kind of creep. If Denny even thought about hitting me, he'd be out the door on his ass."

"Denny would *never* think of hitting you. I think the Junction has the best men on earth, right here under this roof. We've cornered the market."

Avani laughed. "As long as we light a fire under Joey's tail every now and then."

"What is this new store? I hope it's not a bait shop, that's what the building looks like."

"Not any more, they've done a lot of work on it. I guess it's an antiques store. A couple in town are opening it, name is Borrowed and Blue."

"Antiques? Maybe they'll be interested in carrying some of Brigid's stuff."

"I don't know. They look pretty straight. We can ask."

Diana took a bucket, brushes and a bar of the old fashioned handmade laundry soap they used for cleaning instead of corporate chemical products, and headed for the east wing. As she went through the great room, Morningstar climbed to her feet.

"Rassha, will you take me to go see the baby chicks?"

"You have promise not to cry if any of them have died, okay?"

"I won't cry. I only did that when I was little."

"I have to clean up the crash space, then we can go see the baby chicks. No picking them up, though."

"I know, I know." They'd gone no further than the stairs before Morningstar said, as Diana knew she would, "If I help you clean, can I pick one up?"

"We'll see."

"If I clean a whole room by myself, can I pick one up?"

"Maybe."

"If I clean a whole room, and the whole bathroom by myself, can I pick one up?"

"If you do all that, you'll be too tired to pick one up. Oh, wonderful." Diana stopped in the doorway of the first bedroom, wrinkling her nose. "Someone puked in here. They couldn't make it to the bathroom?"

"Ew, stinky, ew, that's so gross!"

"If you clean it up for me, you can pick up two baby chicks. Deal?"

"Nooooooooooo! Ewwwwww!"

"Ha." Diana checked the other two bedrooms, which were merely cluttered, and went to the bathroom to fill the bucket. "Aw, man, the toilet is backed up, too. Did they even tell anyone?"

"Pigs pigs pigs pigs…"

"Okay, Morningstar. Don't say mean things. Can you go pull together all the blankets from the rooms that don't have puke so I can fold them up?" Morningstar ran full tilt down the short hallway, and Diana, sighing heavily, located the plunger and pulled a scarf from her skirt pocket to tie back her hip-length hair.

The bedrooms fortunately were not hard to clean, as each contained only six or seven mattresses, a shelf of folded blankets, and various cushions and throw pillows accumulated from yard sales or curbside freebies. The walls were almost entirely concealed by painted murals, graffiti and a wide assortment of posters, most of them rather tattered. Bright colored lengths of fabric draped the windows: paisley prints, Indian muslins, and in one room, the top of an old patchwork quilt. Avani had posted hand written signs in strategic spots: "no smoking in the house, outside please," "quiet after 9 o'clock, babies sleeping!" "Please ask before taking food out of the kitchen," "NO incense or candles, danger Will Robinson!" (this with a vivid drawing of a house on fire). In the bathroom, a bucket for used toilet paper stood under a sign "Yellow is mellow, brown goes down" aimed at sparing the cranky old septic system. "Use the sunshowers outside unless it's snowing," was only half a joke.

Fortunately, the toilet was not badly clogged, and after it was running and the vomit was cleaned up, Diana washed down the bathroom, brushed out the toilet, swept the bedrooms, folded up the blankets, straightened the mattresses and neatened the rack of used clothes. Morningstar held the dustpan for her, and by laying it out on the floor and going around and around, managed to fold up a blanket entirely on her own.

"Whew. Good job, Morningstar, let's go see the chicks."

"Yayyyyyyy!"

As Diana followed her down the main hall to the back door, she could hear squeals and chatter from the younger children upstairs, where Sorcha was watching them at the moment. *We're going to have to start a school or something.* "Remember, don't let the kitties inside the greenhouse!" Several skinny and very friendly barn cats from the dairy farm had migrated to the Junction. They caught scores of squirrels and mice and other garden-eating varmints, but after the chicks arrived, the cats were usually seen perched by the greenhouse door, listening intently.

The Junction still avoided using electricity as much as possible, but along with the refrigerator, the well and Brigid's kiln, the greenhouse and an old washing machine in the cellar were excepted. Diana smiled at Morningstar cooing at the chicks peeping under their brooder light. They were cute, but after three seasons of raising them Diana saw them mostly as little eating machines that viciously pecked each other to death. She had Morningstar sit crosslegged on the floor and hold a chick in her lap, to the chick's immense dismay.

"Why do you and Troy work all night and sleep in the daytime?" Morningstar asked suddenly as Diana was topping off the chicks' food hopper.

"It's just the way we are. We've always done that."

"Do you have to work at night?"

"We're more comfortable doing that. That's our thing."

"Are you vampires?"

Morningstar's query was so casually inquisitive, exactly like all her other questions, that for a moment it didn't register with Diana. Then she gaped in shock. "What? Morningstar, where did you hear that word? Who's been talking to you about things like that?"

Morningstar huddled down so tightly over her lap, the chick stopped peeping. "Nobody."

"Someone did. Morningstar, that's not a very nice thing to say about a person."

"I'm sorry..."

"Who's been talking to you about scary things like vampires?"

"I don't know."

"Oh, Morningstar...you don't think I'm scary, do you?" Morningstar shook her head. "And you don't think Troy is scary, right?"

"No. I love Troy."

"Then don't say silly things about us. We work at night because it helps your mom and dad and everyone else here at the Junction for us to do that. Now let's switch baby chicks, I think you've worn that one out."

She sat at the great room table watching Morningstar play and sorting out cardboard flats of various sizes for their farm stand, which was due to open Memorial Day weekend. They'd started the stand the previous year, when they were harvesting enough to sell, and direct-to-consumer retail sales were clearly the most profitable option for them. The property extended quite a ways down the road, and they built a three-walled saltbox shed at a spot where there was a wide verge and the ghost of a dirt road leading up into the woods, so there was space for a couple of cars to pull in. The farm stand had been more successful than they expected, especially during sweet corn season. But public attitudes had shifted since 1967, and the Junction members were no longer viewed as quite so freakish. They had become a familiar presence in town, and their views about food and simple living were starting to trend in the mainstream. The first Earth Day a month earlier had been a phenomenal nationwide success. Moreover, as Diana had predicted to Troy, communes were popping up everywhere, especially in Vermont. Some were strongly organized and structured like Rainbow Stone Junction; others were anarchic, do-you-own-thing enclaves which usually ended up attracting burnouts, fugitives, dopers and the cops. One such community, Johnson Pasture in Vermont, had suffered a disastrous fire in April that killed four people. It was this event which led the Junction members—after a week of arguments about supporting an evil corporate monopoly—to agree to have a pay phone installed in the front hall. Up to now, the closest telephone had been the dairy farm.

The proliferation of communes meant that the Junction got fewer visitors; there were other places for the wanderers to go. But those who did show up included an ever increasing percentage of speed-freaks, or meth-heads: shaky, anxious, scrawny addicts of methamphetamine. Speed and heroin had devoured the Haight, and now they had spread throughout the hippie community like a metastacizing cancer.

Tonight the Junction had no visitors, not even townies, but the dinner table was still crowded with eight adults and three children.

"Are we going to have peas and spinach in time to sell for Memorial Day?" Avani asked Denny, who had been out planting seeds with Troy and Joey; Ellie had been working on the stand, since they were adding more display counters.

"We should. But you can make plenty of pies and bread. Those always sell well, and people have picnics and cookouts on Memorial Day weekend."

"Gods, I hope the weather is nice," Diana said.

"Seems to me that we should do another acre of corn," Joey said. "It's always popular at the stand, when we run out, we hear complaints."

Denny shook his head. "We've got all the acreage under cultivation now that this many people can handle. We'd have to bring in more hands, or start using power equipment."

"No power equipment," Brigid said. "Tractors and things, even tillers—commercial farming is one of the most dangerous industries for on-the-job fatalities, and it's all because of the equipment."

"And then you've got gasoline to worry about, too," Ellie said. "It doesn't take much to pollute an aquifer."

"We're probably already screwed on that one," Joey said. "The dairy farm has its own underground tank and pump. You think they've never had a leak?"

"The water has been tested and it's fine," Avani said. "It's an artesian well."

"I don't think power equipment would be that bad," Sorcha said. "If we can make more money that way—how many acres does this place have, Avani?"

"About fifty-two, right now. My dad sold off some of the original acreage, but my grand-uncle donated a lot to the state for the state forest, because he didn't want it developed."

"That was generous of him," Diana said.

"Self-serving, too. I think he and the Maddoxes conspired on it."

"Hey, look, it's not like we're complete purists like some of those people in Maine." Joey grabbed another chunk of bread. "We're not total vegans, we use some electricity, we're not twenty miles down an unpaved road..."

"We're not extremists," Troy said. "That's our strength. Moderation in all things, as they say."

"Depending on your definition of moderate." Avani chuckled.

Denny said, "It's all about our priorities, too. Are we a self-sustaining community, or are we a business?"

"Are they mutually exclusive?" Diana asked.

"Not necessarily," Ellie said. "After all, Brigid and I are kind of running our own sub-business, when you think about it. I do contracting jobs and she markets her crafts. But it all goes to the house."

"Rainbow Stone Junction, Inc? Diversified divisions?" Diana feigned shame at the chorus of groans.

"Some communities have expanded and built more living space," Sorcha said. "We could have a lot more people living here. So much of the land is just growing back up into woods."

Avani shook her head. "Then we run into issues with occupancy, the zoning...we've already got the Board of Health circling over us because of the farm stand. The house can't take more permanent residents right now because of the septic. I don't think we *need* to grow." She chewed thoughtfully. "At least, not this year. Maybe we can talk more in the fall about clearing some acreage, and where another building could go."

"You have to admit," Diana said, "In all these years, we've never had a visitor seriously petition to stay on permanently."

"Too much work," Joey said.

"We haven't made it obvious that we'd take permanent new members, either," Denny said.

"Especially after the strawberry incident," Avani added, her lip curling.

"Still, you'd think...well." Diana stopped as an uncomfortable thought occurred to her. Every visitor, after all, met her and Troy at the communal dinner table. She'd never noticed anyone acting strange around them, but then, she hadn't been watching for it. *Who told Morningstar about vampires—and why?* The house didn't have a TV. Morningstar had never even seen one. But vampire movies were very popular now, along with a fabulously successful soap opera called *Dark Shadows*. Maybe some visitors had been talking about them and Morningstar overheard them.

After dinner and cleaning up, Diana and Troy spent the night doing more planting, since this was a top priority with the last frost date just past. It was far easier than digging, and Diana wouldn't have rejoiced at the prospect of clearing more acreage. But planting in the intensively cultivated raised beds was meticulous and tedious, and they both were weary when they finally retreated from the glow of pre-dawn and the chatter of awakening birds. At least the nights were short, with Solstice only a month away.

"I see your interesting diagram is finished," Troy said. "Can you finally tell me what it's supposed to be?" He couldn't read the dates and notations by the circles; Diana had written them in Gregory's cipher, like her journal. He had been watching her buying newspapers and filling in circles and lines for the past two years, and she knew he had followed the types of reports she picked out. He had kept most of his questions to himself, however, and Diana had not volunteered any explanation.

"It's a sort of timeline."

He raised his eyebrows. "It's certainly a complicated one. It doesn't seem to be linear."

"It's not, at least not in a simple way." It couldn't be. It was the closest representation she could make in two dimensions and a static medium of the network, with its branching tendrils and simultaneous imaging of past, present and future.

"Where does it start?"

She walked over to the first quarter of the diagram. "This is August 25, 1968, the day I started, but I back-filled in some earlier incidents." She moved to the other end and pointed at the last circle, just squeezed into the corner bend of the walls. "And this is Thursday. I'd started projecting when I thought something might happen, and this is the last one I had room for."

"They're all dates?"

"Yes."

"And what is their significance? What does this whole timeline map out?"

Diana swallowed hard. "Chaos."

Troy gave her an odd look, then glanced down at the newspaper on the floor. It was the Lowell *Sun* for May 15, 1970, and the front page displayed a headline, "Two black students killed," datelined Jackson, Mississippi. "August 25, 1968...that was the Democratic National Convention in Chicago?"

"You have a good memory."

He nodded absently, his eyes scanning the wall. "And every one of these circles represents some violent or disruptive incident?"

"Riots, bombings, murders, assassinations, protests...if it made the front page, it's probably on here."

"It's a very impressive array. But what, exactly, are you attempting to document? That the past several years have been violent?"

"You wouldn't agree with that?"

"More violent than Prohibition?"

"The disruption has been more widespread. The gangs during the twenties and thirties were centered in certain cities, and eventually they were brought to justice. This is civilians at war in the streets, everywhere. We've had brawls and beatings right here in this tiny little town."

Troy spread his hands. "Highly emotional times. But most of history has been far more bloodthirsty and violent than the current era. It's only been since the beginning of this century that most people could walk the streets unprotected without risking robbery or worse. Believe it or not, this is an unprecedented time of safety and civility for the human race."

"Be serious, Troy, the Twentieth Century has had two world wars, and how many smaller ones?"

"But put that into perspective. Consider the effects of those wars on a per capita basis. Historically, wars and pestilence have decimated societies. In the first millennium B.C., the victors in a war typically slaughtered every remaining man, woman and child of their opponents. The Black Death had a kill rate of up to sixty percent in fourteenth century Europe. It shattered classes, cultures and the distribution of wealth. Some scholars believe that without it, the modern world would be so different that we wouldn't even recognize it. Taken as a percentage of the total population directly impacted, the wars of the twentieth century have been minor by comparison."

"You must have been a good student at Brown." Diana's tone was a little dry.

"I read. A *lot*."

"Bear in mind that we now have weapons capable of incinerating every square inch of the planet and reducing it to a lifeless piece of rock."

"Does your timeline point to such an apocalypse happening?" He sounded skeptical.

Diana looked soberly back at the diagram. "No. It doesn't have anything to do with that."

"Then what does it mean? Raksha—" he walked over to where she was standing. "Don't you see that this timeline is critically unbalanced? You should also be putting in all the positive changes and beneficial things that have happened over the same range of years. All this upheaval and unrest comes from real change taking place. That's never easy or painless. How many times have I heard you, and our housemates, complain that the news media are biased, and emphasize the negative just to keep people scared? Well, how is what you've done here any different?"

"You're right, I admit it. But I made this diagram to trace the connections between these events, connections that aren't obvious and that other people don't see. All these things are interrelated somehow, they're not just random events. I know that good changes are happening, but I'm not convinced that so much violent reaction to them is inevitable. There's something behind it."

"Something? Or...someone?" She looked away. "You can't talk about it." He sighed heavily.

"It's not that I don't trust you."

"You do realize what you sound like, don't you? We've heard plenty of conspiracy theories and paranoid ideas from our sane visitors, never mind the speed freaks. Everyone wants to find an explanation for what's going on that ties it all together and makes it seem controllable. People fear the unpredictable, that's why fortune tellers never go out of style. But looking for an explanation and believing that you've found it are two different things."

"Oh gods, I wish I could tell you more about the reasons for my beliefs, Troy. I know I can't expect you to understand without more information. But I can't, I just can't."

"Even if you think we're all at risk?"

Remembering how appalled she'd felt with April, Diana felt a pang of guilt. "If there was anything you could do about it, or some way you could protect yourself, I would tell you, and confidentiality be damned. But there isn't. And honestly? You probably wouldn't believe it, which makes telling you somewhat pointless."

The bird song was louder outside, and the light was seeping around the heavy drapes on the windows. Troy yawned. "I'm assuming you don't expect a crisis today."

"Of course not. I just ran out of wall. Let's get some sleep."

As they were getting into bed, Diana suddenly remembered something. The seed planting had involved measuring and recording and marking rows and much discussion and this had slipped her mind. "Troy—I'd better tell you what Morningstar said today."

"Can Morningstar's latest bit of inspired cuteness wait until we get up?" His voice was groggy.

"This is...something else." Apprehensively, she related the short conversation in the greenhouse.

When she finished, there was such a long silence, she thought Troy had fallen asleep. One forearm covered his eyes. "Oh, god," he finally said. "That is not good."

"She's only four and half, she didn't even know what the word meant."

"She knew enough to associate vampires with sleeping all day and being awake at night. You didn't try to find out what else she knows."

"I can't imagine where she could have heard about it."

"Exactly my point. It's the beginning of the end, Raksha."

"What do you mean?"

"This is how it usually starts. It's always the children who notice. They don't rationalize away the unusual like adults do."

"Well...what can we do?"

"There's nothing we can do. But we'd better stay very alert to any shifts in people's view of us. We may have to leave rather suddenly."

26

The planting was finished after a week, and Diana spent the nights before Memorial Day weekend working on preparations for the farm stand's opening. Some visitors arrived on Wednesday, two very young women traveling together and an emaciated, ragged man who bore the unmistakable signs of having been a serious meth-head. He was quiet, but his eyes had the hollow stillness of a building gutted by fire. He swore that he was off the shit, and was just passing through on his way to a community up in Vermont where he said he had friends. Denny and Joey took him aside and made him turn out his pockets and empty the backpack he carried, but found no drugs, and indeed, almost nothing else.

At around 2:00 a.m. on Thursday night, Diana was working in the kitchen making fillings for the farm stand pies when one of the young women poked her head in the door, seeming embarrassed to be bothering anyone.

"Excuse me? That guy? He's totally freaking out."

"What do you mean, freaking out?" Diana said as she hurried through the great room, the young woman trotting to keep up. "Did he try to hurt one of you?"

"No, no, nothing like that, he's just…"

They'd reached the crash space, where the young woman's friend was standing in the doorway of the second bedroom, her arms tightly folded and her shoulders hunched. "He's doing the same thing as when you left."

Diana went to the bedroom door. After a couple of close calls, Denny had outfitted the crash space with 25 watt bulbs in the overhead light fixtures, rather than kerosene lamps like the Junction members used. The ragged man was pacing back and forth in the murky yellowish light, mumbling to himself continuously. He seemed to be holding a conversation with an unseen second party, although he never stopped talking. "Oh, gods," Diana sighed. She'd seen this before. "I wonder if he's sleepwalking."

"Is he okay?"

"Well, no. But I don't know how serious it might get. Did you see him take anything?" They shook their heads.

"We didn't even smoke any grass, honest."

"He was sleeping," the woman who'd come to the kitchen said. "You don't sleep on meth."

"Could you two just hang out here for a couple of minutes more? I need to go get something for him."

Diana went to the kitchen and got a wooden case from a high cabinet, filled with basic first aid supplies and a number of bottles of medical tinctures she had made with alchemical processes. They weren't as potent as the medicaments that Gregory could have cooked up—in his sleep, probably—but they worked. The hard part would be getting these into the ragged man, but the dose was only a few drops, and the tinctures had a sweet flavor.

When she got back to the bedroom, the ragged man had stopped at the far wall and was standing with his hands flat on the wall and his forehead pressed against it. "It's happening it's all happening man it's all coming down stop pushing at me stop pushing at me stop it stop it's coming down man it's coming down man the zombies are out there walking on the wires man can't you see them they're all zombies man it's all coming down..."

"What's he talking about?" the second young woman was shaking.

"Nothing. He's having a psychotic break, he's not even on this planet. Hold this for me." Diana handed the young woman the box. Stepping around the mattresses, she walked over to the ragged man and put her hand on his shoulder. She wanted to see if he would react violently to a touch, which sometimes happened, although far less often than the anti-drug media depicted. But the ragged man didn't respond at all. She took a firm hold of his arm and turned him around. He leaned back against the wall, his eyes partially rolled up, muttering the same ceaseless flow of words in a flat tone.

"Be careful," the first young woman said nervously.

"Don't worry. Look at him, I probably weigh more than he does. Could you bring me the box?"

The ragged man suddenly started to shake and his voice rose. "oh man oh *man* they're hiding the things it's all going to go up it's all going to go *up* they're *zombies* man can't you see it we're going to blow up man..." his arms started flailing and Diana caught his wrists.

"Quiet, they'll hear you," she said to the man in a clear, firm tone. He froze, blinking.

"They'll hear me," he whispered. "Gotta be quiet man they'll hear me *he'll* hear he hears everything he *knows* man..."

Taking advantage of the respite, Diana quickly opened the box which the young woman held and found the sedative tincture and an eyedropper. She carefully dripped a liberal dose of the tincture on the ragged man's cracked and trembling lips. As she'd hoped, he licked his lips by reflex. He hadn't eaten much for dinner and with that and his underweight frame, the medication would probably work quickly.

"What is that?" the young woman asked as Diana replaced the bottle and dropper.

"Oh, a lot of things, but mostly valerian. It'll bring him down, and hopefully make him sleep. Why don't you two go back to your room and try to do the same. I'll stay with him."

The young women seemed all too happy to get away from the ragged man, although they cast guilty looks over their shoulders as they huddled out of the room. The ragged man, still muttering a steady stream of repeated words, swayed, and Diana caught him and half eased, half grappled him down onto the closest mattress. She pulled a blanket over him, as the room was cool and she knew his metabolism was dropping from the sedative. He was starting to shiver.

She sat down on the floor next to him, listening intently to the flow of his words. Regardless of what she'd said to the young women, Diana had been struck by the content of the ragged man's speech. Was he merely delusional and paranoid—or had his drug-raddled brain somehow broken through to another level of reality which he now couldn't comprehend or block off?

"...walking the wires man walking the wires every wire has an end and they're all walking it hiding the shit hiding the shit at the end of wires he's pushing them they're all zombies man he's pushing..."

The ragged man's words repeated over and over, but he was slowing down as the sedative took hold. Diana leaned over him. "Who is pushing them?"

"he is he's pushing them the guy with the wires..." the ragged man wasn't really responding, she realized, simply picking up on an isolated word or two that he heard.

The ragged man's brain was too hyperactive for him to fall completely asleep, although he had quieted and his running speech had reduced to a hoarse murmur. After an hour of listening to the same repeated phrases and asking an occasional fruitless question, Diana had an idea that she couldn't shake off. *Don't do it...it would be insane, this is your home...there are eight people in the house and any one of them could walk in to see what's going on...*but she was losing the argument with her common sense.

She got up and checked the two young women. She'd wondered if they'd be too spooked to sleep, but they were both in deep slumber, their slow heartbeats and breathing and lowered body temperature impossible to fake. They'd seemed completely exhausted when they arrived. Diana went out into the main hallway of the house and listened carefully, but heard nothing against the silence except the distant sounds of sleeping people. Troy was working out in the barn.

She went back into the ragged man's room and knelt down next to him.

Where would be least likely to show… nowhere was foolproof in an environment where casual nudity was the norm. After some thought, she pushed up the sleeve of the ragged man's jacket, which he had never taken off, above his elbow. His arms were so thin, he looked like he'd been liberated from a concentration camp. After pausing to listen carefully once more, Diana leaned down, pressed her mouth against the vein in the ragged man's sour-smelling elbow, and *opened*. The ragged man flinched, said, "whaffuck?" and went silent.

His blood was thin and had an unpleasant taste that Diana knew boded ill for his general health and life expectancy. But she had only one reason for doing this. Concentrating, she enfolded the man's mind mentally and *influenced*, something she'd only done on two previous occasions. As Thomas had warned her, the ability was limited, tricky and far less reliable than straight memory blanking. But the ragged man didn't have much in the way of defenses. *Think clearly and tell me the truth*. She *closed* and sat back up.

The ragged man was breathing heavily, looking straight up at the ceiling. He wasn't talking, and Diana realized he was waiting for a question.

"Who is the guy with the wires?"

There was such a long pause, Diana was about to repeat the question when the ragged man answered. "The guy in the middle of the web. The guy pushing everything."

"What is the guy's name?"

The ragged man closed his eyes, his brow creasing. "My name is Legion, for we are many," he whispered, sounding as though he was quoting. Diana sat back, frustrated. She recognized the phrase as a screen suggestion, designed to pop up automatically and block a memory that might be triggered by association or a question.

"What are the zombies?"

"They all do what he says. Hiding things for him. Thousands and thousands of them."

"What are they hiding?"

"Don't know, man, but it's all coming down. He talks to us in our sleep, man, we're all stuck in the web."

"Who is he?"

"He's the guy in the web, the guy who's bringing it all down."

Diana sighed. "Did you hide anything?"

"I'm no zombie, I pushed back at him, I got away. But he's following me, man. I can't get loose." The ragged man was starting to shake. Tears oozed from his tightly clenched eyelids. "Don't make me look at it anymore, I can't look at it. It's everywhere, it's touching everything, and they're all turning into zombies. We're going to blow up, it's all coming down…"

231

This was obviously as much as she was going to get. "Okay. It's all right. You can sleep now. I'll stay here with you and keep him away." To her mild astonishment, the ragged man sighed deeply and fell asleep. She pulled his sleeve back down and sat by him until dawn, partly from guilt and partly because his breathing was so shallow, she worried that the sedative and slight blood loss might be too much for him. *I wonder who he is,* she thought. *Did he meet Jack in person? Did resisting fry his brain, not drugs? Or is this all a complete hallucination and I'm just interpreting it according to my own obsession?* There was no way to find out for sure.

The two young women were awakened by the early bird song. They packed their knapsacks and slipped out the front door before anyone else in the house was up, saying nothing to Diana although they glanced furtively in at her as they passed the bedroom doorway. *Now I'll have to explain that to Avani, as well as why those pie fillings aren't finished,* Diana thought. But no one could say it was her fault. Everyone could see that the ragged man was a walking breakdown when he got here.

The ragged man slept most of the day, and was contrite when told what a bad night he'd given Diana. "I'm sorry, man, I'm just wasted, I keep having these blackouts." He kept rubbing the inside of his elbow unconsciously, but didn't push up the sleeve to find out why it was sore, to Diana's relief. She didn't want Troy to see the mark—they had agreed years ago not to allow their vampiric needs to invade their safe haven at the Junction, and never to drink from visitors no matter how hungry they became. As thin as he was, the ragged man voluntarily left before dinner, asking Denny if he could have a lift out to Route 24 where he could thumb for rides north. Avani packed some food for his empty knapsack, and Diana slipped a ten dollar bill in with it, hoping that it wouldn't be spent on meth.

"Do you think he'll make it to Vermont?" she asked Avani.

"God knows. I certainly hope so." She folded her arms, her brow furrowed. "Maybe we should have bought him a bus ticket."

27

Memorial Day weekend was cool and damp, but the farm stand did well. Their customers from last year had been waiting for it eagerly, seeing its opening as a harbinger of summer. The peas and spinach sold out on Saturday, and all the baked goods sold. Most of the customers asked what they had planted for sale later on. The Junction had grown a new hybrid sweet corn last summer which had been a smash hit and everyone wanted it. It seemed like a glowing omen for the coming season.

Several weeks later, Diana sat at the table in the barn loft to open some mail that had come to the house for her. It had been a long night tending the seeded garden beds, but the bigger job, setting in plants that had been started in the greenhouse, had begun right after Memorial Day and was all finished. She didn't get much mail; she hadn't given this address to many people. But she received a monthly bank statement, which was quite complicated, since she had multiple accounts. With dawn approaching, she was already sleepy, and it took a moment for one of the account balances to register with her. *Wait a minute... that's not right.* The cash account she used for most of her general activity seemed much too low—about twenty thousand dollars too low. *What the fuck?*

She searched her memory for anything she might have purchased or funded and forgotten about, but there had been nothing that large. She shuffled through the pages, searching for the transaction details. There it was: a wire transfer, to a numbered account with no other identification, which she didn't recognize. She stared down at the paper, feeling cold. It wasn't that losing the money was a hardship for her, although that amount did make a considerable dent. The real issue was where it had gone. Stephen no longer had access to her accounts, and her parents never had. Neither had Jack...but he'd had plenty of opportunity to get her bank information. They'd lived together, and he'd picked up the mail. But if he'd done that, why hadn't he used the information before now?

Or had he? She didn't go through her statements line by line every month; she couldn't be bothered as long as the balance seemed right. *Where is David when I need him? Gods, he'd be lecturing me a blue streak.* She got the metal strongbox with her records and took out all the bank statements from the past four years.

Troy came in while she was in the middle of poring through them, making notes on the blank back of one sheet.

"What on earth is going on? Have you discovered a discrepancy in your accounts?"

"Just a small one. I seem to be missing around thirty thousand dollars." That was the tally so far. She'd found transfers, checks made out to cash, and withdrawals, month after month, all of them small and unobtrusive, none of them traceable from here. She'd never asked for her cancelled checks to be returned, it hadn't seemed worth the nuisance. Now she was kicking herself. *But Jack had known that...*

"That's not a discrepancy, that's a felony." Troy came over to stare down at the statements. "Are you sure?"

"I am now. Someone's been skimming my account all along. They just got greedy and pulled a big chunk. I don't know why, it sure blew their cover."

"Maybe they suspected they were about to get caught."

"Or they decided they never would and got cocky." *Or...they needed a large amount for something. But what?* "Well, there goes my beauty sleep. I've got to get into Boston and see my bankers, today. I'll have to change all these accounts and lock them down."

"And report a major theft."

"The bank will take care of that. They'll be mortified." Her bankers were practically family, Diana's parents and grandparents had banked with them. "Damn...how am I going to get there? I can't go dematerialized in daylight, and Denny needs the truck. Oh, fuck it. I'll pay a cab. The local guy can use a big fare."

She packed the bank statements and other little-used paperwork, like her ID, into a knapsack and started down the stairs to call the cab from the payphone in the hall.

"Wait, minute, shoes."

"Oh..."

"Do you think you might want to put on underwear, to meet with your banker?" All Troy got in response was an impatient dismissive wave as Diana went down the loft steps two at a time, and he grinned.

𝔒**he cab driver balked** at taking the fare; hippies often were refused service, unfortunately for good reason, although the hard-core freeloaders were the minority. Diana gave him fifty dollars up front, which soothed his suspicions. She'd been to Boston a couple of times a year to deal with business since moving into the Junction, as well as checking on the property up in Maine, but she'd been able to plan those trips in advance.

Her banker saw her promptly, and unlike the goggle-eyed tellers, kept his opinions of her appearance to himself. The Chilton family had always been Bohemian eccentrics, although never as way out as Diana's present style, and he'd seen her in recent years, anyway. He was far more impressed by what she had to tell him. He scolded her sternly for not paying better attention to her statements, but he was frankly appalled at the latest wire transfer.

"How could you let this happen? That's what I want to know."

"Miss Chilton—you've been traveling for years, and your parents live in Europe. If someone has all the necessary information to authorize a transfer, we have no way of knowing that it's bogus. You've taken out large amounts on numerous occasions." That was perfectly true: buying the house in Lexington was only one example.

"Can any of this be traced? I'm not saying recovered, I understand that. I just want to know if you can determine where the money went—I mean geographically. It's very important."

"We'll initiate a full inquiry today, and we'll do our utmost to track down all of these transfers. It may take months to get results, however."

"Start with the big one, and work your way back."

"Do you think you know who might have done this?"

She hesitated. "I have an idea, but it's someone I haven't seen since nineteen sixty-three, and he could be anywhere in the world. That's why I want to know where that money went."

"We want to know, too. But it sounds like he's very good at covering his tracks."

"Oh, he is."

All of her accounts had already been changed and restricted, which meant a lot of paperwork, and she'd have to talk to the family attorney about the trust and the various funds and investments. It was all a mare's nest beyond belief, and Diana had been cursing Jack mentally for hours. *Of course, I don't know that it's him, there could be some loose cannon out there...but I can't imagine April, or David, or Troy doing something like this, no matter what Troy was up to in the Roaring Twenties. He's as well off now as I am, and so is April. But Jack...this is exactly the kind of thing he could justify to himself. The second I met him at Beltene, he was crashing in my hotel room on the sly! Gods, I am such an ass!*

But all her fulminations paled before the one overriding question in her mind: *what does Jack need that money for?*

It was late in the day by the time she'd finished with the bank and the attorney, who very luckily had been available. She gave them the number for the pay phone at the Junction, which would be answered if anyone heard it ring. She called and made an appointment for one last stop.

If the banker had kept a poker face when Diana walked into his office, Brad's reaction was gobsmacked enough for both of them. The last time he'd seen her, she'd had beatnik black tights and a short gamine haircut. "Oh, my *god*. You're not living on a commune and taking LSD, are you?"

"Yes to the first, plead the fifth on the second." She plumped down in his office chair. "I know it's been a long time. But I found what I was looking for—"

"You *did?*"

"—and I have you to thank for that, at least in part, so…thanks."

"Well, I mean…you're welcome, and that's terrific. I'd do the same for any paying customer, after all."

"And I certainly paid you a lot. Do you have any time on your schedule for something new?" Brad's eyes looked a bit wistful. His office did not have an aura of prosperity, and she guessed that business was no better than it had been in the 1950s. The last seven years had not been kind to him; he'd gained twenty pounds and was balding, although he still wore the same black-rimmed glasses.

"Is it more weird stuff? You know, I've kept on putting some things aside for you, even though you asked me to suspend your search. They'd just pop up, and I thought maybe I'd see you and get a chance to pass them on."

"Thank you, that was amazingly thoughtful of you. I'll take it. But no, this is something totally different."

"As long as it's not trying to track down runaway kids. That's most of my business these days, and either they turn up dead or they look like you and are strung out on drugs. It's depressing."

"I know. We get those runaways passing through all the time. This is just news tracking, Brad, but I want you to really dig deep. I want to know what's not getting reported or published, even if it's trivial."

"News about what, specifically?"

She sat back looking at him soberly. "Bombs. Explosions."

"You mean—domestic terrorism incidents, like the Weather Underground?"

"Exactly. But I want the stuff that's off the radar. If someone reports a firecracker in their mailbox, I want to know about that. But also, anything that's being kept quiet for, as they say, national security reasons."

Brad frowned. "Could be tricky. That's getting into federal territory."

"Beyond your capabilities?"

He sat up straighter. "No, no, I don't mean that. I'll just have to pull more strings. Could be…" he cleared his throat delicately. "a little expensive."

"Just bill me."

"All right." He smiled faintly, shaking his head. "A commune, really? Up in Vermont?"

"No, down by Fall River. We raise organic vegetables. I'll give you the address and phone number…the phone, you might have to try a few times."

The pile of "weird stuff" Brad had collected was so large, it didn't fit in the small knapsack Diana had brought. He rummaged around and found a large cardboard expanding file holder so she could carry it all.

"I'll get back to you next week, and if you've found anything especially interesting, I may come up here to get it. If you can trust it in the mail, just mail it. If you find something *really* exciting, call me. And here's a deposit, in case you need mad money to get started."

He accepted the bills with the stunned look of a sweepstakes winner. "Will do."

Ｔroy was curious about the "weird" reports. Diana had related how she'd used those reports to try and find clues about vampire activity without letting Brad know exactly what she was looking for. She skimmed through some of them, but she didn't need them now that she'd found what she'd been seeking. Troy, however, seemed to be looking for something else. It took both of them a while to get very far because there was seven years of material and it varied a great deal.

June passed much as it had every year. The garden work got a little heavier each summer even without clearing more acreage. The farm stand sold asparagus, strawberries (replanted after the tragic demise of the first bed), spinach, peas, lettuces, herbs, baked goods and Brigid's pottery, and Denny started to talk about expanding the parking area to either side of the shed. Avani worried about customers who parked on the other side of the road and crossed the tarmac, especially with their children. Since River was not a through road, the main traffic danger was from other customers of the farm stand, but there had been some close calls.

Diana staffed the farm stand in the afternoons after she got up, and they all took turns. She'd stitch on clothing details for Brigid's designs, and Brigid was also teaching Diana to knit, since she was the only female in the house who'd never learned. Brigid and Sorcha wanted to branch out into hand knitted wares, with homespun, naturally dyed wool, to sell during the winter months. Diana sometimes recalled her joke about "diversified divisions" with some irony now, because it was becoming less funny. The more they "diversified," the more work there was to do, and it seemed as though something had to give. The household now had two babies and three children under the age of five.

By Fourth of July weekend, the sweet corn was coming in, along with the first squash, tomatoes and cucumbers. Denny had put in raspberry canes two years ago and those were bearing for the first time. In the midst of all this, Diana got a packet of reports from Brad with a note: "Come up and see me when you get a chance." This meant he had something more that he didn't want to entrust to the mail. Fourth of July was a big picnic and cookout holiday, so it was several days before Diana could make excuses to get away for a trip up to Boston.

"What have you got for me?"

Brad handed her a folder. "It's a number of incidents, but they all follow a pattern. The reason I didn't want to mail them is that they're all being investigated by the FBI, but on the face of it, you can't understand why. They must have some reason for looking into them."

Diana looked through the pages. An empty house on the outskirts of Dallas had been reduced to rubble in a blast that mystified firefighters. It was finally attributed to a gas explosion, but the gas company insisted there was no service to the building. A old warehouse in Illinois imploded at high noon before twenty witnesses who said it was like those controlled demolitions on TV. The building collapsed into itself, even though it was completely empty. No trace of explosive materials could be found. An isolated empty farm house in Oklahoma was found completely demolished two days after a line of severe storms had passed through. Authorities concluded that a tornado must have hit it during the storms, but there was no evidence of a cyclone anywhere else. There were a dozen more similar events, from virtually every corner of the United States. They all had four things in common: the buildings involved were vacant; they were completely demolished, literally smashed to bits; no explanation could be found that seemed to fit the facts, including any known conventional explosives; and the FBI was investigating every case. It was that last detail that was the most mystifying.

"I don't understand," Diana said finally. "Why is the FBI looking into these, when they appear to be accidents or natural disasters? What do they know that we don't?"

Brad just raised his hands in a shrug. "I have no idea, and the only way to find out is to kidnap and interrogate an FBI agent. I don't have any inside contacts in the Bureau. But I'll tell you what I thought when I read these."

"What?"

"I thought, it almost sounds like a lot of dry runs. As if someone was testing out some new kind of weapon—maybe testing how to control the timing and method of detonation, and seeing what kind of damage it does to different types of structures. No one's been hurt so far, but…something this destructive in a big, busy building? It would be indescribable."

Diana's mouth was dry, and she swallowed hard. "You're right, that's exactly what it looks like. Maybe that's why the FBI is trying to figure it out."

"Maybe they've gotten threats or communications from some new terrorist group. They don't want the public to panic, so they're keeping it all classified."

Diana was silent for a minute. Then she put the folder in her knapsack and got up. "Thanks, Brad. This is exactly what I'm looking for. Keep 'em coming."

He gave her a little half-salute. She turned at the door and forced a smile. "Next time, I'll bring you some tomatoes. In three weeks, we're going to have trouble finding the house."

By the end of July, Brad collected another set of incidents like the first, with only one variation: all of these buildings were larger, and six of them were in cities. But the demolished buildings were in neighborhoods devastated by race riots in earlier years, so the inexplicable explosions, or implosions, still had not resulted in any casualties. It seemed only a matter of time before at least an unintentional death resulted from one of them, however. None of the incidents was reported in the news, which in the case of the city buildings, was just plain bizarre. It frightened Diana in a whole different way to realize that the government could prevent a newspaper from reporting on a disappearing building in the middle of a city, as though it had never happened.

But after July, Brad found no more events, and he had no idea whether they were now being covered up even more securely, or whether they had just stopped. Maybe the "test phase" was over.

"I thought of something else, too," Brad said, after Diana had talked to him about her discomfort with the suppression of the events from the news. "This might be something that our government is doing, some kind of top-secret weapons tests. That would explain the lack of news reporting. The FBI could be keeping tabs to spread disinformation and make sure no one else starts sniffing around and asking awkward questions."

"That does make sense. If it's true, though, we could get into some pretty hot water for collecting these reports."

"Well, they won't hear it from me. Anyway, I'm not handing you anything stamped Top Secret or Eyes Only. Just don't pass that stuff around."

Diana left Brad's office pondering just how concerned she must be, if the idea of secret government weapons tests in the heart of American cities actually made her feel relieved. Too bad she couldn't really believe it, because that left her with only the alternative.

In the meantime, Diana's bank notified her that they had some information from their investigation, and once again she had to clear a day. But the Junction had gotten some unexpected help after the Fourth. They now had such a good reputation in town for their industry and integrity that a troop of Girl Scouts asked to volunteer to help in the gardens in order to earn a badge. After considerable discussion, the Junction members agreed that assistance in harvesting, cleaning and packing crops was too desperately needed to reject. A chance to educate middle-class high school students about organic gardening and heirloom seeds also excited Denny and Avani. "It's the next generation," Avani said. "We're finally starting to have an impact."

"As long as we all remember to keep our clothes on while the girls are here," Diana said. "No more communal lunchtime showers to cool off."

"I'll hang some tarps around the sunshower stall." Troy looked very amused.

Diana's banker was completely over any surprise at her present lifestyle and got right to business. "We were able to track where the checks were cashed, and most of the small transfers. The large one, however, went to an offshore bank in the Caymans. We couldn't get any further with it. The FBI tells us that usually, money that's moved offshore is transferred back to the U.S. and converted to cash, which is completely untraceable. Apparently it's a common tactic used by drug dealers and organized crime." He gave Diana a look that said, *just what have you gotten yourself mixed up in?* which she chose to ignore.

"You said the FBI?"

"With a sum this large, and the offshore bank, the police contacted them for assistance, yes. But they haven't turned up anything." He handed Diana some papers. "Here are the locations of the smaller transfers, if it means anything to you."

Diana could understand his caveat. The money had been accessed all over the country in a seemingly random pattern. *Well, what else would Gregory's best friend be, but as brilliant as he is? If only I had half the brains.* "It doesn't, but thanks. I'll study it some more."

"As far as this Jack Garrett, whose name you gave us—not a trace of him has turned up, in connection with any of these transactions or otherwise. But the police will keep on looking."

28

One day in mid-September, Diana and Troy were sleeping after a long night harvesting late corn and clearing some of the beds that were done producing for the year. Avani came up to the barn loft at 11:00 a.m. to awaken Diana. This was a rarity; the other Junction members almost never visited the barn loft, respecting their housemates' odd schedule. Startled, Diana jolted up in bed when Avani shook her shoulder.

"What...what's wrong?" Next to her, Troy half sat up, blinking. Avani's expression communicated something very serious, and Diana's first thought was that there had been a fire or a bad accident.

"There are some FBI agents here. They want to talk to you."

"What? Just to me?"

"Yes. They've asked for a private place to interview you. Do you want them to come up here?"

Diana looked at the timeline diagram, which now continued on the back wall, and imagined what the FBI would make of it. "No. No, I'll come over to the house. Is there somewhere…"

"You can use Brigid and Ellie's room. They want someplace with a table and chairs, and an electrical outlet."

Diana glanced at Troy, and he nodded once. He'd find someplace where he could overhear the interview with his enhanced senses. They both got out of bed hastily and pulled on some clothes. Avani was peering at the diagram in the dim light that filtered through the curtains, looking puzzled, but she didn't say anything about it.

In the house, two conservatively groomed men wearing suits and ties displayed badges and introduced themselves as Agents John McMasters and Douglas Whiting. Agent Whiting carried a large leather case.

"Diana Chilton?"

"Yes. What is this about?"

"We'd just like to ask you a few questions. With your consent, the interview will be recorded."

Diana floundered mentally. Should she request an attorney? Was she in trouble? Would refusing be an admission of guilt? Guilty of what? She decided not to delay the inevitable. "Sure. We can use a room upstairs."

She led them to Brigid and Ellie's large bedroom, which was a complete mess of Morningstar's toys, the baby's crib, clothes, and Brigid's projects. The agents showed no curiosity or interest in the room at all. Diana pulled chairs up to the table, and Agent Whiting opened his case and took some time setting up a recording device of a kind that Diana had never seen before. She assumed it must be the latest thing, if the feds were using it. The agent set a microphone in front of Diana's chair. Agent McMasters, meanwhile, removed a thick file from the case and opened it. The only identification on its tab was a number.

"Speak into the microphone and answer all questions briefly and truthfully," Agent McMasters said. "Are you ready to begin?"

Diana swallowed hard and wished that her mind wasn't so foggy. The light in the room hurt her eyes. She reminded herself to try and show no reaction to anything and to say as little as possible. "Go ahead." Agent Whiting turned on the recorder, which whirred softly.

"Officer 3645 interviewing Diana Chilton, September 16, 1970. Officer 6237 in attendance," Agent McMasters spoke into the microphone. He looked up at Diana. "Do you know a man using the name Carlos Gutierrez?"

Diana thought for a moment, bewildered. She had met so many people during the months she'd spent on the roads, but she couldn't recall this name at all. "No."

"Have you ever heard that name?"

"No."

"Do you know a man using the name Jimmy Marston?"

"No."

"Have you ever heard that name?"

"No."

The same set of questions were repeated for the names Darren McClure, Evan Hannaford and Tom Dunstable. Each time Diana thought hard and gave the same replies, growing increasingly bewildered.

Then Agent McMasters asked, "Do you know a man named Jackson Carl Garrett?" Diana froze. The recorder whirred, and Agent McMasters watched her impassively, but she could see that her reaction had been noted. His pupils had dilated slightly. Agent Whiting, who was monitoring the recorder, glanced up.

"Yes," she finally said. If she'd been mortal, her heart would have been pounding; as it was, she felt a bit dizzy. *Oh gods, Jack, what have you done?* Her overwhelming fear was that Jack had been caught, or had said or done something to incriminate her, and she didn't have a clue what was going on.

"When did you last see Mr. Garrett?"

At least that was an easy one. "November 24, 1963."

"Where did you see him at that time?"

"A house in Lexington, Massachusetts."

"You lived with him there?"

Oh, damn. "Yes. My last view of him was his back. He packed his bag and stomped off. I haven't heard a single word from or about him since that day."

"You have had no contact with him in seven years?"

Diana felt a cold lump drop in her stomach at the words *seven years.* "No word from him, no news of him, no sightings, not even indirectly from other people. He might as well have walked through a door into the Twilight Zone."

"To your knowledge, was Mr. Garrett ever a member of the Communist Party?"

"He said he was, in the nineteen-fifties for a short time. I wasn't in touch with him then."

"But you'd known him since childhood."

Diana wondered what they'd dug up about her and Jack, and who they'd talked to. "We were...educated together as teens." They probably knew that neither she nor Jack went to public school. "Jack went out West in nineteen forty-eight and I stayed in Boston. I had no contact with him at all until he came back here in nineteen fifty-five."

"To your knowledge, was Mr. Garrett ever a member of or involved with Students for a Democratic Society?"

"Not to my knowledge. He went to one of their rallies in Boston and read some of their literature, but he never seemed interested in pursuing it. He was a lot older than most of that group, and he wasn't a student." *You're talking too much,* she lectured herself, but her suspense was reaching critical levels.

"To your knowledge, was Mr. Garrett ever a member of or involved with the group known as the Weathermen or the Weather Underground?"

"Not to my knowledge."

"Did Mr. Garrett ever talk favorably about acts of domestic terrorism?"

Diana swallowed, recalling some of the things Jack had said in their meetings, especially during the Klinghoeffer project. But that had only been about individuals. "I never heard him speak favorably about violent acts."

"Did Mr. Garrett ever talk to you about explosives or incendiary devices?"

"No, he did not."

"Mr. Garrett was in the military, wasn't he?"

"He was in the Navy during World War II. You'll have to talk to them about his service record. He never discussed it with me."

"Did Mr. Garrett ever talk about handling explosives or munitions during his military service?"

"Not to me. He was a sailor, he wasn't in the Army or Marines. I don't know whether he handled munitions at all. He did say—" she broke off, kicking herself.

"What did he say?"

"He mentioned once that he was pretty safe during the war, he didn't see much combat, and he wasn't complaining about that. He thought he was lucky."

Agent McMasters turned over some papers in the file. "You reported that Mr. Garrett had accessed your bank account?"

"I don't know that it was Mr. Garrett. He's on my short list of people who could have gotten my bank information."

"Did Mr. Garrett have authorized access to any of your financial resources at any time?"

"Never. No one did, as far as I knew."

"Did you ever discuss financing Mr. Garrett or supplying him with resources or support for any reason?"

Diana was starting to guess where this was going. *Does the FBI think I'm funding domestic terrorism? That will land me in deep shit...* "I did not. And if Mr. Garrett is ever apprehended, I intend to have him prosecuted."

"Do you have any knowledge of Mr. Garrett's present whereabouts?"

"No. None whatsoever." *And he's damned lucky I don't,* she would normally have added, but she wasn't about to say anything into the microphone that could be construed as a threat, even jokingly.

There was a pause as Agent McMasters looked at a couple more papers in the file. "That's all for today." Agent Whiting turned off the recorder and began to pack it back into the case, and Diana let out a long noiseless sigh.

"Can I know what all of this is about? Besides the obvious—the bank told me that the missing money from my account was reported to the FBI."

"It's an ongoing investigation, Miss Chilton. I can't say any more than that right now." He took out a card case and handed her a card. "If you hear from Mr. Garrett, or anything about him, please give me a call."

"What's he's supposed to have done?"

"That's what we're trying to find out. Thank you for your cooperation."

Troy stayed well out of sight until the agents' sedan had completely disappeared down River Road. Diana found herself wildly wondering whether the agents had placed a bug in the house, but she didn't think they'd ever been left alone. When she and Avani had entered the great room, Brigid, Ellie and Sorcha were all there, and from their attention level the agents might as well have been holding them at gunpoint.

Those three housemates were all sitting at the long table, and Avani came out of the kitchen.

"What was that all about, Raksha?"

"I'm sorry. There's nothing for any of you to be alarmed about. Before I came here, I had a friend who has apparently gotten himself into some pretty deep shit. They wanted to ask me some questions about him. I couldn't tell them much." She held up Agent McMaster's card. "They want me to call them if I hear anything, but I doubt that will happen. We definitely went our separate ways, years ago."

"God." Brigid's hand was pressed against her chest. "We were freaking *out* down here, Raksha. The FBI has been raiding communes. We thought we were all going to be lined up against the walls, the house would be searched, DSS would come for the kids..."

"Good gods, Brigid, get hold of yourself. They wouldn't have asked for me and stood around waiting patiently if that was the scene."

"They are raiding communes, though," Ellie said.

Troy had come in and walked over to Diana. "Not communes like this one. But some of the looser places like Johnson Pasture are easy hideouts for fugitives and drug dealers, and that's why they're targeted."

"We don't have anything to hide," Diana said. "It's all right, really." She glanced at Troy. "If you don't mind, I'd like to catch a couple more hours sleep. We were working until six a.m." Between having been roused from deep slumber, and decompressing after the suspense of the interview, she was about to collapse onto the floor.

Back in the barn loft, Troy said, "I heard it all. Is Jack somehow connected with this timeline you're mapping out?"

Diana sank down on the bed. "I don't want to believe it. But I think he is."

"You think he's planning some kind of criminal act? Or working with people who are?"

"Obviously, I'm not the only one who thinks so." She put her hands over her face. "Gods, I never dreamed that all this would affect Rainbow Stone Junction. I didn't think the FBI would come here to question me. Am I dragging everyone here into this mess?"

"This does not improve our situation here, Raksha."

"I know." She stared bleakly at the diagram. "I've got to do something. I've got to do something...drastic."

"Such as what?"

"I'm still thinking about it."

29

wo days later, the pay phone rang during dinner and Diana, who had finished the small amount she ate, answered the phone so the others could continue their meal.

"Diana? It's April."

"How are you?"

"About ready to murder someone, that's how I am."

"Same as last time I saw you, then. Did the FBI interview you?"

"You, too?"

"They came here on Wednesday. My housemates are still freaked."

"It turns out that Jack has been skimming money from my bank accounts! I hadn't even noticed until they asked me about it. Forty fucking thousand dollars he's gotten away with! That son of a *bitch!* I can't *believe* it! I *trusted* him!"

"He screwed you for forty? He only got thirty out of me."

"That fucking *prick!* You wouldn't believe what I've had to go through to change all my accounts. And what is all this shit about domestic terrorism, Diana? What the fuck has Jack gotten himself into? Is he going to bring all of us down with him?"

"If you mean, our former coven, I don't think so, April. They didn't ask me for any details about that. They were more interested in what I know about Jack now. And I don't know shit."

"Me, neither. God, if I get my hands on him..."

"Careful. This is an open line." She spoke humorously, but April immediately sobered. Years with SNCC and now with the women's movement had made her cagier than she used to be. "April...I actually have something entirely different I need to talk to you about. It's something that has to be discussed in person. Could I come down to D.C. and meet with you?"

"It's that important?"

"It's extremely important."

"Oh. Well, if you can wait a week, I'll save you some trouble. I'm coming up to a conference at Smith College the weekend of the twenty-fifth. We can get together Friday or Saturday night for as long as you want."

246

"That's perfect." Diana stretched up to grab the notepad and pencil that stayed on top of the phone, where Morningstar couldn't reach it. "Give me the information and I'll see you there."

𝔗hey agreed to meet on Saturday, since the conference was hosting a reception Friday night. April suggested a restaurant in Northampton that was popular with the students, but Diana said, "No, we're going to need someplace very private."

"The library?"

"They're not open. Let's walk over to the athletic field and sit in the stands. No one will overhear us there, and this will just take a few minutes." April rolled her eyes but didn't argue.

They found a place to sit, April huddled in her coat. "Now what is so important, and so secret?"

"April…you remember back in nineteen sixty, when Jack said his source for the enhancements had left the country? You made some calls and got us some high quality material."

"Yes…"

"I need you to put me in touch with your contacts for that sort of thing, if there's any way you can do that."

"That was ten years ago, Diana." She wouldn't meet Diana's eyes when she said it.

"Come on, April. Don't bullshit me. I know you're still using. You took more supplements outside of sessions than any of the rest of us, and you were the one who turned me and David into potheads. Look, I'm not laying a big puritan trip on you. I'm the last person in the world who could do that. We all smoke at the house. But I know you. I know you're still in touch with your sources, and I know they're good ones."

April opened her mouth to retort and then stopped. "Okay. But why is this so important?"

"I need an enhancement. I need something really strong. It's not so easy to get anymore, at least material you can trust. Leary's in jail. Owsley's in jail. The mob is controlling the entire black market. You never know what's going to be in street drugs, and most of the psychedelics are contaminated, cut or counterfeit. And I'm looking for something that isn't on the street now, anyway."

"What?"

"I want DOM. It hit the streets in sixty-seven as STP."

"Fuck, Diana, you know the reputation that shit has?"

"I do, and I know that like just about everything else, it's exaggerated. But what it has is staying power. You remember the story I told you about my friend

Gregory, and that concoction he made. I need something that strong and that long-lasting—if I can find it."

April frowned. "I can't guarantee anything, but I suppose if anyone could get that for you, my people could. But are you sure…"

"April, I've taken quadruple doses of acid and it does nothing, just nothing. I used all of Jack's supply, I had a big stash of Owsley acid and I used all of that. It doesn't last long enough, not even if I stagger doses. I've got to try something extreme."

April was quiet for a minute. "This has something to do with Jack, doesn't it. There's something very strange coming down, I can feel it."

"It does and there is. And I can't break through to see what it is by purely magical means. I just can't, certainly not alone. This is the only thing I can think of." As April pondered, Diana added, "I'll pay a lot."

"You certainly will. These people don't come cheap. I'm letting you into pretty rarefied company here, if I do this. I hope you know what that means."

"Of course. Not even under torture."

After another long thoughtful silence, April said, "Okay. You need to pick a pseudonym, one name, make it distinctive. That's your code name. They don't want to know anything else about you. I'll call and tell them to expect to hear from you. I'll give you a code phrase and an exact time to call. They'll arrange a meeting. When you meet, then you tell them what you want, and they'll tell you if it's possible."

"April, I'm seriously in your debt."

"Wait and say that later, if you still can. Of course, I guess you don't worry about brain damage, do you?"

"Not really." Diana stood up. "Come on. Let's check out that watering hole you were interested in. I'll buy you dinner. I want to hear what you've been doing with N.O.W."

April didn't waste any time in following through on her promise. Diana chose the pseudonym Selena during dinner in the raucous but rather fun dive in Northampton. April called the pay phone at the Junction on Monday evening with her code phrase and call time. The phone number was in Cambridge. Apparently, Harvard and MIT still had an enclave of libertarian individuals who went under the radar after Leary was ousted in 1963, and kept on making and distributing pharmaceutical quality recreational drugs on a very quiet and secretive basis. April also hinted that this tight circle of people, which had changed membership over the years, had been involved with some of the CIA research into mind-altering drugs and possibly still were. Diana had heard rumors that the government had actually financed, if not commissioned, the development of several of the scariest drugs out there, drugs that were rarely used by choice but sometimes ended up as contaminants in the Mafia's ersatz psychedelics. These chemical chimeras were the true villains in most of the LSD horror stories lapped up by the media.

On Thursday night, she traveled by air, dematerialized, as far as Quincy, where she could take the Red Line all the way across greater Boston to Cambridge. She got off at Harvard Square and walked briskly down Mass. Ave, keeping her head down, until she turned onto one of the side streets between Mass. Ave and Radcliffe. She found the address, a small commercial building, completely dark and unlighted. As instructed, she walked behind it and down steps into a well for a basement door. She knocked.

"Yes?"

"It's Selena."

"Did you bring the sausage pizza?"

"They only had pepperoni." She had to repress a smile; it was like an old movie about speakeasies. But there was a reason these techniques were timeworn. They were pretty foolproof.

The heavy steel door opened, and she stepped inside, wincing as it slammed shut behind her. After all this, she'd half expected to be standing under a blinding light talking to faceless silhouettes in the shadows. But the room was warm and almost cozy with several small lights on card tables and a TV muttering in one corner. The drug liaison was a cheerful young man in chinos and a Boston Red Sox t-shirt. He looked like a grad student, and was actually rather cute in a dark-eyed and swarthy way. "Have a seat." He waved her to one of several shabby armchairs in the basement room. "I hear that you're looking for something a little different."

She explained. He sat on the arm of one of the chairs, stroking his chin. "Hm. There's not a big market for that. That bullshit in sixty-seven scared people off, and the syndicates buy it up to cut their acid with. I think I know someone who might have a supply. He's got a connection to NIMH, interned there last summer. He's doing some research. I should warn you, he may ask you to fill out a questionnaire or something."

"A questionnaire? About my drug use?"

"It's for his dissertation. Hey, he's a prodigy, he's only twenty-one."

"Very impressive. And you trust him, asking your clients all kinds of questions?"

"Oh, sure. He's cool. I don't refer many people to him, and when I do, I make sure they know what his bag is."

Diana thought about this, completely bemused, and suddenly burst out laughing. "First of all, I'd be there for hours, and second, I'd totally skew his data set. I hope he doesn't ask."

The liaison just smiled. "You might be surprised what's in his data set."

"Would the transaction be conditional on filling out this questionnaire?"

He shrugged. "It might be."

And I guess I can't really make a fuss, can I? Diana thought. "How do I contact him?"

"Oh, you can go right over there, if he's in. Let me call." He went into an adjoining room and shut the door, which was pointless in this case. Diana could clearly hear the phone dialing, and then his voice. "Harry? Yeah. I've got another compensated subject for you. Right. No, she'll tell you. Yeah, I will. Selena." He emerged from the room. "He's expecting you. Here's the address. It's over on the other side of Harvard Square."

"That's it? No more code phrases or secret handshakes?"

He just chuckled. "You're cool, Selena. But you're not done yet."

It took about twenty minutes to walk all the way through the Square and down Mass Ave. on the east side. The sidewalks were busy with college students, and she found herself automatically checking each one for a body heat signature without thinking about it, she'd done that for so many years whenever she was in the city after dark. She almost walked past the address. Harry—she was fully aware this wasn't his real name—lived in a third floor walkup over a bar and a beauty parlor. He came down the stairs to let her in when she rang the buzzer.

"Come on in," Harry said as he waved her into the apartment. It was very tidy except for a long table piled with papers, binders, folders, books and a typewriter. Two large bookcases were jammed with books, chiefly on psychology topics. She noticed a shelf devoted to science-fiction and smiled. The Junction had one of those.

"I heard you're looking for something unusual?"

Once more she explained, and he frowned. "I don't have that on hand. I can get it—I think—but it might take a couple of weeks."

"I can deal with that."

"Okay. I'll call you when it's ready to pick up."

"How much should I bring with me?"

"Ummmm…" he wrote some numbers on a scrap of paper and showed it to her. Diana gaped.

"Are you shitting me? I want a couple of hits, I'm not trying to turn on Los Angeles."

"This is a tough one."

She wasn't in a bargaining position, and she already knew this network's clientele was in a high income bracket. "Okay."

He crumpled up the paper and tossed it into a wastebasket. "Now, you know about the questionnaire, right?"

"That was explained to me."

Harry picked up a clipboard and pen from the table. "This is absolutely confidential. I'm not asking for any information that can be used to identify you, and no name."

"Don't you need basic demographic information?"

"That's correlated independently from the drug history."

Diana sighed. "How long does this take?"

"About ninety minutes."

She managed not to grit her teeth. "All right, let's get started." She sat on the sagging sofa, and he pulled up a straight backed chair. His eyes, behind round rimless glasses, were avid. Diana knew she couldn't tell him everything, not even her real age. Partial truth was safest, but she prepared herself for a tongue-blackening hour and a half of fictionalizing.

After that she could do nothing but wait for Harry to call. Fall harvest was at its peak, and the farm stand was selling corn shocks, pumpkins, winter squash, Silver Queen corn, late season tomatoes, garlic, onions and potatoes, although the potatoes hadn't done as well as they'd hoped and most went into storage for the house. As various crops finished and their beds were emptied, the beds needed to be cleared, dug over, and the soil prepared for next year with fresh compost. Avani was canning every day. After a great deal of discussion, Brigid and Ellie had decided not to enroll Morningstar in kindergarten, fearing that she would be bullied and develop a taste for things like TV, junk food and plastic toys, none of which she had yet been exposed to.

"You were home-schooled, weren't you?" Brigid asked Diana.

"They didn't call it that, but, yeah. There are definitely pluses and minuses."

"Like what?"

"Well, on the minus side, I didn't get as much math and science as I would have in public schools. I couldn't go to college, even if I'd wanted to. On the plus side, I was reading at four and read most of the classics by the time I was twelve." A great deal of her education had been magical, but she dodged that detail.

"We can get textbooks and teaching aids for science," Ellie said. "Most of us took college-level science courses. Avani had pre-med courses, and Denny was in agricultural college, he took biology and chemistry."

"And aced them," Avani called from the kitchen.

"We've got a lot more resources to draw on here than your average nuclear family, no doubt about it," Diana said. "But Morningstar should be reading by now, she's that smart. My mother read to me every night."

"We should get more children's books," Sorcha said. She sounded a little defensive, because she did a lot of the child care. But with two babies and two toddlers, it wasn't easy for her to sit and read to Morningstar, and the other adults were rarely available to do so, either.

Eight grown-ups and no one has time to read aloud to one child, Diana thought. *There's something wrong with that...* Looking at Brigid's and Sorcha's faces, she had a feeling they were thinking something similar. She decided that she would make an extra effort to read stories to Morningstar whenever she could, and try to teach her to read. Maybe she could find some books about baby chicks at the library.

꒳roy had continued to page through the thick mass of "weird stuff" reports from Brad when he got a free moment, and he'd pulled a few things out of the pile and set them aside. One morning when Diana came up to the loft for bed, he said, "I want you to take a look at some of these."

Diana took the pages he handed her and read through them. "Psychic surgery? In Brazil and the Philippines? Troy, these stories have been reported for decades now. Back in the nineteen fifties, the Order looked into some of them. They're all hoaxes. Sleight of hand, dim lighting and a lot of high emotions, that's all there is to it."

"But the Order didn't know about vampires. I admit a lot of it sounds questionable, but some of the reports seem extremely similar to what we do. What if vampires, like us, are using this belief as camouflage?"

"But what would be the point of revealing that you can *open* if you can't drink? There's no mention in those reports of blood drinking, and the so-called surgery seems to be done with plenty of witnesses. I think someone would notice if the psychic surgeon was guzzling from the patients, don't you?"

"You're making a lot of suppositions and assumptions. It would be easy for some surgeries to be done in private—a clever practitioner with high credibility could come up with any number of plausible reasons to work alone with a patient. I think this might be worth looking into. We agreed long ago that we'll never work out what it is that makes us different unless we find more vampires for comparison."

"Are you suggesting that we abandon the Junction and go to Brazil?"

"Well...yes."

"Troy, this place will collapse without us. The eight of us are staggering under the workload now, and it's only getting worse every year. We can't mentor a troop of Girl Scouts every summer."

"Why not?"

"Supervising apprentices and interns is a full time job in itself. We're committed to the Junction, and until we *have* to leave, I think we owe it to them to stay. Avani, Denny, Brigid, Ellie, Sorcha and Joey have all been very,

very good to us. How can we just tell them, 'so long, we're off to Brazil, good luck to you all?'"

Troy was quiet, looking down at the floor. "Yes, they have been good to us. But we aren't going to be able to stay here much longer—maybe two or three years at the most. It's better to leave than to flee. We'll pass through an unending number of temporary homes like this. We're going to be vampires forever, and as it stands, we're profoundly ignorant about our own condition. Learning more about it should be our top priority, because that may enable us to achieve some kind of stability, find a way to live that doesn't require us to roam the world like lost souls. Don't you want that?"

"Of course I do, but…"

"You're young as a vampire, Raksha. You haven't had to leave enough behind to fully comprehend the burden." He took the pages back from her. "We can't just go running off to these countries unprepared, no. We don't know the language and we wouldn't be accepted or trusted in the culture. But I'm going to try and find some guide who is familiar with the local societies, speaks the language and is willing to introduce us to the practitioners. I'm sure that will take some time." He started pulling his clothes off, not looking at her. "You don't have to come with me, you know. It's up to you." He got into bed and fell asleep without saying anything further.

𝔒hree weeks after Diana's adventures with the underground—as opposed to the underworld—drug market, Harry called on the pay phone. Diana had given him a specific time to call, late at night when the mortal Junction members were in bed. But he didn't have the news she'd hoped for.

"I wanted you to know that I haven't forgotten you. I haven't been able to find your preferred product. The manufacturer I hoped to contact is out of business."

"Does this mean I'm out of luck?"

"I don't think so. But I may not be able to fill the order for several more months, possibly early next year." Diana groaned. "I'm sorry. I'll do my best. But these things can't be rushed."

"Well, thanks. I don't have any other options. I'll just have to wait to hear from you."

30

On December 21st, Rainbow Stone Junction scheduled a day-long house meeting to talk about some major changes in their operation. After five years of farming by hand, Denny and Avani wanted to modernize. "We're not Amish," Denny said. An outsider might have needed the clarification, seeing a table full of bearded men, hair in ponytails or flowing to mid-back, the women in Brigid's brilliant peasant skirts and blouses, their long braids worked with ribbons and beads. Massive Denny himself, with bald pate and flowing brown whiskers, resembled the family patriarch he staunchly refused to become. "We're not Luddites. And we're not talking about combines and earth-movers, Brigid. We're talking about tillers, some small yard tractors, power tools, everything on a human scale."

"It's a whole question of balance," Avani said. "We're working ourselves to the bone, and we don't have time left for anything else. Most importantly, we don't have time for our children. If we adopt some technology, it will free up enormous amounts of creative energy for other things. We simply can't go on doing this much longer."

"I think it's fine if we have the right attitude," Joey said. "We treat all our tools with respect. How are power tools different, just because they get their energy from gasoline instead of our muscles? We have a truck, we don't go pick up the compost with a horse-drawn wagon. We use some electricity."

"I'm tired of never having time, and doing everything by hand," Sorcha said. "We work from the minute we get up until the minute we go to bed, and then two of us work all night long. We have Rainbow Stone Junction, the farm that never sleeps. It's like some kind of sweatshop nightmare sometimes."

"I agree with all of you," Brigid said. "I'm just worried that this is a slippery slope. If we start with tillers and a sewing machine, where will we stop? Bulldozers, four cars and a giant TV in the great room?"

"This is what killed fine craftsmen, industrialization," Ellie said.

Avani said, "Ellie, I think you're taking too negative a view. There are still hand craftsmen around and people pay a lot for their work. We're not industrializing. We're talking about quality of life. This isn't just a self-sustaining, closed community anymore. It's a business now. We have to make room to grow. Joey, you tore a rotator cuff in August, and we barely got the mid-season corn in. Denny is getting some arthritis in his shoulders, and he's only thirty-one. Either we pull back and only grow and produce what we need, or we've got to make some changes."

"We're all getting older, like it or not," Denny said. "I don't really want to live below the poverty line. I don't want my kids to live like that."

"And if we keep on growing our business, we have to adopt some modern methods," Avani said. "The Board of Health has given us a free ride on the farm stand. They're treating us like they would a church bake sale. But if we're going to expand our distribution like we've talked about, we'll have to implement some standards. The kitchen will be inspected, and the way it is now, we'd be shut down."

The debate went on and on, interrupted frequently when a baby needed tending or one of the toddlers strayed or started to demand attention. Morningstar had crayons, chalk, and sheets of newsprint from Diana's roll of paper; she already showed signs of real artistic talent. She seemed wholly absorbed in drawing and playing with Michael and Sirena. But Diana knew the five-year-old was listening to every word her elders said. She could sense that this was a critical moment.

By dinnertime, they had come to an agreement. Rainbow Stone Junction would join the Twentieth Century—at least up to a point. Having at last reached that consensus, even final holdouts Brigid and Ellie were bubbling with ideas.

"You know, we could look into ways of generating our own power, so we're not supporting the corporate grid…"

"Passive solar. Maybe we could try windmills. The wind is almost constant at the peak of that hill…"

"Yeah, but we'd have to take down a lot of trees for that…"

"I think we should name all our tools," Brigid said. "Name them, and give them a christening, and treat them like new members of the family. That will prevent us from taking them for granted, and just running them down and always wanting more, more, more." She was bouncing Northwind so enthusiastically that he started to whimper.

"That's a funky idea," Sorcha said. "So let's name the ones we have now. Your potter's wheel, the kiln…"

"Can I pick some of the names?" Morningstar said eagerly.

"Can you write them down if you pick them?" Diana asked. "Have you been practicing?"

"Yes I can, yes I can!"

"Then make a list, and show us," Avani said. Her smile was half doting and half amazed.

After dinner was over, it was Diana's turn to read to Morningstar. Even though she was exhausted from staying up all day for the meeting, she wouldn't have dreamed of skipping it. She and Morningstar sat on the mattress in Brigid and Ellie's bedroom that Morningstar slept on, and Morningstar, as usual, wanted to hear the story twice. Michael and Sirena crowded in with them, mostly because they followed Morningstar everywhere and wanted to do everything she did. Little Northwind was at the age where he babbled and talked to himself for hours in his crib, and his monologue made an interesting counterpoint to the story. After the second run-through, Morningstar took the book and went through it page by page, sounding out the words partly by reading them and partly from memory. Eventually the book had to be rescued from the toddlers, as it belonged to the library.

When Brigid, Sorcha and Avani had taken custody of their children for bedtime, Diana wandered over to the barn, still smiling from the residual warmth of storytime. Troy was flopped on the bed up in the loft; neither of them really slept until dawn approached, but he was weary, too. Diana got on the bed and snuggled up next to him, wondering if they were too tired for sex on a rare night when they had plenty of time. Even the thought made her yawn.

"Long meeting," Troy said, smiling. She suspected he was thinking exactly the same thing.

"Amazing, though. I'm still boggled. Big changes coming."

"And good ones. You know what this means."

Diana's smile faded. "Yes. It means we'll be able to leave. They won't need us anymore."

"We won't be critical to their survival anymore. No one person, or couple, should be such a keystone that a group or endeavor collapses without them. That's either bad planning, or egomania."

"It happens all the time, though."

"Yes it does, so we have endless examples of how badly it turns out. You don't *want* to be that indispensable. It's too heavy a burden."

"I just dread telling them."

"They'll be unhappy and they'll miss us. It's better to leave while that's still the case."

"Yes, I know…ah, let's not talk about it anymore, Troy. Let's fuck ourselves silly. It's been weeks."

"Yes, talking is definitely over quota for the day."

Diana got up, stretched and shed her shirt, boots and skirt with an economy of motion. By the time she'd finished, Troy's clothes were tossed in a corner. They embraced standing, kissing deeply for a while, Diana wrapping one leg around the back of Troy's knees.

"God, I wish I wasn't so tired," he said when they broke off for a moment. "Do you want to get back on the bed?"

"And fall asleep? I've got something new to try. This has been obsessing me ever since I noticed that thing."

"What thing?"

"This big iron hook in the beam. The house in Maine has those, too, but this one never even registered with me—probably looked too familiar." She pulled Troy over and stationed him so they were facing each other directly under the hook. "See, if I jump up, and grab hold, I'm just exactly the right height…" she wrapped her thighs around Troy's hips.

"Will that hurt your hands?"

"Not as much as the splinters from the wall in my back did. I can hang from one hand, for hours. I did it in the woods in Maine a lot." Demonstrating, she coiled her free hand in his hair and pulled him forward for another long kiss. He caught hold of her thighs almost by reflex, sliding both hands around under her buttocks and pulling her more tightly against him. She gripped the hook with both hands again and pulled herself higher so he could suckle at her breasts.

"Come on," she said finally, "Let's see how this works…oh, yeah…"

He thrust up hard but it wasn't enough, and she urged him with her legs like she would urge on a horse, hands white-knuckled on the hook above. "Harder, Troy, don't hold back, just let loose…" Finally she let go of the hook with a cry, wrapping all four limbs around him as Troy sank to his knees.

"Just a bit more," he said hoarsely, and finished with her on her back, legs over his shoulders.

Some time later, as they still lay limp and tangled on the bare floor, Diana sighed. "The best thing about vampire sex? The long, *long* afterglow."

Troy just chuckled. "You seem a little different."

"In what way?"

"You don't seem quite as distressed about leaving the Junction."

"Oh. Yeah." She slowly pushed her hair back from her face. "Contrary to what many people would tell you, I am not immune to common sense. I know you're right. I don't think Morningstar has forgotten that conversation in the greenhouse. And I don't have too much longer before people stop asking for my beauty secrets and start wondering if I'm an android. I'd love to stay…but I don't belong here. It's just taken me a while to accept that."

He smiled faintly, stroking her hair with his fingers. "Does this mean you're coming to Brazil?"

"Are you really going? You found a guide?"

"Not yet. Just asking."

"Oh, Troy…" She pushed up on an elbow to face him, and reached out to touch his bearded cheek, the black hair as silky as a cat's fur. "I don't want to lose you. But—I'm not free. I've got something to finish, and I can't just walk away from it."

Troy looked over at the diagram, which now went on for half the back wall. "You said you'd have to do something drastic. Are you still thinking about that?"

"I've run into a setback, but yes. I may need your help, when I finally get what I'm waiting for."

"I'll help if I can. I just wish you could explain more."

"I know. For what I'm going to ask of you, I may have to. It only seems fair."

"You certainly know how to string a man along. You're worse than Scheherazade."

"I am not."

"I'm getting all tense, and it's not even midnight." He leaned in to kiss her, and Diana's blissful languor tightened, like an instrument being tuned two keys higher. "Let's do this again."

1971

31

She had almost given up on Harry when the pay phone rang one night in late February. He only let it ring three times, so it wouldn't awaken anyone upstairs if Diana wasn't in earshot, and she barely caught the phone.

"Selena? I have your product. Come tomorrow at eight." The phone clicked off.

When she rang the buzzer, there was no response for several minutes, and Diana fidgeted, feeling conspicuous standing there. Finally she heard Harry coming rapidly down the stairs. He slammed the outside door as soon as she was in and double-stepped back up, leaving her to follow more slowly. When she got to the apartment, he was on the phone.

"I'll call you back in an hour, I've got to make a long distance call. I will. Love you." He hung up, a little winded. "Sorry. My fiancée. Her mother is totally freaked out because the only date the chapel was available was April first, and we booked it."

"You're getting married on April Fool's Day?"

"Literally the only open day for weeks on either side."

"Gee, wonder why."

He chuckled. "Lynn and I think it's very funny. Her mother doesn't have much of a sense of humor." Diana thought wryly that Lynn must not be too picky, as Harry wasn't much of a catch. He had the weakest chin she'd ever seen, and with his round eyeglasses and pouty lower lip, he reminded her of a goldfish. He was also financing his Ph.D by dealing dope, but she was in no position to judge about that.

Harry pulled the top drawer of the file cabinet all the way out and peeled a long white envelope off the bottom of it. "Here is your product. I apologize profusely for the long delay. I had to find someone who would manufacture it and it wasn't easy. Things are getting very hostile out there, lots of crackdowns."

"I know. That's why I came to you in the first place. So this is actually custom-made?"

"You could say that. It's exactly what you asked for." He looked as smug as a used car salesman.

Diana tucked the envelope into her bag, pushing it all the way to the bottom, and pulled out her own bundle. "Here's *your* product."

"Thanks." He put it into the file cabinet drawer, which he closed and locked. "Do you have a couple of minutes?"

"I suppose so."

"I've just got another short questionnaire, it's an addendum to the longer one. Actually, it's a simple cognitive test. It won't take long."

"A test?"

"I'm trying to establish whether LSD use above a given threshold affects certain parasympathetic nervous system reactions. You qualify for that sample group. You'd be doing me a huge favor. I've almost gotten the full number of responses I need to be statistically significant, and then I can really start writing."

"All right." He seemed more nervous than when she'd seen him the last time.

"Could you just go over to this chart on the wall?" He picked up a clipboard.

She crossed the room to where a line of tape on the floor obviously indicated the place to stand, facing a chart full of symbols and letters somewhat similar to an optometrist's eye chart.

"Just look at the first four rows. In sixty seconds, I'm going to ask you to turn around and answer some questions."

Dutifully, Diana scanned the figures, trying to memorize them and despairing that the questions would probably be about details she didn't even notice. She hated these things.

"All right, turn around and take this pencil."

She was startled to hear Harry's voice so close behind her, as she hadn't been aware of him approaching. She turned, extending her hand, and Harry reached out, grasped her hand, and very rapidly pressed the object he was holding into the base of her thumb. It wasn't a pencil; it was some kind of sticker device, like the ones used to draw blood samples. There was a little pop and a sharp pain. Diana reeled back, utterly shocked. She felt a rush of sensation up her arm. *Did he just give me some kind of drug?* Harry's face was absolutely impassive, as if he was simply watching to see what happened next. Then Diana dematerialized.

She didn't know why she did it, aside from momentary blind panic. Her hand hurt and whatever the drug was made a tingling sensation but this was nowhere near threatening enough to trigger an involuntary dematerialization. She was trapped between the wall, Harry, the desk and an armchair, she was startled and confused, and she just did it. Now, watching Harry's face turn more fish-like than ever with gulping open mouth and wide eyes, she knew she had to take another action she hadn't planned on. She solidified, dropping an inch to the floor as Harry jumped back with a hoarse shout.

"What was that? What was on that needle? What did you give me?"

His face was gray. "It was just, just a little test, it's harmless—"

"You stuck me with a needle and it's *harmless?*"

"Mild stimulant to, to, enhance your memory—"

"You stuck a *needle* in me, you shit!" She'd backed him up against the bookcase, which was not very stable; it rocked back and forth and a dozen books fell off the top of it and hit the floor noisily. *Why am I so angry?* she suddenly thought. *Mild stimulant. Oh.* She struggled to control herself before she did something both of them would regret.

"I didn't mean, I didn't know…it tests your reaction to the unexpected," he said desperately, sweat beading his forehead.

"Tests my *reaction?* So what do you think, Harry? Where does this one go on your bell curve?" She knew he'd probably assumed she couldn't threaten him because she was so petite, and this infuriated her even more, but some of her anger was with herself. *Why the fuck did I do that?* He was starting to recover from his shock and that was both surprising and a bad sign.

"I've tested forty-nine subjects, you're the last one."

"Sneaking up on people and sticking things into them is just fucking rude, in case your mommy never taught you that. I hope you don't make a habit of it."

"I'm sorry…I…what *are* you?"

"Never mind." She didn't want to waste time trying to hide the mark, and Harry probably would check any sore spot with a mirror no matter where it was. She impatiently slapped his hands out of the way, flung her arms around him as though she was hugging him and pressed her mouth to his neck, down low where his shirt collar would cover it. She moved so fast he didn't even realize what was happening before she *opened,* making him jerk back so hard the rest of the top shelf of books cascaded down on their heads in a cloud of dust. Before the books had finished tumbling, she had blanked Harry's memory, as hard and extensively as she could. He might not even recall shaving this morning.

The euphoria of blood calmed her, and she was left with the dismal sense that she had overreacted. She pulled Harry's limp body up off the floor and stretched him out on the sofa, then picked up and replaced the fallen books. He'd dropped the sticker pen and she picked it up and took it with her, but put his clipboard on the desk. He'd miss the call back to his fiancée, and she knew that she'd pushed his mind so ruthlessly, he'd probably have some lasting disorientation. He'd likely puzzle over the mark; he didn't look like someone who incurred many unexplained injuries.

She didn't want to be seen walking away from his apartment, just in case, and she dematerialized again and ghosted out the window and straight up into the sky. There was a slight risk of being spotted, since it was only about 8:30 in the evening, but it was winter and a bitterly cold night. As she headed southwest, she grew increasingly uncomfortable about this encounter. Her brief contact with Harry's mind had hinted at something very dark underneath the friendly, professional façade. A man who played psychological mind games with unsuspecting people he knew would never report him because they'd come to him for illegal drugs was not someone you'd want for an enemy. Diana had the uneasy and completely irrational premonition that someday, tonight's incident would come back to haunt her.

32

ow, you're absolutely sure that you're cool with doing this?" Diana met Troy's eyes with a hard, somber look. "If you want to back out, this is your last chance. After this, I'll be depending on you."

"I'm sure. We've discussed this at great length, and I swear that I'll do everything I can to keep an eye on you and prevent anything unfortunate from happening. I just hope you're right and you won't dematerialize. I can't follow you or stop you if that happens, so I'll be useless in that case."

"As far as I know, I've never dematerialized while I was tripping. I don't think I could, actually. I don't know what would happen if something forced me to dematerialize in that state, but I hope I never find out. It would take something like a shotgun blast, anyway."

"How likely is it that you might get...out of control?"

"You mean, running around climbing the walls and howling, like in all the TV scare stories?"

"It's not as if I've never seen that happen—although granted, not usually with psychedelics."

"When we did our enhanced sessions, we didn't move, except to fall over. We'd come to sprawled all over the room like cats in a heat wave. This stuff...I have no idea. But this isn't a recreational trip. I'm using this to go inward, and I don't think my body is going to do very much without me. But if it does... well, I'm a hell of a lot more worried about who I might hurt than about what happens to me. That's why I need you here."

"And it really might be three days?"

"It could be. I'm taking all of this, the whole batch. There's no point in going halfway. If this doesn't work, I'm screwed. I don't know what else to try."

"Well..." he made a resigned shrug. "You certainly have plenty of experience with this sort of thing. There's no point in putting it off with more talk."

"No, there isn't. I'm as ready as I'll ever be. We only have this cabin until Sunday, anyway." She shook the capsules out of the white envelope into her hand, hesitated, and popped them into her mouth. It took half a glass of water to get them all down. After a minute, she said, "These have a slow onset, so we'll talk a bit. Once I close my eyes, don't try to speak to me, even if I say something. It's unlikely that I'll be talking to you."

"I understand."

For some time they chatted about inconsequential topics, avoiding anything with emotional associations. The Junction was beginning to acquire its power equipment, mostly well used, and Troy was helping Joey refurbish it. A more neutral subject of conversation would have been hard to think of. It took about two hours before Diana was aware that all her senses were shifting. The interior of the cabin looked as though she was seeing it through clear running water, rippling and distorted, parts of it swelling and other parts receding. Patches of soft light slowly grew and faded on the edges of her vision, and Troy's voice had an odd hollow sound. Although she was sitting with her legs folded, hands cupped in front of her, as she had for their sessions, she had the illusion that she was standing up, and at the same time, sitting on a rough pile of small broken stones that poked into her. Her hands seemed very large, and it felt as though she was holding something in them, something so heavy that it was dragging her hands downward, stretching her arms like rubber. Troy seemed to have stopped talking, and she wondered how long she had been silent, although her eyes were still open. She didn't want to look at his face directly, given what the walls and floor were now doing. She could hear an odd hum all around her. She drew in a deep breath and slowly released it.

"I'm going now." She closed her eyes.

Very deliberately she sank down into deep trance, counting it down to stay focused, although she kept skipping numbers.

She seemed to wander for days in a vast desert, sun beating down on her head. Heat rose up from the sand like hot air from an open oven door. She couldn't make anything out—everywhere she looked, she saw only glaring light. When she looked down at her hands, they seemed to be shriveling, and her feet were blackening. *Why is it always day? Why does the sun never move? Why is it never night?* She sank down to her knees on the burning hot sand, bowed over. *It's a riddle...someone knows the sun will hurt me...someone has made a barrier for me...*she had to get out of this. There was so little time left, everything was moving so quickly...

Time. Time was the tool she had been given, suddenly she realized that. She looked up at the impossibly blue sky, which cut her eyes like glass, and as though a movie projector had restarted, the sun began curving across and down the faded indigo dome, until it sank below the horizon in a glorious bonfire of reds and oranges and yellows. A opalescent starry nightscape stretched over her. The stars seemed close enough to touch, so she reached up and took one in her hand. It was hard and cold, like a diamond, but it had no substance. She popped it into her mouth and it dissolved and she was no longer thirsty. *I wonder if the desert looks like this in New Mexico*...and with that thought, the desert vanished.

She was standing again, but she felt that seasons, years, centuries were rushing past as she somehow remained outside of their turning wheel. She started walking forward, toward the place where the sun had plunged out of sight in such magnificent self-sacrifice. Shapes and colors were rushing past her, and she wished they would slow down and allow her to see, for she thought she was glimpsing amazing things, animals that were neither bird, mammal nor reptile but combinations of all of them, with silver wings and twisted horns of gold and copper, complex buildings of artistry and delicacy that rose into the clouds, their tops invisible, thousand-petaled flowers with colors that had no names and had never been seen in the waking world, growing from seed to bloom and withering all in one instant...all at the *same* instant. Then she knew she was getting close. Past, present and future not merged into one but existing independently all at the same time...where had she seen that before? How many times had she seen that? Millions. Every tendril of the network...the network that wasn't supposed to exist any longer, the network they had built but never really owned, the network that had been hidden from them years and years ago...where was it now? What had it become?

It felt as though wind was screaming by her now, epochs of time passing in a blur, as if she was riding the wings of a jet plane—no, a spacecraft. Everything was accelerating but Diana herself, turning to a mere blur of light, and she had the knee-shaking fear that any second she would smash into some wall or terminus and be utterly demolished by the impact. Did the Universe *have* a terminus? Or would she just shoot out into a void, expanding to dissolve into the infinite as she'd thought would happen the very first time she demateralized? She braced for either or both outcomes, yet the journey went on and on and on, Diana squeezing her eyes shut against the blast of air that would have torn them from their sockets. How many days had this been going on? She couldn't recall how she had gotten here—but she still remembered where she was supposed to be going.

Voices were rising up from her memory...*always spinning patterns and the rest of us are just the threads he uses...you've got the talent to get yourself into more trouble than all the angels could dream of...you're in the eye of the storm you've made...*

Was this another barrier or was she just past her ability to handle what she'd unleashed in herself? She reached her arms to either side and it seemed that the force of rushing air on her hands was less intense, but she couldn't move in either direction and get out of the slipstream. She summoned all her strength and called the name of the one person on earth, if he was still on earth, who could help her.

"Gregory..." she couldn't hear her own voice over the roar in her ears, although she thought she'd screamed as loudly as her body was capable of. She could only feel the name in her mouth and throat.

A large, warm, chemical-roughened hand firmly grasped her left hand, squeezing so tight that it hurt. "It's about time, love. When will you learn that you have to ask?"

The hand yanked her sideways with such force she wondered why her arm was still in its socket, but instantly the roar and the rush of wind was still.

"How do you get yourself into these things, love? One step deeper and I couldn't reach you—and deeper is where you need to go, Di. It's below you, you know the way."

She looked frantically around but saw no one, and she wanted so badly to see him, the face that for almost twenty years had appeared only in her memories and her dreams. "Gregory, where are you? Are you...are you dead?"

He laughed softly. "Are you? I'm around, love. Just busy, that's all. You've got to keep moving, Di. Remember the leaves."

Then he was gone; she felt him go. "Gregory, don't—" But she stopped herself from even thinking it. This wasn't Gregory's job. She hadn't even thanked him. *It's below you...remember the leaves...*

She looked around and saw that she was on a vast open moor, short grass and scrubby bushes stretching as far as she could see on every side. The gray overcast sky above held no clues to the directions of the compass; any way could have been north. But her awareness was opened now. This was another barrier, another illusion. If she walked very far, she thought, she'd run into a wall of mirrors, or a painted stage backdrop. The limitless space was intended to deceive, to set intruders wandering in circles until they gave up or exhausted themselves. *Very clever Jack, oh so clever of you...* She bent down and peered at the bushes closest to her. Yes, the leaves were all facing in one direction. She walked that way.

Before long she came to a place where the ground gaped open in a black hole, invisible until she nearly stumbled into it. All the bushes angled toward the hole, as if they were pointing at it. Under other conditions the effect would have been somewhat comical. She leaned over and peered down into the hole. Icy damp air rose into her face, and the darkness seemed to have substance, as though it was black fog or smoke, not merely an absence of light. Its depth was unguessable, and as Diana looked down, she was overwhelmed by a dizzying sense of height and a keen awareness of her own dense, gravity-dragged weight. She wouldn't even consider dematerializing here, if that was even possible—the gods alone knew what would happen. There was no way to climb down. She drew back, the visceral terror of falling radiating out from her solar plexus in waves, locking her to the ground. Then she seemed to hear Troy's voice in her head; calm, rational Troy, who didn't even believe in magic. *You're indestructible, so what if you fall? You can't get squashed, you're tripping on dope! Fear is just another trap, don't be so gullible.*

She straightened up. "Troy, do you *always* have to be right?"

She walked to the very edge of the hole, her toes extending out over empty space, and spread her arms wide. "All right. Show me." She stepped forward and dropped.

Except that she didn't. There was no drop, no stomach-lurching free-fall, no upward rush of air billowing her clothes and whistling past her ears. Instead there was a shocking jolt and the entire reality she occupied shattered and disappeared, in exactly the way that an extremely vivid dream breaks apart when the sleeper is shaken awake. For several moments she was completely disoriented, and then the new reality—or the actual reality, the one that had been concealed behind all the barriers and traps and illusions—coalesced in her consciousness. She was in the same magical space they had gone to thousands of times in their sessions, the space she had never visited alone and had not seen for nearly eight years, the space that was supposed to have returned to nothingness and vanished utterly when their coven broke its bond by the mutual consent of them all. But it had never been their space. They had just been the laborers who built it. Jack had solved the conundrum which had gotten him banished from the New Mexico group, and all he had needed were magicians powerful enough to manifest his vision, which was no small requirement. But he had found them, and he'd used them from the start. Had it just been a coincidence that he'd run into her, and that she'd run into David, and that they all had such symmetry? Could something like that *be* a coincidence?

Could anything be?

As for the network itself…she was unsurprised, because she had expected this, but at the same time, she was stunned, aghast, overwhelmed by what she saw. Ten years ago, after the election, Jack had blocked off their perception of the network because at last he was capable of doing so. It was all so clear now, and she had been so blind before. For sixteen years the network had been growing, first feeding on their power, until they broke up, then on what else, she could only imagine. Whether Jack had been actively building it alone since 1963 or whether it simply evolved from its own strength and momentum didn't really matter. He had nurtured it, the way the Junction nurtured its gardens. The tendrils, the interconnections, the twisting branches ran to the billions now, far beyond the finite ability of a human mind to comprehend.

But the second she'd arrived here the network had automatically attuned to her consciousness, and a stream of information and images was pulsing steadily through her mind, not invasively, just displayed for her to examine. It was friendly to her, this network, it knew her. It had no reason not to plug right in and do its job. Her first request: *don't let Jack know that I'm here.* It was done, before her thought was complete. Jack could only use the network if it was completely free of constraints. That's why he'd put so much protection on the outside. He didn't even admit the possibility of anyone else accessing the network now—and that, she knew, was his one vulnerability. Only she could have gotten this far, and only because he didn't realize, or believe, what she could do. But then, she'd also had some assistance.

She remained there a very long time, because following tendrils and finding the threads that she wanted was a far bigger job now, and there was so much she needed to know. She had to fight off her growing emotional reactions because they distracted her and interfered with the information. Cold horror, disbelief, anger, grief, all had to be pushed aside as the full extent of Jack's plan unfolded piece by piece. Finally, she focused on pinpointing Jack's location. She saw it, and at last knew where to find him in the physical world, but the melding and confusion of past, present and future left her uncertain exactly what she would confront when she got there. She could only pray that it wasn't already too late.

The drug was wearing off, and as it did she was slumping with a fatigue so deep, it gave her an illusion that she was physically melting into a formless puddle. She had better leave while her mind was still clear, or she might betray her presence to Jack. She had felt him on the network but had carefully avoided any contact with his thoughts or energy. She didn't need that; her next moves would be undertaken in the ordinary world.

She opened her eyes and saw the planks of the cabin roof above her. She was lying on the narrow bunk she'd been sitting cross-legged on at the start, with a blanket over her. She was almost entirely down, but she could tell she wouldn't be completely back to mundane consciousness for a few more hours, possibly a day or two. She could understand now why DOM had gotten its street name of STP, for "Serenity, Tranquility and Peace." She thought of her slow awakening as a vampire that first day, and this was quite similar. In the back of her mind was a mass of information and a sense of terrible urgency, but she was able to disregard that, at least for a little while. It was very quiet, but the sounds of birds told her it was daytime. She drew in a long breath of air, scented with dust and old wood and pine smoke. Finally she looked to her right, and saw that the other bunk had been moved over next to this one, and Troy was on it, deeply asleep. He wasn't off-guard, she realized—she saw a cord tied around his wrist, the other end tied to her own arm.

She didn't want to wake him, although she was very hungry—dangerously so. She hoped they could hunt before they returned home because she doubted she could be trusted around people. She was getting close enough to complete normality to start feeling less tranquil and more fidgety when Troy stirred and awoke. He immediately turned to check on her, and started when he saw her awake.

"Thank god. I was really starting to worry."

"How long have I been out?" Her voice was whispery from disuse.

"This is the third day, but I confess, I thought you had to be exaggerating."

"I'm glad it hasn't been longer, the cabin might be rented to someone else after us." She sat up, working at the knot on the cord.

"Are you all right?"

"As far as I know. I'm starving, though." She tossed the loose cord over to him and he started undoing his own end, slowly, as if he thought he might still need it.

"Was your experiment a success?"

She was quiet for a moment. *If a doctor trying to identify a mystery illness finally proves that it's terminal cancer, would he call that a "success?"*

"It did what I wanted it to do," she finally said. "Far exceeding my most tenuous hopes."

"You don't seem happy about it."

"I didn't expect the news to be good." He was about to say something and she put a hand on his arm. "I have a lot of thinking to do before I can talk coherently, Troy. But I want to thank you again for staying with me. What did I put you through? I hope you didn't leash me because of some close call."

"No, I just couldn't stay awake anymore, and you did walk around some. You were very quiet, really. You went outside once."

"You let me go outside?"

"You got out when I was dozing, but you weren't in any hurry. You just wandered around, so I followed you. That was the first day, about eight hours after you took the capsules."

"That's interesting…"

"Mostly you just sat, or lay down. You spoke a couple of times."

"What did I say? It could be important."

"Well, you called out a name once—Gregory? I believe you've mentioned him, in passing."

"Oh…"

"You were crying." Diana looked up at Troy unhappily. His expression wasn't quite jealous, nor quite hurt, but there was something in his eyes that made her wince.

"Troy, you know I have a past. I haven't seen Gregory in many years."

"I know, but this sounded…well. You were on drugs."

"Exactly."

He looked back up with a quirked smile. "And yes, I do always have to be right."

She laughed out loud. "And I'm really glad, let me tell you. Without your infuriating voice of reason in my head, I don't think I'd have made it." His smile this time was unconditional, and she got up and hugged him. He hugged back, surprisingly hard.

When they finally let go, he said, "Oh, there's one more thing. When I got you back inside, you were holding something in your hand. You had it when I caught up with you. I thought you'd picked something up outside, but it's a little puzzling." He reached over to the small table by the cabin's pot-bellied stove. "I had to pry this out of your hand, it was clenched so tight, but I didn't want it to get lost, if it was something important."

Diana took the badly crumpled piece of tightly folded parchment paper and turned it over, bewildered. It took her a moment to recall who used this kind of paper—the Order's was similar but more modern, Thomas had used white linen paper—and then she remembered. The paper was folded into a complex origami-like triangle and took a moment to undo, especially with her hands trembling. She stared numbly at the symbols on the sheet.

Troy looked at her still face and then leaned over to peer at the paper. "That's the same cipher you write in your journal, isn't it? The one on the diagram?" She just nodded. The paper was Levoissier's, but the handwriting was Gregory's.

"You say I just had this in my hand?"

"Yes. I thought you might have brought it with you."

"And you're absolutely sure you didn't see anyone?"

"I checked regularly. There isn't, and wasn't, a human within ten miles of here. We're in the middle of the woods, and it's March. There are exactly two sets of tracks in the snow, yours and mine." He looked down at the paper again. "What does it say?"

She folded the paper in quarters. "'You have to stop him.'"

33

They returned to the Junction via two stops at farms, so Diana was well-fed. She needed longer drinks than she'd required for some time before she felt satiated enough to be safe for human society. Her fatigue, however, deepened with every step. Once she was back in the barn loft, she curled up underneath the blankets in a tight ball like a hibernating squirrel and slept for twenty-four hours. When she got up, Troy was working, and she made no attempt to find him or speak to their housemates. She sat at the table in the loft and wrote in her journal for hours, recording every detail of the information she'd gleaned from the network and could recall.

When she could write no more, she sat for a long time, thinking. After a while, she stood up and paced around the room, looking disinterestedly at the clothes hanging on a bar that Troy had installed across one corner, the odds and ends like toiletries and incense, beads and ribbons, some pottery bowls and jars that Brigid had made for her. She'd arrived at the house with a bag the size of a large purse and the clothes she was wearing, did she need to take anything more than that when she left? She wanted to travel light, anyway. She hoped Brigid's feelings wouldn't be hurt. She found her bag, and started to pack a bare minimum of items into it, along with her journal. She took down a picture that Morningstar had drawn for her, folded it carefully and tucked it into the very bottom of the bag.

She was pulling down the diagram from the walls and tearing it into pieces she could stuff into the little stove downstairs when she heard Troy close the workshop door. He came up the loft steps, saying "I see you're finally awake—" He stopped when he saw what she was doing.

Slowly he walked up the last few steps and regarded her bag on the bed, the rifled clothes bar and the disarranged personal items on the small table. She kept on tearing down the diagram, not sure what to say.

"Were you even going to say goodbye?" His voice was harsh.

She turned around sharply, crumpling paper between her hands. "Of *course* I'm going to say goodbye! What do you think of me, Troy? I just..." her voice dropped. "...am putting it off as long as possible."

He looked slightly shame-faced but didn't apologize. "How are you feeling?"

"Much better."

"Can we talk, then?"

Diana studied him for a moment. "You've got that look on your face that usually precedes the words, 'you'd better sit down.'"

"Sitting down would probably be more comfortable."

She sat in the chair she had been writing in, and Troy sat on the bed. "When we got back, there was a message for me, from Professor Alberto Herreira at Boston University. I'd contacted him some months ago. He's been doing research for a book on some of the syncretistic sects in Brazil, and he's working directly with several that practice psychic surgery. He's going down there with a team for three months. He initially said he didn't think he'd be able to bring along any non-academics, and he was going to let me know if he heard of anyone else in the field who might work with me. But he's lost two of his team members, and he says you and I can come along with them. They'll be living in the communities and interacting very closely with the local people."

"We can go with him as what, observers?"

"Something like that. We'll be working with the team. You have a passport, don't you?"

"I do. It's in Maine, but I can get it in a day. But what about you? You've only been Troy Stevenson since 1965."

"I had to have one forged, but I started that process months ago. It's all ready to go."

"What about physicals, shots..."

"There are ways around all that. We're going to meet Herreira and his team in Rio de Janeiro."

"We are? Did you tell him that we're definitely coming?"

"I told him that I am. I said you might be. I couldn't commit you to the project without talking to you."

Diana was silent, trying to absorb this radical idea. "When is he leaving?"

Troy hesitated. "That's the part you needed to sit down for." He swallowed and met her eyes. "They're leaving in two days."

"Two days! But Troy, I can't!"

"Raksha, this is an unexpected chance and it's dropped into our laps. We may not get another opportunity so perfect for years. Professor Herreira was born in Rio de Janeiro, he knows these people intimately. We couldn't have a more perfect entree to that culture."

"But, couldn't we go with him on a future trip?"

"This is his last one, after this he'll write and publish the book."

"Couldn't we say we'll be getting down there later, meet him in the village or wherever?"

"He wants us there the first week for basic orientation with his team. I have no idea what villages he's studying, the information is confidential. He's very protective of these people, he doesn't want them to be made into freaks by the media. Raksha—why can't you do this? What are you packing for, where are you going? What is so important?"

Diana covered her face with her hands, inwardly cursing. She shouldn't tell Troy, it violated not only Jack's confidentiality but David and April's. Troy was a cowan and a complete skeptic, he wouldn't believe it, anyway. But she thought of Troy spotting her for three solid days while she took powerful drugs, for reasons he didn't understand and she refused to explain. Did Jack deserve confidentiality, with what he intended to do? *But it's not Jack, it's the principle of the thing...* "Oh, fuck it," she said out loud. Troy raised his eyebrows.

"I'll tell you, Troy. I'll tell you everything. Then you'll see why I've got to leave, now. I don't have much time."

He listened silently and attentively, his expression carefully neutral, while she told him the whole story: how she had met Jack, his proposition, forming the coven, the things they had tried to do, how they had used enhancements and built the network, what had finally happened after the 1960 election. She described all the clues and hints she'd had since Jack's disappearance: what Phoebe and April had told her, the ragged man's rantings, the strange incidents that might be bombings. She finished by telling him what she'd learned when she'd broken through to the network.

"You see, he planned this. He hid information from us, he used us. He knew that Kennedy would be assassinated before the nineteen sixty election. That's why he cut us off from the network, he didn't want us to know."

"So—you're taking responsibility not only for Kennedy's election, but for his death?"

"We *felt* responsible. Entirely responsible? No, of course not, there were a few voters involved and someone named Oswald. But we fucked around with fate, and someone else paid for it."

"And now you think that Jack is planning some kind of...magical apocalypse?"

"Troy, I *saw* it. He's using the network to find and influence susceptible people. He sends them a device and they hide it wherever he tells them to, then forget about it. Eventually there will be thousands of these, all over the country. When he's ready...he'll detonate them. Using the network. All at once. These are *magical* devices, Troy. No demolitions expert or forensic team will ever be able to figure out what has happened—and that's if there's enough left for an organized investigation at all. That's the whole point." She covered her face with her hands, shuddering. "The complete mystery is the real attack. The explosions will cause terror and social chaos, but his real aim is psychological devastation. The survivors of this attack will go to war against one another. People won't be able to trust anyone or anything. Manson thought he was going to start a race war when he orchestrated the Tate murders. Jack is really going to do it—and that's just for starters."

Troy was shaking his head helplessly, and Diana had to fight to keep from shouting. "This is what Jack needed all that money for: he's using alchemical processes to make these devices. He needed chemicals that are rare, very costly, and at least one of them is strictly banned from crossing United States borders. You don't smuggle in that much contraband easily, but you can always do it with enough money at your back. That's what he got from me and April—maybe that's all he really wanted from us, after he had his network." Her voice was bitter. "Once he finished his test explosions, he started large scale production. He might as well be manufacturing a new kind of car."

She had to stop, fighting down an impulse to jump off the bed and run from the room. Troy was studying her, his brow creased in a deep frown. After a long pause, he said, "And you saw all this…during a three day drug trip."

"Troy! That wasn't just a drug trip! Haven't you been listening?"

"I have, Raksha, and I have to admit, I'm somewhat concerned. Do you really not know what you sound like?"

She gaped at him. "Sound like? You mean…delusional? Crazy?"

He sighed. "By your own admission, this…coven…of yours was taking large amounts of mind-altering drugs on a regular basis. You holed yourself up together in that house, isolated yourselves from other people, and built this elaborate belief system that you were performing magic and changing the course of history. But what did you actually *do?* What can you point to and say, 'that would never have happened if it wasn't for us?' History is littered with examples of small groups of people who banded together and invented their own version of reality. Most of them ended up very badly."

"Troy, give us credit. David and I had this same conversation, and we stopped the group from being so insular and isolated. Why did we all revolt, then, and decide we were wasting our time? We all quit, and now April is a political activist, David's in Israel and I've been working on an organic farm for five years. Does that sound like some little cult that goes and sits in a field waiting for the UFOs to pick them up?"

"Please don't get so overwrought. You're right, you all seem to have gotten your perspective back and moved on. But look at what you're doing right now. You say you haven't seen or heard from Jack since nineteen sixty-three and yet you've cooked up this whole massive, elaborate plot in your head, without a shred of evidence."

"The bombs—"

"What connects those with Jack?"

"The FBI interview!"

"You don't know why the FBI was asking about Jack. Maybe he's joined the Weather Underground."

"No, it was the people he was influencing! Some of them slipped out of his control and talked. That was inevitable, you can't control human minds reliably. I could have told him that."

"I suppose that's possible, but you're still speculating."

"What about the money missing from my and April's accounts? Who would have stolen that much money from both of us?"

"You don't know what happened to that money. You just think Jack might have stolen it somehow. Your bank, the police and the FBI haven't found a connection, and they have Jack's name. You and April certainly ran with some colorful crowds over the years. Wealth attracts con artists, it's a fact of life."

"I suppose you'll say the meth-head was just hallucinating, even after I influenced him."

"You said you questioned your own interpretation, didn't you?"

"But—"

"Don't you see: once you've created a paranoid idea like this, everything in the world seems to tie into it somehow. That's how paranoia works. Every tiny little thing takes on some special, secret meaning that only the paranoid person understands, and the whole thing becomes a massive feedback loop. It's almost impossible to break out of."

"You're saying I'm paranoid?"

"Raksha—I know how much acid you've dropped, just since you've been here at the Junction. I haven't said anything, I figured it was your business. But you've never opened up and talked to me about all of this before."

"And you can see why! I knew you'd be skeptical."

"No, I'm realistic. I see how much damage wishful thinking and irrational beliefs do in the world."

Overwhelmed with a sense of futility, Diana stared down at the floor. "If you really think that I'm delusional, and irrational, and a hopeless acid-head… why do you want anything to do with me at all, far less want me to travel the world with you?"

"Because I see all your other qualities, some of them quite amazing. I think you should come with me for a lot of reasons. I think you need to get completely away from the Junction, and magic, and drugs, and all these wild ideas. Come with me to another country, a whole new culture, learn a new language. Come back to earth where you belong."

She couldn't speak for a few moments. "I can't. I have to do this, I'm the only one who can."

"The only person on earth who can save the world from a madman."

Diana groaned. "The only member of our coven who can stop Jack from going off the deep end! You're making this sound more outrageous and fantastic than it is."

"I'm only stating what I hear. I think you're scared of Jack, guilty about letting him down and wondering when he's going to move against you in retaliation for quitting the coven and wrecking his little ego-game. You've inflated that fear into cosmic proportions. I'd be willing to believe that Jack holds a grudge and might try to hurt you and your friends. That's perfectly plausible. I'd believe that he would try to use magic to do that. After what you've shown me, I'd even allow for the possibility that something magical he tries might do you some harm. But this? Mass bombings, mind control of thousands of people, a one-man plot that basically would bring the entire United States to its knees? It's just too incredible."

Diana was silent. She wanted to mention the note, but she knew what Troy would say—that she'd written it herself. It was her cipher, after all, and he didn't know what Gregory's handwriting looked like. Finally she said, "I can't verbally convey to you what my entire life's training and experiences have been. I couldn't do it if I talked for days. In my own defense, I can just say that all that training has not been lacking in challenges, questioning and aligning perception with reality. Maybe you'll say that we still all reinforced each other's belief system. But this is my whole *life,* Troy, not just a few years using drugs. I've fucked up plenty of times and seen other people suffer for it, and that's always been because I didn't take the magic seriously enough, never because I went too far in believing it. Rationalizing is what gets me into trouble, every time. I tell myself something can't be true and everything's fine, despite all my instincts and intuition, and then disaster hits. And I could have prevented it."

He was quiet, and she could see that he was thinking over what she'd said. She'd told him what happened to Brent when the magical working in Maine went wrong. "All right. Certainly people have attempted ambitious and far-reaching acts of destruction in the past. Most of them have failed. But if you think that Jack is really planning widespread bombings, and you know where he is, why don't you call Agent McMasters, right now? Why handle this all alone?"

She closed her eyes for a moment. "I thought of it. Gods, I wish I could. Do you think I wouldn't give *anything* to hand this off to someone else? But they can't stop Jack now. He's working through the network, he could be in solitary confinement in a federal penitentiary, in a mental institution, anywhere, and he could still pull this off. Besides…with the timelines so confused, I'm not certain that Jack really is at the place I saw at this exact moment. I'm going to have to go there and look, and track back and forth if I've got the dates off. If Jack has the slightest warning, he'll disappear."

In the even longer silence that followed, Diana struggled with the chill of fear roiling in her stomach, amplified by frustration and despair that she was losing not just her life at the Junction, but Troy as well. He was glowering down at the floor, his expression conflicted. Finally he looked up.

"If this is so important, then…could I come with you? You may need help. I do have some abilities that could come in useful."

Diana stared; this was the last thing she had expected him to say. "Oh, Troy…I don't think it would be safe. What Jack is trying to do, if anything goes wrong…you might not survive it. I couldn't bear that."

"I might not survive, but you think you will."

"I'm indestructible, Troy, and you're not."

"You say you're indestructible, but how seriously has that been tested? What if you're wrong?"

"Then I'll be…" she raised her hands helplessly. "But I don't want Jack to have anything he can use as a weapon against me. I've given him far too much that he can use already." She looked away. "I underestimated him all along. But he doesn't have that advantage anymore."

Troy got up from the bed, came over and took both her hands in his. "Don't do this, Raksha. Let it go. Come with me to Brazil. *Please.*" He squeezed her hands, trying to get her to look up at him, but she bowed her head.

"I can't."

He let her go and straightened up. After a long heavy silence, he said, "Where are you going, then?"

"Binghamton. It's in central New York state. "

"I may not come back from Brazil after three months. I may go on to the Philippines and look into those stories, too. I'm going to have to change identities again soon. I won't be using this one when I return to the United States, whenever that is."

She just nodded. "Maybe someday we'll run into each other, and you can tell me what you found out."

"I hope so." There was light filtering around the curtains and the birds had been singing for half an hour. Troy looked around the room, his eyes a bit lost. "I think I'll go over to the house and sleep up in the attic today. You need your rest."

ᴩerhaps it was Troy's sudden shift in sleeping arrangements that forewarned the Junction members, or perhaps they were just perceptive. But there was less surprise around the dinner table the next evening when Diana and Troy broke their news than Diana had expected.

"We're going to miss you," Avani said. "I don't know what we'd have done without you, especially at the beginning."

"You said the Universe would send us the right people," Denny said to Brigid. "And you were right."

"You're not leaving because you don't want us to use machines, are you?" Sorcha asked.

"Of course not," Diana said. "And you certainly can't think that about Troy."

"Fuck, no," Joey said. "I was sort of counting on you to help keep it all running."

Troy smiled. "You're doing fine. You're a motorcycle mechanic, after all. The Junction doesn't need two mechanics, unless you plan to open a garage."

"Hey, now there's an idea..."

"No," about five voices said at once.

"It's the right time for us to leave," Diana said. "It's not personal and it has nothing to do with you. I'm going to miss all of you, every day. These have been the best six years of my life."

"You can come back and visit, can't you?" Brigid said.

Diana hesitated. "I might. It depends how things go with this whole family mess."

That was all: no tears or histrionics or emotionalism. Just as the Junction members had accepted their arrival as something intended by fate, they accepted the need to say farewell. Diana wondered what they might suspect about her and Troy and never mentioned, and whether on some level, Rainbow Stone Junction was quietly relieved to see them go. The rest of the dinner conversation revolved around what to do with the clothes and belongings they were turning over to the household, starting the spring soil preparation with the new tillers and equipment, planting for the coming year, and Morningstar's schooling.

The following day, Troy packed a smaller bag than Diana's, saying that he'd buy clothes in Rio, so as to blend into the local environment as much as possible. He went into town to a barber shop and returned with his beard trimmed short and close, and his hair still a bit long but just brushing his collar. He left behind Brigid's beads and tie-dye and wore his simplest work clothes, jeans and boots and a plaid shirt. He'd gone from hippie lifer to New York writer in the space of sixty minutes; he would have no difficulties with the cab he'd called to take him to Logan airport. Diana also dressed in her garden work clothes, jeans and boots and a pullover, and she bound her hair into one long braid, all ribbons and feathers undone and left on the table in the barn loft.

She walked out with Troy when the cab arrived.

"You're sure you won't change your mind?"

She shook her head. "Good luck, Troy. I'm know we'll see each other again."

He looked as if he was about to say something, then stopped. "Good luck in New York." He bent down and they kissed, rather chastely.

"I don't know if you'll get any news from the States down there, but watch for something about Binghamton." Troy nodded, then he got in the cab and was gone.

Diana sat with the household for one last dinner. It was a quiet meal.

"Are you calling a cab, too?" Sorcha asked.

"Someone is picking me up down by the farm stand."

"I hope they don't have trouble getting through town," Denny said as he helped himself to more potato and lentil soup.

"Why would they?"

"The whole town is on holiday," Brigid said. "Jerry Standish has given the mill a free day off with pay."

Diana blinked. "That doesn't sound like Mr. Union-buster. What's going on?"

"He's a daddy," Ellie said. "Hello to little Veronica Standish, silver spoons in her mouth and all."

"Yeah, I wonder if fatherhood will mellow him out any," Joey said. "Maybe he won't be so gung-ho about the war if he's got a kid to think about."

Avani chuckled. "Miracles have been known to happen."

After it was fully dark, Diana took her bag and walked down the road until she was out of sight of the house. No one saw that she walked west, toward the dairy farm, and not in the direction of the farm stand. Even with her pressing sense of urgency, she had to force each step away from the Junction, Sheridan, and the last six years. She passed through the dairy farm grounds so noiselessly, the dogs didn't bark. Beyond the main buildings a dirt road climbed to the peak of a grassy hilltop. *I won't look back…I won't look back…*she repeated as she walked. But at the top of the hill, she stopped and turned around. Trees half hid the sprawling house at the Junction, but the hundreds of square beds radiated out from it in an uneven mosaic. To the southeast, the lights of Sheridan spattered the darkness with yellow, orange and white. Red beacons blinked on the tall smokestacks of the Standish Mills. *Goodbye, Morningstar, and Michael and Sirena and Northwind and Arwen…and even you, little Veronica. With luck, you'll have a world to grow up in.* Movement in the sky caught her attention, and she saw the lights of a plane, low enough to have just left Logan. *Of course it isn't,* she thought, but her eyes followed the plane until it was almost out of sight. Then she gave the strap of her bag an impatient tug, turned, and started down the hill.

34

*N*o one would ever guess, she thought. *Perfect protective coloration. No one would ever dream what's really in here.*

She was standing in deep brush watching a two-story industrial building on a state road leading out of Binghamton, New York. She was idly curious as to how Jack had located this site—isolated, screened by surrounding trees, and probably cheap given its condition—but maybe he'd just read the commercial real estate listings. The building had no windows; a section in front that probably had been the company offices had once had windows and glass doors that were now heavily boarded over. Several shipping docks punctuated the rear wall of the long building, but their large pull-down steel doors were closed and tightly secured, as well. Potholes pocked the crumbling asphalt of the parking lots in front and back. Around the perimeter, a rusting eight foot high chain link fence held back several acres of chest-high weeds, thick with brambles and saplings.

But there was something going on here. She'd been watching for almost twenty-four hours and she'd seen six deliveries so far, fairly large packages. Nothing seemed to have gone out, and she hoped that part of the timeline was still in the future. It probably wouldn't be long, though. Thin smoke trailed from a tall steel chimney on the building's roof, probably a vent for the heating system. She'd caught a whiff of it a few times and she recognized the smell. Jack had an athanor in there.

She should have realized how good an alchemist Jack was when he'd mentioned helping Gregory build his athanor. Gregory would never have asked her to do that, and as far as alchemy went, she was a fairly solid B student. But Jack...maybe he learned more from the New Mexico group, but he was even better than Art. Certainly, he was far more innovative.

If Troy thought she was grandiose, fantasizing about saving the world, it was only because he had no idea how thoroughly humbled she felt now, after breaking through to the network and seeing Jack's true intentions and actions with piercing clarity. He had never been able to exert mind control on her directly, but she had been as fooled by his blocks and barriers and misdirection as April and David. She'd wanted to be fooled. She'd wanted so desperately to find a kindred spirit, someone who didn't think her passion to change things magically was arrogant or misguided or crazy. Most of all, she'd wanted someone who would join her in immortality, and if Jack had agreed, she would have done it. Every time she thought of that now, such a sickening horror gripped her that she had to instantly force the thought from her mind. But maybe she had Troy to thank for that. Jack had been so repulsed when he was drunk from and his memory erased, he couldn't accept what had to happen for him to be changed. *Are there any coincidences, ever?*

Does Jack know I'm here? She doubted it. The network was still obeying her command. She knew this because now, after cracking herself open with that massive dose of drugs, she could access the network herself. Jack had redesigned the entire foundation and purpose of that working so it would be available to individual members of the group that made it, just as April had said he wanted to do. But in so doing, he'd created his own downfall. His barriers around the network were almost unassailable. Nothing human could have pushed past them and survived; if she hadn't realized that, she'd have been begging April and David for help. But she didn't need their assistance, as much as she wanted it. Now that she had broken through, she could access the network not only in trance, but constantly, in a waking state. Jack had changed that for his own purposes, and all that power was hers, as well. He had placed some magical protections around this warehouse, but those were chiefly to keep cowans from paying attention to the place, like the ones they'd used on the Woburn house. She'd expected them and had no trouble avoiding them.

She still wasn't absolutely certain Jack was inside the building. Someone was opening a door in the back for deliveries, but they'd remained out of sight. She tried to sense a presence but she couldn't feel anything, leaving her unsure whether there might be more people in there than Jack alone—or just other people, while Jack was someplace entirely different. That would complicate matters considerably. She had to get inside.

She had been circling the building dematerialized, because the brushy undergrowth outside the chain link fence was almost impassable. But she couldn't work magically that way because it wasn't possible to focus enough—just staying dematerialized required considerable concentration. She had to stay in touch with the network, and that meant fully solid and feet on the ground. But her delay in approaching the building wasn't merely from caution.

All the way here from Sheridan, sometimes by air and sometimes walking a mile or two because she needed to ground and clear her head, she had struggled with her own principles. The conversation they'd had during the Klinghoeffer project kept replaying in her mind:

"Are you suggesting that we actually murder people?"

"It's not considered murder during a war, Diana."

"That's the kind of thinking our enemies fall prey to. There are always alternatives to killing."

"Not always. And even when there are, you don't always have time...we have to be prepared to take extreme measures, if they're required."

She'd been the one insisting that killing was never necessary, and no warning bells had chimed in her conscience at Jack's talk of extreme measures. He'd seemed to back down, and she'd taken that for granted. They all had. But now her principles were meeting the ultimate test. How could she stop Jack without killing him? What kind of reasoning, what appeals to emotion, what sort of binding or impairment short of death would turn him aside from this insane path?

For hours her mind had chased this dilemma in circles. She'd played over every conversation, every argument, every statement she could wring from her memory. She'd recalled those idyllic teen years when she and Gregory and Jack had been the trouble-making whiz kids of the Order, breaking the rules and getting away with indulgent wrist-slaps because of who they were, like rich prep school students whose parents paid off the judge every time they wrecked the car. But she and Gregory had finally run face-first into the brick wall of consequences—Gregory when he poisoned himself and was banished, she when she hit the Order's glass ceiling and was censured. Jack had suffered no such reality check—his expulsion from the New Mexico group obviously hadn't impacted his ego.

The vent on the roof had stopped smoking and that meant another batch of chemicals was finished and cooling. She had to get inside the warehouse.

She left her bag in the weeds and ghosted through the chain link fence and across the open expanse of broken asphalt to an emergency fire exit on the side of the building. It had no exterior knob, just a keyhole. She started to slip through the crack of the door, which should have been simple. But she couldn't do it. She was so shocked, she solidified six inches off the ground, dropped, and staggered backwards a step. *What the fuck?* Even if there was something solid across the door inside, she should have been able to get through it. Cracks were easier, not essential. She dematerialized and tried again, but she was completely blocked. She circumambulated the building and tried the loading dock doors, another emergency exit, the boarded up door and windows in front, and even the chimney vent—all with the same result. She couldn't penetrate the walls directly, either, so the barrier wasn't restricted to exits and openings.

Well this is a fine mess... Thomas had told her that he'd encountered magical barriers that stopped them when they were dematerialized. He'd also said those barriers didn't work if they solidified. But the doors and locks themselves had that angle covered. She might be able to break in physically, but not without making a lot of noise that would immediately alert anyone inside. The doors had keyed deadlocks or padlocks. She wouldn't be able to escape the building dematerialized, or easily in any form. *Jack knows I can dematerialize, and he figured this out, just in case…did he suspect I would find him, or was he just covering all his bases?* She stepped back from the building, thinking. *Gods, Troy, I could use someone who can open locks right now…*but lacking that, she would just have to be resourceful.

She went around to the back of the building and carefully moved a battered empty trash can to the edge of the loading dock. She sat down by the door she had seen opened when the deliveries arrived, and waited, her ear pressed against the hard metal. Even with her vampiric hearing, she detected only silence inside. But after about an hour, she heard footsteps. Someone had come into the area near the door and was moving things around; she thought she heard the sound of a box cutter opening a carton. She got up, kicked the trash can off the dock, and dematerialized, fading back to the closed door. The can sailed in a graceful arc and landed with enough crashing and clattering to be audible to the closest neighbors. She had to wait a few moments; she heard the deadbolt key scraping on metal. The door jerked open and a man came out, holding a long iron pry bar in one hand and the deadbolt key in the other. He looked around wildly and then went to the dock and peered down at the trash can, still rolling back and forth. Diana solidified and ducked inside the door, hurrying back through the shadows. She hadn't even taken a good look at the man, who had come inside for a large flashlight and was now scanning the parking lot. Could she dematerialize inside a completely enclosed magical barrier? She tried. *Nope. I better stay on my tip-toes.*

The lower level of the warehouse was filled with rows of broad industrial shelf units, stretching to the ceiling fifteen feet above. Diana drew back between two of the sections, pulled herself hand-over-hand to the top shelf and flattened herself tightly down on it. The man had come in from the dock, slammed and locked the door, and was walking down the center aisle shining his flashlight down every row of shelves, and taking his time. She would have heard his breathing change if he'd spotted anything, but he couldn't see her this high up without climbing himself. After a pause, he returned to the loading area, got some smaller boxes from the carton he'd opened, and walked back. She heard him clanking up metal steps to the second floor.

She dropped lightly to the floor and extended her awareness and her enhanced senses, seeking for any hint that another human being was inside the building. But as far as she could tell, she and the pry bar-wielding man were alone, and locked in. With double keyed locks on every solid steel door, he wouldn't be able to escape fast, either.

She walked around the dark space, using sight, feel and magical sense to examine the contents of the shelves. Most of them were stacked tightly with unsealed, unmarked cardboard shipping boxes of uniform size, each containing a loosely wrapped package about the size of a brick.

She'd seen what the bombs consisted of: a tiny amount of volatile compound capable of transforming several pounds of apparently harmless putty into a magical explosion when triggered. The bomb created no flame or heat—just a massive shock wave that reduced anything within a very wide radius to particles, much as the Schuller house had been. But unlike the exploding athanor, these bombs would instantly disintegrate living things as well as wood, metal and masonry. Each device was attached magically to a tendril of the network. One thought sent down the tendrils and it was all over.

The shelves contained thousands of the boxes. But none of them were armed with the triggering compound, and finally Diana let out a long sigh of relief. Jack's plan wasn't as far along on the timeline as she'd so desperately feared. He'd made all his base packages ahead of time. She should have known that, when she considered how recently Jack had stolen the large amounts of money. This was his last step; he'd spent the previous eight years building the network, finding and controlling his army of unconscious drones—the zombies the meth-head had raved about—and laying out his plot to the last detail. The sheer magnitude of what he was doing would have been awe-inspiring had it not been so horrific.

She took off her boots so she could get up the metal steps silently. The second floor was a large open room, with shelves only along the outer walls. Two rows of lights, dimmed with years of grime, hung from the ceiling. At the far end of the room Diana saw the athanor, quite a large one, its vent connected to the pipe that rose up the wall and through the flat roof. Long work tables end to end in front of it held a complex array of chemical equipment and several alcohol burners. The man was standing at the end of the tables, his back to her, unpacking the boxes he'd brought upstairs. Diana glanced around and stepped noiselessly to stand at the end of the wall shelves, completely concealed from view. She closed her eyes and sent awareness out around both the room and the network. Yes, the bombs up here were complete, and hooked to the network. Hooking them in was the last part of the process of making them, and not a simple one. She let her mind trail down the tendrils that touched each one. There were less than fifty so far.

Taking a deep breath, she started walking silently down the center of the room toward the man. He smelled like Jack, although it was hard to be sure because this man hadn't washed in some time. Thinning greasy hair hung several inches below the collar of a stained denim jacket with a splitting armhole sleeve. His jeans bagged over his butt and legs, which seemed much thinner. The muttering voice was familiar…when she was about twenty feet away, she stopped.

"Hello, Jack."

Jack whipped around, slamming back into the table. A beaker shattered on the cement tile floor. Even prepared, Diana was shocked; his face was haggard and lined, and a stringy, filthy beard hung to his sunken chest. His eyes were more dilated than they should have been, and she didn't think drugs were the cause. He stared at her for several long seconds, then his body relaxed and he straightened his shoulders, putting his hands on the edge of the table behind him, his mouth in a cynical quirk. *The old Jack isn't dead yet,* she thought, with a ping of irrational hope.

"I *knew* it was you. The second I saw that trash can, I knew you'd gotten inside that door. Fuckhead me for leaving it wide open."

"After eight years, that's how you say hello? You're not surprised to see me?" She looked around at the brick walls and the exposed steel girders of the roof overhead. "I guess not, given what you've done to keep me out."

"I thought you might try to track me down."

"I just bet you did."

"So it's a crime, wanting a little privacy? Not wanting to wonder if some astral spy is hovering over me every second? Why didn't you just knock on the door, babe, if you wanted to see me so bad?"

"Would you have let me in?"

His mouth grimaced in a sneer, and she saw broken, graying teeth. "Why should I? You three deadbeats couldn't get rid of me fast enough in sixty-three so you could run off and play with your new toys. Oh, yeah, I know what you've all been doing."

"Really? How?"

He caught a breath, then his eyes glinted. "I hear things, babe. I hear things. I've seen April's name all over the newspapers. Excuse me, her fake name, I mean."

"Oh. I thought maybe you were watching us on the network, you know, like we all used to do."

"The network? Are you fucking with me? You all killed the network when you quit. Eight years, flushed down the crapper."

"No one said you had to leave, you know."

"Right, like I was going to hang around with a bunch of backstabbing traitors."

She walked forward a few steps and saw him stiffen. "So, where have you been all this time? We've really been curious. David thought you might cool off and come back for a while. April even went back to New Mexico to ask them."

"Oh, don't pretend any of you gave a fuck. I could have been starving in the gutter for all you cared."

"Pretty harsh, Jack."

"You're one to talk."

"You think maybe eight years is an awfully long time to hang on to all this anger?"

Jack spat on the floor. "Don't gag me with any of that fucking hippie peace and love bullshit. I've had a crawful of that."

"From whom? You don't look like you've been very social for a while. Have you actually had a bath since you left Lexington?"

"Fuck you. If you don't like it, get the fuck out. And don't come back."

She gestured casually at the apparatus behind him. "What's all this? Looks impressive."

"This?" He looked behind him as though just noticing the tables and athanor. "Gotta eat, babe."

"Um. Doesn't look like you've been eating much."

"Yeah, it's a tough old world out here. You wouldn't know about that, little missy Mayflower rolling in bread. Not so easy to earn an honest living when you don't have a trust fund."

"So I hear. So...what are you doing? Drugs, is that it?"

His eyes shifted uneasily. "What do you care?"

"Something illegal, isn't it? Is it drugs? What are you manufacturing here?"

"None of your fucking business. Where do you get off moralizing, you're a fucking bloodsucker! How many people have you killed?"

"Actually...one."

"Bullshit. That's still one more than me, so fuck off."

She folded her arms, forcing a half smile only because she knew it would infuriate Jack. "Make me." *Let's see if I'm right...*

He stood rigid, staring at her with eyes so wide, she could see white all around the iris. The *Newsweek* cover photo of Charles Manson came to her shrinking memory and she suppressed a shudder. But then Jack's pupils contracted and she felt it—a wave of something, flowing over her with tiny prickles, instantly vanishing like a puff of smoke in wind. Jack's mouth fell open and a look of utter shock crossed his face, and she knew her guess was on the mark.

"Ah-ha. I thought so. You can't shoot that cute little ray-gun blast inside your own magical shield, can you?"

He'd already recovered, or at least submerged his dismay into rage. "Well, so the fuck what? You can't do that vanishing act of yours, either, babe. We're even."

"Oh, you think so?" She took another step toward him. He jumped back, scrambling on the table for the pry bar, which he raised menacingly. Diana could only laugh. "Oh, be *serious!* Come on, try and hit me. Go ahead!"

He stood frozen, then suddenly he shouted "Fucking little *cunt!*" and flung the pry bar to the floor so hard it struck sparks, then bounced across the tiles with an ear-piercing series of clangs. "What are you doing here? What the fuck do you *want?*"

Angry herself, Diana was tired of playing verbal ping-pong. "Oh, I don't know. How about my thirty thousand dollars?"

"Your...*what?*"

"My thirty thousand dollars. And I'll take April's forty, while we're at it. Come on. It must be here someplace. What could you possibly have spent it all on?"

"I don't know what you're *talking* about, babe. Do I look like I have thirty *cents?*"

"Actually, no, which is quite a mystery. Whatever did you do with it all? Come on...Carlos Gutierrez."

"What?"

"Or should I say, Jimmy Marston? Tom Dunstable? Which is it this week? 'My name is Legion, for we are many.' Not very inspired. I spotted that one the second I heard it."

"You are fucking *tripping,* babe."

"I wish I were. Stop playing stupid, Jack. The FBI interrogated me. Some of your mind control slipped, and your distributors talked. But you knew that would happen, that's why you planted those screen memories in them. I met one of them, actually. No, really, he wandered into our commune. Small world, isn't it?" Emotions churned over his expression like bubbles in boiling water. She felt a pressure in her forehead and suddenly was outraged. *I can't believe it!*

"Stop that!" She pushed back at him as hard as she could and his head jerked as if he'd been slapped. "You never *learn,* do you? What are you making here, Jack? Why did the FBI ask me if you knew anything about munitions? Why did they ask me if you ever talked about acts of domestic terrorism? Are you actually making explosives? Are all those boxes downstairs bombs? What the fuck are you *doing,* Jack?"

He wiped away the blood trickling from one nostril with the back of his hand. "All I'm doing, babe, is what none of you had the balls to do. You wanted real change? How the fuck did you think that would happen? Nothing, *nothing* can shift the balance of power but pure revolution. The people in this country are *never* going to do that, half of them are shitting their pants scared and the other half are too busy feeding their fat faces at the trough. So I'm doing it for them. That's the only thing that's going to work."

"The world is what it is, Jack. You can't just weed out what you don't like and mold it to suit you. We have to take what's given to us."

"Oh, listen to you, little Miss Sell-Out! What happened to forming a society of immortals to lord it over everyone?"

"I was cured of that for good a few days ago. Funny how really seeing for the first time can change everything. I guess I have to thank you. You've shown me just exactly what my ideas can lead to. I'm just sorry it's taken so long for me to get a fucking clue."

"You don't have a fucking clue, babe."

"Oh, you're wrong, Jack. I know everything."

"What are you talking about?"

"I've seen the network. I'm there with you."

He stared, his mouth moving. "You...you can't."

"Look." She focused, found the tendril she'd avoided up to now, ran along it and touched his mind. He lurched back as though he'd gotten an electrical shock. "Here I am."

Even after their conversation so far, she was shocked at Jack's reaction. He wrapped both arms around his head, his entire face clenched as though a red-hot spike had been driven through his skull, and his first word was a prolonged howl that split her eardrums. *"NO!* It can't be, you can't! *It's not possible!"*

"It certainly wasn't easy. I'll give you credit for that much. It took me three days, with people helping me. In fact, if it hadn't been for Gregory, I'd never have gotten through."

He'd gone even whiter when he heard Gregory's name, but she thought it was the whiteness of pure rage now. "You're lying! He would never do that!"

"So he's in on this, too?" Jack opened his mouth and then stopped, and his frustrated expression assuaged her fear on that point. "You wanted him to be, and he wouldn't do it."

"I haven't seen Gregs since nineteen fifty. He's dead. He has to be."

"Well. So am I. As April never tired of pointing out. April told me why the New Mexico group banished you. She didn't believe you could do what you've done. I don't think she'd believe it if she saw it. I'm just...aghast, Jack. It's mind-boggling. And all of it so you can do something that's so...you used all of us, you used us from the start. You lied to the group in New Mexico, you lied to all of us, you stole from us...and I don't understand why."

"Why?" He stared at her as though she had said something incomprehensible. "After all our sessions, after all we talked about, you don't understand why? You've been on the network. You know what I've seen, what I see now, every moment, day and night, I can't shut it off! I don't have to spell it out. You want examples? There was a little village in Vietnam called My Lai."

Diana swallowed hard. "I heard about that."

"But you didn't *see* it! I *saw* it, babe! You remember what it was like to experience shit on the network! I *lived* it! Every fucking bloody unbearable second of it! And that was just one of them, there were a thousand My Lais! You think what gets into the papers is all there is? What gets into the papers is only the shit that slips past the censors. But nothing gets past me, doll. I see it all. I have to see it."

"You don't, Jack. You can shut it down. You're not God. The human mind isn't built for omniscience, it's driven you mad. Why do you think we all quit?"

"What difference does it make whether I shut it down or not? It's still happening, and I'll know it's all happening! It doesn't stop because no one is watching. It will only stop because someone pays attention, and fucking does something about it!"

"Damn it, Jack, this is not your responsibility! Who do you think you are? Innocent people, Jack, you're going to murder millions of innocent people, and make life a permanent nightmare for tens of millions more. How does that make you any better than the men committing atrocities in Vietnam, or the cops gunning down Black Panthers, or any of those others you're condemning—how are you different? You're worse than all of them put together."

"There are no innocent people in this country, Diana. Everyone is complicit, everyone is guilty, everyone is feeding the engine. You go to the store, you turn on the TV, you drive your car, you're feeding the system! This country is grinding the world up to stuff the coffers of the rich. Everything this country does is just to keep the corporations and fat cats bloated, everything! It's all about the money, and nothing else! When I'm done with this, when it all comes down, we'll be starting all over again from scratch, level playing field. We won't make the same mistakes."

"If you really believe that, you're an idiot. 'After the Revolution, people will be different,' that's what they always said. People are people. They're greedy, using, cruel, vindictive, ungrateful, corrupt…but there's more than that, Jack. You're only seeing one side of the picture. You tuned the network, you decided what it would key in on. David said it, remember? You tuned the network to show you evil—and now that's all you can see. You can't even imagine how narrow a view that is. It would take a hundred networks as big as this one to show you even a fraction of the good that offsets all that darkness. And you're blinded to it."

He stared at her for a moment, his lip curling. "Wow. You really have done a lot of drugs. Who ever thought the great crusader would turn into good morning starshine?"

"Retune the network, Jack. It will do anything you say. Retune it. I'll help you."

He burst out laughing. "Aw, *man!* You are *deluded*, babe! You really think

I'm *choosing* to see this hideous shit? When did we *ever* choose what we saw? This is reality I'm seeing. Life on this planet is hell, because people make it that way. I used to be just as glassy-eyed as you are, I know that. I actually thought there were good guys and we were on their side. Now I know better. There is no side of the angels. There's only not being on the side of the devil."

"And blowing up half the country is it?"

"Stopping what's going on is it. Whatever that takes."

There was a long silence after that. Diana looked down at the floor, aware that Jack was watching her intently, waiting for her to make some move. *I won't kill him and he can't kill me,* she thought. *That leaves me with my last option.* She'd hoped it wouldn't come to this, because Jack was irrational enough already. "I guess we're at an impasse."

"What does that mean?"

"It means I give up." She looked up at him and shrugged. "I came here to try and reason with you, but you're lost to reason. There's only one thing left to do." She walked over and picked up the pry bar from the floor. "I'll just have to wreck your laboratory. Watch out for the flying glass." She strode rapidly across to the tables and swung the pry bar in a wide arc, shattering the elaborate web of glass tubing and retorts suspended from their metal framework. Sparkling crystals showered to the floor around her, covering her shoulders and head, and a gurgling puddle of greenish fluid seethed on the tabletop.

"Hey! Stop that!" She'd known he'd never let her get within ten feet of him without putting up a violent struggle, and she knew why—his deep fear that she would drink from him, and try to influence him. She wouldn't have bothered; she knew, after what Troy told her, that Jack was too resistant to vampiric influence for that to be a solution. But as she raised the pry bar to sweep another complicated apparatus off the tables, consciously moving much more slowly than she was capable of, he rushed up to her and grabbed her arm. "Let it alone!"

She half turned, letting him wrest the pry bar from her right hand. As he did so, she dipped her left hand into the pocket of her loose-fitting jeans, pulled out Harry's sticker pen and jabbed it hard into Jack's forearm. He yelped in pain and jerked back, dropping the pry bar as he clapped his hand over the stuck place on his arm.

"What the fuck...what did you give me? What is that?" He was already staggering and after two more steps he sank to his knees.

"Something new. It's called ketamine, but I've tweaked it a bit. Don't fight it, Jack. You're going under. And I'm going with you."

She knelt down next to him and reached to cup his face with her hands. He tried to recoil but he was too impaired by the drug's anesthetic effect to do more than twitch back, and his eyes were turned up under their lids. She closed her own eyes and sank down into trance, immediately surrounded by the unimaginably vast twining web of the network, constantly moving, constantly branching and growing in new directions, touching new incidents, splitting again, conception, execution and result all displaying at once, all of time compressed into one unending present moment. Tendrils uncountable and all of them pointing to something ugly, some cruel or ghastly or tragic deed…it was a wonder Jack wasn't even more insane, watching all this every moment, waking and sleeping, never taking a respite. Who wouldn't finally want to just wipe the earth clean and start over, confronted with such a relentlessly hopeless and repellent picture of human nature?

But she knew it was a terrible illusion, one that she was partly responsible for helping Jack create in the first place. As she traveled from Sheridan to Binghamton, and during the long hours she'd been casing the warehouse, she had allowed her consciousness to work with the network, ever so carefully so as to avoid attracting Jack's notice. She remembered Troy's words last summer: *Don't you see that this timeline is critically unbalanced? You should also be putting in all the positive changes and beneficial things that have happened over the same range of years. All this upheaval and unrest comes from real change taking place.* She'd admitted to Troy that he was right, but dismissed him at the same time. She understood more now.

She caught hold of Jack's wavering consciousness and pulled him around to face the tendrils she had been retuning and nurturing over the past few days. Like vigorous young plants, they were growing and expanding much faster than anything else. Touching each one sparked a burst of euphoria in her soul's center, like the ketamine euphoria but more profound and less physical. *Look, Jack. Look at these. Come with me…* She felt him turn to follow her direction, with none of the defensiveness or resistance she'd expected. The drug had dissolved those, at least briefly. But she had so little time…ketamine did not last long, and her tweaks to make it take effect faster only shortened its half-life. *All right,* she said to the tendrils. *Show us.*

The tendrils caught them both up, Jack clinging to her psychically as if this was the first time he'd ever been here. With a dizzying sense of careening velocity, they were off, swooping and turning as though on a roller coaster ride, launching off the end of one tendril and on to the next. The air seemed to be full of laughter, but more musical than earthly laughter, more tactile than mere sound. Diana wished she could slow down the visions, for they came so fast and thick it was difficult to absorb them. Couples in love celebrated their weddings, babies were born, homes were built, communities formed. She saw teachers in crumbling inner city schools, young children forgetting their bruised faces as they traced lines in books with their fingers, their growling stomachs appeased by food the teacher had bought for them out of her own pocket. She saw supposedly spoiled teenagers from affluent suburbs volunteering to pick up litter on filthy beaches. She saw straight men in a bar stopping two of their buddies from beating a homosexual man who'd stopped in to ask directions. She saw a middle-class woman in a small Texas town operating a safe house and underground railroad, single-handedly, for battered women escaping their drunken and abusive husbands. Even the war looked different…a soldier was hit three times as he ran through sniper fire to pick up a wounded platoon member, but kept going and got his comrade to safety; a company of exhausted GIs went miles out of their way to take several women and children to a neighboring village after their own had been hit by carpet bombs. Pinpoints of light in the darkness, but they were there…

But there was another reason that Diana couldn't pay as close attention to the flashing images as she desperately wanted to. While Jack was distracted, and seemingly transfixed by what he was seeing, she had discovered how to unhook the completed bombs from their triggering tendrils. She thanked Mother Goddess that it was much easier to unhook them than to connect them, meaning that Jack would not be able to rearm the bombs easily if he realized what she was doing. If she could unhook them all, if she could destroy what Jack had done so that he would have to start all over from the beginning, if she could make that impossible even if she couldn't change his convictions… she had three of them, now four. She kept control of the tendrils, but he could always grow others. Only if the network was dissolved forever would they be truly safe, but she had no idea how to do that.

She kept stopping, because the visions unfolding at the ends of the tendrils were becoming so wondrous. *Troy was right, the world is changing, and will change, in amazing ways, and I wasn't even seeing it.* Twenty…twenty-one… *The Berlin Wall? No. No, I don't believe it!* Twenty-eight…twenty-nine… *Am I really seeing all of them? Are the ones on the shelves all there are?* Thirty-two…thirty-three… *A Negro elected as Massachusetts Governor? and President? No, it can't be! It can never happen!* Thirty-five…thirty-six… *Penobscot Bay is clean? And the river in Sheridan? When will this happen? Or am I seeing the past?* Forty…forty-one… *Who is that woman? Is that April? But she looks younger—no, it's—it can't be Morningstar…* forty-six…forty-seven…*Is that all of them?*

But the visions were slowing down now, and she could feel Jack growing restless, his mind clearing. She had no idea how long it had been, but the ketamine was obviously wearing off. Gathering together the tendrils she had collected, she nervously felt around Jack, the warehouse and the disconnected triggers with her psychic senses, searching for anything she had missed. But she had counted forty-eight completed bombs on the shelves and she had forty-eight tendrils firmly under her control. Jack was returning to a waking state, and she brought her own awareness back to the grimy cavernous room. Broken glass gritted under her cramped knees as she bent towards Jack, her voice a hoarse whisper.

"You see, Jack? You see how much more there is? Would you stop all that from happening, too? Would you destroy all those futures?"

He was bowed over, his shoulders shuddering. Was he sobbing, terrified or enraged? She couldn't tell. But he was shaking his head.

"Doesn't matter…it doesn't matter."

"Why doesn't it?"

"It's weak. Good people always lose. They fight and fight and they always lose. *We* always lost."

"We didn't! Jack, we succeeded more than we failed."

He raised his head and she saw now that his face was wet with tears. "We never succeeded, we were only deluding ourselves. That's why you all quit. There is no victory in this war. Every flower is just trampled down. There isn't any point in fighting."

"Maybe there isn't a need to fight at all. Maybe that's the real lesson we were meant to learn. Fighting itself is giving in to the darkness."

He still shook his head, more tears running into his ragged beard. With a qualm, Diana recalled that the more euphoric the drug trip, the harder the crash at the end. There was no more ketamine—the sticker pen only held one dose.

"It wouldn't matter if I sat and watched this stuff all day, babe, with popcorn and a soft drink. I'd still know. I'd still know what else was going on, every second, whether I watched it or not. I can't ever forget it. Nothing can wipe my head clean after what I've seen."

"Then you have to live with that. But you have no right to deny life to others. I'm sorry, Jack. That's the oldest law there is—and I've broken it once, so I know what the consequences are. Trust me on this."

"I do." He closed his eyes, letting his head fall back. His voice was stronger. "It's still going to happen, you know. All those pretty hearts and flowers, all the good will and Boy Scout shiny clean in the world, it's not going to stop it. If it's not me, it will be someone else. It might be New York, or Waco, or Oklahoma fucking City, but it's coming down. You won't stop them all. It's going to happen. I've *seen* it."

"You may be right, Jack. It might not stop here. It might still happen. But it's not going to be you. It's not just the people you'll hurt. I'm not going to let you do that to your own soul. We spent half a life together. We're fellow Initiates. It's my obligation to stop you."

He smiled faintly. "To save me from myself? Diana. You still want to be the big hero."

A bit stung, she straightened her shoulders. "I'm not going to see your face on the cover of *Newsweek,* that's for sure."

He gave a little snort. "And you disarmed my bombs."

"I had to. All forty-eight of them."

He was quiet, looking down at the floor, where chemicals from his broken apparatus speckled the shards of glass. He mouth quirked into a slow smile as he whispered, "Forty-nine."

For a moment she didn't realize the full implications of his words, and that was one moment too long. With a gasp she focused on the network, seeing the tendril, the bomb that had been sitting on the worktable hidden by boxes, the last one he'd connected, its tendril not yet bundled with the others so it could be triggered simultaneously with the rest... "No! No, Jack, no! Mother Goddess..." A surge of power made the network turn blindingly bright in her mind's eye, and then everything flared into pure white energy and was gone.

35

She saw flashing red lights for some minutes before she slowly became aware that she was a conscious mind, and real enough to perceive lights. The lights were painfully bright, but they held her attention as she felt herself condensing, bit by bit, as though individual molecules were wandering back from wherever they'd been blasted to and reluctantly settling into place. The red lights acquired a blur of movement around them, and then sounds, the distorted voices of emergency vehicle radios. She remembered what had happened. If there were still fire trucks here, at least days hadn't passed. She was relieved when she had eyelids to close against the glare, and by then, she was almost entirely back. She tried moving. Nothing seemed to be just exactly the way it was before, but this might be an illusion that would fade. She was lying on her side outside the chain link fence, where she'd dropped her bag. No wonder the moving shapes around the lights had seemed to be going in strange angles to the ground.

She sat up, making sure her joints bent the right way and flexing her hands. *Well, I'm still here,* she thought. *I guess I am indestructible. Or at least, it will take a bigger bomb.* She was cautious about moving, not wanting the firemen or police to notice her.

There was nothing left of the warehouse and a large amount of the surrounding parking lots except a crater in the ground filled with what appeared to be gravel or tiny pellets. She knew what that was; she remembered awakening covered with the pulverized remains of the Schuller house all too vividly. They would find no trace of the athanor, the packages, or anything else. Of Jack, nothing would be left but bits of bone distributed through the rubble. She saw a man in a jumpsuit and coat bending down and examining the debris. He appeared puzzled. The firemen were mostly standing around talking, since there had never been any fire, smoke or heat. She could see a small knot of curious people in the parking lot entrance, huddled against the early spring chill and staring at the empty lot. She knew there must have been one hell of a boom, and probably the closest neighbors had some broken windows.

She was in no rush to go anywhere, and sat watching quietly as the firemen stowed their trucks and pulled out. The police officers stayed a bit longer, and she had to duck into the bushes when one carefully paced out the fence perimeter, shining a flashlight through the mesh and looking for anything untoward. The cruisers pulled out and one stopped while an officer stretched crime scene tape across the driveway. Then all was quiet and still.

Diana closed her eyes, opening her awareness to see what had happened to the network. For some minutes she searched patiently, but she wasn't surprised by what she found—or didn't find. The network was gone, vanished as completely as the warehouse itself. Jack's Intention had kept it in existence after their coven had disbanded, and with Jack gone, the network had dissolved into the limitless field of potential from which it had been made.

She ghosted through the chain link fence and walked shakily to the crater's edge, looking down at the debris. The particles hurt her bare feet—she'd left her boots at the bottom of the metal steps. She squeezed her eyes shut, but couldn't block off the running stream of memories that tortured her—Jack at fourteen tagging after her and Gregory; in his naval uniform, never knowing how dapper she'd thought he looked; scarfing down steak in the Hilton after Beltene in 1955, lean and weathered as a cowpoke; leading their coven into building the network and changing history. Was it fair of her to accuse him of conniving the whole plan from the start? Maybe he'd simply been taking advantage of opportunities and making it up as he went. *Don't we all do that, when it comes down to it?* She knew now that some of the time he'd spent alone in Lexington had been spent on the network by himself, and that had been the beginning of his madness. Only the validation, support and reassurance of the group and its union had given the rest of them the strength to bear what they saw. David had commented on Jack's solitude suspiciously and she hadn't paid attention. She had been too preoccupied with tracking down Troy.

She impatiently wiped tears from her face with her already soaked sleeve. *I did it again, Troy. I fucked up and someone else paid.* Abruptly, she heard Troy's voice in her mind—*So, who made you God? You can't take responsibility for everything.*

"Oh, shut up, Troy," she said out loud, but she was smiling, for a moment. She straightened her shoulders, taking in a deep breath. "Good-bye, Jack."

But she had an odd feeling that she couldn't leave yet, which made no sense, since hanging around here was clearly a stupid thing to do. She noticed something by the back fence. She walked over to it and found the trash can, much the worse for wear, lying on its side. She turned it upside down and set it by the fence so it wouldn't fill with water or roll in the wind—as if anyone would care. She turned away, thinking *I really need to split before anyone comes back.*

"Well, Diana. It's certainly been a long time."

She whirled around, her jaw dropping. Comfortably seated on the upturned trash can was a man with sandy brown hair, a Roman nose and quite stylish clothes. His deadpan sober expression belied the eyes that glinted with glee—the glee in a cat's eyes as it plays with a dying mouse. She hadn't seen him since 1952, but she was fairly certain he wouldn't say the same thing about her.

"Levoissier."

"And I must say, it's worth the wait. Brava, my dear. I'm very proud of you."

"Oh, so *now* you're proud of me? Kick me out the door in nineteen fifty-two, spend twenty years hiding from me, sit by watching me commit two truly magnificent screw-ups, and now you're proud of me?"

"You really must get over that, Diana. All fledglings have to leave the nest, and holding grudges is such a waste of energy. Of course I'm proud of you. I have been all along."

"I don't give a fuck whether you're proud of me or not, you know."

He smiled. "I do know that. It's wonderful to see one's protégées grow up."

Diana rolled her eyes. Ten years ago, she would have had a lot to say to Levoissier, but none of that seemed to matter anymore. "Do you have some reason for popping up here tonight?"

"Not particularly."

"How is Gregory doing?"

Levossier's expression looked a little wistful, like a doting parent's. "Beyond my most optimistic hopes. Oh, by the way, he gave me your message. The one about me being a son of a bitch."

"Oh, good, then I don't have to repeat it. Just out of curiosity, where is he?"

"He's around. I keep him very busy. I'm sure you two will run into each other someday. After all, you have all the time in the world."

She was silent, digesting this offhand comment. "Just because I have a lot of time doesn't mean I think any of it should go to waste."

"Ah, you do understand. But then, what constitutes wasted time is a matter of opinion, isn't it?"

"Only up to a point."

Levoissier just smiled.

"I've got to get moving, I don't want to be seen here."

"Where are you going? You seem to be at a point of transition."

She was quiet, looking past him at the tangled foliage behind the fence. "Home," she said finally. "I'm going home."

"Where's that, then?"

"Maine. I think I'll plant a garden. It's disgraceful to let that field grow up into scrub."

"I should think you'd had your fill of gardening."

"Not at all. I've gotten quite a taste for it. There's healing in the earth, you know. Healing, and stability and…strength. It's wafting around on the astral that I've had more than enough of for a while."

"Then you've found true magic, Diana. Not many do."

"Maybe a piece of it." She thought back to the day that Morningstar was born. "Maybe a couple of pieces of it." She looked at him. "Do me a favor? When you see Gregory, tell him I said thanks."

He raised his hand in a half-salute and then he was gone. After a second, Diana stepped over and touched the trash can where he'd been sitting. It was as cold as the fence behind it.

Ah Mother Goddess, no more enigmas! I don't even want to see a crossword puzzle until at least nineteen-eighty, all right? There were only a couple of hours before dawn, so she'd have to make good speed. Strange that the stone house no longer seemed lonely or empty to her. She was looking forward to seeing it. She dematerialized and headed northeast.

Made in the USA
Charleston, SC
01 October 2013